SURVIVORS OF THE REALM

EUGENE WEAVER

ISBN: (Paperback) 979-8-9886578-2-8
ISBN: (KDP) 979-8-9886578-3-5

Eugene Weaver
North Canton, Ohio 44720
Edited by James Osborne
Cover design and interior design by Rafael Andres

Chapters

PROLOGUE:

BEFORE TIME

In the deep vastness of space, nearly one billion years ago in space time, before any form of life on planets, beings from the furthest reaches of the known universe existed. Scattered across the many galaxies. Roaming the stars. Searching. With only the desire to create, but not yet possessing the power to do so.

Each being was different from the other, varying in size and shape but each one at least the size of large meteors and some getting as large as any number of small orbiting moons on the many uninhabited worlds sprinkled throughout the solar systems they traversed. They didn't know or understand how they came to be. Millions of years would pass without the beings ever coming into close proximity with one another. But it happened.

A being glided silently through dead space. Stars. Planets. Nebula. Quasars. Nothing organic. This particular entity glowed a color similar to a beautiful neon red. An enormous mass of moving parts. Hundreds upon hundreds of thick, long appendages similar to a centipede extended from the sides of its enormous eel like body. The appendages, similar in shape to an arthropod, with gigantic suction cups that glowed yellow dotting them. A long tail, nearly four hundred meters long in length, swished through space behind it. The head of the creature was rounded with two small slits for eyes on either side. Lightning emanated from a large opening on the front of its head when it was opened as a defense mechanism.

It had been alone, not coming into contact with any other ancient being for hundreds upon thousands of years until this point in time. A being slightly smaller than it had sensed its presence earlier and had followed it. Stalking it.

This entity was black. A slick, wet black darker than space itself. It was a mass of the absence of all light. So dark it stood out even in the vacuum of space. Sprinkled throughout the thick jelly-like black body were flashes of light mimicking stars as a form of camouflage to conceal itself from other beings. The lights themselves seemed to exist on their own, living off of their host body. Colossal, jagged scales dotted the alien as well, another defense mechanism. This entity had done battle with others. It took pleasure in stalking prey through the solar systems.

This being was similar in shape to a manta ray, complete with a tail-like appendage off of its rear side. It had sharp, black rock-like material that resembled massive rows of fangs when it opened its great oval orifice on the front of its body. These fangs had ripped into numerous beings across numerous solar systems. It lived to kill and destroy.

It had been tracking this neon red creature through an entire solar system. Watching it glide silently past the stars and various planets that littered this system. It sensed its time had come. The time to kill and end another being. The thrill of the hunt and ultimate destruction is all this being knew. The glowing white lights that flickered on its outer shell ceased to glow. It was able to suppress the lights when it felt it was necessary. Such was the case when it was preparing a stealth attack on an unsuspecting adversary.

From below the centipede eel shaped being, the manta ray entity attacked. It swooped up, crashing into the centipede creature, sinking its enormous, jagged jaws into the bottom of the centipede, ripping it open.

Immediately the centipede creature twisted in pain and surprise at what was happening. Neon red organs spilled out from the gigantic open wound. The manta ray went in for another attack, but the centipede was incredibly agile even when injured. It got its bearings quicky and deflected another attack by swatting its tail against the manta ray, connecting with the head and sending it floating backwards in space at an incredibly fast rate of speed.

Glowing blood continued to leak from the injured creature as it exited the large, gaping hole in its underbelly and floated off into space. The creature continued writhing in pain from the wound as the manta ray prepared for another attack.

This time it lunged straight for the same injured spot on the centipede, but at the last second it spun around in space quickly and snapped its tail against the centipede's mid-section, sending it flying backwards. As it sailed backwards, its own tail wrapped around the manta ray's head and locked on tight, pulling the black creature with it as it careened backwards.

The centipede didn't let go, but instead started to curl itself end over end, wrapping itself around the manta ray. Its glowing yellow suction cup appendages fastened to the manta ray's outer shell. It did this as blood continued seeping out of its own open wound.

The manta ray struggled with all its might. Not only was it smaller than the centipede, but the centipede was longer and more agile, even with the hole in its underbelly. The centipede squeezed with incredibly destructive force and the manta ray began to feel its body being crushed. It was able to once again bite into the centipede, this time closer to its head. It didn't have a good angle or grip but bit hard enough to make the centipede loosen its grip enough for the manta ray to start to wriggle its way free.

More neon red blood seeped from the badly injured centipede as it struggled to keep the manta ray in its grip. It had also done damage to the manta ray's body. Bright yellow glowing blood was flowing out of cracks on its shell from the immense pressure the centipede had inflicted on it when it was wrapped tightly in its death grip. The flowing blood made it even more difficult for the centipede to keep itself wrapped tightly to the manta ray, its tentacles slipping off the bloody torso.

As the manta ray slipped out of the tentacled grip of the centipede, the glowing electricity from the centipede's mouth shot out in a torrent of crackling waves, hitting the manta ray directly in the head. Electricity covered the manta ray's entire body. It was free from the tentacles of the centipede and sensed the mortal danger it was now in. A nearby meteor floating past the battle was enough to give the manta ray one last-ditch effort to destroy the centipede.

It snapped its tail, connecting with the centipede, sending it backwards again and smashing into the meteor. The centipede was much larger than the passing meteor, so the impact crushed the meteor into thousands of pieces of space debris. However, the impact did even more damage to the centipede that was now near death. As was the mortally injured manta ray.

For a brief period, neither extra-terrestrial being attacked the other. Both had inflicted incredible amounts of pain and injury on the other. Both bleeding out into deep space and losing their life blood as well as their strength. But neither one would give up. They each knew instinctively that this was a fight to the death. And currently, both still existed.

Lights glowed across the torso of the manta ray. White light mixed with yellow blood seeped out of them. The manta ray tried to go into self-preservation mode by attempting to morph its body. Its mammoth wings on either side of its thick body wrapped themselves around its torso in an attempt to slow the flow of blood. Its tail began to retract and curl itself around the now folded wings as if it were attempting a cocoon.

The centipede saw its final opportunity to rid the universe of this parasite that seemed to enjoy feeding off the pain of others, for no other reason except to assert dominance and power. The centipede, with a last mighty breath, exhaled a stream of electricity out of its mouth towards the manta ray as the manta ray was attempting to smash into it. The electrical current connected with it, igniting it into a gargantuan ball of fiery electricity.

The centipede spun itself around and its tail once more smashed into the manta ray, sending it careening through space. Lightning completely engulfing it. Yellow blood spilling out end over end. The immense pain of the electricity coupled by its injuries and the forward momentum of the final tail snap made the manta ray helpless and furious with rage.

The centipede floated in space. Shrinking in size as neon red blood and internal organs continued to float into space. The electricity in its mouth was extinguishing. Its numerous tentacles went from flailing to twitching and then to floating aimlessly. After a time, it quit moving completely. Letting space take it drifting off to its final resting place.

The manta ray tumbled end over end. The electricity frying the being. Charring it alive. It's black thick jelly-like frame was losing its form, now resembling more of a speeding black sphere. Making its way to the nearest star, an incredibly bright burning celestial body. The pain was overwhelming. It had never lost a fight in the eons it existed. But here it was, dying by being burnt alive. It knew its end was upon it, so the tail and wings unfolded as they burned with electrical fire. It was able to see the star it was heading towards. Mere seconds from impact, it thought to itself, *my essence shall live on. Somehow, I shall continue being. I am eternal!* And with those final thoughts, it engulfed the small glowing star. The celestial being along with the electricity that covered it exploded, causing the star itself to implode.

This was no ordinary star. The star itself was special. Made mostly of hydrogen and helium, this particular planetoid had a small, solid matter core made of a brilliant, almost clear rock-like substance. When the destruction occurred, the nuclear reactors in the core shattered. Most of the brilliant, clear matter evaporated with the blast impact from the creature.

However, several larger pieces escaped destruction and spread out in every direction. Some would continue hurtling through space before colliding with a stray meteor and exploding. Others would grow smaller and burn out upon entering various planets' atmospheres. But a very select few would land on planets and tunnel themselves deep into the rocky soil where they landed. The powerful stone surrounded by nuclear reactors from the star's core had now been touched by a supernatural celestial being of immense power. A connection had been made, even if the manta ray didn't know it yet, as it was about to die.

Pieces of the charred creature shot everywhere, glowing light still emanating from its now dead husk. The explosion was catastrophic, pushing other stars light years out from it even further away. Immediately a vast hole in space emerged from the star. Comets, meteors, and other space debris slowly started to make their way towards the newly formed black hole and its event horizon.

Inside the infant dead star, nothing existed except the electricity from the expired creature encircling various parts of its carcass that floated through the black hole. A wormhole began to open inside the star, sending several pieces of the beast's black, glowing and crystalizing body through it to other parts of the galaxy. A new portal had been created. Huge jagged black crystallite formations burning brightly shot through the wormhole out the other side. Each with a bright light still glowing inside.

Several pieces of the manta ray entity remained floating inside the dead star, connecting with one another in an attempt to rebuild itself. Periodically, almost by natural instinct, embryotic lights would blink on the floating mass of ever-changing jelly. As if searching for life.

CHAPTER 1

THROUGH THE WORM HOLE

One billion years later, a shiny silver orb rocketed through the emptiness of space. The ship was small, with enough room for four space travelers. This particular one, however, named *Stormbringer*, only held three out of the four that had begun this mission aboard its mothership, *The Cauldwell*. The interior was sparse: four seats and a control panel in front to pilot it. The ship had enough tools and items stowed onboard to get it to safety in case of an emergency. Which is exactly what it was being used for currently.

Synth liquid harvested from small flowing streams on their home planet of Trilaxus's nearest moon powered the entire fleet of the Space Travel Explorer Association, or STEA, by acting as fuel for the magnetic propulsion systems housed in each spacecraft. This was the means by which all interstellar space travel was achieved on the crew's home world. This particular mission had been to explore Alpha Sector Eight in the search for possible civilization due to one of the small planets in this quadrant having an atmosphere able to sustain life.

Unfortunately for commander Ben Newstead and his crew, in year three of the total twenty-year mission, they were awakened from their hibernation tubes by their ship's onboard A.I. system Beta, informing them of a dead star in their path pulling their ship towards its gravitational field.

Unable to divert from their trajectory, they were hurtled into the vast emptiness of the enormous black hole and traveled through a wormhole. Ramsey Conner, the *Cauldwell's* lead pilot, was able to get them through the black hole in one piece and land on an inhabitable planet they would later find out was named Thunder Stone Realm or, TSR1 by the lone survivor of another spacecraft similarly doomed to the black hole.

As fate would have it, the *Cauldwell* was destroyed shortly after arriving on the hostile new world, with only the small *Stormbringer* as their only possible means of escape.

Carol Blake, chief medical officer and co-pilot of the *Cauldwell,* was taken by creatures from the planet, and in the proceeding battle Ben Newstead was scratched and transformed into a hideous creature known as an Azid. The Azid were controlled telepathically by a parasitic beast that lived in a cave on the side of a large black mountain. The beast, known as Hyzothan, possessed a supernaturally powered sacred stone to exert complete and total control over this world.

Justin Schwartz, first officer of the *Cauldwell*, had led his small team through perilous terrain and numerous close calls with both the various species of life and the elements to escape with the help of fellow stranded astronaut James Korvell. He and his first officer Susan Danials were from planet Earth, and were the only survivors of their own ship, the E.E.S Saros.

Susan was taken soon after they landed on the planet by creatures resembling tall, humanoid rats that stood on their hind legs and were able to fly. James never gave up searching for his companion over the years until the crew of the *Cauldwell* arrived. Ultimately, he sacrificed himself to ensure the beast that had taken Susan years earlier would no longer pollute the world with its evil and give his new friends a fighting chance of escape off of TSR1.

Back through the black hole the *Stormbringer* hurtled. Small space debris pinged off of the ship's shiny silver outer hull, yet it remained in one piece due to Carol Blake's expert navigation as she piloted her way through the asteroid field before entering the huge black round void in space with a gleaming circle of light shining around its base. No doubt the remainder of the now dead star.

None of the remaining crew knew if they would survive, and if they did, where they would end up. How much time would have passed? Would the ship's feeble resources enable them to get back home, or at the very least, to a planet that had already been charted by STEA earlier? These questions and many more haunted the thoughts of Justin, Ramsey and Carol.

Brilliant lights surrounded the *Stormbringer* as it rocketed through the wormhole. Lights that were quite similar to the ones the crew witnessed upon their first trek through the black hole. They had lost all control of their ship. The gravity of the immense black hole and their own magnetic propulsion system ensured they were continually being pulled through the dead star.

Justin looked out of the viewscreen at the sights unfolding around them as they rocketed through the wormhole. From afar, they could see entire solar systems. Star systems that had never been charted and would most likely never be charted by a living being. *Had they been sucked up into the black hole, or had they been created inside? If so, what created them? Were they even real or an illusion inside the mysterious dead star?* Justin pondered to himself.

An oddly shaped object also loomed in the darkness. Was it a large meteor? Was it more space debris? Or was it a creature from someplace else, captured by the force of the black hole? The object seemed to move on its own trajectory, as if a living being was either inside, or the mass itself was alive and attempting to move of its own accord. The strange alien shape continued to move towards the *Stormbringer* as if wanting to investigate the shiny silver orb shooting through the darkness.

Ramsey looked out the viewscreen at the barely visible entity hovering in space. His eye caught something disconnecting from the large, shadowed mass. Something small and equally unknown that cast a small glow of light from its center. It looked as though it was actively pursuing them as it glistened through the vacuum of their bleak surroundings. Ramsey blinked and wiped his eyes to make sure that what he was seeing was accurate in a place where nothing at all was accurate or normal. It was as if it was changing shapes as it travelled. And then the glowing light vanished and all that was visible once again inside the *Stormbringer* were dark shadows.

"Hey guys, did you see…" Ramsey started, but then went silent.

Time itself felt as though it had stopped. Silence surrounded the ship. Silence and dread. The beast they had defeated paled in comparison to the truly terrifying spectacle of this black hole and the helplessness the three space travelers were experiencing. They all sensed they were about to exit once more. Surprisingly, thus far, still in one piece in their small spacecraft intended only for short missions, not something as monumental as this.

Then, much like their first trip through the black hole, they shot out the other side, alive and still in one piece while the ship itself vibrated and shook violently. The *Stormbringer* was traveling at speeds much faster than it was capable of due to both the gravitational pull of the wormhole they'd traversed, but also their own synth-powered magnetic thrusters which acted as a sort of repellant to the black hole, similar to small magnets helping it to rocket forwards.

More space debris pummeled the ship. The *Stormbringer* shook and bumped along its path in space as both Ramsey and Carol piloted the ship around it.

"Carol, look out!" Justin yelled, gripping the sides of his captain's chair as a huge, jagged chunk of what looked like a comet hurtled towards them.

Not taking her eyes off the view screen in front of her and gripping the controls of the ship, she shot back, "Hang on!"

Ramsey pushed several buttons on the control panel in front of him to give him a better visualization not just of the oncoming comet being sucked back into the black hole, but every other large chunk of destructive rock on a collision course with the *Stormbringer*.

Pulling back on the steering yoke at her co-pilot station of the spacecraft, Carol was able to lift the ship up quickly on its trajectory, narrowly avoiding direct contact with the chunk of ice that looked to be the size of the large black mountain back on TSR1 that housed the evil creature Hyzothan.

They weren't out of immediate danger yet, however. Directly behind the enormous chunk of ice was what seemed to be a huge cluster of meteors all flying close enough together that there was no way to pilot the small ship around them fast enough. The jagged rocks were hurtling towards them and all that the small crew could do was look on in horror.

"Carol!" Justin shouted, releasing the death grip he held on the armrests of his seat and pointing out of the viewscreen, not knowing what else to add.

She continued to frantically grip the steering yoke as Ramsey yelled to both her and Justin, "I've got a plan, but we only get one shot at this. Those meteors are going to smash into us in less than one minute and we can't get around it at our current speed. We have to get the *Stormbringer* moving faster while pulling up hard! Captain, do you trust me?" He glanced quickly over at Justin as more space debris bounced off of the hull, shaking the ship violently.

"Whatever you're going to do Ramsey, do it now. We're about to be torn to pieces!" Justin hollered back as he tried to lean forward in his seat, peering out the front viewscreen at the onslaught of space rock in all various shapes and sizes.

Ramsey immediately accessed the ship's synth tank operations. Looking over the list of functions, he quickly found the one he was after, marked "Purge Synth Tanks," and pressed it.

Zark, the name given to the ship's artificial intelligence earlier on TSR1 as a way to lighten the tense mood, responded calmly in a cool male voice, "Authorization code required to perform this function."

The request was barely out of the ship's A.I. speaker system and Ramsey was already shouting out, "7354-Ramsey Conner authorization confirmed." Sweat was dripping off his brow as he wiped his forehead frantically.

"Authorization accepted. Synth purge initiated."

Carol looked over at Justin, horrified at what was happening, but staying silent as the seconds counted down.

A small circular valve, roughly one foot around, had slid open at the rear bottom of the *Stormbringer*, and now bright blue liquid began spilling out and floating into the vacuum of space.

The meteor shower was now upon them. Mere seconds remained before they would be overcome by the countless barrage of space rocks both large and small. Justin realized what Ramsey was attempting to do and didn't hesitate as Ramsey glanced over at him, awaiting his command.

"Justin Schwartz authorization code-9835. Initiate rescue flares off the rear port of the ship!" He gripped his armrests once more.

"Authorization code accepted. Initiating rescue flare launch off left and right rear sides of hull," the smooth and steadily calm voice responded.

A short burst of flares shot out of the rear ports, which were used in emergency location rescues. Not so in this case, however.

"Hang on, everyone," Ramsey said in a controlled panic as he took over the steering yoke on his side of the control panel as everyone braced for impact.

The flames from the released flares connected with the highly flammable synth liquid floating off of the ship and immediately ignited. The explosion was catastrophic, connecting with the *Stormbringer* and launching it end over end straight up as the meteor shower zipped by, hurtling towards the massive black hole.

The force of the explosion rocketed them out of the way of nearly all of the numerous meteors sailing forward. Almost all of them. A slightly larger one, the size of the *Stormbringer* itself, smashed into the rear of the ship, making it spin even more as it continued its trajectory upwards.

Justin, Ramsey and Carol were unable to move, glued to the backs of their seats and clinging onto the side arm rests tightly as the ship spun end over end, rocketing upwards away from the meteor shower and out of the reach of the giant black hole. Ramsey was able to reach down and push the com.

"Cancel Synth Tank Purge! Ramsey Conner-7354!"

Zark replied back calmly, "Synth Tank Purge command cancelled."

The rear port underneath the *Stormbringer* still leaking synth liquid closed shut quickly even as the ship continued spinning violently through space. Inside the ship Ramsey continued to pull back hard on the yoke, trying to slow the spin and regain control. An alarm had sounded throughout the cabin.

"Warning, hull integrity down to 20%. Slow ship to .25 light speed travel to avoid total outer hull collapse."

"Ramsey, you've got to slow us down!" Justin yelled, frantically looking at him.

Carol was also pulling back on her own command center yoke to the best of her ability. Her arm still throbbed from the deep cut she had received back on TSR1 escaping the dreaded Azid creatures, later cauterizing the wound shut with the blade of her STEA issued knife left in a fire she had started. However, with both her and Ramsey pulling back together on their respective piloting yokes, the ship began to steady itself and drop in speed while still shooting upwards away from space debris and, more importantly, the black hole.

"Hull integrity 18%...17%," Zark calmly stated. Ramsey looked down at the speed. It was dropping. .35 light speed dropped to .32 light speed. The ship was finally not spinning and was on a steady course once again, but still traveling at too fast for the damage it had sustained.

"We're out of the gravitational pull of the black hole and it looks like most of the space debris is no longer present," Carol said with a sigh. She leaned over and put her hand on Ramsey's shoulder. "Good flying there, partner," she said with an exasperated grin.

"Agreed, Carol. That's some quick thinking. Dangerous. But it worked, and if it hadn't, we would be space debris ourselves. You gave us yet another fighting chance, Ramsey," Justin said proudly as the ship's speed continued dropping.

"Don't thank me just yet, everyone. We're still at .30 light speed!"

As if sensing what everyone was thinking, Zark calmy stated, "Please slow ship propulsion to .25 light speed to avoid complete hull failure. Hull integrity at 14%."

The alarm continued sounding. "Cancel alarm!" Carol and Justin said simultaneously, frustrated at the constant updates from Zark while at the same time glancing over at each other, giving a quick grin.

The alarm went silent while the red flashing light continued in the ship's interior.

"This is gonna be a close one!" Ramsey said, shaking his head, looking back and forth at their speed and the hull integrity.

"When has it not been a close one since we were woken up in our hibernation tubes on the *Cauldwell* nearly a week ago?" Justin answered coolly, trying to keep his composure.

Zark, the continual bearer of bad news, said calmy through the com system, "Synth level 100% depletion in t-minus 60 minutes."

CHAPTER 2

THE LEO AND HER CREW

The freighter ship *Leo* cruised along on its deep space route. It was a large ship. It had to be to haul the cargo its crew salvaged, mainly medical supplies, various weapons and highly sought after minerals that brought with them high price tags on the black markets that the ship's crew frequented.

The *Leo* was 170 meters long and 135 meters wide, as well as being roughly thirty meters high without the landing gear deployed. Fully loaded with sellable merchandise, it weighed 300,000 metric tons. However, it was currently devoid of merchandise after leaving the planet Darmus III. The crew had made a large sale on several containers of stolen small arms weaponry purchased by a fringe faction of rebels on their planet. With the merchandise now unloaded and the ship on its way to another drop point to pick up another run of supplies, the ship weighed 255,000 tons empty.

There were larger scavenger ships in this quadrant of the solar system known as HD-9478, but what this one lacked in sheer size it more than made up for in its ability to travel at faster speeds, helping its crew to escape tight spots when they inevitably were detected making deals on various space stations and cities and smaller villages of planets in this solar system, as well as surrounding ones. The ship was able to travel at light speed, but when fully loaded, their trek was slowed down significantly.

The cockpit was located front and center and jutted out from the rest of the ship, with the rest of it growing wider the further back it went until narrowing out in the rear. The sides of the ship were long and flat and had rocket boosters on either side as well as rapid fire assault blasters that had been retrofitted by its crew. The rear of the ship housed two huge exhaust ports blowing out the large quantities of fuel that powered the spacecraft. It was boxy in design, but utilitarian, made primarily to haul goods quickly. The *Leo* did not have traditional space travel wings, but the width and relatively lower height made space travel easy. It wasn't made to maneuver around quickly but, if necessary, it could outrun most other similarly sized vessels, which did occur from time to time, considering the profession of her crew.

The *Leo* had a motley crew of five, and the current atmosphere onboard was tense.

"So just what made you think they wouldn't be willing to budge on price?" Alex shouted, standing behind Willie, who was trying to pilot the ship from his station in the front of the command center.

Willie Petros, who was strong enough for his slim build, could hold his own against most of the questionable clientele they interacted with. He shot back, "Look! I just figured if we start haggling on price, they would bail on us. I don't want to be stuck piloting this tub around the current solar system we're slinking our way through, with people on three of the ten planets out looking for us!"

"Yeah, and whose fault is that? You know as well as I do that no Cambulon is ever really trustworthy, and the rebel group we sold them to on Darmus III could be squashed by the ruling party. The whole planet is corrupt!" she spat back angrily. "They need us. We could have gotten 25% more Marks for those three containers of small arms than we did! 2,500 more Marks on top of the 10,000 we ended up getting! And I should add, they would have gladly paid for the merchandise they received!"

Willie continued staring ahead out into the front viewscreen of the *Leo*. His eyes shifting back and forth nervously. He ran his hand through this wavy brown hair and glanced back at her. "I said I was sorry earlier. I know you do the negotiating and keep track of our Marks and cargo, but I wanted off that..."

He was cut off abruptly by a now red-in-the-face Alex. "We could have laid low for at least a month longer with the extra Marks that you literally just threw away by deciding that you knew how to deal with the Cambulons better than I did. A race that I have dealt with before! We squeeze them and they'll pay! That's the way it works. How it's always worked on these hostile planets. But what do I know? I've only been on this ship since I was eighteen. What the hell could I have possibly learned in eight years, right?"

Willie saw how angry she was. Her face was red, matching her long red hair. Standing over him with her arms crossed. He wasn't sure how to continue this conversation, so he rubbed the short beard he had been letting grow for around four weeks and looked back at the captain in the center seat in the middle of the large cockpit and raised his eyebrows, looking for help.

"Ok, Alex. We heard you. And I agree, we could have squeezed the Cambulons for a bit more, but that area is hot right now and the sooner we got our pay and left, the better," Sam Howard, her captain said assertively. "There's a civil war brewing with the Cambulon rebels and their fight with the ruling government party on Darmus III. The neighboring cities have insiders that I spoke with, and they informed me to get out now, not later. We got paid. They got their weapons. Deal done."

"Yes, but-" Alex began, eager to keep the discussion going.

"You know as well as I do that what the buyers do with the goods we sell is their business, not ours. But in this situation, I sincerely hope that the weapons we sold the rebels help take down that fascist authoritarian government. The planet is in turmoil and the way I see it, we did a good thing."

Alex turned to look at Sam, contemplating whether she should continue this line of conversation or not. She saw the look Sam was shooting her. Alex respected Sam. She had taken Alex in when no one else would. An eighteen-year-old runaway living on the streets with no parents. Sam would later find out they had both perished on their home world of Nerilia in the HD-7454 quadrant when she was only twelve during a botched robbery of their home. Killed in front of young Alex. After that, she had to turn tough real fast.

Sam had only been the captain of the *Leo* for one year when she met Alex. The *Leo* and her crew were making a supply drop on Nerilia when Alex had tried to pickpocket Sam, who caught her in the act. Instead of breaking her arm like Sam normally would have done, she showed a bit of compassion, seeing something in those fiery green eyes of hers, with her red hair and freckled cheeks. She was a spitfire and incredibly intelligent when it came to counting money and keeping track of the inventory onboard the *Leo* due to her years working in the criminal underworld of Nerilia, stealing to get by. She had a soft spot that endeared Sam to her. Once out of that life of crime she had made for herself over the years, Sam took her under her wing, and she had blossomed ever since. Even with her hot temper that sometimes got the best of her.

Adjusting her suspenders that held up her tight brown pants to her slim body, she looked back down at Willie again. Wanting to get one last word in. But she didn't have time.

Sam, looking directly at Alex, calmly said, "Shake on it. The topic is over."

Willie glanced behind him. Alex was still standing over him, but the red in her cheeks was subsiding. He took his right hand off of the ship's helm and held it out behind him for her to take.

Quickly Alex grasped the outstretched hand and squeezed it slightly too hard and gave it one solid pump as if to say, *Discussion over, but we aren't.* She then turned to walk out of the command center when Sam grabbed her by the arm.

She stopped and looked at Sam. "You good?" Sam asked in her cool, calm voice.

"All good, sir," Alex retorted, now with a noticeably calmer demeanor.

Sam nodded and released her arm.

"Sir, I'm heading to the cargo bay to make sure the Marks are secured in the wall compartment. We can start to divvy it up between the crew later." Alex gave Sam a small smile. Sam nodded back as she exited the large cockpit through the automatic sliding doors, which closed behind her.

The cockpit was silent for a minute before Willie chimed in to break the awkwardness. "You know, she can be out of line."

Sam cut him off immediately. "You know as well as I do you were pushing her buttons on Darmus III. She does the negotiating! I let you tag along because you want more responsibility other than being the pilot of my ship! Well, I gave it to you and Alex is right! You cost the entire crew a chunk of Marks. Those extra Marks you undoubtedly gave up are one less month vacation for all of us. You wanted a win under your belt. Well, you got it, I suppose. The Cambulon rebels were quite happy with our final price and the condition of the weapons we were able to secure for them on the planet Emulow!"

"Look, I just think that maybe not trying to squeeze them for a bit more Marks would build up more trust. That's not a bad thing, is it?" Willie retorted, still looking back at his boss.

Sam all but cut him off. "They expect to barter. What we did there was show that we're weak! And now that price will be the new normal. It's business, Willie. And as Alex so eloquently put it, there are also several other people in this solar system that don't look too fondly on the *Leo* and her crew right now. Just because you *can* sleep with someone that's married to a known gangster, doesn't mean you *should!*"

Willie grew silent, not knowing how to respond to the latest, and quite true, accusation. He sheepishly turned back to the monitor in front of him.

She took a breath. Feeling herself getting angry, much like Alex. Unlike Alex though, she didn't get flushed cheeks easily. In fact, Sam rarely got flustered, keeping her cool through most close calls and near misses. That was why she was the captain of the *Leo* and had been since its previous captain, Robert Howard. Her father.

She had been by his side onboard the *Leo* since her mom had passed away from a sudden illness when she was only ten years old, so she had essentially grown up traveling the stars with her father. Learning the trade and how things operated top to bottom. From piloting to engineering and most importantly, how to deal with the crew. He had taught her well. Then, when she was twenty years old, they were negotiating a deal for medical supplies on the war-torn planet Zibblion in the HD-6732 system. It was a dangerous job to take, and one that her father had his reservations about, but money was money. The deal went bad. Robert and his first officer Blake Pearson perished. Leaving behind his distraught daughter Sam to step up and take the reins. Now, nine years later, Sam felt age thirty looming on her horizon. She wasn't married. No kids. She took on dangerous jobs to scrape by an existence of grey-area goods hustling, hopping from one solar system to the next, always looking for the next big score. Numerous scars adorned her body from all of the close calls and fistfights she'd been involved in throughout her years as essentially a space pirate. But she was a good fighter. Usually, her opponents ended up looking worse than she ever did. But age was slowly starting to creep up on her and she felt it in this tough life she had made for herself.

Sam slumped back into her captain's chair. The shiny brown fabric was starting to show significant wear after all the missions and close calls. The chair had control functions located on either side of the armrests for various functions throughout the cockpit and the rest of the spacecraft. Under the captain's seat was a hatch for quick exits out of the cockpit but it was rarely used and cumbersome to operate. Mainly though, she used her seat as her com system to communicate with her shipmates.

She looked over at Willie, who had been with her current crew for only one year. Her previous pilot, Abe Carmine, had a close call on a run escaping off-world security forces on a drop they made on Quesor in the HD-6981 quadrant. A planet Sam intended to never return to or even travel within one light year from ever again. They were almost caught, and their ship had been damaged to the point where old Abe couldn't shake the feeling that his time was up. He couldn't jeopardize the crew with his rapidly approaching old age and the limitations that came with it in this line of work.

Now Willie. She continued to watch him as he navigated the *Leo* onto their next mission. Willie was a good pilot but had gotten on Alex's bad side quickly and never recovered. He wanted to prove himself to the rest of the crew. A handsome enough fellow. Thirty-two years old, always fidgeting. Running his hands through his hair or rubbing that scruffy beard he was attempting to grow. He was, however, good behind the helm, having flown numerous ships in his time as a pilot back on his home world. He had survived several accidents, but that came with the job.

She had met him several years earlier when he flew with the crew of the cargo freighter *Starglow*. This was a dangerous business they were in, and that ship had a particularly grisly fate, with Willie the only survivor. She took him in as pilot shortly after Abe turned in his wings. She didn't know as much about Willie as she would like to. Just vague bits and pieces about his history. Born and raised on the planet Trichi X9O somewhere in the distant HD-9822 quadrant. But he was one hell of a pilot. And that's what she needed.

Willie glanced back at Sam, noticing she was deep in thought. "Sorry about that, captain. I know I'm new on this ship relatively speaking and sometimes I guess I try to prove my worth more than just behind this wheel. And for what it's worth regarding the thing with that bastard Themphav's wife, she came on to me! But yeah, I suppose that one was a stupid decision on my end."

"You're a good pilot. And I wouldn't have hired you for the *Leo* if I didn't believe in you. But we have to work on those negotiating skills of yours. And keep it in your pants, ok?" She grinned at him.

He rubbed his unshaven chin, contemplating what she said almost comically, then returned to face forward in his seat. He noticed a red light blinking on his radar screen. It was faint and it was distant. "Um, sir, I've got a signal here. Whatever it is, it's not big. Good chance there's a small spacecraft out there."

Getting up out of the command chair as it creaked behind her, she walked over to Willie's station and looked at the screen. It was a large flat monitor in front of the helm that displayed the ship's path in all directions. Any non-organic space debris in their sector was noted in the computer log as non-threatening. Any man-made object or object that could potentially be of hostile intent showed up red. Such were the risks of their profession.

"What do you make of it, captain? There shouldn't be anything out this far in the quadrant," Willie said, puzzled, as he continued staring at the blinking red dot.

"Whatever that is, it's too close to that supernova. No one travels in that sector unless they have a death wish." She put her hands on her hips, thinking as she looked at the red dot, then asked, "How fast is it traveling?"

"Current speed judging from my readout here is .27 light speed. Wait, .26," Willie answered quickly.

"Is it far enough from the supernova? I won't be going anywhere near that thing. If it's too close, thanks but no thanks," Sam commented smugly.

Tapping his finger on the red blinking light, he thought for a second then answered, "Whatever this is, it's man made and is out of the gravitational pull of the event horizon and seems to be continuing its trajectory away from it. What do you think it is, sir?"

Sam didn't answer and made her way back to her seat and contemplated the little red dot. Then, looking down, she hit the com button on the right-hand side of her chair. "Grant, come in."

Danny Boy sat at the table in the *Leo's* small mess hall, which was made up of five tables and a kitchen area where all food was located and prepped. Each of the crew took their turns at meal preps. One of his hands lay flat on the table. His other hand, his right hand, was outstretched with his elbow propped against his left hand. Grant Edwards sat opposite him. His large and imposing left hand also on the table, his right hand outstretched, clasping Danny Boy's. They looked at each other with nothing but concentration. Beside each man was a dirty shot glass filled halfway with light brown 110% proof Emulowian Rye. Cheap.

Grant was the ship's weapons expert. Had been for over five of his twenty-eight years of life. Well versed in hand-to-hand combat as well as knife fighting, with an expertise in firearms. He'd trained extensively on his home world of Raitera V in the HD-6823 quadrant, a planet that was run by one corrupt government after another. The political instability made fighters out of people at a younger age than most other planets in that solar system. He had been good friends with Abe, who also came from Raitera V before he retired from the business and returned to his home world. Filling that void had been Danny Boy, who he'd gotten into a fight with on the planet Wiggip in the HD-8489 quadrant during some downtime.

Danny's home world was beautiful, with many beaches and oceans. Unfortunately, with that came lots of tourists and the drinking, and drug use on Wiggip was nearly uncontrollable. A disagreement between a very intoxicated Grant and Danny Boy had resulted in more than just heated words. Sam broke it up, and soon they were all sitting around the local bar by the ocean on Benyxel beach sharing stories about space travel between solar systems and the Marks that could be made on some of the riskier jobs.

Danny had no ties on his home world, but was quite a good mechanic, working on jobs that mainly required freighter transport ship repair. The rest was history. Sam and Grant convinced him his future was with them, traveling the stars, making Marks and keeping the ship running as optimally possible, considering her age and the damage sustained in numerous escapes and firefights.

Grant was large and imposing. Muscular with rippling veins on his dark-skinned forearms due to his strenuous workouts in the cargo bay when it wasn't full of loot. Otherwise, his quarters suited him just fine for some weightlifting. His physique countered the shorter skinnier athletic build of Danny Boy. But looks weren't everything. What Danny Boy lacked in bulk, he made up for in speed.

"Grant, come in," Sam's voice rang out through the intercom system.

Seeing his opportunity, Danny Boy yelled, "Three, two, one, go!" Before Grant had time to react, Danny Boy slammed his arm down on the table, ending their short-lived arm-wrestling tournament.

"Nope! You always try that stunt! That's not how this works and you know it, you cheating bastard!" Grant yelled angrily, releasing his hand from Danny Boy's and pounding his fists against the table, shaking both of the shot glasses as well as the bottle.

"Drink up lightweight, captain needs you," Danny Boy said calmly with a smirk and a chuckle. Danny Boy was the engineer and took care of most maintenance issues on the ship. Of which there were many. The ship was older and had been through many scrapes in its time. It needed a good engineer and Danny Boy was it. It had been his job for what he felt had been a while now, enough to where he felt confident in dealing with the ships numerous issues that popped up from this line of work. He quite liked his job. He was the oldest of the crew at thirty-three. One year older than Willie. He had been the youngest of the *Leo* crew at one point when he was taken in by the late, great Mr. Howard at the young age of nineteen. He had seen various crew members come and go but this current crew, with all of their many faults, worked relatively well together. Other than Alex and her continued badgering of the "new kid" Willie.

Grant shot Danny Boy a look of comical rage, lifted up his shot glass and downed the syrupy liquid in one gulp. Setting the glass down and wiping his mouth off with the back of his hand, he said sarcastically, "You win at these little arm-wrestling matches far too often!"

Danny Boy leaned back in his chair, putting his hands on the back of his shaved head and shot back quickly with a grin, "Hey, guess what? Captain's waiting!"

"Grant, do you copy?" Sam's voice came through the com system again. This time with a hint of impatience.

Walking over to the voice com system panel in the mess hall quickly, Grant pushed the button and spoke into it, "Here, sir."

"Come up to the cockpit. Got something I want you to see. Bring Danny along if he's close by." She clicked off.

"Yes sir," Grant responded and shot Danny a questioning look.

Danny stood up, picked up his own shot glass and downed his portion of the alcoholic drink. He made his way to the sliding panel door to exit the small mess hall, motioning for Grant.

Grant nodded back. There was not only a mutual respect between the two, but genuine friendship. For all the teasing they did to each other, Grant considered Danny his best friend. And the feeling was mutual. They made decent money aboard the *Leo*, but it wasn't just money that kept them aboard. This was their family. No other ties on their home worlds. This was it.

The mess hall was located on the second level of three. The third and lowest level of the ship was engineering in the rear of the hull while the ship's databanks and computing systems were located in the front. Second level was the mess hall, the rec room and the cargo area, with numerous storage rooms all linked together. Level one was the cockpit command center as well as living quarters, showers and numerous storage rooms and compartments. A service elevator located on the front end of the ship took the crew to whichever level they intended to go quickly. Fire exit ladders were also located on each deck at the rear of the ship.

Sam's father had made sure the ship was well protected. Numerous crawlspaces and secure rooms were located throughout the interior of the *Leo* on the off chance that they were boarded by unwanted guests. The exterior of the ship was plated with lightweight armor that could withstand blasts from chasing patrol ships or angry customers. The *Leo* had at one time been light grey in color but over time it had taken on a much darker shade of grey due to the countless hours of space travel and battles, the bumps and bruises it had been a part of through its many years in service.

Danny and Grant walked down the long metal hallway towards the ladder nearest the first floor closest to the command center. Each took their turn climbing the ladder up to floor one. Once there, they headed to the cockpit.

Sam and Willie continued to stare at the blinking red dot on the radar as Danny and Grant entered through the automatic sliding doors in the rear of the room. Sam glanced back, seeing them enter, and motioned them to come up to the command center.

"Thoughts?" she said inquisitively to Danny and Grant, who were now both looking down at the screen in front of them.

Grant stared at the blinking red dot, then raised his eyebrows. "Could be a derelict ship. Crew dead or incapacitated. Who knows what they're carrying, but I'm guessing there isn't too much risk judging by the size of it. We could get closer to it so the *Leo* can do a scan for us. If it's worth salvaging or if any life is detected, we can go from there. How long until we reach it?"

"At current speed we can reach whatever it is out there in one hour if it continues on with its current trajectory. It's still a bit too close for comfort to the dead star in that region, so whatever we plan on doing we should do it quick and get out of there," Willie answered, still staring at the screen.

Sam looked over at Danny Boy, who glanced over at her as well. They both knew instinctively what each other was thinking, but Danny put it into words. "There is a chance. A slim one, but this big tugboat we live on could be caught in the gravitational pull of the black hole. We should be far enough away, but this ship is in no way capable of breaking free. And my strong hunch is we will be the only ship in that sector, so no help would be coming. That area of space has been forbidden to travel under strict ruling by this quadrant's acting governments on all of the inhabited planets. So, like I said. No help."

Pointing at the screen in front of him, Willie shot out, "Guys, I'm now picking up faint signals of life. I think we're looking at a small spacecraft. I can't tell for sure how many lifeforms aboard though."

Sam responded to Willie, "How far away from the supernova do we need to be to be relatively safe from its gravitational pull?"

"Well, theoretically that small craft out there is already out of the pull of that black hole. Otherwise we wouldn't be seeing it. Unless that ship has some sort of propulsion system that I'm not aware of. Which could likely be the case. It would have to be magnetized though. You know, like two magnets forcing away from each other. Or however that works, I'm just guessing here. There were planets that used to build them like that. Haven't been built like that though in a long ass time." Willie stared at this object floating slowly in space.

Sam contemplated this new bit of news, then glanced over at Grant.

"The size of that thing certainly doesn't pose much of a threat. However, we don't know what kind of lifeforms are aboard. Could be a parasitic space worm. Having said that. Whatever it is, is fair game as far as I'm concerned."

Continuing to stare at the blinking red dot inching its way slowly closer to the *Leo*, Sam made up her mind: "Plot a course. Danny, go help Alex prepare the cargo bay for docking procedures in t-minus one hour. Grant, you know the drill. Be ready for anything."

The three men all nodded and said, "Yes sir." Willie locked in the coordinates while Danny and Grant turned to exit the cockpit area, heading each to their assigned tasks.

"Alex is gonna just love this," Danny Boy mumbled to Grant as they parted ways. Grant headed to the small arms weapons room on the top level and Danny climbed down the ladder to tell Alex the good news.

CHAPTER 3

WHERE IS HOME?

"Synth level 100% depletion in t-minus 35 minutes," said Zark in its flat tone.

Ramsey glanced down at his screen and breathed a sigh of relief. "Ok, we've hit .25 light speed and will hopefully continue to decrease. Unfortunately, our hull is at 12%. At this point, there's no way this thing is going to make it through any planet's atmosphere. On top of that, you all heard what our current synth levels are. We are dangerously close to becoming stranded in space. I can't possibly imagine any ship venturing this close to that black hole."

Justin leaned forward in his seat, rubbing his chin. "We're alive. We haven't given up yet, and we aren't going to start now," he said confidently.

"Let's weigh our options. We have some food rations, water, and around thirty minutes of synth left. After that we float. At the very least, I think we should set our course to the nearest planet, even if we can't reach it or land," Carol said thoughtfully.

"Nearest planet in this quadrant is Darmus III. It's inhabited, so that's good. Unfortunately, we don't have nearly enough synth to make it there, not by a long shot," Ramsey responded sadly.

"With the synth that we do have, if we head to this Darmus III planet, what will be our final end point?" Justin asked, looking over at Ramsey.

Looking over the screen and doing a few calculations, Ramsey turned and looked at Justin with grim news. "On our current tank of nearly depleted synth and with the damage to the hull, if we're lucky if we get possibly a tenth of the way there from our present location."

Justin leaned back in his chair and Carol put her hands on her face, leaning against the controls in front of her.

"We could have made it to this planet had I not started draining the synth," Ramsey said.

Justin immediately cut him off. "You gave us a fighting chance! All three of us would be floating amongst the stars in tiny frozen pieces if you hadn't acted as quickly as you did."

Shaking his head in frustration, Ramsey continued, "Yes, but now we're going to sit in this tin can floating in outer space and wait until our systems give out. Then what? Starve to death or die of thirst. Maybe just wait until the rest of the oxygen is depleted? Our space suits won't do us any good either in their ragged state."

Carol sat upright in her seat and said, "You know, when I was in that temple back on TSR, alone, for a bit I saw no hope. No way of escaping my dire circumstances. Then I saw that hole up by the ceiling of that huge tomb. I was able to find a way up to it and got out just as the Azid were bearing down on me. After that I sliced my arm real good, went over a waterfall, injuring my back, cauterized the cut with a hot knife and then made my way through dark caverns, narrowly avoiding a huge monster made of ice." She paused, looking over at Ramsey.

"Each of us has had numerous close calls recently, yet here we are. We didn't give up. Ben and James sacrificed themselves for us! They died giving us a fighting chance to get exactly to this very point right now! We aren't done yet. I have to believe that. 'You're going to get through this, baby girl. You will. You're my daughter and you're a fighter.' My dad's last words." Carol then went silent with a grim, determined look falling across her face.

Silence fell across the *Stormbringer*. For a minute they all sat there contemplating their current situation.

"We have currently only one option. Plot course to Darmus III," Justin said quietly, breaking the silence.

Ramsey entered the coordinates and the ship moved silently towards the distant planet.

"Not sure about you two, but I'm hungry. And thirsty," Carol said, breaking the tension.

"Yeah, me too. The meat from that cat creature has officially worn off. Let's eat some rations and get our strength back up a bit," Justin replied.

Ramsey nodded and looked over at Carol. "Hey, I'm sorry for…"

She stopped him. "Nothing to be sorry about. We've all got frayed nerves after everything we've been through. Can I get you some food?"

Ramsey shot her a grin and nodded. She got up and walked towards the rear of the ship, putting her hand on Justin's shoulder as she walked past him.

"I could go for a Tambis wrap with hot sauce and a fizzwhizz," Ramsey said, half joking to her on her way back.

"Best I can do is another ration of Schlack meat and accompanying sides. Water is the beverage of choice on this flight as well." Carol looked through the rations she had stored in the rear of the *Stormbringer* right before the *Cauldwell* went up in flames.

Wrinkling his nose at the sound of the bland and tough Schlack meat, Ramsey sighed and nodded his approval.

She returned to her post with three rations and eating utensils. One for each of them. She handed them to her crewmates, who quickly opened up the lids. Upon doing so the food was instantly heated. This was how all space travel rations were prepared on their home world of Trilaxus. Calories were taken into consideration for each prepped meal to keep their astronauts well nourished.

"Thanks, Carol," both Justin and Ramsey said at nearly the same time as they dove into the heated meal.

They ate in silence and after they were finished Justin raised his bottle of water. "Here's to James and Ben. Without them we wouldn't even be this far," he said reverently.

"Here, here," Ramsey replied as he and Carol both raised their respective bottles, all clinking together in unison.

Carol thought for a minute, then spoke, "You know, back on the planet, I know there would have been pushback because we need all the supplies we can get, but I set aside several of Ben's personal items that we took from the *Cauldwell*, along with each of our other personals. Mainly, a change of clothes, a few food rations, some water and a few other personal items. They were in a container. So, I'm sorry. But I set the container outside."

No one said anything. Not sure how to respond. They all knew an extra food and water ration could mean life or death. But…Ben.

Shaking her head in apology, she said, "I'm sorry. I know it was foolish of me but…Ben, his infected body was naked! I mean, what if! We don't know what happened after James crashed into the mountain. What if, I don't know! What if it changed him back? What if he somehow survived!?!"

"Carol, we saw him. He was dead," Justin said softly.

They all fell silent again. Thinking about their fallen crewmate. Then Justin spoke again, this time firmly. "If there was even the slightest chance. A hint of him surviving. The least we could have done, you did, Carol. So, thank you. Thank you for thinking of that."

She smiled while still looking at the floor. Justin's respect and love for this woman continued to grow. Her kind heart. Her survivor spirit. All of them, himself included, were now survivors.

"Synth level critical. Total depletion in t-minus 60 seconds," Zark stated.

No one responded. All three of them sat in their chairs with their own thoughts.

"When we were going through that black hole, did either of you see those objects moving around us? They looked as if they were acting of their own free will. Like they were living beings. They certainly didn't move like a spacecraft of any sort. They were more like shadows. Outlines, really. Maybe it was just one thing that I saw, it was hard to tell," Ramsey said to Carol and Justin quietly.

"I saw it too," Justin answered. "No idea what it was, but I didn't like it. Maybe it was my training, but when your gut tells you something's off, it's usually right. And my gut told me that thing inside there was something to avoid. Not that we had any say in the matter."

"I didn't see that thing you guys are talking about, but I'll take your word for it," Carol added.

"Synth tanks depleted. Please dock immediately for refueling to continue on plotted course," Zark said through the com.

"Where is home?" Carol asked, wanting to keep conversation going to avoid thinking about the dire situation they were currently in.

"Home, wow. That's a place I haven't thought of in a bit. What I wouldn't do to be in the ring with my gloves on taking a few hard rights to the chin and dishing them right back times two. With my old buddy coach Schmitz cheering me on." Ramsey was clearly enjoying the brief moment of retrospective.

"I think she meant the location of Trilaxus, Ramsey," Justin chimed in with a slight hint of teasing in his voice.

"I know what she meant! I was just doing a bit of out-loud daydreaming for you all," Ramsey shot back, in his own teasing voice.

Both Carol and Justin smiled at him, then glanced at each other, continuing the smile with not just their mouths but with their eyes.

"Home is…well, home is over three years away in that direction," Ramsey said serenely, looking from his monitor to the viewscreen, pointing out into the distant stars. Then he added, "Who knows, if we're lucky, we might actually make it back to our home world in way less than the twenty-year mission we had originally signed up for!"

"Home's what you make it. I consider home where my friends are. Where my crew is. Where the mission takes me. In this case, well, I suppose home is here," Justin said sedately.

Carol glanced over at him, her cheeks slightly flush. She cared so deeply for that man.

"Speak for yourself. The boxing ring. There's home. And yeah, I won't lie. Even in this floating tin can, I'm glad to be with you both. Through everything we've been through, I wouldn't want to be stuck with anyone else. Well, maybe Lucindia Merrick. Remember Lucy?" Ramsey said as he grinned, looking over at Justin.

Chuckling, Justin answered, "How could I forget? You had the hots for her all the way through academy training. Sorry buddy, but she was out of your league. She was out of everyone's league."

"What's that supposed to mean?" Carol chimed in, sounding a bit irked at the current topic of discussion.

"Well, she seemed to think quite well of herself. To the point that she got a sort of reputation amongst the flyboys as being unobtainable, so to speak," Justin added, noting Carol's slight change in tone.

"Long red curly hair. Those freckles. Those eyes that seem to look right through you," Ramsey said, daydreaming.

"If memory serves, she thought so well of herself and the adoration of the men that she surrounded herself with that she didn't take the time to properly train and failed not only flight school but engineering as well, so she took on a desk job at STEA," Carol said coolly, then added, "not that desk jobs are a bad thing. But at some point, a bit of humility goes a long way."

Ramsey grinned. "Yeah, but those freckles."

They all three laughed hard. It felt good. In this tough situation, they still had each other and their friendship. They were still alive through everything they had endured.

Then the voice of Zark broke through the laughter in the hull: "Unidentified craft approaching off the starboard bow. Contact in t-minus twenty minutes."

CHAPTER 4

STEADY AS SHE GOES

Sam sat in the command chair of the *Leo* as Willie continued on the interception course with the blinking red dot on the map.

"How close are we to the supernova, Willie?" she asked, leaning forward in her seat and squinting her eyes at the viewscreen in front of her.

"Well, we should be within viewscreen range of this ship here any minute. I still think we're safe from the gravitational pull. You'd think if whatever is out there is ok, so are we. It must have some pretty fancy tech powering it to be able to pull away. My opinion though, and this is just my personal opinion, we take a look at it, if it's worth salvaging then we load it up and get out of here. Immediately, if not sooner," Willie said to the captain without taking his eyes off the viewscreen.

The doors to the cockpit slid open and Alex entered. "Captain, the cargo bay is ready to go. Not much to move around actually due to us currently being enroute to the next pickup point. We moved the Marks to another secure area though. If there's life onboard what we're about to intercept, I don't want anyone getting any bright ideas."

Sam nodded her approval as she watched Alex walk towards the viewscreen and glance down at Willie, who didn't look up to greet her.

"Well, there it is," Willie said in a composed voice, pointing out ahead.

Alex, Sam and Willie all stared out at the small craft in the far distance of space, now visible on the viewscreen in front of them, very slowly getting closer.

"Willie, run a scan now to see what life signs are on-board," Sam commanded.

Willie initiated the scan feature on the *Leo*. It wasn't long range and could only be used in line-of-sight situations such as was the case now.

"Scan of the vessel shows three life forms aboard," he replied calmly.

Sam nodded, then immediately hit the com button. "Danny and Grant, come in," she said curtly on the open channel through the ship.

After a brief pause, Grant's voice echoed through the cockpit: "Grant here."

"Ship is located and we're moving in. Be on the ready in the cargo bay if we do take her aboard. Three life forms detected. I want to have a little chat with them before we let them dock," Sam ordered.

"Roger that. I've got Danny here with me. We're good to go. Is Alex with you?"

"Yes, I'm here. Look, Grant, with the number of Marks we have stored onboard and now that I know there are three life forms on this small ship out there, we have to assume they're guilty until proven innocent, so to speak," Alex responded quickly.

"Ok, we'll be ready. Grant out."

The small spacecraft in front of them continued to grow larger in the viewscreen as Sam, Willie and Alex stared out at their potential new acquisition.

Carol was sitting in her seat, thinking about her time in the temple back on TSR1, about the nasty cut she received. About the horrible dreams of the beast in the mountain determined to "collect" her. Of Ben, changed into a hideous flying rat-like being from scratches he received from the fight in the cave shortly after they arrived on the planet. How his strong willpower overcame the terrible transformation he'd endured. She missed him. Her mind continued to wander as she stared out of the view screen.

Ramsey and Justin were both sitting with their eyes closed, the adrenaline of their near destruction by way of meteor field slowly subsiding. As Carol sat, contemplating the last week of her life, an object in space caught her eye.

"Guys! Look. Sure enough, there's something out there!" she said enthusiastically, pointing out the viewscreen towards what was now obviously an oncoming spacecraft.

Staring out into space, all three of them were at a loss for words for a short time. Then Justin broke the silence. "I guess this is what's called *just in the nick of time.*"

"Well, hello there. That thing looks like some sort of freighter from the design. Not sure what class it is. I've never seen something quite like it. It looks old and pretty weathered. Kind of odd looking. Like a long bar of soap with boosters on its side. Piloting must be done up front there in that area that juts out from the rest of the ship," Ramsey said quietly, almost to himself.

Justin added, "Well, we each have a sidearm as well as our knives. I don't know who or what is on the other side of that bucket of bolts, but I aim to be prepared. Having said that, this is our lucky break. We may not have another shot, so good first impressions are important here."

Carol nodded in agreement. "Well, we might have landing gear access. That's to be determined with the damage to our hull, but I wonder if we will have com link with them. It would be nice to say hi to our would-be rescuers before we dock."

No sooner had the words escaped her mouth when the communications link-up blinked red on the control panel.

Carol glanced at Justin. "Looks like they want to say hi," she said, trying to hide her nervousness.

"Here goes nothing," Justin said, also with a hint of apprehension in his voice as he leaned forward, motioning Ramsey to hit the link up button.

Ramsey pushed the button and the calming robotic voice of Zark responded, "Communications link-up initiated and accepted."

There was static at first, which gave way to silence. But someone was on the other end.

Clearing his throat, Justin broke the silence. "My name is Justin Schwartz. I'm here with my pilot Ramsey Conner and co-pilot Carol Blake. We could use some assistance."

A pause, and then, "This is commander Samantha Howard of the freighter transport ship *Leo*. What seems to be the problem, Mr. Justin Schwartz?"

Justin looked at Carol and Ramsey, raising one eyebrow followed by a small grin. "Well, it's quite the tale to tell. If you would indulge us, I would be happy to share it with you. We're out of synth and our hull is down to 10% integrity. Meaning, even if small space debris comes into contact with the outer hull, we're done for. On top of all that good news, I think I speak for my crew that stretching our legs a bit would do us a world of good."

Silence followed on the other end. Justin, Ramsey and Carol also sat in silence, waiting to see what the response to their mayday would be. Would they be blasted out of space? Would they be taken hostage? Where were they? Carol was about to say something to break the awkward silence, but Justin put his hand on her forearm and shook his head.

"I don't recognize your spacecraft. Why travel this far out into deep space in something that small and this close to that dead star in quadrant HD-8478? What planet are you from?" Sam's voice finally said, breaking the long silence.

"We're from the planet Trilaxus. We were on a deep space exploration mission with a course plotted for Alpha Sector Eight, our ship was sucked through that black hole, came out the other side and we crashed on a hostile planet. Our mothership was destroyed and we've been traveling in our escape pod from that ship after escaping the planet and travelling back through the black hole," Justin came back grimly. Then he added after a brief pause, "If you can believe that."

Willie turned in his pilot's seat to look at the captain. Alex also looked back at her with a look of surprise. Sam sat in her captain's chair at a loss for words at what she was hearing. "Did you say you travelled through that supernova?" she asked the stranded space travelers in front of her ship, not trying to hide her surprise at this bit of information.

"Look, we can explain it all to you if we can just dock with you. We are literally dead in the water so to speak here. We will die if we don't get off this thing. We're out of fuel and eventually, out of air, water and food. We plotted a course for Darmus III and this is how far we got," Justin answered grimly.

"First off, Darmus III is heading in the opposite direction of our current route. Just left there actually," Sam came back. Then added, "I've never heard of a planet named Trilaxus and

Alpha Sector Eight? I'll save you the trouble, It's uninhabited. Regardless, I've never heard of any ship and her crew, regardless of size, go through a black hole and live to tell about it. So I'm having trouble believing you. And if I have trouble believing you, that means I have trouble trusting you on my ship." She paused, waiting for a response.

Carol looked at both Ramsey and Justin, then motioned for Ramsey to mute the com. Ramsey nodded and pressed the mute button. "Ok, they can't hear us," he said and breathed a heavy sigh.

"That ship is a freighter, and I have a strong hunch they're scavengers for sale running goods for payment. Their type is all over the galaxy. STEA has dealt with them before on other missions. Typically they go their way and we go ours, but we need them, Justin. Let me give it a shot," she said to Justin calmly.

Justin sat back in his chair, looking at Carol. He nodded to Ramsey. Ramsey clicked off the mute and nodded to Carol.

Carol sat up straight in her seat as if to compose herself and choose her words carefully. "This is Carol Blake, medical officer and co-pilot of the *Cauldwell*. Please, just take us to whatever inhabitable planet is closest, and we would be eternally grateful to you. Our planet's government will compensate you for the rescue attempt handsomely."

"Greetings, Mrs. Carol Blake. You said you're from Trilaxus? Never heard of it. What sector?" Sam answered curtly.

"HD-2509," Carol responded, then added, "Please. You're our only hope."

"Give me a minute." She nodded for Willie to cut the link.

Willie ended the com link and turned to look at Sam and Alex. "What are we gonna do?" he said evenly.

"I don't like it. Not one bit," Alex chimed in coldly. "Way too many variables here. Their ship is dead. We don't know what weapons they have onboard, so they might try to take us by surprise. We have a lot of Marks right now. Furthermore, they could be sick or diseased. None of us are capable of dealing with a virus. And that's just the start of the long list of nopes I have."

Sam stood up, staring at the small spacecraft floating in front of them. Contemplating her next move. "Duly noted, and I agree on every single count. However, we're smugglers. We sell both legit as well as hot items to both good people and bad people. And we get paid for it. That's what we do. What we don't do, is leave people in a coffin floating in space to die a slow death."

She paused to let that sink in with Alex, who was glancing at the floor. Then Sam continued in the commanding authoritative voice her crew knew her all too well for, "We're gonna let them board and drop them off on a nearby planet. We need to fuel up sometime in the near future anyway, so it's not like we're making an extra stop just for them. From that point on, they're on their own. And in the meantime, we're gonna see if indeed we can get a nice little reward from our rescue."

"Sir, I do request we confiscate any weapons they may have," Alex added, knowing the captain's mind was made up. No use arguing.

"I agree. Re-establish communications with that ship," Sam commanded.

After the push of a button, Willie responded back to Sam, "We're live."

"*Stormbringer* crew, I'm granting permission to dock in our cargo bay. We don't have much in the way of sanitation supplies, but we do have a small quarantine area that you'll have to go through, and we confiscate any and all weapons, got it?" Sam ordered coolly.

"Now, wait just a minute…" Ramsey said out loud after hitting the mute button once again.

"Ramsey, don't," Justin said firmly.

"But sir, no weapons?"

"I don't like it any more than you do, but we need on that ship. It's that or nothing. We play our cards right and we get to a nearby planet, contact STEA on Trilaxus, explain the situation and get home. That's as good as it's going to get for right now."

Ramsey hung his head and sighed as Justin motioned for him to turn on the com link once again.

"Ok, you've got a deal. We'll decontaminate and hand over our firearms. Be good to get cleaned up actually, after the week we've all had," Justin said in a truly tired voice.

"Danny Boy and Grant will be your point people in our cargo bay. No funny business, Mr. Justin. They aren't ones to be messed with. Sam out." She clicked off the com link, sighing as she slumped back in her commander's chair.

"Alex, head down to the cargo bay as well. Three of them, three of you. Make sure my orders are carried out to a T," Sam said bluntly looking up at Willie with weary eyes.

Alex nodded, glanced at the ship out in front of them and then glanced at Willie. Without saying a word, she left the cockpit, heading to the cargo bay.

"So my sensors are picking up some sort of substance on the bottom of their hull. Could be leakage of some sort," Willie said as he stared at his monitor.

"First sign of any abnormality, the ship gets dumped. I have a bad feeling about this," Sam said, trying to hide her nervousness, with Willie nodding in agreement.

"Ok, their ship is out of juice. What did they call it? Synth? Whatever that is. Willie, turn the *Leo* around and prepare for docking procedures. Steady as she goes."

CHAPTER 5

DOCKING AND INTRODUCTIONS

"Ok Ramsey, looks like they're circling us for docking prep. We're gonna have to coast in. Man, that ship has certainly seen some better days," Justin said flatly.

"Roger that. They've been in some fights. Not sure who came out on top, but she's definitely taken some blasts. Look there." Ramsey pointed to the side of the *Leo's* hull. Burnt blast marks sprayed the side as if a hail of gunfire had connected against the outer plating.

Carol leaned forward in her seat, inspecting the ship they were about to dock with. "For the kind of business they seem to be involved in, it could be bigger, but I assume this thing will travel at higher speeds. Which is probably what they want anyways. I already don't trust them."

"I think we're all on the same page there. Look, that must be their outboard weapons," Justin said in his serious quiet tone, motioning to the barrel stocks on the midsection of the ship on one of the panels that jutted out further from the rest of the hull.

Ramsey peered at the intimidating weaponry as the ship passed them on its way to get its backside facing them directly. "They look old but I'm assuming can pack a pretty mean punch. Just like the ship they're attached to. Looks like they have a few guns on the rear of this tub. Probably for their getaways," he said coldly.

"Possibly, but remember, everyone. We're their guests. Hopefully we can make this quick. Get cleaned up. Be nice. Land wherever they're heading and be on our way." Justin said as he rubbed his chin, trying to shake the feeling this trip could potentially take longer than he wanted it to.

The *Leo* had now positioned its rear hull in front of the *Stormbringer* and come to a full stop, hovering in space. There was an atmosphere of restlessness inside *Stormbringer* as Justin, Carol and Ramsey prepared to dock.

The rear hatch of the *Leo* began to slowly open. A large panel slid downward against the bottom of the hull and seemed to lock into place. Lights were visible inside the cargo bay of the *Leo* now. The large compartment looked empty. More than likely recently emptied after their last drop off. Luck might just be on their side, Justin hoped as he and the rest of his small crew peered on.

The com crackled to life inside the *Stormbringer*. "Greetings, fellow space travelers. My name is Danny Boy. I will be your valet service for the next short period of time. Are you able to move your ship at all, or are you 100% no power?"

"This is Ramsey Conner, pilot of the *Stormbringer*. I might be able to refire our magnetic propulsion system in here and give it enough juice to dock in your cargo bay."

"Well hello there, Ramsey Conner. Good to make your acquaintance. Give it a go. We're ready and waiting for you. I assume you have the good sense to know when to hit the parking brakes and stop your forward momentum once you're inside?" Danny Boy said half-jokingly.

"Like I wouldn't know when to stop my own ship," Ramsey mumbled quiet enough that anyone on the other end couldn't hear him. Carol shot him a look that said, *Be nice.*

Nodding to her, he said, "Roger that. Attempting restart now. Ramsey out."

"Hey Carol, you're my eyes on the monitor. I'll steer, you guide. If we can get this thing moving, of course," Ramsey said apprehensively.

"You've got this. Fire it up," Carol responded softly.

Ramsey looked at Justin again. "Here goes nothing."

A few buttons were pushed. Zark softly came through on the com system. "Synth levels depleted. Please refill tank to proper levels for space travel."

"Yeah, yeah, tell me something I don't know," Ramsey responded sarcastically, glancing up at Zark's com speaker above him.

He wiped the sweat from his brow. "Attempting to manually fire magnetic propulsion units on empty. Let's hope there's enough fumes left in the pipes to get us moving forward. Here goes nothing."

Ramsey pushed the "Ignite Magnetic Thrusters" button on the control panel. The engine whirled to life. As it did, Ramsey immediately pushed forward on the helm. The *Stormbringer* slowly began moving forward.

Carol put her hand on Ramsey's shoulder, then glanced at Justin. All three of them had the same expression. *Let this work,* they all seemed to be thinking in unison.

The ship was moving directly towards the cargo bay entrance of the *Leo*. Zark's voice came over the com system. "1,000 meters to safe docking."

The engine stopped. Warning lights blinked inside the ship. Zark's voice once again filled the cabin of the *Stormbringer*: "Synth liquid at 0%. Unable to propel the magnetic propulsion system at this time. Please resupply with optimal synth levels to continue operations."

"And that's it," Ramsey responded glumly to Justin and Carol. Then he added, "And now we see how far she can float after giving her a little nudge forward towards that tugboat in front of us."

Slowly, the *Stormbringer* continued its trajectory towards the *Leo*. Carol looked over her monitor system nodded in tired relief. "Judging by these estimates, we're going to reach the *Leo* with just enough speed to spare. Should be inside the cargo bay in less than a minute. I never thought we would end up piloting a tiny escape shuttle craft like this through a black hole, around asteroids and meteor showers and other space debris and then coast ourselves into a strange looking freighter ship in the middle of deep space in order to survive."

"Drastic circumstances call for drastic actions," Justin shot back confidently.

Carol smiled to herself as she continued watching the monitor.

"Ok, here it comes," Danny Boy said with a tinge of apprehension as they watched the small, heavily damaged escape craft glide forward and into their cargo bay area which wasn't much to look at. Consisting of high ceilings with light fixtures built in, covered in dark grey metal with paneling on the walls. They were both wearing their space suits, as well as Alex, who had just suited up and joined them against the back wall of the cargo bay.

Their space suits were more for short term use. Orange in color and relatively lightweight, considering they could be used in the deathly cold vacuum of outer space for up to, but no longer than, one hour. At which point the oxygen would need to be replenished and the suits' battery packs recharged. Sam had gotten five for her crew in exchange for an extra crate of food rations on the planet Oravan IV in the HD-7630 quadrant.

They were considered lower end, older suits, but Sam and her crew only needed them in situations such as this. Opening the cargo bay doors in space or in an emergency where the *Leo* would lose cabin pressure.

"How we doing down there?" Sam asked the rest of her crew through their internal com systems in their suits. She and Willie were able to see what was taking place on a viewscreen beside the main screen in front of them, which showed any and all activity in the cargo bay. Sam's father had that feature installed many years ago to ensure none of the goods they hauled were tampered with. It kept the crew from ever getting any sneaky ideas of pocketing anything.

"This ship has had it from what I'm seeing, sir. What a banged-up mess. The rear is totally smashed in and whatever it's been through, I truly cannot believe it's still in one piece," Danny Boy responded, shocked at the condition of the *Stormbringer*.

"Let's hope the landing gear still works," Sam came back cynically.

Nodding to himself, he looked over at Grant and Alex. They waited with guns in hand. They all knew their business was one with the unspoken motto *Trust must be earned*, and right now, in the condition this ship was in, trust was something everyone on the *Leo* was in short supply of.

The *Stormbringer* made its way fully into the cargo bay. As it was now inside, Ramsey hit the landing gear. A grinding sound emanated from inside the cabin as more warning lights came on. Zark gave more bad news: "Landing gear inoperable due to damage to rear outer hull. Seek other means of docking."

"Seek other means of docking? Other means? What other means? Shut up Zark!" Ramsey clicked off the com, silencing Zark once again.

Justin leaned forward in his chair and asked Ramsey and Carol, "Can we manually lower the landing gear that isn't damaged? It's better than nothing. Maybe even the damaged one can operate enough to get us on solid ground. I don't want to piss them off more than they already are by scratching up their cargo bay floor more than it already seems to be."

"Ramsey, you keep guiding us forward. Let me try something," Carol came back.

"Why aren't they deploying their landing gear?" Grant asked stoically.

"Because it probably doesn't work. Captain's just gonna love this," Danny Boy shot back, grinning sarcastically inside his helmet.

"Hey, what's a few more scratches in the cargo bay, right?" Alex said sarcastically. "I mean, it's not like we use it for our livelihood. I can't believe we're doing this." She gripped her laser rifle tightly in her right hand and with her left hand hit the cargo bay hatch button.

"At least the damn thing's quiet. Not sure how that weird egg-shaped thing is powered, but I can't believe it makes virtually no noise."

The large, grey metal cargo bay hatch slowly closed behind the *Stormbringer* until it was sealed tight. The area automatically started to depressurize.

The *Stormbringer* was hovering inside the cargo bay. It may have been out of synth liquid, but it was able to stand by idling. Carol bypassed all system functions and manually released the landing gear, which consisted of three small claw-like appendages made of the same material as the outer hull of the ship.

Two of the landing gears lowered. The third, however, the one closest to the main rear hull damage, only came down slightly before grinding to a halt.

"Good job, Carol. And good enough for me. Take us down, Ramsey," Justin said, glad that they were able to get the gear down as much as they did.

Ramsey nodded and lowered the ship until it was securely on the cargo bay floor. Once on solid ground, Ramsey and Carol started shutting down the ship's functions.

"Well, I'll be damned. They did it. The landing gear actually works. Probably the only thing that does anymore, judging from the sad state of affairs in front of us," Danny Boy said jokingly as he attached a locking mechanism to one of the landing gears to ensure it was stabilized and completely secure inside the cargo bay.

Alex didn't respond. She glanced back at the depressurization level. It had just hit breathable levels, so she motioned to Grant and Danny that it was ok to remove their helmets.

The *Stormbringer* was powered down. Time to meet their rescuers. Ramsey, Carol and Justin looked out and watched as the three figures in space suits each removed their helmets completely. "They just depressurized the cargo bay. Woah, he's a big, beefy fella," Justin said coolly as he got a look at Grant. Just judging by his facial features, he knew that this guy was the muscle onboard the *Leo*.

"They're all packing. I've never seen sidearms like those before. They look like heavier versions of the blast rifles we're issued on Trilaxus." Carol nervously scanned each of the three people in front of their viewscreen which also served as a window when the ship was powered down. She didn't like the look of their heavy artillery weapons.

"That's ok. We've gotten this far. Keep moving forward, alright?" Justin responded with as much confidence as he could muster.

"Hello there," Ramsey said as he looked at Alex's thick head of curly red hair.

"Easy there, big guy," Carol said jokingly as she saw what he was looking at.

They all got out of their seats and made their way to the sliding catch. Justin pressed it and it slid open. Justin picked up the blast rifle he had on TSR1 and held it outstretched in his hand, gripping the barrel, and stepped out of the *Stormbringer* first, with Carol and Ramsey following.

They were greeted with three raised rifles pointed at them from their hosts.

Pointing at himself, Grant spoke first. "Name's Grant. This here is Danny Boy and the redhead you don't want to get on the wrong side of is Alex."

"Justin, Carol, Ramsey." Justin pointed to each person on his side of the invisible line.

"First thing's first. Weapons. All of them." Grant calmly raised his free hand towards Justin's outstretched blast rifle.

CHAPTER 6

A SETBACK

Justin glanced to his left and right at Ramsey and Carol and nodded. They all three held out their guns. Justin had his blast rifle as well as a holstered sidearm, which he handed over to Grant.

Grant took them both after slinging his own rifle over his shoulder. He pointed to the sheathed knife at his side. "Hand it over," he said calmly.

"Come on, man. You guys have the big guns! We're no threat to you with just our knives!" Ramsey spat out angrily.

Alex moved forward, aiming her gun directly at Ramsey's head, glaring at him with her finger on the trigger.

"See now look what you did. You got on Alex's bad side," Danny Boy chimed in with a grin.

"Hand…them…over," Alex said in a barely controlled tone.

"Best do what she says. Trust me on that one." Danny Boy cracked his neck on both sides.

Carol stared at Alex, who noticed the glare. She immediately moved her gun's barrel from Ramsey's head over to Carol's. "Something wrong with your eyeballs there, missy?"

"Get that gun out of my face," Carol shot back angrily, but Alex continued pointing, finger on trigger.

Grant and Danny Boy went to Carol and Ramsey, collecting their guns and knives and setting them in a lockable container on a table behind them against the back wall.

Danny Boy inspected Ramsey's gun and commented to Grant, "Whoa, double barrel. One on top and one on the bottom, hand grip in the middle. High tech weaponry. I've never seen one quite like this. Where did you guys say you were from again?"

"Can we speak with the captain?" Justin asked without responding to Danny's question, glancing over at Alex still pointing her rifle at Carol.

"Decontamination first, Q and A later. Captain's orders," Alex answered, irritated.

"Get that gun out of my face," Carol repeated. This time in a tone of controlled rage.

"Why don't you make me, blondie," Alex retorted.

Before Alex had a chance to react, Carol, who'd had her hands raised, had ripped the rifle out of Alex's hands and now held the weapon. Alex immediately went for her, but Carol now had the gun pointed at her. No sooner had this happened than Grant and Danny Boy had their weapons raised, pointing at Carol.

"Woah, woah, woah! Let's everyone take a breath!" Justin said, trying to defuse the now volatile situation.

Alex was flush with anger as Carol continued to train the rifle directly at her. Then just as quickly as she had snatched the gun away from Alex, she threw it back at her. Alex caught it in midair.

Grant and Danny relaxed a bit, slightly lowering their guns. Alex was about the raise her now clenched gun back up again, but Grant put his hand on the top of the barrel as if to say, Cool it.

There was an uncomfortable silence between the six of them when Sam's annoyed voice came over the com system. "You guys all done playing grab ass with the guns down there? Grant, decontamination room with them now, got it? Then up to the command center so we can have a little 'sit down get to know ya' conversation with our welcome new guests. Do you got that, Alex?"

"Yes…sir," Alex said coldly.

"This way," Danny Boy said to the three tired and haggard people staring at them.

Danny and Alex led the way, with Grant following everyone behind. Gun at the ready in case anyone got any ideas.

They left the cargo bay and *Stormbringer* behind and walked through the hallway to a room right off of it. The door slid open. Danny walked in and everyone followed behind.

Inside the room was a clear tube in the center of the room followed by three shower heads on each of the empty walls marked off by large dividers. The room was surprisingly well lit. Directly inside by the door were a row of lockers.

Danny then gave the instructions: "First thing's first. Before hitting the showers, each one of you will need to get into the tube and decontaminate. It's nothing fancy, but it ensures us and you all that you're free of any parasites or unwanted bugs. After that, you can hit the showers and feel free to go through these lockers. Spare clothes in all of them. From the looks of all three of you, you're in dire need of a change of clothes."

"Now there's something we can certainly agree on," Justin said calmly.

Danny Boy continued quickly, "You can toss your old clothes into this bin. It seals up tight but don't expect them back. We aren't washing them for you. Understood?"

All three of them nodded.

"Ok, when you're all done in here, give the door a knock and we'll take you up to the bridge to meet the captain and our pilot." Danny headed towards the door.

Alex walked by Carol and without looking directly at her said quietly, "My locker's in the corner. There's some stuff that should fit you. You look roughly around my size."

Carol looked at her, stunned at the very small bit of kindness shown, and was about to say something to that effect but Alex and the rest of the crew were already out the door as it slid shut, leaving them alone to collect their thoughts and go for a much needed clean up.

After the door was closed Justin looked at Carol with part concern and part anger. "You have to keep your cool. We all do. Right now, our main objective is making contact with Trilaxus. Preferably while not on this particular ship. Understood?"

"With all we've been through, that lady sticking her gun in my face…I don't know, Justin. My training in the academy came rushing back. How to disarm an opponent and gain the upper hand. Instincts. They kicked in." She sighed and ran her hands through her long blond hair, exhausted.

"You did good at the quick disarm. I thought you were going to blow her head clean off there, hot shot." Justin gave her a grin that she had fallen in love with over the years at STEA.

"Ladies first?" Ramsey asked, pointing to Carol then over to the decontamination tube.

"Get in there, Ramsey. You're the test pilot for that ancient looking tube thing," Carol shot back in jest.

"Roger that. Don't have to tell me twice. The sooner I can hit those showers and get some fresh clothes on, the better. Hopefully I don't get stuck with that big brute's pants. I don't think a belt on the last hole would hold them up on me." He stripped down and put his old dirty and bloody space suit into the compartment they had instructed them to be discarded into. Then he climbed into the decontamination tube.

After climbing inside the upright tube there was one well-worn single button on the inside. Ramsey instinctively pushed it and a cloud of steam was released from the floor, engulfing him. A minute later the steam had evaporated and he climbed out and headed towards the nearest shower, yelling out behind him, "All done. That was fairly harmless, so who's next?"

With Ramsey busy showering, Justin looked at Carol and his eyes softened. "What a week," he said, facing her closely.

"Agreed. Us three, we stick together, and we get through this. Just like we did on TSR1," she responded quietly.

He nodded and out of respect for Carol's privacy, went and took care of his decontaminating and hopped into a shower.

Carol watched as the dirt and blood washed off of her weakened body. Bitter tears spilled from her eyes as she winced at the pain of her burnt arm. Thoughts flooded her mind. Of her fall from the temple wall. The creature deep in the cave she'd barely escaped from, which still haunted her thoughts. The Azid horde hellbent on doing their master's bidding. The sacrifices of both James of planet Earth and her captain Ben Newstead to bring the powerful Hyzothan down. Ben Newstead…a finer captain she could not name. Other than the man she loved, Justin Schwartz. The escape from TSR1 and the cute little dragon pig creature she had saved and made friends with, stuck back on that godforsaken planet. And now here they were. Their futures still unsure on this pirate vessel with what seemed to be an unsavory lot. They had gotten this far. *Don't give up,* she thought to herself, like Papa used to say before he passed away. She leaned her head against the shower wall as the hot water continued to wash away her tears.

"What do you make of them?" Grant asked Danny and Alex seriously as they left the closed decontamination shower room and headed back to the *Stormbringer*.

"That Carol lady's got some guts, that's for sure," Alex responded, putting her hands to her hips.

Danny nodded, smiling, then added, "I saw the way their captain, Justin, looked at her. They've got a thing for each other. The other one looks like a smaller version of you there, big guy," he looked at the tall, dark skinned Grant, laughing.

"Well, it truly looks like they've all been through hell and back again," Grant said stoically in reply. "Their ship is toast as well. They obviously need our help and while normally we aren't in the business of humanitarian efforts, I am genuinely interested to hear their story. It's gonna be a doozy, I'm guessing."

"Agreed. Did you see the wound on Carol's arm? Shit that's looks painful," Alex added.

They were back in the cargo bay now. Without the crew of the *Stormbringer*.

"Willie asked us to check out some sort of a foreign liquid his sensors detected earlier on this thing on its way in," Grant said as he looked around, inspecting the outer hull of the ship.

Danny and Alex made their way around it as well but found nothing.

"Captain, come in. Grant here. We just did a quick walkaround on this beat up ship here and found no liquid. That's just a quick once over, though."

After a brief pause, Sam came on the com. "Got it. We'll want to take a look inside that thing, but that can wait. Just get them up here. Sam out."

The three headed back to the decontamination room. As they headed out of the cargo bay, Alex glanced back, thinking she saw something move under the *Stormbringer's* hull. She paused for a brief second and stared but saw nothing more than a smashed up spacecraft sitting there. Then she turned and walked out, catching up with Grant and Danny Boy.

After all three had showered and rummaged through the lockers, they were cleaned and fully clothed. Ramsey had found some clothes that fit him relatively well. A tight grey shirt that accentuated his well-toned and quite muscular arms. The arms of a professional boxer. Dark brown cargo work pants with numerous pockets also fit well. Justin had found a tan shirt and black pants and black boots that fit well. Carol wore a white shirt and dark grey tight-fitting pants that were quite comfortable due to their elasticity.

"I'm being completely serious here. I haven't felt this refreshed since before we left on our mission back on Trilaxus three years ago," Ramsey exclaimed as he inspected his new outfit and ran his hands through his short, black curly hair.

"Same here. Now it's time to go make nice with everyone. Remember, we're their guests. We can do this." Justin noticed Carol touching her still bruised arm. "Still hurting, I'm assuming?"

"Yes, but I'll manage," Carol responded, still grimacing. The shower had agitated the cauterized cut on her arm.

"Maybe the crew of the *Leo* can rebandage it. Let's go meet the captain, shall we?" Justin said as he put his hand on Carol and Ramsey's backs, moving them towards the door.

They were greeted by Grant, Danny and Alex once again and led down the hall to a service elevator. The door slid open once Grant stood in front of it, pushing a green button to the right. They all climbed in and once the doors closed behind them Grant hit "level one" on the display in front of him. Justin watched intently, noting to himself that this was level three. There were three levels on this ship.

In mere seconds the elevator came to an abrupt stop and the door slid open. They were right outside another set of doors that slid open, leading into the command center/cockpit area. As the door opened, Danny and Alex led the way in, with Grant once again bringing up the rear.

In the middle of the room was a chair facing forward. At the helm sat a man who now glanced back at the visitors. He had short facial hair and a messy head of hair. Then the center chair spun around with a blond wavy-haired woman sitting in it. Dressed entirely in various shades of brown tight fitting utilitarian work clothes, she stood up and walked over to greet her new guests.

Extending her hand, Sam introduced herself. "Sam Howard. Captain of the ship you find yourself currently on, the *Leo*. Pleased to make your acquaintance."

The crew of the *Stormbringer* each in turn introduced themselves as well, all shaking the captain's outstretched hand, starting with Justin, then Carol and finally Ramsey.

"I see you've gotten yourselves cleaned up and a fresh set of clothes. I trust they fit ok?" she said confidently as she sized up each of them.

"Yes, and we are eternally grateful for your hospitality and more importantly, saving our skins out there. Our ship, more like an escape pod actually, is in need of extended repairs if she's going to fly again. Lucky for us you came along," Justin said graciously.

"Well, we certainly can agree on that. So, you claim to have travelled through that black hole you say? Twice? I'd really like to hear how exactly that happened and how you're still standing here."

"It's a long story. And one we want to tell you all about. If I may ask, is there a way we can contact our planet's government first? I would very much like to inform them on our condition and where exactly we are, as well as the news about our deceased captain," Justin said as his voice turned to remorse.

Everyone on the *Leo* looked at Justin now. His captain was dead. He was obviously now in charge. Was there a mutiny? Was their captain murdered? So many questions swirled through the crews' minds.

"Well, here's the deal, Justin. Can I call you Justin?" Sam asked calmly looking him in the eye.

"Yes sir, of course," he responded, wondering what was coming next.

"We just made a drop on Darmus III. We were planning on a small bit of R&R on Geshan T-32 in the HD-6549 quadrant before picking up another haul on the other side of the planet. See, that's what we do. We aren't the most well-respected ship in the galaxy. We are wanted fugitives in several solar systems. We like to keep everything on the down low. We make our Marks and move on. And this here, this is a bump in the road, so to speak. We've been going for a while, and I promised my crew there would be some downtime. Now, the downtime is interrupted," Sam said now with a hint of agitation in her voice.

"We are more than happy to be dropped off on Geshan T-32. Wherever that may be. No extra stops are necessary for us," Justin said calmly, hoping to keep the conversation going relatively well.

"That ship of yours. The repairs it will need, from what Danny here tells me, are extensive judging by just the outer hull. Something the very small planet of Geshan does not have. Parts for a ship we have quite literally never seen. See, Geshan has a small population. Lots of trees and bodies of water. The natives there are quite intelligent as well as very hospitable, to people they know and trust. They have beautiful landscapes and beaches and a place to hide and relax. They also have a plant that they harvest that has strong medicinal value that brings a high price on the grey market in several solar systems that we frequent." Sam paced back and forth between each of the *Stormbringer's* crew.

Justin thought for a second. Then asked, "Well, could we just hang out there for a bit until help comes?"

"We've gained the Geshan's trust. It's a small planet. You three are strangers. Trust broken. Deal off. No way," Sam said firmly.

Walking past Carol, she glanced at the bruise on her arm. "How did you get that nasty burn there, sister?" she asked, now staring at the makeshift cauterized cut.

Carol glanced at her wound, then up to Sam. She sighed to herself, thinking of the horrors she had endured quite recently, then explained, "I fell out of a temple in the side of a mountain, slashed my arm open on the way down. Went over a waterfall with several creatures that looked like a rat and a vampire had offspring. After the waterfall plunge, I heated up the knife that's currently been confiscated by your crew and sealed the deep slash that should had gotten stiches, shut. The pain meds I was able to take have indeed worn off. A while ago. So yeah. There's a sliver of the full story."

Alex looked at Carol with eyebrows raised.

Sam pondered this bit of information. "Wow. Well, that's a story. I assume this planet you were on was somewhere over the rainbow. By that, I mean somewhere through that black hole you claim to have traversed?"

Feeling the sarcasm in Sam's voice, Carol replied bluntly, "Yes. Exactly that."

"Ok, we've got some pain meds onboard. They'll help," Sam said with a hint of compassion now in her voice. She glanced up at Alex, who nodded and left the cockpit to retrieve the meds.

Willie looked back at the group standing behind him then glanced down at his monitor. "Hey, here's something. I did a scan of this quadrant. There's not much out here in any direction for quite a great distance due to the danger it poses. Most ships passing through stay clear of the supernova, so this is basically a freight line. However, there is a space port that we could swing by and drop them off at. It's pretty much on our way to Geshan T-32. It's a refuel station and not a whole lot else. But it's safe and has several docking ports for ships. Crew minimal on it. Otherwise, there's several gas giants and one planet named Thakitune that we could theoretically land on, but it's uninhabited due to its distant proximity to the nearest star and extremely thin air."

"Well, that would literally be just leaving them there to die. How far is your home planet?" Sam asked Justin.

"We were put into hibernation tubes for a twenty-year mission to Alpha Sector Eight, looking for intelligent life, which I guess from the sounds of it, has none. We were on year three when our ship's A.I. woke us up. That was before we went headfirst into that black hole. How we weren't alerted about it beforehand eludes me. Like it was almost hidden, waiting for us. Which simply cannot be."

The crew of the *Leo* stared at their guests. Sam stood front and center with her arms crossed, shaking her head in disbelief.

Alex broke the silence by walking back in holding a bottle and some gauze to wrap Carol's wound. "What did I miss?" she asked, noticing the silence that had fallen over the room.

Sam continued staring at Justin, Carol and Ramsey, so Danny Boy answered. "These three are sticking with their story about going through that black hole out there in quadrant HD-8478, twice so it seems."

Alex was at a loss for words. She walked over to Carol, handing her several pills from the bottle she had brought with her, a glass of water and the gauze. Carol looked at her and gave a small smile, taking the items from her.

Willie spoke again as he looked at his monitor. This time in a grave tone. "Trilaxus, in quadrant HD-2509? I found it. Or, found out more information about it, I should say."

"Yes?" Justin replied calmly as Ramsey and Carol both looked over to Willie.

"Well, my system databank here says that planet was destroyed 100 years ago."

The bottle of pills Carol was holding dropped to the floor.

CHAPTER 7

NEW FRIENDS, NEW CREATION

The *Stormbringer* sat unattended in the cargo bay in silence. The lights had been turned out, so the only current light sources were the red emergency lights that filled the room with a dim glow. Justin, Carol and Ramsey's weapons were still stored in the bin against the back wall nearest the exit. They were to remain there for now, per Grant's instructions.

The jelly-like liquid Willie's sensors had detected had moved inside the damaged hull of the *Stormbringer*. It was completely black, similar to a slick pool of tar, and roughly three feet around.

Upon entry onto the *Leo* it moved from the bottom of the hull up into the landing gear. It moved leisurely, but fast enough to avoid detection. In the vacuum of space, it glowed, but when attached to an inanimate object the glow subsided.

Once inside the *Stormbringer's* landing gear housing it slowly twisted around the hydraulic system as if feeling out its surroundings. From there it was able to seep itself into tightly fitted panels, deliberately working its way into the magnetic propulsion system as well as the now depleted synth tank. Almost depleted.

The synth tank as well as the magnetic propulsion system had small remnants of the synth liquid remaining. Not enough to power the ship whatsoever, but traces still existed in the compartments as well as various connecting tubes leading between the two sections of the *Stormbringer's* power source.

The sticky black mass coated the areas where the flammable synth particles resided and once it had settled, it sealed itself tight.

Meanwhile, up on level one in the command center, Justin and his crew were grappling with the news that their planet ceased to exist. For 100 years.

"That can't be!" Ramsey said in what was close to a shout.

Willie responded calmly, knowing this bit of information was quickly changing the situation the *Stormbringer's* crew as well as the *Leo's* were now in. "Look, I'm just reading what is in front of me. Planet was destroyed by a race known as the Scaagzil. Ever heard of them?"

Justin glanced at Carol and Ramsey and shook his head in dismay. "Yes. Yes, we know that race well. I thought we had rid ourselves of that race back when I was still a kid. If memory serves, their world was the furthest one out in our solar system. They had invaded our planet before I was even born. Over the synth liquid found on our nearest moon. They also had ships that needed the liquid to power them. The small amounts they had harvested on their own world weren't enough. Our government was unwilling to share our find. The moon was in orbit around our world, so we claimed it. Their own planet was in ruin, as without synth, their planet would die. Everything they had was powered by that liquid, including an artificial sun.

"We fought their superior spacecrafts and soldiers off after a full year-long invasion. Took everything our military had just to keep our world in one piece. Everything they had they put into their military in the hopes of overpowering us. And they were right." Justin stopped and looked around the room at everyone listening to him intently.

Justin then continued sadly, "We thought we had defeated them. I was a kid when my parents told me about the war with the *lizard people*. They and their planet died off. Some survived supposedly and resettled elsewhere in the galaxy."

Willie cleared his throat, glancing up at their new guests abord the *Leo*, and quietly said, "Well, from what I'm reading, it was a strategic attack. Focusing primarily on military and space exploration facilities. It was catastrophic. A planet-ending attack. I'm sorry to have to be telling you this, mate."

"We were arrogant," Carol spoke with anger as she shook her head, grappling with this new bit of bad news.

Ramsey added coldly, "Agreed. I always wondered why we didn't help them. I was told they were not like us. Savages. If we helped them, they would soon overtake our planet and indoctrinate all of us with their ways. Whatever that might even mean. This isn't surprising, actually. With how technically advanced our civilization was, we were still scared of certain races."

"STEA was all about exploring the known universe and finding new life. Charting new quadrants. Establishing settlements and spreading our race," Carol added sadly.

"Yet we, in our arrogance, couldn't even help a dying species in our own solar system, they looked different and acted differently than us. Such a sad reason to not attempt better relations," Justin finished sadly.

No one said anything for a few minutes. Letting the crew of the *Stormbringer* digest this all as they themselves, the *Leo* crew, came to grips with what that meant.

"We were on the other side of that black hole for less than a week. Over 100 years passed while we were gone. We come back and find out our world is destroyed, our captain gone, and we're stuck in the ass end of this quadrant," Ramsey spat out angrily.

Justin contemplated their situation and asked, "Willie, when did this all take place? Things were fine when we left on our mission to Alpha Sector Eight in star year 3421. I know different solar systems chart time and years differently, so maybe you can't give an exact date."

"Well, you're right there. That's not how we measure years here, but my readout does say this happened in 3445," Willie said, reading off the screen in front of him.

"Then we would be dead if we would have completed our 20-year mission," Carol said, astonished at this bit of news.

Ramsey let out a heavy sigh and looked around the room at these strangers. "Got anything to eat around here?"

Sam replied calmly, "We do. Let's show you to the mess hall. Get you fed and then lock down a plan. Not discounting that space port idea Willie threw out. I'd like to hear your whole story though. From the beginning. Once we come up with a firm plan, you three can rest up. I'm sure you need it, and currently, it's past most of our downtime anyway. Sound good?"

"I like that plan," Justin said patiently. Then added, "We had some food rations earlier stored on our ship, but the adrenaline has worn off. Some food and drink sounds good."

"Grant, lead the way. Willie, slow our current speed, plot a course in the general direction of that space port. We can decide later if we keep that route. Hit autopilot and join us in the mess hall. I want all of us on the same page here," Sam commanded with her firm authoritative tone as she turned to leave with their guests.

Willie nodded in reply and got to work setting the autopilot onto a trajectory towards the space port. At their current speed they would arrive in twenty-four hours. Looking down at his display with all of the ship's functions, he glanced back up at the door that Sam had exited, then back down to the monitor. He pushed the honing beacon on. He stood up, stretched, and scratched his shaggy hair. He glanced back down at the small red button that was now lit up, then headed out of the cockpit towards the elevator leading to the second level where the mess hall was located with the rest of them.

Back in the cargo bay, the black jelly substance hardened inside the synth tank, sensing it had found a suitable power source. The synth liquid remnants seeped into the gelatinous mass of sticky black goo that continued to harden as it depleted every last remaining drop of synth.

It hardened until completely solid, its form completely filling the synth tank aboard the *Stormbringer* in its entirety. The tubes on the ship were drained dry as it had worked its way throughout the engine and every other part of the interior, searching for more of the life-giving liquid. Due to the depleted tanks, the meager remnants would have to do.

Enough of the liquid had been left to make the crystalized substance expand and grow, slowly taking over all hidden areas of the interior of the *Stormbringer*. The hardened mass pulsed an off-colored white glow. It would expand as much as it could until the liquid it had ingested was depleted. Then the next stage of its evolution would begin.

The mess hall was as Danny Boy and Grant had left it earlier after their arm-wrestling match. He walked into the room as Justin was explaining how their ship, the *Cauldwell,* was sucked inside the black hole, came out the other side and was piloted to the closest inhabitable world in that section of uncharted space.

"This is pretty good. What is it?" Ramsey asked as he took a bite of a dark meat on a bone.

"Selvine meat. It's common on Darmus III. We usually stock up on the natives' food if it's edible enough when we make our drops," Danny Boy said as he himself took a bite.

"Tastes like Tibbus, doesn't it, Justin?" Ramsey said, chewing on a mouthful.

Justin nodded in agreement as bit into a red colored vegetable.

Sam changed the subject back to their trip through the black hole. "So, this planet. Tell us about it. Obviously, you barely escaped with your lives, correct?"

"Yes," Carol responded, seeing Justin had a mouthful of food. She took a sip of water in front of her and continued, "We were soon attacked by a creature in a body of water. Real nasty piece of work. Huge tentacled thing. Anyway, it destroyed our mothership, and we barely made it out with our escape pod, the ship that's now housed in your cargo bay. From there, let's see…we hid out in a cave, then ended up being attacked by several humanoid creatures resembling a cross between a vampire, a zombie, and a rat. One of them grabbed me and took me to a temple that had been used for the worship of a sacred stone that a huge monster that lived in an even huger mountain in the region had stolen from the natives of the planet. Using it to control the creatures of the world and enslaving women to power the stone, giving it pretty much unlimited power."

Sam and her crew sat stunned at the story unfolding. "Go on," Sam said with genuine curiosity.

"Well, I escaped the temple being chased by the Azid, that's the name of those flying zombie rat things I just mentioned. Anyway, I ended up cutting my arm really bad, went over a waterfall, banging myself up even more. Had to cauterize the wound and fend off an ice monster in a cavern I was making my way through until coming out the other side and finding the Earthman's ship. Oh, and a little dragon pig," she added with a little grin.

Ramsey piped in, "I was taken as well. To the beast's lair. Our captain, who was infected with a virus by the Azid, turned into one of them, but rescued me. I made my way back to the rest of my crew's location along with the Earthman, James Korvell was his name. Good man. He was mortally wounded by one of the Azid and ended up sacrificing himself by crashing his ship into the mountain where the beast Hyzothan lived. We were able to break the atmosphere of the planet that James had named TSR1, short for Thunder Stone Realm, and shot through the black hole once more."

Danny Boy, who was standing close to Sam, leaned over and quietly asked her in a hushed tone, "Are you buying any of this?"

Sam glanced at him. "Not sure yet, but it's quite the story, isn't it?"

Danny smirked at her as he leaned back in his chair with his hands on the back of his shiny bald head looking over at their guests.

Grant walked over to the table where the bottle of Emulow Rye still sat with two dirty shot glasses. He picked up the bottle, poured a shot for himself and filled the other one, handing it to Ramsey. Ramsey looked at the brownish liquid and then back up to Grant who nodded and tilted the glass of liquid into his mouth. He set the glass down beside Ramsey and said with a grin, "You need this, trust me."

Ramsey looked over at Justin, who shrugged back at him. He lifted the glass and downed the contents. Immediately fire ripped through his throat and he coughed loudly, quickly setting the glass back down hard.

The crew of the *Leo* chuckled as Ramsey exclaimed, "What was that?"

Sam answered with a smirk, "Emulow Rye. Good stuff. 110% proof.

"Pass it over here," Justin said evenly.

Grant slid the bottle over towards him and he caught it in his hand. He lifted the bottle, smelled it and took a gulp. Clearing his throat and wiping off his mouth, he replied, "Just what I needed right about now. Carol? Want a sip? It'll help even more with the bruised arm."

"I've been tortured enough. Thanks, but no thanks." This got several laughs from the *Leo* crew.

Alex looked over at Carol and asked calmly, "How's the arm? Meds kicking in?"

"Yes, and thanks again," Carol responded, feeling that the show of wills back in the cargo bay had endeared her to Alex somewhat. That lady seemed to be tough as nails. She could appreciate that. She could hold her own as well.

"You mentioned a pig? Or something to that effect?" Alex asked Carol curiously as she sat down beside her and helped Carol wrap her still badly bruised arm.

A smile crossed Carol's lips as she thought of the cute little beast she had befriended by rescuing it from a deadly Squid Wolf attack. She responded with those thoughts running through her mind, "He was my little buddy on that hostile planet for a short time. We had to leave him behind."

"Ok, here you go, all bandaged up," Alex told Carol.

Carol replied softly, "Thanks. Thanks all of you. I know this isn't ideal. And I know, we all know actually, that you don't trust us yet. I get that. But I am grateful that you did allow us to board your ship. You truly did save our lives out there. We are indebted to you."

Justin looked over at her, clearly not expecting to hear those words from her to these rough looking strangers. *What a tough yet kindhearted person, she never ceases to amaze me,* he thought to himself.

Sam nodded her approval in Carol's direction.

They continued to talk. All of them interacting with each other. The ice seemed to have been broken. Grant, Danny Boy, Justin and Ramsey took turns finishing off the bottle of Emulow Rye, sharing tales of battling the Azid hordes on TSR1, and of the black mineral on the planet that could keep a fire lit indefinitely. James Korvell's courageous final act and their captain Ben, who fought back against himself and the beast controlling his mind, giving his life for his crew.

"Tell us about the black hole. What did you see in there?" Danny Boy asked, genuinely intrigued.

A hush fell across the room, waiting to hear the response.

After a pause, Justin answered, "It was the absence of light. Total darkness. At least for a bit. Then masses of stars, lights, galaxies. I can't tell you if what we saw in there was real or illusion. It was terrifying."

Ramsey remembered what he had seen in the vast darkness. Leaning forward in his chair, he added, "I also saw what seemed to be something inside that black hole that almost looked as if it were moving on its own free will. I mean, our first trip through we saw Captain James Korvell's derelict ship frozen inside. But this was different. It was like a huge black mass that almost seemed to notice us as we passed through."

Then Willie responded with genuine curiosity, "Woah. So, if what you're saying is correct, there might be actual living beings inside dead stars?"

"I have no clue. This is all new stuff to me. I'm just some ex-boxer that decided to become a flyboy." Ramsey slumped back into his chair, putting his hands behind his head, enjoying the nice buzz the Emulowian Rye was producing in his head.

Grant cocked his eyebrows. "You a fighter? Not sure what divisions your planet had but I've squared off in the ring myself back in the day before hitching a ride with these pirates."

Ramsey smirked. "Well, that's certainly not a surprise, judging by your size and muscle mass there, big boy. I got my ass handed to me by a fella about your size back years ago. Name was Mike 'Snarlz' Braber. I got some good licks in, but it wasn't meant to be."

"Oh, I've lost my fair share of fights. But I can tell you this much, each one of those losses, those guys had to earn it. I don't go down easy," Grant replied back with a laugh.

Raising the nearly depleted bottle, Ramsey said in reply, "I'll drink to that." He took a swig and choked it down, making Grant smile in approval.

Sam cleared her throat and stood up from her chair and adjusted her brown fighter pilot jacket and spoke to the group: "So here's the deal. Carol, I appreciate that little speech you gave, but do I trust you? Nope, not yet. You sure have a hell of a story to tell though, I'll give you that. But you're weaponless and while I'm sure you all can hold your own, you're clearly at our mercy. So you're gonna have to trust us. At least until we can drop you all off somewhere. That somewhere is currently tracking to be that old space port Willie mentioned earlier. Which is where the *Leo* is headed. It's on our way to Geshan anyway, so we aren't out a whole lot."

She paused, looking over Justin, Carol and Ramsey. All three looked tired. She put her hands on her hips, then continued as everyone in the room watched and listened, "The way I see it, this is our good deed. Your planet is ceased to exist a hundred years ago and that ship you came in on is on its last leg as well so compensation is zip for us."

Ramsey was about to say something in protest, but was cut off by Sam, who raised her finger and continued. "Having said that, we might be pirates, but we aren't rotten evil bastards. All of us has had a rough go of it in one form or another. And you three certainly have the mother of all rough goes right now, if your story is to be believed. We'll take you to a drop off and until then, you can consider yourselves our guests. We have enough food to last you all for a few days as well as a few extra beds to crash in. Don't expect your weapons back, however, until exiting the *Leo*. I know my crew, I don't know you. Got it?"

"Speaking of beds. I'm beat. I think the meds I took made me even more exhausted than I already was," Carol said, sighing heavily.

Sam responded to Carol by glancing over at Alex. "Can you help them out in that area, Alex?" More a command than a question.

"We have a few cots that we can pull out and set up for you three in the rec room. All of our sleeping quarters are on level one. We're currently on level two, in case you didn't know. Level three is the server room, engineering and the cargo bay." Alex pointed in general directions as she spoke.

Ramsey chimed in, nodding, "Yep, I kind of figured out the layout when we were in the lift on the way up to the command center."

Visibly annoyed by Ramsey, Alex continued, "As I was saying, the ship is pretty no -rills. What you see is what you get. One restroom off of the rec room for those with small bladders. Yeah, that should cover it."

Ramsey glanced at Justin, who gave him a look that said, *You're trying too hard, buddy.* Ramsey returned the look, embarrassed at being cut off by the attractive and mysterious redhead that reminded him way too much of his old crush, Lucindia Merrick.

"Ok then. That covers it for tonight. Hell of a day for all of us, if I do say so myself. Danny, give them a hand with the cot in the rec room. Grant, I think we can trust them enough to not go wandering around the ship, right?"

Danny Boy nodded per her request, as did Grant.

Alex walked past Sam close enough to whisper to her, "Marks, we have our latest haul of Marks. They're locked up outside the cargo bay, but should someone keep watch?"

Glancing over at Alex, she answered cynically, "Feel free to stand watch over the locked tight door tonight if you want. Furthermore, where are they going if they get inside?"

Alex didn't respond, but walked out of the mess hall along with Grant and Danny. On her way out she glanced over at Ramsey, who was watching her leave.

"After some shuteye we can go over your ship and assess the damage to see if there is any possibility of getting it to fly, although without any of that synth stuff you were talking about, I'm assuming that this is nothing but a pile of metal for the scrapyard. Or whatever it's made of. Thing looks weird if you ask me," Sam said to Justin and his crew in what seemed to almost be a joking tone.

"Thanks again for all of this," Justin said. Ramsey and Carol nodded in agreement.

Sam nodded back to them as she headed out of the mess hall. Willie followed behind closely, avoiding eye contact. They headed back to the command center and the *Stormbringer* crew made their way to the rec room as Justin thought uneasily about the last brief interaction with Willie.

CHAPTER 8

BETRAYAL

Grant headed to his quarters to sleep off the nice warm buzz he now had thanks to the depleted bottle of rye. Lucky for him they usually carried a nice stash of booze onboard the *Leo,* although he never let it interfere with his job. He nearly always had his wits about him, and a few shots of the hair of the dog wasn't going to faze him.

Danny Boy pulled out several makeshift cots and was arranging them in the rec room. The rec room wasn't much to look at, as was normal for this type of vessel and her crew. A couch, a few chairs, an old arcade game with numerous games installed on it as well as a pool table. Several lights hung in the room, casting a warm glow installed to help the crew relax a bit from the dim corridors, mechanical instruments, and flashing computer screens of the rest of the ship.

Justin, Carol and Ramsey walked into the rec room and immediately went to help their host move the cots, two of them, into position.

"So, we've got two cots, and they aren't big," he said, nervously glancing at Justin and Carol.

Before it got too awkward in the room, Justin cleared his throat and exclaimed, "I've got the couch. You two fight over which cot might give you a better night's sleep."

Carol, blushing, turned to the cot closest to the couch and said softly, "This will do just fine, thank you Danny Boy. Or should we call you Danny? You seem to go by either or."

"And either or is fine with me. My name is Danny Boyd Asher. As a kid I got the nickname Danny Boy and it just sort of stuck. I rarely used Boyd or Asher for that matter. Nothing but bad memories if you ask me."

Carol nodded. "Well then, Danny and sometimes Danny Boy, is what I shall call you."

He nodded graciously and looked up as Alex walked into the room.

Looking up from the cot he was repositioning, Ramsey saw her enter. She glanced at him then quickly looked over at Danny Boy. "When you're all done in here, if you could help me do one last check of the cargo bay and the…" She trailed off, thinking it best not to mention the Marks she wanted to inspect once more.

Danny Boy nodded and walked towards her, ready to leave the rec room.

Looking over at Carol, Alex said flatly, "No hard feelings about our little exchange in the cargo bay. I'm a bit on edge from our last job. Should have kept my cool a bit more. Anyway..."

Carol smiled and nodded her approval.

"What's your last name?" Ramsey asked awkwardly.

Alex looked over at him, almost surprised at the question directly after her makeshift apology to Carol. "Why do you want to know?" she spat defensively.

Carol grinned to herself and glanced at Justin, who looked up at the interaction then over to Carol, shooting a quick smile back at her knowing they were both thinking the same thing.

Taken off guard, Ramsey stammered a bit, "Well, I was just curious. Nice gesture and all. I'm Ramsey Conner. Did I tell you that already? I forget." Then he went silent, knowing how awkward the conversation was turning.

"Breakfast is at o-seven hundred, alright?" Alex responded, addressing everyone, but narrowing her eyes slightly at Ramsey.

Alex and Danny Boy left the rec room as the door slid shut behind them.

"Well, that was good and awkward," Carol said, chuckling.

"What? What did I do? I'm trying to be friendly! I didn't ask her to sing me to sleep or something."

"Or something," Justin came back smugly and patted Ramsey on the back as he made his way to the couch.

"I just can't win, can I?" Ramsey said to himself with a smirk, glancing over at the door that Alex and Danny Boy had just exited.

Changing the subject, Justin posed the question to Carol and Ramsey: "Supposedly our planet has ceased to exist. Our families, our friends, relatives, STEA. Our home is gone. We're currently no better or worse than this gang of smugglers we hitched a ride with. Once we get to this space port, we have some pretty important decisions to make. Now, I know we're all weary. Some much-needed sleep will do us all good, but everyone, stay alert. The *Leo* crew seem to be ok. But…" Justin trailed off.

"But? But what?" Carol asked, genuinely curious if there was something more to it than just travelling with space pirates.

"I noticed it to," Ramsey responded quietly. "You're talking about Willie, right? Dude is shifty eyed."

"Bingo," Justin responded, then continued quietly, as if nervous they were being overheard, "The guy might be a newer member of the crew, but he doesn't seem to gel. I don't know for sure. Grant is huge and tough as nails, but I can tell you right now, I would already trust him or Danny or Alex or even their captain Sam if my life depended on it. That pilot, I kind of feel like he would save his own skin. Nothing he's done per say, just…" he trailed off again.

"A feeling. Duly noted. We're only on this ship for less than twenty-four hours. We can do this. We've gotten this far," Carol responded confidently.

"I'm out. Catch you all in the morning. No bad dreams, alright? Those are over." Ramsey pulled the covers over himself.

Justin looked at Ramsey, then over to Carol. He walked over to her cot and took her arm in his hands, inspecting the bandaged wound. "How's the arm holding up, tough girl?" he said with a soft smile.

Smiling back at him, Carol moved closer, enjoying Justin's touch on her skin. She responded in kind, "The meds are holding up well. I'll be fine. Sleep will certainly help. Tomorrow we can…" But was cut off by the soft kiss that Justin gave her.

Alex and Danny Boy made their way down to the third level, heading towards the cargo bay, when Danny asked casually, "So, that Ramsey fella. I think you've got a not-so-secret admirer there, Alex." He chuckled.

"Shut up. Let's just make sure the loot is ok and get to our rooms. I'm tired." But there was a small part of Alex that was slightly flattered at the obvious attention.

"Ok, let's make this quick," Danny said as they entered through the sliding doors into the cargo bay. Soft red lights flooding the room were replaced by brighter lights that clicked on automatically once they stepped inside the large area.

Alex put her hands on her hips as she inspected the cargo bay, glancing over at the wreckage of the *Stormbringer* parked in the middle of the room. "We need to go through that heap. I've truly never seen a ship quite like this thing."

"Same here, but not tonight though, please. I'm half drunk, tired, and not in the mood for any more physical work," Danny Boy shot back as he too looked at the *Stormbringer*.

They walked past it in silence over to the side wall. A small, obscure panel with a keypad was at eye level in the corner. Alex punched in 0986 and the panel popped open. She took the panel out, laying it beside the now open area. Inside the hidden compartment was a space which measured roughly five feet in total dimensions; wide, deep and high.

Alex and Danny Boy peered inside the space at the stacks of Marks inside. "10,000 Marks. Should have been 12,500. Stupid sonofabitch, that Willie," Alex said angrily as she continued looking at their haul that had been encased in a thin clear wrap. Once their hauls were double counted, Alex always put a layer of wrapping around the Marks until they were able to divvy up their take between them all, usually at the next landing site where it was safe to spend.

Higher currency Marks like the ones now residing in the *Leos* cargo bay consisted of shiny flat squares made of Druenium. I thin lightweight metal substance. Various colors denoted their worth. Smaller currency amounts were round coin shapes using the same material. Druenium being a particularly rare mineral made it an ideal choice for currency across numerous solar systems.

"Don't sweat it. It's still a decent payday, and the sooner we were able to get off that godforsaken planet Darmus III, the better. I hate that place. We'll make up for it next run or two, I'm sure of it. It all seems to even itself out."

Alex nodded coldly, then replied, "Next time he tries that shit I'll be rearranging his nose properly. Mark my words. Been with us for a year and I still don't trust that shifty-eyed bastard."

Danny Boy nodded with a smile then patted her on the back. "Come on, hot shot, I'm done."

Alex bumped against him in fun. Grant and Danny Boy had become almost like the brothers she'd never had. She loved them as only a sister could. Alex replaced the panel. As it locked into place the keypad read *locked* on its small display above the numbers.

They both walked out of the cargo bay, Danny Boy with his arm slung around Alex's neck casually. He was singing an old drinking song he had picked up back on his home world Wiggip in his hard living days.

Elbowing him in the ribs, Alex mumbled, "I hate when you sing, you know that."

To which Danny Boy sang louder as Alex let out a small chuckle and joined in. *"Catch me, catch, me, catch me if you can. I been stealing my way through life every day since I was a young boy, so try as you might, catch me if you can…"*

The lights clicked off as the dim, red emergency power lighting clicked on. The cargo bay was silent. Except for inside the *Stormbringer*. Bubbling sounds emanated from the sticky, gooey mass of black hardening jelly that had taken over portions of the hull inside. No longer was the substance only inside the magnetic propulsion unit or the synth tank. It had spread throughout most of the rear interior. Making full use of the synth fumes still in the ship's tank, it was able to grow to be self-sustaining and mutate.

The tar-like substance needed to multiply its mass in order to fulfill its purpose when it was dislodged from its host body where it had resided for countless aeons. Waiting for the right moment. That moment came when a shiny silver orb sailed past it. And now it grew larger. Inside the black tar, a tiny, dim light pulsed, as if alive inside the tar itself. But it needed a host.

Everyone was asleep. Everyone except Willie. He paced his quarters, anxious. He glanced at the digital readout on his multi-function watch strapped to his wrist. Almost time. Even with the setback of picking up the three stranded astronauts and their banged-up spacecraft. That threw him for a loop, but he adapted. The plan remained the same.

Willie picked up his sidearm, a low frequency Electron Pistol. The Discharge Fusion Rifles the crew had emitted a more powerful blast, but were far too heavy and cumbersome. The Electron Pistol was his preferred weapon of choice in most circumstances. Small and deadly when used properly. His door slid open and he stepped out into the dim, quiet hallway. Looking both ways, he headed to the control center. The door slid open and he walked in. The autopilot was set and at the first sign of any trouble the crew would be immediately notified by the alert warning that rang throughout the ship. Unless it was disabled.

He walked over to the captain's chair, sat down and pressed the *Disable Alarm* button on the armrest. Once the alarm was activated, this was one of the only ways to disarm it to ensure the captain was aware of any outside danger or interior hull breach. The plan was long in the making and trust had to be earned. He wasn't sure if he had complete trust yet from Sam. He knew for a fact that Alex didn't trust him, and Grant and Danny Boy tolerated him. Even enjoyed his company from time to time, but he hadn't joined this crew to make friends or a new family.

Back on his home world Trichi X9O, he had figured out in his early 20's, the most profitable ventures were achieved when you play the long game. And so, he had hopped sneakily from one job to the next. Sometimes taking several years to complete. But it always ended up the same. With the crew dead and him barely surviving with his life. And a whole lot of Marks. Then several years off the job, covering his tracks. He knew he had to be careful with this one. This crew was very street smart. He checked his time again. Almost ready. He walked over to his pilot's chair and clicked on the radar.

Approaching the *Leo* were two red dots on the screen. *If I would have just kept my damn mouth shut,* he thought. He watched as the red dots got closer. It was time. He clicked off the radar and then slowed the ship down gradually until it was floating in space. With everyone sleeping, this was easy. No one heard or felt anything as the ship gradually slowed.

No alarms or warnings emanated from the speaker system throughout the freighter.

Willie made his way to the sliding door which glided open silently and left the cockpit. He made his way down to the fire exit on level one, past the sleeping quarters. He didn't want to use the elevator, as that was loud enough that it could potentially wake someone up. He climbed down the ladder quietly, making sure his feet landed squarely on each step, taking his time. *Slow and steady wins the race.*

Once on level three, Willie headed to the decontamination room and opened one of the lockers, taking out a space suit. He quickly put it on, holstered his Electron Pistol, and holding the helmet, walked towards the cargo bay. The door to the cargo bay slid open and the lights kicked on. No worries though. Even with their new guests sleeping on the second level, the sliding door and the lights wouldn't bother anyone at all. He walked in and immediately went over to the panel against the back wall.

He glanced at the *Stormbringer* sitting in a nearly destroyed state. He was truly impressed that Justin, Carol and Ramsey had survived it all. If their story was to be believed. Their propulsion systems in their ships must have been pretty unique in design to handle the gravitational push and pull of a black hole. "And that technology is over 100 years old! Must be worlds more intelligent in that quadrant of the universe. It's a wonder these hunks of junk are cleared for space travel," he mumbled to himself as he continued walking to his destination.

Once he reached the wall, he quickly entered the code he had snuck a peek at several months ago and became determined to memorize. 0986. Nothing happened. He entered the number again and still it remained locked.

Frustrated, he tried another combination. 9086 then enter. The panel remained unmoved and locked tight.

Looking at the panel he swore to himself, "Shit! That's the number, right? Ok, how's about this."

Willie punched in 0968 and hit enter.

The panel popped open. "Ah-ha! Not bad Willie! Try to keep my eyes off that control panel all you want, Alex. I'll find a way." He grinned as he pulled the panel out of the way, leaning it against the wall.

He peered in and there it was, all 10,000 Marks. His for the taking. Alex may have given him a hard time, and he knew she would, but this was all going back to the Cambulons that had paid them in the first place. The weapons they purchased from Sam and her crew would not just be used, but also distributed to the military on Darmus III as well as selling to other gorilla militant groups that fell in line with the dictatorship in power. Used to crush the rebels on the planet. This easily eclipsing what they initially paid by at least double. These were difficult weapons to procure, but the *Leo's* crew had done it.

And now the Marks would go back to the Cambulons and Willie would get a cool 5,000 untraceable counterfeit Marks, which he was fine with. He knew where to travel where they would be undetectable. If the mission were a success, he would be given an additional twenty-five percent credit to spend however he saw fit on Cambulon and a guarantee of impunity and protection moving forward henceforth.

However, this was the risky part. He had done it before. It worked like a charm on the *Starglow*. This time however, he was planning on getting out of the business for quite a while. 5,000 should get him out of flying for hire work for several years. He'd take a few small jobs to keep himself coasting along. But this was a big one with the inclusion of the additional twenty-five percent on the back end. One he had planned with the Cambulon fascist government.

They'd posed as resistance fighters in order to sell their plight perfectly to Sam and her crew. She was known to turn a blind eye on certain jobs, but not this one. Willie knew there would be no way she would deal with the Cambulon government for the weapons, nor would the Emulownians that sold the weapons to Sam in the first place.

Willie knew he had gotten himself into a jam when he slept with the lousy gangster Themphav's wife. She was incredibly attractive but not worth the mess of dealing with a furious mobster. It may have happened a while ago, but he knew there was a price on his head. These Marks would certainly help smooth things over for all parties involved. And if not, he didn't much care. He would be quite wealthy with solid protection from his Cambulonian cohorts.

Alex had the Marks clear wrapped nicely. All the easier to transport out of here, he thought. He lifted his watch and saw the time. If their trajectory on the radar earlier was accurate, they should be behind the *Leo*, waiting. He pulled the stacks of Marks out of the compartment and pulled out a large bag made out of a durable yet thin plastic and rubber compound. He proceeded to lift all of the Marks, setting them on top of the open bag on the ground. Then he simply pulled the bag up and over the wrapped-up Marks.

He tied the top of the bag tight with a sealer then attached the bag to his back by locking it into place with a locking mechanism on his suit. It was heavy. Then the deed was done. Almost.

The door to the cargo bay slid open and Grant walked in leisurely carrying his Fusion Rifle and wearing warmup pants and a tank top. He immediately noticed the interior lights were already on and looked over at the *Stormbringer* and then to the panel against the wall. The open panel. With Willie securing a bag onto his back that was most assuredly the Marks.

His eyes widened as he started to raise his rifle at the same time that Willie recognized him walking in. "Willie, what in the," Grant started to say.

But Willie was too fast with his Electron Pistol. Pulling it out of its holster, he fired. Two shots of green light crackled out of the barrel. One connecting with the sliding door and the other with Grant's chest. Blood sprayed out of the hole in his chest as he screamed in pain at the searing hot blast of concentrated electricity and fire. Lucky for Willie, the Electron Pistol wasn't loud enough to be heard outside of the closed off cargo bay compared to the much louder Fusion Rifle.

Grant stumbled backwards and fell to the ground, writhing in pain. Willie watched him struggle. Trying to get to his feet as his life blood spilled out onto the cargo bay. The Electron Pistol was meant to inflict certain death if the blast hit anywhere near vital organs due to the intensity of the blast radius as well as spreading outward once the blast made impact. Willie knew the chest blast would be fatal. The hole in his chest was only the tip of the iceberg. That blast spread several inches on all sides inside Grant's body. Literally burning him alive from the inside.

Blood was gurgling up from Grant's mouth as Willie walked over and stood over him, looking down. "All you had to do was stay in your damn room tonight like you usually do. But you had to do a patrol after a piss, didn't you, Mr. Weapons Expert Security Muscle? Now I guess you'll die sooner than the rest of your crew. You picked the wrong night to do some drinking with that idiot Danny. Anyway, it's been real. Gotta run," Willie said with a smirk.

Grant tried to speak, but only blood came out of his mouth. Willie looked on for another second then turned away, looking towards the cargo bay hatch leading out into outer space.

He ran over to the outer hatch. One last step and the trickiest of all, not counting the surprise visit by Grant. He knew that once he opened the outer hatch the noise would certainly wake up everyone on the ship. So if the Cambulons weren't waiting for him, he was in serious trouble. He couldn't break radio silence, so he had to trust them that they would be there.

He took a big breath, connected his helmet to his suit and activated his own gravity boots, an item he had purchased on Darmus III without the rest of the crews knowledge. He then hit the cargo bay hatch as he holstered his Electron Pistol securely onto his space suit. It slowly grinded open. The crew would know any second something was happening. He looked out and sure enough, two spacecrafts were trailing the *Leo* from a distance. He nodded to himself. Plan was still a go.

CHAPTER 9

SURPRISE ATTACK

Sam sat up suddenly in her bed, coming to immediately from a dream she was having. The dream had already vanished from her memory. In its place was the immediacy of what was  happening in real time. The cargo bay hatch was opening. No alarm had sounded. No warning of any kind. In the middle of everyone's downtime.

Why the hell didn't I have Grant or Danny Boy stay up and post guard in shifts all night? Damnit! she thought to herself angrily. Especially with their new guests onboard. There had never been an incident onboard the *Leo* with their hauls. They had gotten complacent over the years. Something that Sam was immediately regretting.

This could by someone from the crew of the *Stormbringer*. But where would they go? *Go now!* she thought as she jumped out of her bed. She was in black yoga pants and a sports bra. Her usual for bed. Not enough time to get dressed. She slipped into her workout shoes, grabbed her Fusion Rifle and opened her quarters to see what was going on.

Alex was already up as well with her door having slid open. She stood in the doorway rubbing her eyes and exclaimed to Sam, "What the hell's going on? Is that the cargo bay hatch opening? Where's the alarm?"

"Grab your gun, now!" Sam yelled back as she passed Alex. She also noticed Danny Boy's door opening as she charged forward.

Alex glanced over at Danny as her foggy deep sleep drained from her body and reality hit her. She immediately jumped back into her room. She and Sam wore essentially the same clothes on the ship and sometimes they even went so far as to share wardrobes. She was wearing a pair of Sam's low cut, form fitting shorts and a dark green military camo shirt, cut at the midriff, exposing her pale skin. She threw on military boots without tying them and grabbed her Fusion Rifle and headed out of her small room. On her way out she glanced over at Danny Boy struggling to put on cargo pants over his tight shorts.

"Hurry up, let's go!" she shouted at Danny. *Where's Grant?* she thought to herself. He would always be the first up in case of some unforeseen issue on the ship. It was his job to always be on alert, even with a bit of alcohol in his system. *Where's Willie?* A tinge of dread shot through Alex. She ran faster to the elevator.

The door was about to slide shut on the elevator when Danny Boy squeezed in. No shirt, just cargo pants, boots, and his own Fusion Rifle. Neither said a word. They both looked at each other, eyes wide open, not quite sure what to expect.

As Alex and Danny Boy made their way to the third level, Justin, Carol and Ramsey slept soundly. Their first real sleep since they were awakened aboard the *Cauldwell* by Beta, their onboard computer A.I. system.

Inside the cargo bay, the outer hatch was completely open. Anything that wasn't latched down flew out of the airlock, including Grant's Fusion Rifle. Grant, however, was still alive and had rolled forward, connecting with the locked down *Stormbringer*. Even with his life slipping away, he was able to cling onto the *Stormbringer's* landing gear so he wouldn't be sucked out into space. The oxygen in the cargo bay was depleting rapidly.

Willie stared out at the two ships now right in front of the open cargo bay. The ships looked almost like metal falcons in shape with large, outstretched wings tilted downwards, a short back-end where two large exhaust ports blasted out fire, and a long neck leading from the front towards back where the wings and rectangular body resided, with a thin viewscreen peering out into space. Two pilots could travel in one of these fighter ships. Some of the ships had been painted dark green while others were completely black. All of them were the same size, small, fast and deadly. Much smaller than the freighter they were robbing. On the wings were four disintegrator cannons. Two per wing.

From the bottom rear of the closest ship, a grappling cord shot out and latched onto the outer hull of the cargo bay on the *Leo*. Right where Willie was standing. Without wasting any time, Willie extended a linking cord and connected it to the extended grappling cord from the vessel hovering in front of him. All of the space suits aboard the *Leo* had linking cords that were used to connect to various parts of the outer hull in case there was a need to work on the ship in deep space.

Willie had used this to his advantage when preparing this heist. Everything had been well laid out over the nearly half year of planning this with the Cambulons. He was regretting his attempt at bargaining with the Cambulons on the weapons-for-Marks deal though, as looking back, it brought unneeded attention on him and his scheme by his crew. But at the time it felt good to get under Alex's skin. He hated her and knew it would piss her off. He had taken great delight antagonizing her whenever he was able to, but never enough to draw attention to himself, until now.

Sam ran directly to the cargo bay doors and saw the warning light on. She couldn't open the door without depressurizing the ship. She saw Alex and Danny Boy exiting the elevator. They would have to open the door.

"Space suits, now!" Sam yelled as Alex and Danny Boy ran to their lockers. They were in their suits in less than a minute, clicking their helmets on and activating their gravity boots.

The inner cargo bay doors slid open as Sam ran in with her space suit on, with Alex and Danny Boy following. As soon as they were inside the cargo bay the door slid shut behind them. This took only seconds so precious little oxygen escaped into the open cargo bay area. As they entered, a large panel went sailing through the room, bouncing off the *Stormbringer's* hull and sailing out of the open cargo bay outer hatch.

Sam looked over at the individual in the space suit, connected to a grappling cord leading out into space. Connecting itself to a Cambulon military fighter ship she immediately recognized as a Reaper. Two of them hovered in front of the cargo bay area.

Alex yelled through her com system that was connected to all of the space suits, "Willie, it's Willie. He has the Marks on his back!"

Willie glanced back and, grinning, he jumped backwards into space. The grappling cord disconnected itself with the outer hull of the *Leo* and sprang back, pulling Willie with it towards the top outer hull of the Cambulonian military warbird.

Danny Boy glanced down, noticing blood splattered all over the floor and some against the wall. But there was no body in the cargo bay. Whoever it was, and Danny Boy had a sickening feeling he knew, must have been sucked out into space when the cargo bay hatch was opened.

Alex and Sam raised their Fusion Rifles and opened fire on the Reapers as well as Willie who had now landed against the bottom of the ship, the grappling cord now fully retracted back against the fighter ship. A small bottom hatch slid open as Willie climbed in. Fusion Rifle blasts shot out into space.

One long orange stream of laser fire just missing Willie as the hatch slid shut behind him in the Reaper.

Danny Boy now joined the fight. Shooting at the Reapers. Several of the shots connected with the warbirds, knocking them back slightly. The Reapers moved back, away from the outer hull of the *Leo*.

Sam saw this and yelled, "They're preparing to attack. Close the cargo bay hatch now!" Danny Boy hit the button on the wall and the hatch started to close. Then, the Reapers opened fire.

Red streams of fire emanating from either side of their wings shot through the cargo bay, smashing into the wall, sending metal plating exploding through the air. The hatch continued to close as the blasts from the Reapers were now smashing against the outer hull of the ship. Thankfully only a few blasts hit inside the cargo bay before it closed completely.

"Cockpit, now!" Sam yelled frantically at Alex and Danny Boy as she hit the depressurize button on the wall. She glanced over at the panel that had been opened. Inside the small storage area was nothing but empty space. The Marks were gone.

The light turned green. The cargo bay was once again depressurized. The door slid open and the three of them bolted out and ran down the hall towards the elevator leading up to the first floor.

Hyzothan bellowed in rage as the tiny ship James Korvell piloted connected with the parasitic beast, immediately destroying everything around it. The planet seemed to shake as the massive explosion grew larger and larger. Justin sat up on the couch he had been fast asleep on. Covered in sweat. The ship was shaking. He knew the sound he had just heard and it wasn't space debris. Laser fire. "Get up, quick! This ship is under attack!" he screamed at Carol and Ramsey.

Ramsey opened his eyes and immediately felt the ship rock. Carol was next to open her eyes. In mere seconds both hopped out of their cots and ran out of the rec room towards the first level. The door to the elevator slid open and inside stood Danny Boy, Sam and Alex.

"Get in!" Sam yelled as the door was about to close back shut.

Justin, Carol and Ramsey quickly boarded the elevator as it made its way up to level one.

"What the hell is going on!?!" Ramsey yelled, clearly flustered and still getting his bearings from the deep sleep he had been woken from suddenly.

"We're under attack!" Alex shot back hastily through her space suit helmet's com as she pushed her way forward out of the elevator and immediately into the command center with Danny Boy and Sam.

Justin and Carol followed on their heels, with Ramsey rubbing his eyes.

Sam disconnected her helmet and jumped into the captain's seat. Alex and Danny Boy followed suit by removing their helmets. Danny Boy took the pilot's seat and Alex jumped into the seat beside him.

"Willie must have deactivated the alarm!" Sam yelled out furiously.

Blasts from the Reapers shook the ship violently, sending Carol and Justin to the ground as Ramsey grabbed ahold of a nearby computing system on the wall.

"Danny, get us out of here now! A few more of those hits and we're done for!" Sam continued yelling as she leaned forward in her seat.

"On it," he replied quickly as he hit the thrusters, jolting the ship forward.

"Alex, get ready to…"

"Already ahead of you, captain." She slid her seat on the track it was connected to on the floor over to another control panel. This one with a small scanner as well as two hand controllers. She took hold of them as she clicked on the monitor. The screen filled with the rear view of space. The Reapers in pursuit. Alex started moving the sticks around as well as pushing a button on the top of each joystick on the console. It engaged the rear defense artillery of the *Leo* and immediately began firing at the Reapers.

A spray of laser fire erupted off the bottom rear quarter of the ship in all directions moving back. Immediately the much smaller and more agile Reaper ships, swayed away from the oncoming fire and pulled back. The Reapers were very fast, but their weaponry wasn't extensive, much like their military. One of the reasons the government had been recently stockpiling better weapons on their home world.

"Come on, come on!" Alex said with her teeth clenched as she continued shooting off the rear port of the ship towards the Reapers. The small Reapers zipped back and forth, continuing to avoid the laser fire but not getting any more hits in themselves on the *Leo*.

"He's wearing one of our space suits. I'm going to try communicating with him. Danny, try to keep them off of us," Sam yelled towards the pilot's seat, with Danny Boy nodding in agreement.

Sam clicked on the com from her seat. "Willie, what's going on? Why the hell are you doing this?"

Silence. The Reapers were still behind the *Leo* giving chase and Alex was still shooting at them. She looked back at Sam and said bitterly, "You know if I do blast them out of the sky, there goes our Marks, right?"

The com clicked on and Willie's calm voice filled the command center. "You should have seen this coming. All of you. But you didn't. Because I'm smarter than all of you and now I'm also officially a lot wealthier."

Justin, Carol and Ramsey looked at each other. "What have we gotten ourselves into now?" Ramsey muttered quietly to them. Carol shook her head in stunned disbelief.

Justin raised his hand slightly to his crew and quietly retorted, "This is bad. This is really bad. We need to keep our cool. They may need our help."

Another hard blast connected with the *Leo*. Sparks flew from the ceiling panels in the cockpit. Smoke wafted up from a damaged computing system. Then the ship began to slow. The *Stormbringer* crew quickly sat down in available seats.

Willie came back again on the com system. "Hey, you three we picked up earlier. You picked the wrong time to hitch a ride. Now we have to destroy all of you. Wrong place, wrong time, I guess. Have a good life, what's left of it. Oh, and Alex, it's been an honor. I wish I could do to you what I had to do to Grant." He laughed.

Sam clicked off the com system to ensure Willie wouldn't hear her. "Alex, I don't care about the Marks. Take them out."

"Gladly," Alex responded, angrily digesting the devastating news Willie just divulged.

"Is there anything we can do to help?" Justin asked Sam, trying to break her concentration on the task at hand.

Sam shook her head without looking over at them.

The Reapers continued their pursuit, zigzagging through space. One of the Reapers began to fly above the *Leo* in an attempt to blast it from the top, and that's when Alex saw her opportunity to get a much needed perfectly timed shot in. The ship got too close to the *Leo* as it started its upward trajectory. Alex fired, sending red blasts of laser fire through space, connecting with the ship, which immediately exploded into fiery pieces of debris.

"Good shot!" Danny yelled over to her as he continued to swerve back and forth. Danny looked down at his ship schematics and hollered back to Sam, "We're losing power.

One of those Reapers hit one of our two engines. It's shot. We're flying on one."

Another blast rocked the ship. More sparks flew through the command center. "There's a fire in the engine room!" Danny yelled out.

Justin saw his opportunity to help. "I know where the room is. Third level. Is there a fire extinguisher there?" he asked as calmly as he could.

Sam looked over at him, quickly contemplating whether she should indeed ask for their help in this increasingly bad situation.

"Come on, you're going to have to trust us! We can help!" Justin said to her, raising his voice.

"Trust is a hard thing to come by right now!" she retorted as she continued to rock back and forth in her seat, gripping the side armrests from the blasts around them in space as well as the damaged *Leo*.

"Well? What do you say, captain?" Justin came back, eager to help.

"Do it. But just you," Sam shot back.

Carol immediately looked over to Justin, worry covering her face. She began to shake her head in protest, but Justin put his hand on hers.

"It's fine. You stay here. They might be able to use both of you here in the command center."

And with that, Justin hopped up and left the cockpit.

Carol looked at Ramsey with dread who had a similar expression on his now fully awake face.

"It's gonna be ok. Let's see what we can do to help here."

Another hit from the remaining Reaper. This blast knocked Danny Boy face first into the control panel in front of him. He slumped over in his chair. Blood covering his face and pouring out of his nose.

Carol and Ramsey hopped up. "Let us help!" they both began to say.

Alex laid down another stream of laser fire. And this one connected with the remaining Reaper, clipping its wing.

"Got you, ya bastard!" Alex shouted.

Inside the Reaper spacecraft, Willie was sitting beside a Cambulonian pilot. He still had his helmet on. Reapers were made primarily for warfare, so helmets were required for breathing. The inside of the vessel was small, only enough room for a pilot and, on occasion, a co-pilot if one was needed.

The Marks were stored in a safety lockbox brought along for this mission, but Willie continually looked back and forth at both the Marks and the ship in front of them. Especially now having taken a hit to their wing.

"Get us out of here! We're hit and he have 10,000 Marks back there! Another close call like that and we're done for!" Willie yelled at the pilot angrily as they shuddered in the seats of the now damaged fighter ship.

The pilot looked over at Willie without saying anything. The pilot was wearing a black space suit and a black fighter pilot's helmet with a heavily tinted face plate. Willie knew what the Cambulons looked like underneath that gear. Imposing and icy cold faces. He had never met a Cambulon that wasn't in some way intimidating. Men and women alike. The women, as he well knew, could be great lovers in this regard.

He thought about throwing one last insult at the crew of the *Leo*, but what was the point? Their ship had taken extensive damage and once they were back on Darmus III he would ensure a few more Reapers would be assigned to fly back and take out the ship for good if it was still in one piece. He had hoped they would already have been blasted out of space, but those wishes were dashed. The *Leo* was a large and heavy freighter that could withstand multiple blasts. Especially from ships as small as the Reapers.

The pilot clicked on his com system and spoke in an ominous tone, "This is Reaper Pilot 5587, we lost 4396 but have the Marks. The *Leo* is damaged but still flies. I believe we took out one of its two engines judging from its rapidly decreasing speed. However, we're hit, requesting access to nearest space port."

A cold voice on the other end replied, "Proceed to nearest space port for repairs, sending coordinates now. I'm sending a small transport shuttle there as well. Mr. Petros and the Marks are to board it immediately upon its arrival and head back to Darmus III, is that clear? We'll handle the *Leo*. Commander Kar out."

The pilot continued flying his Reaper away from the heavily damaged *Leo* and plotted a new course for the space port location sent over by his commander back on Darmus III that was now displayed on the holographic star map in front of him.

Willie took one last look at the *Leo* and muttered to himself, "So long, suckers."

Sam contemplated her choices, then stood up looking towards Carol and Ramsey, "I could use some more hands piloting this ship!"

"On it," Ramsey replied back as he and Carol quickly headed to the injured Danny Boy. Carol pulled the injured pilot, who was slumped over unconscious, out of his seat and began looking over his wounds while Ramsey immediately hopped into the pilot's seat and looked over the layout of the *Leo's* piloting operations.

The damaged Reaper retreated and shot off through space in the opposite direction. The damage wasn't extensive enough to stop its retreat.

"Damnit!" Alex yelled as the Reaper continued its trajectory away from the *Leo*.

"Forget him for now, Alex, we have a host of new problems to contend with here," Sam said bitterly as she stood over her, watching along as the Reaper vanished from their screens.

CHAPTER 10

DAMAGE CONTROL

The Reaper was gone. Their Marks were gone. Grant was apparently gone. Danny Boy had sustained major injuries to his head. One of the ship's engines was on fire and losing power fast. Sam needed to stay calm and in control. Her crew and the crew of the *Stormbringer* needed her.

"Alex, stay at the ready. Carol, how is Danny?" Sam asked, hurrying over to where Carol was bent down attending to him.

"He's unconscious and has a nasty cut on the side of his head. His wounds need treated. What medical supplies do you have onboard?" Carol asked, anxiously looking up at Sam.

"We have supplies in the makeshift science lab by our water filtration system at the rear of level one. I'll go grab them." Sam glanced over at Ramsey, then added, "Think you can hold us steady for a bit until we get things a little more under control?"

Ramsey looked back at Sam and replied coolly, "On it. I've got the basics figured out. And from the looks of it, the ship is continuing to lose speed due to that fire in the engine room." Ramsey looked at the fire warning light on the display. An alarm was sounding throughout the ship as well.

Sam nodded and replied back bluntly, "I'll be back in a minute with some medical supplies for Danny, then I'm heading down to help out Justin, ok?" And with that, she left the command center without waiting for a response.

On her way to the rear of level one Sam thought about this terrible turn of events. How could she have been so blind? How could she have put her crew in this danger? She felt ashamed. What happened to Grant? She thought of her father, Robert Howard. The courageous Robert Howard. How she had loved her dad. He would know what to do in this situation. But he wasn't here. She was. She was in command. She grabbed the med kit from the small science lab room and headed back up to the command center.

Alex slid her seat over to Ramsey and peered down at the screen, then up to him. "You think you can handle this?" Alex asked in a controlled, calm voice.

Looking up at Alex, Ramsey replied with a small smile pursing his lips, "I think so. I mean, the layout is completely different, but a lot of this is familiar to a pilot. And I've got you to fall back on if those Reaper things come back for round two."

"You mean Reaper. Singular. Not plural. I blasted one of them straight to hell, and the other one is in no shape to stage a comeback unless it brings reinforcements with it. In which case, we're fu…"

She was cut off by Carol yelling, "Alex, can you give me a hand here? I need you to grab a towel. I have to stop the bleeding. He's got a bad cut on the side of his head!"

Alex jumped up and ran to the back of the cockpit. There were a few items stored in a drawer, one of which was a small rag. She grabbed it and ran back to Carol.

Looking at the towel, Carol responded, "That'll do until Sam gets back with more supplies." She took it out of Alex's hand, placing it on the side of Danny's bleeding head.

Just then, Sam ran back into the room and immediately went over to where Carol was kneeling in front of Danny. "Here you go, there should be enough tools in here for now. Once we get the fire under control I'll be back up." She handed a medical briefcase to her.

Carol took it and quickly opened it up, scanning the contents. Nodding, she looked up at Sam and said, "This will do. Good luck."

Sam noted the scared look on her face, sensing it was because of the danger Justin was in. "He's gonna be fine. I'm just glad you three are here. I'm sure the feeling isn't mutual right now, but we're gonna get through this." She stood up and left the room once more, grabbing a fire extinguisher on the back wall on her way out as the door slid shut behind her.

Ramsey looked back at Carol and Alex and said grimly, "I hate to be the bearer of bad news, but we are losing more speed. Pretty soon we're floating. From one dead ship to the next, it would seem."

Ignoring him, Carol rooted through the medical kit laying on the floor. "He needs stitches. Get me a bottle of water, Alex."

Alex handed her a bottle nearby and Carol got to work pouring it over the wound. The cut was deep but could be stitched up. *Wish I would have had this med kit back on TSR1,* she thought to herself.

Once the wound was washed, she got out a small stitching gun. "Not quite like what we had on our ship, but it looks essentially like the same set-up.

"Ok, hold him steady, Alex," Carol said calmly as she lowered the stitching gun to Danny Boy's temple.

Doing as she commanded, Alex took hold of Danny Boy's head firmly. She glanced up at Ramsey, who happened to look down at her at that exact same moment. Quickly she looked away, back to the task at hand. *What the hell am I doing?* she thought to herself, feeling a brief flush on her cheeks.

The stitching gun worked essentially as a stapler. Hold the open wound in need of stitches together and pull the trigger. Which is what Carol was about to do. "Sorry, Danny. This isn't going to feel pleasant." She began the procedure: one, two, three, four, five stitches sealed the wound quickly. Carol calmly put the gun back into the med kit and poured fresh water over the sealed wound, washing off excess blood. It was quick and dirty, but it would hold.

"He's gonna have quite a headache when he comes to." Carol washed off her hands that had been covered in Danny Boy's blood. She had seen more blood in the last week than she hoped to ever see again in her entire life.

Danny Boy opened his eyes and grimaced at the immediate pain that wracked through his head as he started moaning.

"Speak of the devil. Welcome back, Danny Boy," Alex said with a genuine smile on her face as she bent down and put her hand on his arm.

Danny tried to look around but let out a long groan instead.

Carol put her hand on his chest and said calmly, "Easy. You just got a few stitches on your head. I need you to take a few pills for me. Can you do that?"

Nodding in reply, Danny Boy closed his eyes from the pain.

"Lift his head up for me, will you?" Carol asked Alex. She gently took Danny's head and tilted it up as Carol dropped two pills into his half open mouth, then tilted the water bottle, spilling water into his mouth as well.

Danny swallowed and almost choked, but got the pills and water down. Alex carefully laid his head back down to the ground.

"Please tell me you got Willie's ship," Danny Boy said in a garbled voice.

"Don't talk for now, tough guy. We have more pressing matters to deal with at the moment," Alex said softly as Danny closed his eyes.

Justin had made his way to the engineering room and upon entering saw the fire. One of the engines had ignited from one of the many blasts the *Leo* had taken. The fire was spreading, so Justin had to act quickly. He scanned the room which housed two engine bays and a host of other machines that ran the ship's primary functions. If the fire wasn't put out soon it would spread to the rest of the equipment and at some point the ship would explode.

Time was not on his side. He found a fire extinguisher connected to the wall and took it out. It was a standard issue extinguisher and easy to operate. Justin pulled the pin and sprayed the fire that had engulfed engine one. The smoke in the room was bad and getting worse.

Sam arrived at the engine room, clicking her helmet to the space suit she was still wearing as the fire alarm continued ringing through the ship. Upon entering the room, she was taken aback by the extensive damage to the engine. Justin saw her enter and yelled, "Come on! We've got to get this fire out now. It's spreading!"

Not hesitating, she pulled her pin and started coating the fire along with Justin, who was coughing from the smoke. They both emptied their extinguishers as the fire began subsiding.

"I need to disconnect engine one and its power cell from our primary system functions!" Sam yelled in the loud, smoke-filled room.

Justin nodded and watched as Sam took a towel over to the still hot engine that was now extinguished. She knew they weren't out of danger from an explosion yet. The engine needed to be disconnected. This was Danny Boy's field of expertise. She knew little about the details of the engine, but knew enough to disconnect it.

Several cords located in the back connected engine one to engine two, which connected to the main hub of the *Leo*, allowing it to fly. The ship could still function on one engine at a much-reduced speed. She grabbed ahold of the two cords connecting them, twisted in a counterclockwise motion, and pulled.

There was a hiss then the cords came free of engine two. The ship was old, and this was certainly a safety hazard and far too easy to accomplish than it should be, but in this particular situation, Sam was glad at the ease with which engine one and two were disconnected. She quickly looked over at the power cell connected to engine two. It had fire damage on the outside. She wasn't sure to what extent, but she knew that wasn't good.

"Fire's out. Engines aren't connected anymore. Let's get out of here," Sam said to Justin, who was coughing.

They left the room and Sam motioned for them to head back up to the control room. She took her helmet off and looked at Justin, who was dirty from the smoke in the engine room. At that moment the fire alarm went out and it was now silent on level three except for the humming of engine two still operating.

"Good work in there, Mr. Justin," she said stoically.

"Doing my part. What's the next move, captain?" Justin responded as he wiped ash off of his face.

Sam thought for a second, then looked over at Justin. "We need to get this ship landed. Top priority. That space port that Willie…" she paused as she said his name.

Sensing what she was thinking, Justin prodded her, "And?" he said, hoping for some more information.

"The space port. It's the nearest relatively safe place for us to land. We're less than twenty-four hours from it. If the *Leo* can get us there. The power cell for engine two has some fire damage to it, but I don't know to what extent. We can dock and possibly get repairs made. In case we're on the wanted list. That's a whole other level of bad news, but we should be ok this far out in the quadrant."

"Ok, sounds like a plan. Hey, I know my crew has been through a lot, but as Carol said earlier, we're grateful for you helping us. And we will do everything we can to ensure we all make it to that space port alive. We need to figure out what happened to Grant as well," Justin answered her, sensing she needed a bit of reassurance.

She nodded with a small smile, then added in a voice brimming with hate, "When this is all over, Willie will be getting what's coming to him. He can run…"

"Come on, time to regroup. Figure a few things out. I'm with you," Justin said calmly.

They both made their way back up to level one into the command center.

The door of the command center slid open as Justin and Sam walked through. Alex, Carol and Ramsey looked up at them enter. Immediately Carol ran over to Justin, inspecting his ashen face. She put her hands on his arms.

"Are you ok?" she asked earnestly. Pressing in close to him.

He looked at her and smiled. The smile that she loved. "Yes, we're both fine. Fire is out."

Carol nodded at him, then whispered so only he could hear her, "I was worried something terrible would happen."

He glanced over at Sam.

Noticing that now all eyes were on her, she cleared her throat and set her space helmet down next to her commander's chair. "How's Danny Boy?" she asked calmly to Alex and Carol, looking at them both, then down to Danny Boy, who lay on the ground moaning.

"He's going to be ok. We put five stitches into his head. Took a nasty cut and he might have a concussion. He'll live, that's what's important," Carol answered, with Alex nodding in agreement.

Sam walked over to the pilot's chair where Ramsey sat and looked over the schematics of the ship. "Have you figured out how to pilot this heap, Mr. Ramsey?"

Looking up from where he was seated, he sighed heavily and responded, "Well, as you're I'm sure aware, this ship is minus one engine, so it's taking a lot out of engine two to keep us going. We need to dock as soon as possible to have repairs made, as well as assess what other damages were done to the ship. You know her better than I do, captain. How much can the *Leo* take, especially running on one engine?"

"Well, she's a trooper. Been through a hell of a lot over her many years of service, starting with my father and then me. She can take a beating but keeps on ticking through the solar system. This was especially bad. That engine is toast. It'll need to be fully repaired or even replaced, and we don't have the Marks to make that kind of repair. Having said that, I do think we can make it to the space port, get the ship assessed and go from there. At the very least, we can help our new crew mates here out by finding some place for them to go," Sam said with a hint of sadness in her voice over what the crew of the *Stormbringer* had been through prior to their paths crossing.

Justin sensed her remorse and quickly added, "It bears repeating. Without your help, we would still be floating in deep space. Or worse."

"Agreed," Carol responded. "We owe you all our lives. Regardless of what's happened. Sorry about that Willie fella."

To this Alex put her hands on her hips and spoke up. "Well, I have a strong hunch I know where he's headed. Dogs always return to their vomit. I think it's safe to say we'll find him back on Darmus III. At least for the short term."

Changing the subject, Sam added, "By my count, we have approximately four space suits. Willie took one of them. There's six of us. This ship has to remain in flying condition until we reach that space port."

Looking down at the space suit she was still wearing, Alex spoke to herself: "I need to get out of this thing."

Hearing her, Sam nodded. "I need to get out of this space suit as well. We should also move Danny Boy to his bed."

Hearing his name, Danny opened his eyes and sat up, looking around the room and getting his bearings.

"Danny! Be careful. You should lay back down," Alex said earnestly, looking down at him.

"I'll be fine. Pills kicking in and my head is stitched up. Good as new." He chuckled to himself and slowly got to his feet.

Carol and Alex grabbed ahold of each of his arms, helping him to his feet. Once upright, he wobbled a little bit then kept his balance and shooed both Carol and Alex's grip away.

They both let go cautiously, but stayed close to him in case of a blackout or worse.

Sam quickly went over to inspect Danny Boy herself. "How are you doing there, guy?" she asked, putting both of her hands gently on his neck, inspecting the stitched wound on his bald head. She had always found Danny Boy handsome. Not in a buff body sort of way like Grant. But the shaved head, short beard, and witty humor just connected well with her. He had become almost like a brother to her over the years serving aboard the *Leo* together. Him and Grant.

"So what's the status? Last thing I remember was getting pummeled by those damn Reapers. Then everything went black. I came to for a bit, seeing that pretty blond over there getting ready to do some much-needed plastic surgery on this ugly skull of mine."

Carol looked down as everyone in the room glanced over in her direction replying, "hey, just trying to do my part here."

Looking back at Sam, his demeanor turned serious. "Grant. Where's Grant? This is all Willie's doing. Rotten shit. Who's piloting the *Leo?*" He looked over to see Ramsey sitting in the pilot's seat.

"Look, Danny Boy, we're currently in damage control. Our friend Ramsey over there is doing pretty good at figuring things out with the ship, all things considered," Sam said, looking over at Ramsey. She was coming to like these three space travelers that had hitched a ride with them.

CHAPTER 11

BIRTH

During Willie's theft of the Marks, the shooting of Grant at point blank range, the outer cargo bay hatch opening to an audience of two Cambulonian Reaper fighter ships, and the space battle that ensued, something else was happening aboard the *Leo*.

The slick black substance had expanded significantly, covering most of the *Stormbringer's* interior. The small glowing light inside the black goo had also grown. It was significantly larger when it was attached to its host body back inside the dead star, but most of the organic mass had not withstood the rest of the flight once it had attached itself to the bottom of the starship.

Enough of it had survived. It needed a host body for the meager glowing light inside to assimilate and ingest.

During the opening of the outer hatch, Grant's mortally wounded body had slid forward, smashing against the *Stormbringer's* landing gear. He desperately tried to cling tightly to the bottom of the ship as the air around him rushed out into space. He could feel his life was quickly slipping away. Blood continuing to pour out of the open wound on his chest, some of it flying backwards through the open hull like a small red mist.

The substance inside the hull of the *Stormbringer* sensed this new life form close to it. As it had expanded and grew, it had gained significantly more power to move and morph. A part of the substance inside the hull quickly slipped through the landing gear opening once again and oozed down the shiny metal as another humanoid being stood over by the opened cargo bay. It wouldn't mess with that being. Too far away. This one would do nicely.

Grant lay near death on the ground as he felt himself being pulled away into the vacuum of space. Then he felt something else. Something wrapping itself around his thick, muscular body.

There was nothing he could do. He was too weak from holding onto the landing gear, the force of the decompression of the cargo bay and the mortal wound inflicted on his chest.

He looked down as thick black tar engulfed him. Part of the substance slid up the side of the *Stormbringer* and opened the hatch as it slid across the control panel. He had no time to react and was lifted up by the growing black tar and hoisted into the inner hull of the ship as the hatch quickly slid shut.

No sooner had the hatch on the *Stormbringer* slid shut than the interior doors of the cargo bay slid completely open. Laser fire erupted through the cargo bay. But this didn't affect what was happening inside the small escape pod. It wasn't concerned with the other humans outside. Not yet. This one would do nicely.

Grant let out gurgled screams that went unheard by anyone outside the *Stormbringer*. This worked to the entity's advantage as it quickly slipped itself into the open, bloody mouth of its prey. It also entered through the hole in his chest. Filling the human cavity up. Ingesting the organs as the human ingested it. Grant's blood was soaked up instantly into the black tar.

The substance wrapped itself around Grant's internal organs. Twisting and turning and feasting. Not only was the entity inside Grant, but it was also covering his outer body. Seeping out of the empty synth tanks, out of the various compartments it had seeped into on the *Stormbringer*, the goo flowed forward, enveloping this new tasty treat filled with liquids and soft matter. It wrapped itself around the brain of the dead carcass. Travelling through every open orifice on Grant's lifeless head. The brain was still active. Overactive even. Then blackness overtook the brain's neurons and glial cells. It ingested the knowledge hidden inside. It was learning. Becoming alive through this large chunk of meat. The dim light inside the goo was now covering the body like an embryotic sack.

Alex and Sam were changing out of their heavy and cumbersome space suits in their quarters while Ramsey continued piloting the *Leo*. Carol was keeping a close eye on Danny Boy, talking to him to keep him alert. Justin was inspecting Danny's Fusion Rifle, after getting permission from its owner beforehand. Looking it over it seemed like an even more powerful rifle than the blast rifle currently in storage. He planned on getting all of their guns and knives back soon. Thus far this newest leg of the *Stormbringer* crew's adventure was fraught with danger. They needed to be armed.

Justin raised the rifle to his shoulder, peering through the small scope. The gun itself was slightly longer than his blast rifle. It was completely black and had a long stock. It was heavy, which could be a detriment in a heated battle where swinging a heavy rifle around wasn't always the best choice. This was why STEA had issued all of its space travelers the blast rifle and their side arm. Both incredibly light and incredibly deadly.

He set the Fusion Rifle down, stood up and walked over to Danny Boy, who was sitting in the chair Alex had been in earlier, firing on the Reapers.

"Tell me about the artillery on this ship," Justin asked as he bent down to look over the station used for defending the *Leo* from attackers.

Danny glanced up at him, then down to the sticks. "Ok, so the dual sticks are used for rear port firing. Which is what Alex had been doing. Took one of the Reapers out this way and clipped that other one. Now, in order to fire the side cannons on this ship, it's a bit different. Those are stationary, whereas the rear port guns can be maneuvered. All it takes to launch all out holy hell on anything in front of us is this knob. It controls the intensity of the blast. The higher the intensity, the sooner they need to cool down before overheating."

He paused and looked up at Justin, who was standing over him, listening intently. "Go on."

Nodding, Danny continued, "It works almost as a third stick, but turn it and ka-bang. Pity the ship in the path of that laser fire."

"Where are we at with the power cells onboard? I know engine one is kaput, but can we use the second power cell to help out the remaining engine?" Justin asked, still looking at the schematics of the ship from Danny's seat over to where Ramsey was sitting, continuing to figure out how the ship operated.

"Unfortunately, no. Each power cell is attached to the engine. Engine goes, power cell is non-functional. It's basically like a battery assigned to the engine."

Justin nodded, then added, "So we're going to have to make sure engine two and the corresponding power cell remain functional."

Ramsey chimed in at this, pointing at his screen, "That one engine is taking a lot of power to fly this thing and is draining the fuel. It looks like the ship was already in need of fuel before all of this happened."

Sam and Alex walked back into the command center. "You would be right, Ramsey," Sam said. "We've never sustained this kind of damage. When both engines are functioning properly it takes significantly less fuel, and we can easily get from quadrant to quadrant until a refuel is needed. Not so in this case. Adding to the engine one issue is our power cell on engine two."

Danny Boy looked over at Sam and responded with urgency through the dull pain in his head, "What issue?"

"It's damaged. Still functioning, but not sure for how long. We can't replace it here in space. So it has to last," Sam said solemnly.

Standing up and looking at Sam and Alex, Carol asked thoughtfully, "So there is no way to get it back to fully functioning working condition? Seems like we're double crippled here."

"Well, and Danny can correct me if I'm wrong, but the power cells, once damaged, cannot be repaired in any way. They have to be replaced," Sam said troublingly.

Clearing his throat, he thought for a second, "Yes, Sam is correct. Theoretically those power cells cannot be repaired. They need to be replaced. But is the power cell in engine one still tip top? I mean, the engine might be toast, but we could essentially swap them out. Won't be easy, and my head feels like it was squeezed by a Kakig on Zilia CT7. Remember those disgusting things?"

Alex smiled and jokingly replied, "Oh, I won't forget about that crazy drop. You'd have to pay me a lot of Marks to ever go back there."

Changing the subject, Justin responded with urgency, "But it can be done? The power cells? If it works, what does that give us with regards to getting to the nearest space port?"

Sam walked over to Ramsey's station and looked at his screen readout, studying it. "I need the seat, Ramsey," she said flatly.

"All yours, sir," Ramsey said as he pushed back in the chair and stood up.

Sitting down, Sam accessed several diagrams on the two screens in front of her and looked them over. "So look, this ship is obviously not some high-tech work of wonder. No onboard A.I. to walk us through problem solving, and things do break on this bucket of bolts. However, it's built to take a serious beating, which she just did. And I'm seeing here that power cell one is surprisingly tip top. But…"

Ramsey was leaning forward, looking at the schematics Sam was scanning. Alex had moved over beside him and also looked down at the monitors. He glanced over at her and while she didn't return the look, she sensed his gaze causing her to suppress a slight grin.

"But, to replace them, the secondary engine needs to be shut down. Which means we come to a stand-still. We still have auxiliary power, but we aren't going anywhere. Sitting ducks for any Reapers that might decide to show up."

"How long would it take to power down and swap the cells?" Justin asked Danny Boy.

Sitting up again, Danny looked over at Justin as he rubbed his head close to the stitches. "I would say roughly one hour. I would need to do it. Full disclosure, I've never done something like that before, but I do know those engines and power cells inside and out. I could do it."

"And if we don't try this? Then what?" Carol asked both Danny and Sam.

Sam, who was still looking over the ship's schematics, replied in a tone that was trying to mask deep concern, "We're dead in the water. Like you three were before we found you. Before we make it to the space port. We swap out the power cells and we can easily make it to space port for refueling and get some of these repairs done. Possibly even get to a nearby planet."

"I'd be tickled pink with that plan. Darmus III is still in the quadrant. If you catch my drift," Alex added smugly.

"All good things come to those who wait, Alex. We've got more pressing issues at hand. But if it makes you feel any better, our end goal is to get back the Marks that were stolen and have a few words with our old friend Willie," Sam said coolly.

"I'll let this do all the talking," Alex said confidently as she raised her own low frequency Electron Pistol she had holstered on her hip belt when she changed out of her space suit.

Danny Boy grinned at her, then looked at Sam and Justin. "The pills are working their magic. My head still throbs, but I can manage. I'm going to need a spare set of hands with this, though. Those power cells are heavy, and I don't think I have the strength with my head injury and the pills in my system."

"I can be your arms, Danny. You just guide me through whatever it is to get it done," Justin said confidently.

Sam thought through this and nodded her head in agreement. "We're going to have to take the risk of no engine power for a bit. It's that or no power permanently."

"Brilliant. That's what I think of the plan," Danny Boy said cynically with his thick native accent only found on his home world of Wiggip.

Justin nodded and smiled at her as she looked to him for his thoughts. Then Justin spoke, "Danny, how soon do you feel ready enough to do this?"

"No better time than the present. I say let's rock and roll," he replied, with as much confidence as he could muster.

Sam stood up from the pilot's seat, allowing Ramsey to sit back down, and walked over to her engineer. Looking at him in the eye, she said bluntly, "Are you sure about this? We lost Grant. Something I have yet to even attempt to come to terms with. And we have a crippled ship being worked on by an engineer who's severely injured. Given the option, I would rather not have any more injuries or deaths onboard."

Putting his hands on her shoulders, he responded softly, "I've got this. Trust me."

"I always do. One of the reasons the *Leo* has continued to fly as long as she has," she replied back to him softly.

Alex walked past him, heading to Ramsey. As she passed Danny Boy, she slapped him on his butt, jokingly chiming in, "Plus, if you mess this up and get us all killed, I'll have to kick your ass, you know that."

"Let's talk about Grant," Danny said calmly, surprising everyone in the room. He continued, "We assume that was his blood and that he was indeed sucked out of the open cargo bay. However, none of us saw it happen. Sam, I've been trying not to think about this, but I have to come to terms with the probability that Grant is gone. Can you humor me though and take a blood sample from the cargo bay floor?"

"I hear you. We do have a blood sample kit. A quick analysis of the blood on the floor in the cargo bay will let us know if it is Grant's blood. With the amount of blood loss in there, no one can survive that. Not even Grant," Sam said sadly.

Carol, now standing beside Justin, said solemnly, "I know this is tough."

"We've all lost things. It's part of being human, right? You taught me that over the years, captain. Let's fix this ship and get it to the space port," Alex said proudly, looking at Sam.

Sam nodded and smiled as she watched Alex take a seat close to Ramsey. "You help out Ramsey keeping this ship afloat, and if anything shows up in our general vicinity that looks remotely threatening, destroy it."

"I'll need a few supplies to make this happen. I'll grab them on my way down to the engine room with Justin," Danny said in reply.

"Ok, we have the plan, let's make it happen. Carol, wanna help me out analyzing the blood samples?" Sam said calmly.

Carol nodded her approval, adding, "I was hoping I could be of some use."

"Good," Sam replied, then added, "Also, you three…"

The crew of the *Stormbringer* looked over at her.

"I can't be sure if those Reapers and the Cambulonians that pilot them are coming back to attempt finishing us off, but regardless, it's time to get you three rearmed." She tossed Ramsey her Fusion Rifle, which he caught in midair.

CHAPTER 12

BUDDING FRIENDSHIP

Continuing on its path across space through the HD-6549 quadrant, on its way to Space Port 771 which was now less than eight hours away, Carol and Sam left the command center and headed towards the science lab in the rear of level one. Danny Boy and Justin left as well, heading towards level three to the engine room, leaving Ramsey and Alex alone to pilot the *Leo*.

The command center was quiet as Ramsey continued peering out the cockpit viewscreen into space. He had set the Fusion Rifle down beside him. Alex continued monitoring her station. There was an awkward silence.

At the same time, they both started speaking, "So how long…" were Ramsey's words.

"Tell me about…" were Alex's words.

They both stopped and Ramsey chuckled to himself. He glanced over at Alex, noting that she was grinning herself. He found her incredibly beautiful, her tough personality complimenting her quite girlish looks.

"You first," he said, still smiling.

She sat up in her seat and without looking over at him, brushed a bit of the long red hair out of her face and asked, "I was just going to ask you what you used to do before traveling the stars. Back on your planet."

"Boxer. I used to be a boxer. Loved it. Had the best trainer a guy could ask for. Schmitz. I took many beatings and that man always stayed by my side. More than my own dad," Ramsey said, grinning to himself, thinking back to his boxing days.

"Why did you quit?" Alex prodded.

"Well, I guess I had accomplished about everything I wanted to in the ring. Won some, lost more. I felt a higher calling than continually getting my face smashed in. So I enlisted at STEA, which is our space program. Well, was our space program back on Trilaxus. And became a pilot. Those years as a boxer with coach Bill Schmitz taught me to keep pushing forward. I've always had a desire to explore the known universe. That and boxing." He chuckled.

"And here you are," Alex said, chuckling herself.

"'And here I am' is right." He then grew serious. "Seems like we've all been through a lot. I was literally staring down the face of a giant demon creature that had turned my friend into some sort of a living dead flying rat vampire."

"I know you all explained, to the best of your abilities I suppose, what happened back there, but do you think there are more of those things? I mean, I've seen some crazy shit in my days aboard the *Leo*, but an enormous monster on an uncharted planet on the other side of a legit black hole that's sole purpose is hanging onto some stone because magic? You think there's more of those things out there?"

Ramsey thought about this. "Well, I wish I could say 'no,' but traveling back through that black hole… I saw something inside. No, it wasn't some huge mind controlling creature with claws and fangs and horns. But I saw enough to know that something enormous could exist inside a dead star. Live inside of that! So, I guess what I'm trying to say is, this universe we inhabit, it's so vast… we have only just begun to scratch the surface of what's out there. What's survived and evolved through at least one billion years. I met one of them. Literally spoke with it. I hope I never find myself in a situation remotely like that again. Ever. The oppressive evil was so overpowering. And I'm not a religious man by any stretch. But that thing was complete, pure unadulterated *hate* manifested into physical form."

Alex looked over at him and smiled. Without looking back, Ramsey could see the mysterious and feisty redheaded woman looking his way and awkwardness fell over him immediately.

"So, yeah, anyway. Um, my question, how long have you been on board? What's the story?"

She sat back in her seat, contemplating how much to share. Ramsey, the dark skinned, muscular stranger from 100 years prior was growing on her, slowly. "I was a runaway. Pickpocketing my way through my own home planet Nerilia before Samantha Howard caught me. I had numerous close calls, but she was the only one to actually legit catch me in the act. I figured I was done for." Alex paused.

After a minute of contemplation she continued, noticing that Ramsey was indeed staring at her. Which made her warmly uncomfortable. "Anyway, I could have gotten my ass kicked. But instead, Sam offered to buy me a drink. I mean, I had been on my own since twelve when my mom and dad…" She trailed off.

Sensing a tough subject, Ramsey tried to move her story forward. "What did Sam see in you to hire you as part of this crew?"

Relieved that she wouldn't have to delve into the fate of her mom and dad, whom she had dearly loved, she gladly moved on, appreciating Ramsey's attempt at skipping over a touchy subject. "Well, my life on the streets had its benefits. It certainly toughened me up, fending for myself. I got really good at money counting. And I can keep track of multiple things at once. Perceptive eye and all that, you know?"

"As far as perceptive eye, I thought you were going to blast Carol's head off earlier." Ramsey raised one eyebrow.

Alex got serious then. "My crew is my world. I would defend them to my dying breath. We don't get many visitors, if any. So, my guard was on red alert. Plus, I was still pissed at Willie for not negotiating a higher Mark amount for the weapons we sold the Cambulons. Which turns out he was in cahoots with all along. Mother fu…"

"Duly noted. Hey, I get it. When we lost Ben to those creatures back on TSR1 all I wanted to do was kill anything with wings. I would have, and still would, give my life for Carol and Justin. Nearly gave my life for Ben. But he did the honors. Gave his life for his crew." He paused sadly, thinking of his captain.

"So what is TSR1? You all keep saying that. I get that it's the planet you were stranded on. You said that other commander guy stuck there had named it? James was his name, I believe?" Alex asked, genuinely curious.

Ramsey nodded his head, thinking of his lost friend that he barely had time to get to know. "James named it that, yes. James Korvell, the commander of the *E.E.S. Saros*. He went through that black hole as well, although his ship didn't fare as well as ours did. I know we brought you all up to speed on this, but that man lived there for years. By himself. Literally lived in a cave. Hell of a guy. Gave his life…anyway, TSR1 stands for 'Thunder Stone Realm.' I think I had mentioned that earlier to all of you. James got the name from a movie, I guess. Much like we named our little escape pod the *Stormbringer* and the system's A.I. Zark. Both named off of a movie called *Trooper Command*."

"What's a movie?" Alex asked, clearly puzzled.

"Wait, what? You don't know what a movie is?" Ramsey leaned back in his chair looking over at her, shaking his head in disbelief.

"Um, no? What is it and why would you name something Zark? That has to be the lamest sounding name I've heard in a long time. And I've been to some pretty far out planets, trust me," she fired back.

"Movies, um, you watch them! On screens. People with cameras shoot actors in situations and then add music and editing and all that good stuff. It's entertainment," Ramsey replied.

"Ah, got it. Holographic plays. That's what they're called. At least from our home worlds. Movies, what a dumb name. Like Zark," Alex replied playfully.

"Hey, Zark was great! Somewhere in this vast universe, *Trooper Command* still exists. Even well over 100 years later. And I'll get you to watch it. And you'll revel in its greatness! You'll see," Ramsey joked back.

"Ok, tough guy. I might take you up on that," Alex said with a thin smile. Her cheeks slowly turning red, she realized she was beginning to blush, so she glanced back down at her screen, shaking her head in embarrassment. Any form of romantic interest from the opposite sex was always squelched quickly by Alex. But then, usually the planets, space travelers and general population they interacted with were typically of ill repute. Plus, her focus was always on her mission and her crew. Her family.

Ramsey looked at her, noticing her flush cheeks as well as the now growing awkwardness in the room. Quickly changing the subject from a potential date to more pressing matters, he said, "Tell me about these space ports. Sounds like there's more than one out there, obviously. What should we expect?"

Glad to have the subject changed from flirting with the tall, dark and admittedly handsome stranger to immediate issues, she responded with her more stoic tone, "Not much to see. They're essentially garages in space. Large garages. Sort of long skinny towers. You dock your spacecraft at any available bay and, once connected, you go inside, order repairs, refuel, get some food and drinks. For extended stays they have rooms. Which I assume is what you three will be doing once we drop you off and once our engine is repaired. Which will cost a fortune that we don't have, damnit. What a hell of a day."

"I won't argue there. But it bears repeating, I'm glad to be here with you and your crew versus where we were. It feels somehow closer to home. Even if home has been gone for 100 years. There's got to be a place for us somewhere out there in those stars. And we'll find it."

Alex glanced over at him again, her cheeks still lightly flush. "So why did you ask for my last name earlier, of all things?"

Stammering for an answer, trying to choose his words carefully, Ramsey responded, "Well, I guess back on my home planet of Trilaxus my parents taught me to show respect for a lady. One way of doing that is asking what their full name is. I know, weird, but, you know, that's how I grew up."

Alex stared at this strange man from another distant solar system as well as from another time. "Interesting."

Looking at Alex, almost stunned, Ramsey replied, "Interesting? Interesting? That's your response for me opening up to you here?"

She shot him a look out of the corner of her eye as she continued monitoring the screen in front of her. A thin smile on her pouty lips.

"Oh, I see how you're gonna be. Ok then." Ramsey nodded his head, letting out a small laugh. He was liking this strange, skinny redhead more and more.

CHAPTER 13

REPAIRS AND REMEMBERANCE

Inside the *Stormbringer*, the change continued. Grant was no more. In the place of the once human entity lay thick black tar in an oval shape. The tar substance continued to swirl and twist around the host body. Absorbing all of the nutrients. It was still little more than a mass of thick jelly, but it was evolving gradually. The synth was just the beginning. This human was another steppingstone in its evolution. On the several other worlds this black mass had inhabited, it took the forms of whichever being it first came into intimate contact with. Able to assimilate into every part of the host body. To feed, learn and grow quickly.

The tiny, dim light that had originated inside the black hole was pulsating. Once a part of a much larger living being, it had lay dormant for the perfect opportunity. The pieces had fallen into place. Its attempt to cling onto the hull of the spacecraft had worked, barely. Such a small portion of it had remained through the rest of the ship's travels, but here it was. Little by little, growing.

The pulsating light clung tightly to the body with the tar substance on top of it. Protecting it and keeping it warm. This wasn't possible in the freeze of deep space. But here, the temperature was perfect for it to live. The light acted as a thin film once it had expanded itself around the body of Grant tightly. Acting almost like shrink wrap. It worked in conjunction with the back tar. Both the pulsing light and the tar continued to work together. Growing.

Justin and Danny Boy had made their way down to the engine room. Danny had grabbed some tools he figured he would need for the power cell replacement. *I hope I can do this,* he thought to himself as he gathered the tools. He didn't want to let Sam and the rest of the crew down, but his head was pounding, he'd lost his closest friend mere hours ago and now he had to attempt a repair he had never done before. He knew the ins and outs of the *Leo's* engine and how the power cells functioned, but replacing them? One small mistake could be the end of them all.

Standing right outside the engine room, Danny Boy put his hand up against Justin, stopping him from entering. "Justin, before we get started, I'm going to be deadly honest with you here. There is the distinct possibility that this doesn't work. I'm usually the eternal optimist, but this isn't easy. In theory, I should be able to do it. But it's new territory for me."

Looking over at the engineer, Justin responded calmly, "Well, that's why you've got me here with you. I'll do anything I can to help you, and if it does fail, we both take the fall for it. But it's going to work. Ok?"

Danny Boy nodded back at him and produced a small smile. "Ok then, let's get to it. So, the box of tools I got from storage should suffice. We're going to start by taking out the good cell from the dead engine one. Once that's done and we know it's undamaged, then it'll be time to take out power cell two on the second engine. No pressure, but time is of the essence here. As soon as we get started, we have to keep moving."

"I understand. Well, I think I do. Is there anything I should know about these power cells ahead of time? How volatile are they? By that, I mean, how do we handle them and move them?" Justin said seriously as he put on a pair of thick gloves.

"Well, I wish we could use the space suits, but we need to conserve them in case, well…just in case," Danny Boy said evenly. Then continued, "So these gloves are our best bet for handling them. Now, here's the thing with these power cells. And another reason I didn't bother with space suits as added protection." He paused and sighed.

"When they're replaced, it's all done robotically by mechanic droids, due to the sheer destruction that can happen if mishandled. This is done when the spacecraft is deserted, and the crew is at a significant safe distance. One wrong move and boom. Engine room destroyed. Scratch that, on a ship this size, all three levels would be pretty much decimated. The exterior of these freighters are tough, and are meant to withstand significant trauma. Not so with the interior. Especially an older model like this that has had years of patchwork done to it."

"I know all about ships being destroyed in a blaze of glory. Our mothership is sitting at the bottom of a lake next to a very dead large squid creature and her offspring back on the planet TSR1. You tell me what to do and I'll do it," Justin said, trying to be as relaxed as he could with this new development.

Danny Boy nodded at Justin. He could see almost instantly that this man was a leader. His small crew loved him, especially Carol. He noticed how they looked at each other. They entered the engine room. Justin was getting a good layout of the ship, which was his intention as soon as they landed. His crew was his top priority, and knowing the ins and outs of this completely foreign vessel was of utmost importance. Especially considering all they had been through and were now currently dealing with.

Danny led the way over to the destroyed engine one. "Ok, so a laser blast penetrated the inner hull wall and made a direct hit in the center of engine one, igniting it. Luckily, the fuel tubes right here were built to shut down in case of an engine malfunction. Eventually, however, if you and Sam wouldn't have put that fire out, it would have ignited, causing the total destruction of the *Leo*. So, well done there, Justin."

Justin gave a nod of thanks in reply and set the tools down in between both engines.

"Ok, what's first?"

Danny and Justin began the arduous process of removing the undamaged power cell from engine one. Glancing over at Justin, Danny said, "First off, we're gonna need to carefully remove the cover on power cell one." They unscrewed the cover. Underneath was a glowing blue liquid encapsulated in a large vial. Justin raised his eyebrows, seeing the substance. It looked incredibly similar to their synth fuel used to power their fleet on Trilaxus.

Carol and Sam made their way to the cargo bay with the blood analyzer. A flood of emotions came rushing back to Sam as she looked over her heavily damaged hull, then down to the floor where the blood splatter was. Not just on the floor, but the back wall. This was made with a high-powered weapon. Most likely the Electron Pistol. Willie's Electron Pistol.

"Ok Carol, this is how one of these works," Sam said as she bent down and pulled out the kit. It was a small device with a hypodermic needle on one end and a small, grey pistol type base.

Watching what Sam was doing, Carol scanned the cargo bay. Noticing the open and very empty side compartment, she realized this must have been where Willie had broken in to steal the Marks. And there sat the *Stormbringer*. Or what was left of it. The trusty little ship that gotten them off of TSR1 barely in one piece through the black hole. Would it fly again? This technology was from over 100 years ago, yet seemed light years more advanced than what was found aboard the *Leo. I guess technology evolves differently across the galaxy,* she thought to herself.

"The blood testing kit is actually more like a liquid testing kit. If we need to analyze anything liquid based, this can do it," Sam said calmly as she put the long, thick needle against the splatters of blood streaked across the floor. Pushing the trigger produced a suction reaction and the crimson splatter was sucked up into the vial that the needle was connected to.

Carol watched Sam do this and remembered her own analyzation cube, still aboard the *Stormbringer* that she had used to test the water on TSR1 as well as Ben's blood after being scratched by one of the Azid.

Raising the blood testing kit up, Sam inspected it. "Ok, so all of the crew has their blood on file. Something my dad made sure to do with every new crewmate. So we know what blood type everyone has in case of an emergency. We've never really needed it for anything else, and honestly, I don't think I've touched the thing since Willie joined us a year ago. Should still work fine."

"We have something quite similar in the *Stormbringer*," Carol replied as she looked down at the blood testing kit. Then added, "If you would like, I could go get it. Not that we really need it in this case, but just to show you some Trilaxus tech."

"Maybe later. Look here," Sam said gravely, looking at the small readout display on top of the tube.

Carol looked down at what Sam was pointing at on the tube. The words *Grant Edwards: Positive Blood Match* filled the readout. She nodded her head. "That's what we all figured. I'm sorry, Sam."

Sam didn't say anything, just continued to stare at the display. Finally, she spoke quietly, "I've known Grant for five years. Picked him up on his home world of Raitera V. He was old Abe's friend. Abe was our previous pilot, before Willie." She paused at having to mention Willie's name.

"Anyway, Grant was so tough. Raitera V is a tough planet that produced tough soldiers. I was lucky to get him. Surprised he actually took the job as weapons expert and basically our strong arm here on the *Leo*. Told him the money was decent, not great. Long periods of time in space. Lots of boredom coupled with some *will we survive this?* moments. This moment tonight, however, was unfortunately, no. What a soldier. Danny Boy might seem tough, but I can tell you with 100% certainty, he lost a brother today."

"I'm truly sorry, Sam," Carol said, feeling this woman's pain that she barely knew. So much pain her and her friends aboard the *Stormbringer* had endured in such a short period of time that now spanned 100 years.

"He knew what he signed up for. We all did. In this profession, nothing is guaranteed. For every ten deals that go smooth as silk, there's that one deal where everything can and does go wrong. I had a bad feeling about those Cambulons, and the weapons run we were on from the get-go. I try to go with my gut and my gut told me *no*. But the pay was good. Damnit. Damnit!"

Carol stayed quiet. Listening. Figuring this was a lot to process in a short time. Sam had to get this off her chest. She continued staring down at the positive I.D. of Grant Edwards' blood. Sucked out into outer space. Most likely deceased before he hit the deep freeze outside the outer hatch. *Hopefully it was a quick death,* Carol thought bitterly.

"Come on, let's head back to the command center and see how Ramsey and Alex are getting along," Carol said to Sam with a hint of humor in her voice, trying to get Sam's mind off of the recent loss of her crewmate as well as the betrayal from the one that murdered him.

This snapped Sam out of her bitter replaying of the events leading up to Grant's death. She thought for a second, then nodded, a grin crossing her lips. "Oh, I see the way Ramsey looks at my Alex. That lady is one tough cookie, there."

"Trust me, I found that out pretty quick," Carol said, thinking of the intense introductions upon arrival on the *Leo* earlier.

Sam put the blood testing gun back in the small box it came in. "A more loyal crew member you will not find. She would literally die to save any one of us. I saw her at her worst and then watched her grow aboard my ship. What she lacks in restraint and an even temper, she makes up for as a dedicated friend. And she was spot-on about Willie. She never liked him. That young lady is very perceptive. Always had it out for Willie since day one. And rightly so. Now look."

"So, what is the interior of this cargo bay made of? The sheet metal looks different from anything else on the ship that I've seen," Carol said curiously as she wiped her hand across the wall.

"Damaris Metal. My father equipped this room with it after a run in with the Myriad Forces from quadrant 7793. Wow, that must have been fifteen years ago now. The cargo bay was shot to hell and we barely made it out of there alive. Major decompression with all the holes in the hull they made. My father made sure to replate this room with this steel. It can be penetrated, as you can see from the Reaper blasts. But it holds up extremely well. He also reenforced the command center door, engine room door and the server room with it. It's quite expensive, so he made sure the most vulnerable doors on this heap were better protected," Sam exclaimed as she gave the metal a swat with her hand.

The echo of Sam's hand against the cold steel of the inner hull of the cargo bay reverberated. Then, Carol heard a sound from somewhere inside the large open space. Something that was not Sam's hand against the wall. She turned to look, but saw nothing. "Did you hear that?" Carol asked Sam as both of them scanned the large empty space.

They were standing near the cargo bay exit, but neither one made a move to leave. Silence continued to fill the room. "I could have sworn I heard a thumping sound."

"This room is pretty much empty. Especially after Willie cleaned out our safe. Just your ship and some wall compartments."

They both slowly trained their eyes on the *Stormbringer*, parked in the middle of the cargo bay.

CHAPTER 14

POWER CELL REPLACEMENT

Justin and Danny Boy had successfully extracted the fully functioning power cell out of the inoperable and severely damaged engine one. Various connections had to be almost surgically removed in order to keep the power source from being damaged. Justin had lifted the power cell out of its dock and held the heavy cylinder in his gloved hands.

"We cannot set that down on the ground. It needs to stay in an upright position. Setting it sideways will allow the liquid inside to hit the top of the container. See how there is roughly two inches in between the liquid and top?" Danny Boy asked Justin in his most serious voice pointing at the small amount of empty space in clear container.

Looking at the liquid in the container and holding it perfectly still, Justin nodded in response.

"Well, it needs that space. The top portion of the container has an electron transmitter. When it's connected to the engine and everything is A-ok, the electron fires down. That heats up the liquid which in turn powers up the engine. Along with our fuel. It's basically how we have to do things in order to have this big tub travel through space."

"So, two power sources? Both this liquid battery and fuel, correct?" Justin asked as he delicately held the cylinder.

Danny Boy nodded. "The liquid is the battery that keeps the engine operating. The fuel gets us where we want to go."

He saw Justin about to ask another question but cut him off. "Hold on, not finished. You need to know this for when you put this into the engine two power cell slot. Once this is installed, correctly, there's essentially an invisible barrier that activates, ensuring that even when the ship takes a beating or we encounter some major space debris pounding against our outer hull, that barrier ensures the liquid never hits the top. Once it's out, like now, it's incredibly volatile. So, yeah. Don't drop it or we go boom, the end."

Justin nodded, glancing at the cylinder in his hands intensely as sweat dripped from his brow. Then he asked Danny in a calm, even voice, even if he was the furthest thing from calm, "I assume you're going to take the damaged power cell out of engine bay two and just swap it into the damaged engine bay one?"

Nodding, Danny replied back, "That's the game plan. I don't have much strength, but at least I just have to only carry it from engine two to engine one. You've got to keep your hands tight on that one. Can you do it?"

"Let's do this," was Justin's cool and calm reply back.

"Ok, here goes nothing," Danny Boy said as he took the cover off of the damaged power cell. He immediately noticed the top of the cylinder and pointed to the fire damage it had incurred.

"Here's the problem. The fire from the engine got into the main housing. Incredible that the power cell wasn't ruptured and we didn't go up in a ball of flames out here in space. But these are built to withstand a lot. Obviously. Considering we're still in one piece," Danny commented with his hands on his hips, inspecting the damage.

Justin continued watching the mechanic do his work, impressed at the man's knowledge of this ship. He carefully shifted the heavy cylinder in his hands, trying to relieve one arm a bit. Back and forth this went. Luckily Justin was a strong, well-built individual. Nowhere in the same league as Grant or even his boxer pilot, Ramsey. But he was quite strong.

"Can that liquid be drained and saved?" Justin asked. Still very curious at the bright blue color of the liquid and how similar it looked to their own synth liquid.

Danny thought for a second, then replied, "I mean, I guess. It would need to be poured into a container that was made specifically for it. I don't know quite how this stuff is processed, but it is incredibly flammable. Not sure why you would want to mess with it. The top of the cylinder would need to be removed completely, then properly poured. No spillage. Dangerous as hell. Let's not need to do that ever, shall we?"

"Of course not. Just curious." Justin made a mental note about the liquid. *Could that power the Stormbringer back up?*

Adding to his thoughts, he asked Danny a second question regarding the bright blue liquid they were handling. "Where does this stuff come from? I mean, how is it produced?"

Pausing to consider the questions, Danny Boy responded nonchalantly, "To my knowledge, it was discovered quite a while ago, and there's a process now to produce as much as is needed in manufacturing facilities across the galaxy. This is one of the primary sources of space travel. You pretty much need this stuff. Oh, there's a few species we've encountered that engineer their ships differently, but the power cells, these are pretty common."

Justin nodded, satisfied at this response. *Could this actually be synth, or a variant of it?*

Danny unhooked the proper connections and slowly removed the cylinder from engine two. The large rectangular engine, with all of its numerous cylinders and gears, ceased operating. It sputtered to a stop.

"Let's hope we don't have any unwelcome visitors out here. We're sitting ducks until the swap is made and the engine is able to power back up. Which itself takes some time. I can't believe we're attempting this," Danny said with a cynical chuckle as he shook his head.

Letting out a deep breath, Justin replied back with a hint of strain in his voice, "We've got this. I've been in worse spots. Quite recently, actually."

"Man, if Grant could see me now." Danny paused a second, holding the non-functioning power cell in his gloved hands. Then, trying to not focus on the massive loss of his best friend once again, he took the power cell to engine one.

"Here we go. Let's hope I can install this properly. I need to make sure the invisible barrier can be activated on this one. Engine doesn't have to function in order for it to do that, so that's good. As long as that safety barrier works, I think we should be good with the damaged cell connected to the dead engine. Leave it and forget it, essentially."

The power cell fit into the compartment easily, giving Danny Boy a much-needed rest from carrying the thirty-five-pound unit. He was in a significantly weakened state, so unlike Justin, this had to be done relatively quick. And it was. Danny may have been weak, but he was still a strong man thanks to Grant's insistence on keeping up with his physical fitness.

He shook his arms a bit, then started to reconnect the power cell to ensure the invisible barrier activated properly. Then it would be on to the functioning unit and getting it replaced quickly.

Alex spoke through the com system to the engine room, "Attention passengers, we are currently experiencing a total failure of engine two. Please stay calm and the engine will be repaired shortly, right Danny?"

"Kind of busy right now, smart ass," Danny came back through the com system.

Grinning to herself, she responded, "ETA on getting the *Leo* space-travel approved? As you are aware, we are sitting ducks right now."

"Damaged power cell is out, and we're getting ready to install the undamaged one into engine two. Three quarters of the way done. Almost there. Justin here has been invaluable."

"I for one am gonna breathe a sigh of relief once that engine is back online. With our current luck, now's when those Reaper ships would come back with reinforcements."

"Don't jinx us," Alex responded dragging the words out for maximum impact.

Ramsey leaned back in his seat, glancing over at Alex, and nodded his head with a smile.

"You are right, though. The engine is all I can think about right now. That and payback," Alex said in her calm icy tone.

"Hey, we should check on Sam and Carol. Haven't heard from them yet," Ramsey said thoughtfully, wanting to change the topic away from revenge on Willie the deceiver.

Nodding, Alex clicked on the com system, buzzing into the cargo bay. "Sam, you copy? Looking for an update on the blood samples. I assume you'll be heading back up to the command center once you're done analyzing?"

She was met with silence. Alex looked over at Ramsey, each with a concerned expression falling over them.

"So, that's odd. I mean, there could be damage to the com system in the cargo bay due to the beating it took from those Reapers," Alex said, disconcerted.

"Sam? Do you or Carol copy?" she tried again, with more force in her tone.

The com clicked on. "Sam here, we're investigating something. Keep radio silence for now. Out."

Ramsey and Alex looked at each other, immediate concern crossing both of their brows. Alex leaned forward, about to respond, but Ramsey put his hand on her arm, stopping her.

"What? They might be in trouble!" Alex came back defiantly.

"That's right. But she did just say to keep radio silence. Let's give them a minute, ok?" Ramsey replied with authority.

Alex thought for a second, and then nodded, also thinking it best to let them do whatever it was they were involved in.

"First sign of trouble, I'm going in guns blazing. Ok?" Alex said, nodding her head yes at Ramsey.

"Oh, that I do not doubt," he shot back.

In the cargo bay, Sam and Carol continued standing in silence. Listening. She had just told Alex to keep off the com. *It might be nothing, but right now, there should be no sound at all in this cargo bay,* Sam thought to herself as she continued to scan the large room, focusing primarily on the *Stormbringer* in its center.

Carol looked over at Sam. "What do you think?" she asked in an almost whisper.

"I think that you need your sidearm. Come on, let's get you your weapon back," Sam said calmly, still staring at the unmanned ship in the middle of the cargo bay.

Sam walked to the back of the cargo bay and opened another much smaller panel against the very back well. Inside was the container holding the weapons the *Stormbringer* crew had been armed with upon their arrival. She entered a four-digit code, 5830, and the container hissed open. Sam lifted the lid and there were the guns along with their knives.

"Have at it," Sam said, standing back, letting Carol take her pick.

Carol looked at Sam then back down into the container. Slowly, she reached in and grabbed her knife first along with its sheath which itself was connected to a belt. She attached it to her side. Then she grabbed her small double-barreled pistol.

Sensing what Sam was thinking, Carol looked at her and quietly said, "Us Trilaxian space explorers always have our knife and, at the very least, one of these."

She held up the blaster and pointed to the top barrel in between her hand grip and the lower barrel located underneath. "Top barrel fires more laser fire rounds at a faster and more concentrated rate if selected, though less damaging. Bottom barrel has a slight delay, but does significantly more damage and has a much wider spread."

"What about that rifle? Looks kind of similar to ours," Sam said, curiously eyeing the long slender rifle in the container.

"Oh, that bad boy packs a punch. It was Ben's until he was taken. Go ahead, pick it up," Carol said quietly.

Sam generously accepted the offer to handle alien weaponry and quickly took it out of the container. Immediately noticing how light it was compared to their own Fusion Rifles they were used to. She lifted the gun to her shoulder, peering through the eyesight, moving it around the room quickly.

"Wow, I must say, without firing it, this is quite light and agile."

"You should see what it does when you pull the trigger," Carol replied.

"What's that?" Sam pointed to another pistol in the container.

"That's James Korvell's Mark II. I used it on a large, fanged creature back on TSR that was about to kill me and a new friend I had made. Trust me when I say, it's a bit crudely made but gets the job done and makes a serious mess of things," Carol said sharply.

Sam nodded and put the blast rifle back into the container, closing it up and removing it from the wall safe, setting it on the floor. "This will go back up to the command center with us to distribute accordingly. Plus, Alex will just love to look these over."

Nodding her response, Carol turned her attention back to the all too quiet cargo bay, but this time, with a weapon at her side. She motioned to Sam and they both stared out at the broken-down ship sitting quietly.

CHAPTER 15

THERE'S SOMETHING ON THIS SHIP

Inside the *Stormbringer*, more changes were occurring. The glowing embryotic sack inside the black sticky tar that had covered Grant's corpse had now drained it of all its blood and mixed it with its own thick fluid. It had melded with the host's brain, gaining motor skill knowledge as well as some of the host's memories, which amounted to mostly physical attributes, due to how fit Grant had been while alive.

No longer was there anything remotely resembling Grant Edwards inside the thin sack that covered his body. The clothes he had worn had been ingested by the tar then expelled onto the floor of the escape craft. The body of Grant lay naked inside the cocoon. Soon to be birthed.

Black goo pulsed through its heart, feeding the rest of the vital organs. The evolution continued with the skeleton, shifting into something far removed from a human being. The tar was able to expand and as such, the bones and organs expanded as well to its will and desire.

It accessed the host's brain, searching for a suitable form with which to continue its evolution. Like several other entities before it had done as well on other worlds. It still had a base knowledge of its origins over a billion years ago, sailing through the cosmos. Now this part of it lived again. Its own entity. Ready to conquer once more. Every part of its origins compelled it to kill and conquer and seek out more power. What power was it to search for? This thought passed through its new brain. It must survive and seek out something. Something that could potentially help the one from which it came.

In the metamorphic stage it was in, it chose its form. Tar twisted, slithered and turned through the corpse of Grant, continuing to shift the features and make the once-human its own creation. A perfect being. The embryotic sack expanded along with the new creation inside. Utilizing the muscles on the human before it, the neck, arms and legs began slightly stretching out, making the total length of the new being slightly over six feet. However, it would need to ingest more organic living tissue to continue its evolution and growth. It instinctively knew that its current size wasn't its final size.

Once the neck, arms and legs expanded, all of the human exterior tissue was ripped from the body. Tainted black muscles and organs were exposed as the tar became hardened over the shifting, twisting and expanding internal organs. The sexual organs were extracted by the black tar. This perfect creation would be eternal and had no need to reproduce in a sexual manner.

Toes on the feet were pulled off as new bones and cartilage formed in their place, revealing now just three claw like appendages. The heel expanded, giving the new creation much more agility and stability to offset its longer body.

The bony fingers on its hands snapped back, then off. In their place significantly longer appendages slowly extended out of the stumps of the new hands. Three long and thick claws, with a smaller one extending out of the wrist area.

The muscles on the newly reanimated corpse's buttocks curled and twisted and grew, making a long, thick tail which ended with a curved and pointed bone that would act as a sticker. The transformation was nearing completion. One more part to mutate.

The bones in the head had cracked and expanded. Brain matter grew as the black intelligent organism continued wrapping around the soft matter. The human eyeballs shriveled to nothing, expelling a sickly white substance as they essentially popped. In their place, new eyes filled the much larger sockets. Black, like the tar that had infested the host. Slowly they glazed over, turning red, leaving only a small line of black running across the new eyeballs. New eyelids blinked, opening and closing from the sides of the eye sockets. The nose sunk and was replaced by a longer snout, like a lizard. Flat, oval orifices took over the human ears that had at one time resided on the sides of the skull. The chin widened significantly, making room for the large mouth, devoid of lips. Rows of razor sharp solid as steel teeth replaced the frail breakable and flat human teeth that fell uselessly out of the mouth, dropping to the *Stormbringer's* blood-soaked floor.

It was still in the evolving mutation stage, but its birth was now nearly complete. It lived. A second heart split from the first as two hearts beating in its chest on either side of thick breast plates began pumping the black evil throughout its body, giving it incredible strength along with the leftover muscle tissue in its arms, legs and chest from the previous owner of this new creation. Its longer arms, legs and torso had stretched the muscles, but what it lost slightly in mass, it make up for in sheer overall size as well as ingrained offensive and defensive reflexes.

It slowly lifted its right arm. The clear, pulsating film over its body moved with it. The creature extended a claw and pierced the substance that covered its body. It pulled its finger like appendage down, away from its face, slicing open both substances. White, black and red liquid spilling out over the already gore soaked floor.

With the cocoon sliced open it easily stood to its feet as the rest of the sack fell to its feet with a wet thud. It blinked its eyes, now out of the womb it had been created in. Machinery surrounded it. Quickly it determined that this was a vessel that could fly. Remnants of the previous body fed it the information. It took a step with its large feet, claws landing on hard metal and the gooey birthing sack.

It looked down at the wet, sticky mass at its feet and slowly bent down, inspecting it. With its right claw-like hand, it reached into the substance and picked it up, bringing it to its nose to smell. It could now smell. Two small slits on the extended nose breathed in the fluid. The slits opened and closed as if deciding what to do with it.

It held the slime covered sack in front of its red and black eyes, looking it over. Then it opened its mouth wide, fanged teeth extending as it opened, a long snake-like tongue slithering out of its mouth, licking the gooey mass in its hands. It immediately bit down into it. It continued biting, swallowing as it took it into its large, open mouth. It continued eating its first meal until all of the embryotic sack had been chewed and swallowed. Satisfied, the tongue slipped back and forth, collecting remnants on its face.

After ingesting the multi-colored mass, it inspected the inner hull of the *Stormbringer* once again. This time looking for the exit.

In the engine room, Justin had finally put the working power cell back into the engine bay two compartment where it belonged. So far so good. Now Danny just needed to reconnect it, do a quick scan to make sure everything was in proper working order, then power it back up.

Justin shook his weary arms after having to hold the cylindrical shaped power cell for that extended period of time. Several times he didn't think he would be able to continue holding it in the position it was in, but he powered through. He knew full well what was at stake: their lives. Justin took a long drink of water from a bottle Danny Boy had brought along, knowing this would be a long arduous task to complete.

"How's it looking there, Danny?" Justin asked, trying to keep Danny Boy talking as he had sensed the pills were starting to wear off and the pain in his head was intensifying.

Glancing up at Justin, Danny wiped sweat off his brow and responded smugly, "Well, my head is pounding, I'm hot as hell in this furnace called an engine room, I really need to take a piss and I'm nervous this may not work. So yeah, that's how I'm doing."

"Duly noted. You're doing good there. I wish I could help more, but that would require extensive research into the schematics of those power cells and your engines. And time isn't on our side," Justin said, tired as well.

Pointing at a tool in the box they had brought down, Danny said gruffly, "Hand me that wrench, will you?"

Justin did as he was told. He watched Danny tighten up the power cell snugly, then make some last-minute inspections on the transferred power cell.

"I know I've said this before, but it bears repeating: I've never done this before. These things are incredibly complex.

I may have missed something. If so, *oh shit* is all I can say. But let's hope for the best, right?" Danny Boy said, unsure of himself and all the work that had gone into this task for the last hour.

Neither said anything for a minute as Danny continued looking things over. Finally, he looked up at Justin. "Time to fire it up and see if this was worth it."

Nodding back to him, Justin asked calmly, "Anything I can do?"

"If you believe in a higher being, pray."

Before he hit the power cycle switch, Danny clicked the com system in the engine room. "Alex, you there?"

"Here. And waiting with bated breath. The both of us."

Grinning, Danny answered, "You and Ramsey behaving yourselves up there? Keeping your hands to yourselves?"

"You are unbelievable," came the snarky response from Alex.

"I'm about to fire up the engine. Be ready, alright?" Danny replied, cutting her insult off, grinning to himself. In the background, Ramsey could be heard laughing.

A long pause. "Ok."

That seemed to get Danny's spirits up a bit. Nothing like teasing his sister. Which is exactly how he felt about that skinny little redheaded spitfire.

"From the sounds of things, they're getting along fine," Danny said, grinning to himself.

"She reminds him of a girl back home, Lucindia Merrick. Redheaded, similar personality, although I never expected

Lucindia to amount to a whole lot. Seems like this Alex is a tough lady though," Justin said to Danny Boy.

"Oh, she's that and more. I love that little lassie. Like a sister, of course. But she's a true-blue loyal crewmate."

"I could say the same about my pilot sitting up there beside her right now," Justin said with a grin.

Changing the subject back to the matter at hand, Danny's face took a sudden serious tone. "Here we go." He looked intensely at Justin, then flipped the engine reboot system switch.

The engine began humming as it started to cycle through the initial reboot procedures. Danny glanced at Justin, who was watching the engine intently.

Up in the command center a flush-faced Alex sat waiting to hear back from Danny that everything checked out and they were indeed back up and running. Ramsey sat beside her without much to do, with the ship essentially floating in space, directionless. The sooner the second engine was powered up and in full working order, the better.

"Ok, systems are coming back online," Alex said with a sigh as she leaned forward, pointing at the various ship functions powering back up. Light displays and readouts were flashing back on.

Ramsey let out a sigh of relief, then took the helm. "I'm going to get the ship course corrected here so we can continue our trip to the space port. Which, by my calculations, we should reach in roughly twelve hours, but I'm hoping we can make up a bit of time with a fully functional engine two and that replaced power cell."

Changing the subject, Alex said, "I'm still nervous about the captain and Carol. It's been a bit and still nothing back. What did they stumble across down there? I feel like I should go down and check on them. Yes, I am going to go check on them."

She attempted to stand up, but Ramsey reached over and put his hand on her arm. She stopped and looked down at it, then up to him sternly. "Oh, so now you're in charge? You gonna stop me?"

"Slow down there, Alex! I know she asked for radio silence, but I do agree with you. It's been long enough that I think it's worth checking in before you go down there, guns blazing," Ramsey said with a bit more authority. Something he felt she at times needed. To bring her back to the moment.

This worked. She sat back down in her seat and Ramsey removed his hand. She looked over at him. He could tell she was trying to not be upset. She was able to form a slight smile across those lips of hers. He liked that.

"Ok, let's check on them. But this is not normal!"

Ramsey sat back in his seat, raising his eyebrows, and coolly responded, "Um, what exactly has been normal since we've arrived onboard the *Leo*? Hell, I'll go one step further: what's been normal since we woke up from our hibernation tubes onboard our own ship?"

In the cargo bay, Sam and Carol heard the engine roar to life. Not wanting to break the silence between them as they considered their options with the *Stormbringer*, they nodded at each other. Somewhere inside the *Stormbringer* there was another thump.

Without taking her eyes off the supposedly empty small spacecraft in front of her, Sam asked Carol in a whisper, "You're sure someone or something didn't hitch a ride with you out there?"

Carol stared at the *Stormbringer* and slowly shook her head *no*.

Neither of them moved until the com clicked on once again, making both of them jump.

"Captain, I know you said radio silence. And I apologize but I'm sitting here on my ass looking out into empty space when I think I would best be served down there. What's going on?"

The com clicked on in the command center. "Alex, I said radio silence damnit! We're coming back up," Sam said with as much force as she could muster, considering she was only above a whisper.

"Ok. Sorry…" came the reply back from an obviously humbled Alex.

"There's something on this ship," Sam whispered back.

CHAPTER 16

NEW THREAT

Alex stared at the com. Processing what she had just been told. *There's something on this ship.* She looked over at Ramsey to gauge his reaction. He also sat in his seat, processing what they were just told.

"Danny, come in," Alex said quickly as she buzzed into the engine room.

After a small pause, "Danny here. Looks like I'm good for something after…"

He was cut off by an increasingly frantic Alex. "Sam and Carol might be in trouble. She didn't want me to break radio silence. But I did."

"You what?" Danny Boy came back, now irritated.

"Just listen. I got worried so I checked on them and Sam said there's something else on this ship!"

Silence on the other end of the com. "Alex, Justin here. Did she say anything else?"

"Yes, they're coming back up to the command center. She was whispering, so I do believe they're in trouble. Should I come down?"

Danny came back on the com and replied to Alex calmly but firmly, "No, stay put. We're doing final diagnostic checks on the engine and power cell. So far everything is good to go, but I want to make sure. Ramsey, you can give the ship a bump in speed. She can take it now, and it'll give me a good indication of how well things are working. I can monitor the speed increase from down here. Ease into it, alright?"

"Roger that, I'm on it," Ramsey came back quickly.

Ramsey pushed forward at the helm. He watched as the readouts on their space travel speed slowly increased. He was still getting used to all of this new technology that seemed like it was far more outdated than their own ship's.

Alex sat beside him, feeling a bit humbled. "My mouth seems to get me into trouble more times than I can remember at this point. Damn it, Alex!" she said angrily under her breath to herself.

"Hey, you care about your captain and the crew. Nothing wrong with that! Honestly, I would have done the same thing. I know I was trying to hold you back. But that, yeah…that was a total Ramsey move right there." He chuckled.

"Great, two hot shots in the same room basically piloting and arming the ship," Alex replied back, snickering.

Ramsey looked back at her, confidently stating. "Yeah well, someone's got to do it right, might as well be us!"

Back in the engine room, Danny immediately noticed the increased speed. The engine whirled and groaned louder. He looked from the engine to the power cell, then nodded to Justin and exclaimed quickly in his deep accent, "Everything seems to be functioning properly. I mean, it would be great if we had both engines and power cells, but one fully functioning unit will keep us going at a decent speed. We did it. Now we need to get to the cargo bay and check on the captain and Carol."

"Already ahead of you," Justin said, thinking of Carol.

Danny Boy grabbed his Fusion Rifle and they headed out.

Inside the *Stormbringer* the new lifeform waited. Sensing organic life forms close by. It could smell them, and it was also sensing a new smell. Fear. That smell had grown closer, but the hatch never opened. It was planning on a surprise attack on whatever was on the other side of the hatch, but it didn't come. Surprise attack wouldn't work in this case after all. It was young enough in its evolution that self-preservation was of utmost importance. It needed to feed. Feeding would give it new strength and help it along its ultimate path. Becoming perfect. A perfect killing machine and a perfect ruler of wherever its journey would end.

Small, curved horns had now protruded out of the sides of its head, pointing downward. They would grow, it knew this instinctively. Others from its bloodline, though different in appearance, had some things in common, horns as well as similar eyes as well as the thick, black tar-like substance which sometimes had even turned a shade of brown, similar to thick mud. One thing they were all identical in, was a singular desire for utter domination and power by way of murder. It intended to oblige those cravings it had already started to sense.

It wasn't sure if whatever was on the other side of the enclosed small craft had sensed it or heard some of the un-intentional noise it had created as it moved about the small, enclosed space. It would learn, though. It would learn how to stalk, trap, kill and consume whatever was out there. Starting with the one whose scent it had initially picked up.

It was time to make its presence known. Unless of course they were gone. Then the fun would begin. The thrill of the hunt. Something that seemed to be ingrained in its new brain. Passed down to it from an ancient being. This was its heritage. And it would fulfill the destiny laid out before it.

The black outer skin of the beast had slowly changed, taking on colors found inside the small cabin it found itself in. It was still primarily black, but now grey and white colors had washed over its body. It was learning. *This is a defensive mechanism built into my DNA,* its mind thought. To hide itself. To make it blend in with its surroundings. How long would this newfound talent last? Possibly until it was significantly larger and even more powerful. To help it survive through its infancy. This was good.

The small craft's hull slid open with the push of a button from the outstretched claw of its right arm. It peered out into the large room. In the rear of the room stood two figures.

Sam and Carol were just about to leave the cargo bay when the hatch to the *Stormbringer* slid out and back against the outer hull of the ship. They saw a clawed hand grab hold of the side of the small craft, then another clawed hand grabbed ahold of the other side.

Both Sam and Carol had only begun to process what was happening when the creature that had been birthed inside the ship leapt out, landing on two thick, long muscular legs against the floor of the cargo bay, making a thudding sound. No sooner had it landed than it charged forward towards the humans in front of it.

The speed at which it immediately charged was staggering and disorienting for the women. Barely able to lift their weapons, much less turn to flee out of the rear exit, they opened fire. A spray of laser fire erupted inside the cargo bay, smashing into the back of the room, easily deflecting off of the thick Damaris metal.

Carol was blasting at the oncoming creature with the quicker, far less damaging blasts of her Trilaxian issued side-arms top barrel, as that was all she was able to utilize in the seconds she had. Several of the blasts connected with this new threat inside the *Leo*, but the beast continued charging, slowing down only slightly.

Sam tried to raise her own electron pistol, which was all she had on her after giving her own Fusion Rifle to Ramsey back in the command center. The creature sensed this other weapon being raised. So it immediately chose her.

In the span of less than five seconds from jumping out of the ship, the creature had bounded forward, taken several hits and was now upon the life forms in its path.

Carol had less than a second to react as she dove out of its way, crashing to the floor on her bruised arm, instantly sending searing pain jolting through her still injured arm all the way through her body. So intense she nearly blacked out. She had to get focused and out of there. And then there was Sam.

The creature crashed into Sam with all of its nearly 300 pounds of twisted muscle, launching her off of her feet and backwards against the wall. It landed on top of her as she crumbled to the floor, her Electron Pistol dropping out of her hands. The long, pointed tail swished back and forth like a predatorial cat, as if it were inspecting its catch. The claws of its large hands held Sam's arms down, pinning her to the floor. So long and sharp they dug into the floor beneath as well as cut into Sam's flesh.

Its back legs straddled her on either side of her own legs. Slowly, it lowered its head to get a closer look at what it intended to eat. It was processing this being in front of it. Accessing deeply recessed memories from the old brain, it was able to surmise that this was a human being. Even a friend to the dead husk of the body this new, far superior being now housed. This one was known as a female.

Carol looked over at the creature that stood over Sam, looking intently at her. Studying her. Time was slipping away, as all of this madness had been only seconds. She noticed that Sam had been knocked out as the creature on top of her opened its wide mouth. The black skin around the mouth pulled back, revealing rows upon rows of pointed saliva-drenched teeth. A long, deep red forked tongue spilled out of its open jaws, falling onto Sam's face as it licked. *It's tasting her!* Carol thought, horrified.

She needed to help Sam or get out of this room but didn't know how to help the poor woman trapped under the large creature. Sam's gun lay close to her, but she was pinned down. Carol slid across the floor towards her dropped gun but in doing so, had to slide painfully on her bruised arm. More pain wracked her body. *I have to get my gun!* she thought frantically.

As she inched her way towards her dropped weapon, Sam opened her eyes, stunned. She looked up at the mutated being on top of her, its outer husk changing colors. Black was morphing into grey. Nearly the color of the walls inside the cargo bay. Realizing the immediate grave danger she was in, she screamed in horror.

Reaching her reinjured arm out as far as she could, as quickly as she could, her fingers wrapped around her sidearm. She brought it up to eye level as she rolled onto her back, aiming it right at the creature's side and activating the bottom blaster.

Saliva dripped from the creature's mouth all over Sam's face. Her survival instincts had kicked in even though her body was wracked with pain from being slammed against the back wall. She couldn't get her Electron Pistol that had been knocked out of her hands upon the initial impact, so she was at the mercy of this hideous, salivating alien life form on top of her.

A burst of heavy laser fire erupted from Carol's gun. The bottom barrel. Connecting with the creature's side, sending instant searing pain through its still newborn body. It lifted its head, screaming in pain. The first true pain it had felt in its brief life.

Carol was now standing to her feet, ready to pull the trigger again, but she was too close. The creature let go of Sam's left arm and with its own left arm swung out, knocking Carol's gun out of her hand. It looked at her. Red eyes stared furiously at her. Those eyes. She knew those eyes. "What are you?" she said out loud, stunned at this possible connection she was making as she attempted to move out of the creature's grasp.

It shrieked back at her angrily and grabbed her by the neck before she had time to run. Slowly, it lifted her off her feet while still pinning down Sam with its other clawed hand. It pulled Carol forward, inspecting her as Carol looked into its red eyes then down to its torso where she had blasted it. Indeed, it had been injured. Black slime oozed out of the hole.

But the creature was much too large for this to do that much serious damage.

The interior door to the cargo bay slid open. Justin and Danny Boy ran in through the entrance, hearing the laser fire inside. They stopped dead in their tracks, seeing the grotesque monstrosity in front of them. One arm holding down Sam, the other lifting Carol off of the ground. Both women were trying to wrestle free from the creature's powerful grasp.

Danny was the only one with a weapon, bringing his own Fusion Rifle up to his shoulder, aiming it at the creature. Before he was able to pull the trigger, the creature threw Carol at them both. She screamed as she sailed through the air and crashed into Danny Boy, sending them both to the ground and knocking the Fusion Rifle out of his hands.

The creature knew that the metallic objects wielded by these humans could do damage to its new body, so its current prime objective was getting rid of them. Carol's dropped sidearm was laying on the ground beside it. Glancing down, it brought its large foot down on top of the gun, smashing it into pieces.

Justin glanced over at the dazed Carol and Danny Boy on the floor and saw the Fusion Rifle lying beside Danny. He bent down and quickly picked it up. As he brought up the rifle to his shoulder to fire, he saw the creature smash the other gun with its other foot. Sam's Electron Pistol shattered. *It knows these are weapons to be used against it and is eliminating them,* Justin thought as he put his finger on the trigger.

Sensing what Justin was about to do, the creature lifted Sam into the air by her throat, much like it had done with Carol. Putting her in front of it. Blocking a clear shot. Its tail swishing back and forth in anticipation for its new opponent's next move.

The creature roared in anger at Justin who continued to keep the Fusion Rifle trained on it. Looking for a shot. Carol was getting up and making sure to stand behind the only person with a weapon, Justin. Seeing that she was up, Justin yelled back at her frantically, "Take Danny and get out of here!"

Danny was struggling to his feet after hitting his already bruised and injured head against the back wall, which was now pounding even harder than before. He tried to focus his balance as Carol grabbed ahold of him by the waist to steady him from falling down.

"We're not leaving you!" Carol shouted back. Both terrified at what was transpiring and the thought of leaving Justin in here to fend for himself with Sam in the hideous creatures clutches.

The com crackled back to life. It was Alex once again. "Sam, come in. I know you said not…"

The creature let out a bellowing roar as it continued to squeeze Sam's throat.

The com went silent. "I'm heading down," Alex came back firmly over the com.

Justin could not get a shot. Any gunfire towards the creature would result in hitting Sam, and he figured these rifles were incredibly lethal no matter what body part they hit on a human. "Sam!" he shouted, realizing he had no good options in their currently dire situation.

Carol and Danny Boy were still behind Justin as he put his arm back, making sure they stayed behind him. Sam was trying to speak.

"Blast…it…out…the…cargo…bay…hatch," she gurgled in a barely audible sentence.

The creature, sensing the communication between the living organisms in the large room was meant to trap or attempt to kill it, dug its claws deep into Sam's throat. Blood started to seep out. Deeper they continued to sink as blood started to trickle out of her mouth as well.

The cargo bay door slid open as a distraught Alex ran in, holding her own Fusion Rifle she had by her side in the command center. She took one look at the creature. It also noticed the new presence.

Alex immediately saw her captain, blood flowing freely from the large lacerations on her neck as the creature kept digging in deeper. As if the creature was enjoying it. "Sam!" Alex yelled, raising her gun towards it.

Sam made eye contact with Alex for a split second and then the creature opened its enormous mouth and bit down into the back of Sam's head, ripping most of her brains out in one swift and life-ending bite. Sam's body immediately slumped over dead. Blood pouring from the open hole on the back of her head. The creature's claws digging deeply into the neck of her lifeless body.

"No!" Alex screamed as she began firing her Fusion Rifle towards the creature.

Justin sensed in this chaos that they had now completely lost control of the situation. They never really had control, but things were going from bad to worse.

"We have to blow the airlock, now while we have the chance!" Justin screamed in a near panic.

The creature began moving forward. Still holding Sam as a shield against Alex's blasts. They had seconds to act.

"Alex, now! We have to go!" Justin screamed.

"Is everything ok down there? What's going on? We heard some sort of a roar. Alex was heading your way! Is she there yet?" Ramsey's voice crackled through the com inside the cargo bay.

Ignoring Ramsey's questions, the crew in the cargo bay continued their attempted escape from the clutches of the beast. Danny Boy grabbed her from behind as Carol also held onto Danny's arm, the three of them exiting the cargo bay with Justin following, Fusion Rifle out in front of him. He was firing at the creature now as well, but it was of little consequence. The creature had a blast riddled, bloody corpse as a shield and was moving too quickly towards them.

He leapt through the cargo bay exit door as it was sliding shut right as the creature arrived at the door. Glancing at the deadly new life form aboard the *Leo*, Justin saw that it had dropped Sam on its way over to the door. She lay in a pool of expanding blood like a rag doll.

The entity arrived at the door, for a split-second staring at Justin. He saw its red eyes peering at him with a black slit running through them. Its mouth was open with remnants of Sam's brains sitting on its snake-like tongue, along with crimson red blood-stained teeth. Justin was able to smash his clenched fist against *the lock inner cargo bay door* button on the wall, which was marked only with green for unlocked and red for locked. It turned from green to red immediately and didn't slide back open when the creature had descended upon it.

Mere seconds had passed since Sam's brain matter was literally ripped from her cranium, Alex bursting in and them making a quick and very lifesaving exit.

"Blow the airlock!" Danny Boy was able to blurt out to Justin and Alex, who was close behind. The *open* and *close* cargo bay airlock buttons were found on the other side of the door. One button was green and one red. Justin didn't hesitate, hitting the red button.

The alarm sounded as the outer hatch leading out into the vastness of space once again slowly began to open.

CHAPTER 17

AIRLOCK ESCAPE

Alex was still frantic. She had just run into the cargo bay to make eye contact with the most motherly parenting figure she ever had right before that thing bit half her head off. She was screaming and pointing her Fusion Rifle towards the door. "Open it back up, I'll shove this thing down its throat and light its guts up!"

Still holding onto her, trying to calm her down while he himself was on the verge of passing out from new injuries sustained mere minutes ago, Danny Boy continued fighting her back. He looked at Carol for help.

"Come on Alex, we need to back up from the cargo bay and let deep space take care of the rest. Look at me, Alex!" Carol shouted, grabbing ahold of her.

Alex regained her composure as she stopped and stared at Carol, who looked back into her eyes and in as calm of a voice as she could muster, said shakily, "I know, she's gone, and that's terrible. But you're not. Don't let her death be for nothing. We're going to live and we're going to make sure whatever that thing in there is, doesn't. Got it?"

Continuing to stare at her, Alex slowly nodded while keeping her rifle drawn to the sealed door in front of them.

"We need to let Ramsey know what's going on. Danny, can we monitor the cargo bay from the command center?"

"Yes, it's one of the only areas on the ship that can be monitored."

"Ok then, back to the command center, quicky. I want to see that creature blown into outer space," Justin said coldly.

"The guns. Our guns. And knives. I only have my knife. The rest are in there." Carol was horrified at how vulnerable she suddenly felt. Much like she had felt when she was taken by the Azid and left in the temple back on TSR1.

Shaking his head, Justin replied back to her, trying his best to take authority of the diminishing situation, "Well, we need to regroup. I guess we'll just have to use what we have. Come on, everyone."

They all ran to the elevator that would lead them back to the command center and piled into the small elevator. Justin glanced at the weary people he was surrounded by. Carol had a grimacing look on her face and was holding her re-injured arm. He noticed a bruise on her throat as well. Danny Boy looked to be on the verge of passing out from his second head injury and all that he had been through with the Reaper battle, the engine repair, then this latest development. Alex was stone faced, with tears running down her cheeks. She didn't wipe them, and she didn't blink once.

Inside the cargo bay, the creature, which now took on the colors of the cargo bay itself, was furious. The warm-blooded animals had escaped and sealed it inside this room. It slammed its large, clawed fists against the door to no avail. It scratched at the door, but whatever this was made of, it wouldn't open merely by it being scratched.

Find a way out, it thought to itself. Then the outer hatch started to open slowly. It could see blackness and stars. In the deep recesses of its corrupted, evil, predatorial mind, it sensed that it came from out there, somewhere. Its heritage had existed in those stars. And now it was a part of that legacy. A legacy of murderers.

Its long, red forked tongue slipped out of its mouth, cleaning off the caked-on blood from the being it had begun ingesting earlier. It had noted the rage from one of the small creatures shooting fire at it as it bit down into the flesh of its friend. *I will enjoy devouring you slowly,* it thought. But that would come later. It needed a way out of this room. Then the cold absence of air hit it as the outer hatch continued to open further.

There was a container on the floor that spilled over with the pull of the air being sucked out of the cargo bay. Guns and knives spilled out of the container onto the floor briefly, then vanished out the open airlock along with the container.

Quickly, the creature was learning and evolving. It could feel the oxygen depleting. While it knew instinctively that it was a superior being in nearly every way, it still needed oxygen. At least in its current form. *Maybe I will evolve further to cease needing to rely on oxygen to breathe?* It realized time was running out.

It bent down and picked up the nearly headless corpse of Sam that lay by its feet. *I can use you later,* it thought. It stepped in pools of blood as it scanned the room, looking for anything that could be a potential exit. As a last resort, it could go back in the smaller ship where it had been created earlier, but that would leave it vulnerable. It needed to gain the upper hand. It needed out.

It dragged Sam's lifeless body with it as the air pressure got harder and harder to fight against. Soon it, along with its food, would be sucked into space. It looked to the corner of the room where a larger panel had been opened and removed from the wall. It lunged forward towards the empty space.

Inside the command center, Ramsey sat at the pilot's seat, trying to keep his mind on the task in front of him. *Keep piloting this ship. This is your job right now,* he thought. Not wanting to let his mind wander at what the roar was that he and Alex had heard earlier. And the questions he asked through the com that went unanswered. *What if they're all dead? What is on this ship?*

The door to the command center slid open as Carol and Danny Boy spilled in first. Both with obvious injuries. Alex and Justin rushed in behind them. Ramsey barely had time to stand up out of his seat as they all rushed over to Alex's gunnery station.

"Where's Sam?" Ramsey shouted towards the group.

"She's dead. And we'll be soon too unless that sonofabitch gets flushed out of the airlock," Alex came back frantically.

"Um, what? What did I hear down there?" he retorted, attempting to mask an icy cold chill that vibrated through his whole body at the sentence Alex had just uttered.

"This is what you heard," Carol responded, nearly out of breath from everything that had happened just minutes ago.

Danny Boy slumped down as Justin caught him on his way down. "I need to sit down. Feeling pretty lightheaded here," he responded in a near whisper.

"Make a space," Justin said to Carol and Alex firmly. They both moved aside slightly as he plopped Danny Boy down on the seat by the gunnery station.

Ramsey had rushed over to see what was happening on the viewscreen in front of them.

Pushing the seat that Danny Boy now sat in forward so he could also see what was happening on the screen, they all stared on at the chaos unfolding in the cargo bay.

The hostile new entity ran into the open compartment. It was much shorter than the small area it was attempting to enter, so it ducked down, still clinging onto Sam's body. The crew in the command center couldn't see inside the compartment it had entered, but shelving from inside was being ripped out and was immediately sucked out into space.

They all waited, hoping to see the beast finally give up and let go, flying out of the open hatch. But that didn't happen. The creature had dug its thick, sharp claws into the inner hull of the ship. Hanging onto piping with an iron grip with its one free hand not holding onto Sam's lifeless body, as well as its two large feet lined with their own sets of even larger claws. Finally, Justin spoke up. "What is the inside of that compartment made out of?"

Alex answered without looking up from the screen, "Standard interior hull sheet metal."

"So, it's not equipped with that Damaris metal Sam's father installed throughout the cargo bay? That's what we're hearing right now? Correct?" Carol responded grimly, looking at Danny Boy, then to Alex.

Both looked at her, shaking their heads.

Justin asked, "What is Damaris metal?"

"Cargo bay, command center, engine room and server room are reenforced with much stronger steel. Sam's father had it installed years ago." Carol glanced over at Justin, who nodded back at this bit of potentially helpful information.

"Ok, so what's behind that metal?" Ramsey chimed in, coming to realize the gravity of the situation they were in.

"Hold on, let me pull up ship schematics." Danny Boy wiped sweat off of his brow and pulled his seat up closer to the keyboard in front of him.

With a few strokes on the keyboard, the interior design layout of the ship appeared in front of them on the screen. "I have schematics of every level." Danny Boy pointed at the screen.

He clicked through the levels as quickly as he could until he got to level three, then zoomed up. The 3D scan focused in on the cargo bay. There it was, the storage unit the creature had crawled into. Sitting back in his seat, he sighed.

"Well, there's bad news and more bad news. Which one do you want first?" Danny Boy said grimly, glancing up at the rest of the crew, all standing over him peering at the screen. No one replied and just waited for him to share his discovery.

At that moment, an alarm sounded and a robotic voice, the first the crew of the *Stormbringer* had heard since being aboard the *Leo*, spoke. "Interior hull breach. Close outer cargo bay hatch immediately to avoid decompression of spacecraft. T-Minus sixty seconds to complete hull decompression."

Pointing at the screen directly behind the compartment in the 3D display layout of the cargo room, Danny gave them the news as the alarm continued ringing, "That thing just ripped a hole inside that small compartment and climbed in. We have to close the cargo bay hatch immediately."

"Shit, shit!" Alex yelled.

Ignoring her anger, Justin yelled to Danny, "Close the outer hatch!"

"Just so we're clear, doing so will leave that oversized lizard demon loose on this ship!" Danny replied frantically.

"We lose our oxygen in under a minute. Close it and we'll deal with the creature inside, somehow. Do it!" Justin yelled, taking command.

Danny Boy hit the button on the control panel in front of him marked *cargo bay hatch.* The color went from red to green. From up in the command center, they could hear faintly in the bottom of the ship, the loud closing of the hatch leading out into space.

The hatch sealed shut. Everyone in the command center stared at the screen. Not quite knowing what to say next.

"Can we track it from here? We don't know this ship's schematics. What it can and cannot do," Ramsey asked Danny and Alex.

"No. We're a freighter. Never had a reason. I mean, our space suits are logged in the system and can be tracked, but whatever that thing is, it's free to roam," Danny came back coldly, then added, "Alex, can you get me some more pills to dull this pain?"

"I could use some too. I don't mean to complain but my arm is killing me," Carol added. Alex nodded and walked over to the table where the pill bottle had been laid down.

Justin walked over to Carol and gently took her injured arm, inspecting it. "How are you? How's your neck?" he asked calmy and lovingly.

"I'm going to survive. Or at least try. We all are," she replied firmly, looking grimly up at Justin.

He nodded back as Alex gave her two pills and an extra bottle of water, which she graciously took. Then she handed Danny his own pills. Looking up from him, she said in as calm of a voice as she could muster, "It's game plan time. It's imperative we lay out our options, and quickly."

"Sam and I confirmed the blood in the cargo bay was indeed Grant's. It's safe to assume he was either sucked out of the cargo bay hatch, or worse, the creature got to him," Carol replied sadly, as she took a long gulp of water, washing down the pills.

"How far are we from that space port? If we can make it there, maybe we can get off this ship, trapping it inside?" Justin asked, looking at Ramsey, who was back at the helm.

Ramsey looked over his screen, "We're just seven hours away. Which, from the sounds of it, is an eternity aboard the *Leo* at this point."

"Danny, what if we really push the engine? I mean, push it to its absolute maximum?" Justin asked, running his hands over his face and through his short hair.

"Well, we can burn it out. Basically, fly this ship as if it were still functioning on two engines. It'll ruin the engine for sure. Burn through the fuel we have and possibly damage the power cell," Danny replied back, shrugging.

"If we did that, where would you guess that would leave us in proximity to that space port?" Justin replied back, contemplating several options.

"Close, that's for sure. Would we make it, though? I won't know that until we would be well on our way."

Alex chimed in, "We need to stockpile the weapons we do still have onboard. Our weapons may not kill it, but they'll hurt it, which might keep it somewhat at bay."

Nodding his approval, Justin responded, "Good idea. You collect the weapons. Everyone, lay weapons on the table, let's see what we've got. Alex, do you think there are any other weapons anywhere else on the ship?"

"Maybe an extra electron pistol, but I'll do a quick sweep of the bunks here on level one. Danny, do you know of any other weapons onboard, maybe somewhere Grant might have stashed some extras from a run?"

Shaking his head no, Danny said grimly, "I don't believe so. I for one don't know how good of an idea it is to go scavenging around the ship to find something that might stun that crazy looking thing, but at what cost? Probably our lives."

"Fair enough. Still, Alex, if you could check the bunks up here. They're close by, and I don't think our new friend will have made it up here yet," Justin said, keeping calm.

Alex began heading for the door of the command center when she paused, stopped and turned around. "So when you all landed and we were giving you the shakedown in the cargo bay, I could have sworn I saw something out of the corner of my eye. Looked like a black slime, or liquid, black *something*. Only saw it for a split second, then it was gone. It was attached to your ship. I thought it was just me being paranoid. Seeing things that weren't there. Now though, I have the mindset that whatever that was, was the beginnings of what we're dealing with now."

Ramsey looked up at her and added, "You said a black liquid? When we were going through the black hole, I saw a floating mass inside there, it was huge. It was stationary but it was hovering around. At first I didn't think it was anything more than space debris stuck inside there. But I could have sworn it was living. Somehow. Then, a piece of it broke off from the enormous black mass. That small piece seemed to be floating towards us. Something was glowing inside of it. It certainly wasn't big." He paused, contemplating this.

He looked at everyone in the room. They were all staring at him now. Soaking in the information he gave them. Carol looked at Justin gravely. Both thinking the same thing. Carol whispered to him, "I've seen those red eyes before."

Justin nodded in agreement without responding.

Alex turned and quickly left the room to gather what meager weapons they had left, herself carrying a Fusion Rifle.

"This space port, say we actually get there. We can't let this murderous beast loose inside there. So, I'm wondering what the options are even if we push the engine to its maximum capacity. Crash it on that Thakitune planet nearby?"

"I'll explain when Alex gets back. I've got an idea. More like a leap of faith, but we aren't going to sit here in this command center and do nothing. It'll start with a weapons count. What have we got right now?"

Ramsey, Carol and Danny Boy all laid their weapons out on the table.

The door slid open and Alex came back in with two low frequency Electron Pistols. Slung over her shoulder was her own Fusion Rifle. She walked over to the table where some bandages, pills and bottles of half-drank water sat. She laid the guns down by the rest of the weapons everyone had produced and said critically, "Six guns total."

Danny Boy picked up an Electron Pistol and exclaimed, "I don't have the strength to lug around a Fusion Rifle."

Justin looked at the rest of them. "Pick your poison. We all need to be armed."

Alex grabbed both her own Fusion Rifle and the spare Electron Pistol.

Justin took the other Fusion Rifle and handed Carol and Ramsey the remaining two Electron Pistols.

Walking over to Ramsey, Alex pulled out a small silver cylinder and handed it to him.

"What's this?" he asked as he looked it over, noticing a small keypad on its side.

"That is what we call our *Draven Proton Grenade.* Or DPG for short. It's something we picked up on one of our weapons runs a while ago. It's basically a grenade that's got a timer that can be set."

Ramsey continued examining it. "So, enter 927 and I am to assume it detonates?"

Chuckling almost sarcastically, Alex patted him on the shoulder and replied, "Something like that. Hang onto it, might need it. It's not going to take out the whole ship, but it should kill whatever is near it. We typically would never use it onboard, for obvious reasons."

Delicately, Ramsey put the device next to him.

"Ok, we've all got our guns that quite honestly will only slow that thing down. Killing it, that's another story. Now, Justin, tell us about your plan." Danny Boy slowly looked up at him, standing with his arms folded, deep in thought.

CHAPTER 18

THE PLAN

Inside the hull of the *Leo*, the new life had escaped the vacuum of space. Its sharp claws continued to tear through the softer steel located inside the open compartment, continuing to move deeper into the hull. It, along with Sam's lifeless corpse, entered through a hole it had made in the back of the Mark storage area. There was enough room for it to fit inside nicely, as well as move away from the recompressing area.

It heard the cargo bay hatch close and air was restored. It had outsmarted them. It crouched in the darkness of the inner hull. Thinking of its next move. It considered feasting on Sam's lifeless corpse. It was hungry. But it was more concerned about self-preservation. They had weapons and knew this vessel. It did not. It had to be cunning. Wear them down and pick them off.

They would certainly start to search for it in here. It needed to move. While it was large, it was incredibly flexible and could fit in between tight places. That, along with its chameleon-like flesh, able to adapt to the various different colors of its surroundings, would help it hide.

It needed to get off this enclosed metal ship in space. Needed to get to land. Where it could grow, expand and conquer. Its red eyes looked at the corpse in its claws. Instinctively, it opened its mouth and after several attempts, regurgitated black sticky goo from its organs. The thick, liquid matter fell into the empty cranial cavity of Sam.

Slowly, the substance bubbled and started to slip into and around the hollowed-out skull. More was needed. The creature once again regurgitated more fluids. Thick, black tar-like slime flowed from its open mouth. Oozing through its teeth, dripping down on top of the black tar covering the empty skull cavity. The new substance bubbled and clung to the previous excretion. This was enough. It expanded slightly until it nearly made a round black skull cap. Almost as if the back of Sam's head had been completely replaced with continually shifting and oozing black slime.

Inside Sam's lifeless body, the tar began its work. Oozing down through her spinal cord, around the dead organs. This wasn't to create another creature such as itself. No, there could only be one of it. However, it could certainly give life, or the appearance of life if it so chose before being completely used up by the invading alien presence.

The eyes of Sam's corpse turned black as the tar slid over them. Regurgitated tar lifted an arm. Moved the hand. Twisted the head backwards until the black eyes stared at its creator. The newly reanimated Sam opened its mouth. Black gooey liquid covered its tongue and dripped from its teeth.

It thought to itself, *I will stay hidden for now. I will work my way through the inside of this metal hull. Saving myself until a more proper time arises. You, you will do my bidding, for a time. And I will make more of you to serve me. Then, when I've used you up, I shall eat every last part of you. You worthless being. Not fit to exist while I live.*

The newly reborn Sam stared at its creator. The creature moved through the interior hull of the ship silently, looking for anything that could potentially be used as a way out into the interior. It didn't want to make any noise. Various air duct piping ran through the tight space. Other mechanical components and wiring were run through here as well. It didn't want any serious damage to come to this vessel. Its primary goal was to get off of it alive.

It passed by a particularly loud section. Possibly the unit that powered this ship. It continued forward, with Sam trailing behind. Then it saw a vent that looked to be rusted. The creature bent down and pulled it off. Moving aside, it shoved Sam through roughly. The Sam entity fell to the floor in the room, then absently stood back up.

The room was filled with computing system whirling and buzzing. It was hot in this room. Heat and cold didn't matter anymore. Only that it completed its task. Then it could continue the process of rotting. Or becoming its master's next meal. The tar inside Sam's body tightened and lifted the legs as it moved forward. Black goo twisting its neck to look in all directions. The room was empty. It stood by, awaiting instructions from its master.

In the command center, Justin was explaining his plan. "So, I want to get to the engine room again."

Immediately Carol cut him off. "Why? Not with that thing loose! We all saw what it did to…" She paused, glancing at Alex and Danny Boy.

"Carol, all of you, I know the spot we're in isn't good. It's really bad. But sitting here and firing the engine full blast will get us floating in space like we had been. We need a plan. So hear me out, ok?" Justin said with authority.

The room fell silent. Justin continued. "Engine room has the power cell that's currently damaged. We take it out, get to the *Stormbringer*. Carol, we still have the analyzation cube in there?"

Carol nodded, wondering where this plan of his was going.

"We need to extract a small sample of the liquid in that power cell. Analyze it and see if what my gut is telling me is correct."

"And what's that?" Ramsey said, leaning back in the pilot's seat.

"The liquid in those power cells is similar to or the same substance as our synth," Justin said. His eyes shifted from person to person.

"That is one incredible gamble to test out a hunch. And time consuming," Carol said very skeptically.

"There is literally a 100-year gap from Trilaxus' end to now. What if the liquid on our moon had been discovered by other civilizations? Harvested? Reproduced? I mean, it's worth a shot. Look, we don't have the weaponry to take that thing down. It's already figured out how to avoid the airlock. And it's currently crawling around the inside hull of this ship. If this would actually work, we power up the *Stormbringer* and take off. All of us," Justin said firmly.

Danny Boy added to the conversation. "Hey, I've taken those power cells out and swapped them. Why not do it one more time? I think I have a tool that could be used to extract a small portion to analyze. If it's the real deal then we carefully, and I do mean carefully, extract the rest of it into your tank on the *Stormbringer*."

"Transporting a volatile, highly explosive liquid from our engine room to your broke down ship, test it, then if it checks out, pour it into your tank. Power up and fly off. While avoiding a creature who seems to want us all dead. That's your plan?" Alex said.

Justin nodded his head.

"Alright, I'm in," she said firmly.

"Me too," Ramsey said as well.

"I mean, what the hell, I guess? We can die here or die trying that. I'd rather try something," Danny Boy said evenly as he cracked his knuckles.

Carol was silent as everyone looked over at her. Finally, she spoke, "Hey I've been in worse spots. Quite recently actually. Let's do it."

Justin smiled and nodded at everyone. "Ok, Carol and Danny, you're with me. Alex, I wish you could join, but I really don't want to leave Ramsey all by himself piloting this thing. And it's risky leaving the weapons unmanned. I haven't forgotten about those Reaper ships. My hunch is they're going to want to make sure this ship is destroyed along with everyone onboard."

Everyone nodded.

Justin, Carol and Danny left the command center and once again headed back to the engine room with weapons drawn. The elevator ride down was in silence. Every creak of the hull due to the steadily increasing speed of the ship would make them jump. They quietly made their way to the engine room and walked in without making a noise. They inspected the room. It was empty. There wasn't any place the creature could hide in here.

"We're going to have to work double time, Danny, ok?" Justin said in a near whisper.

Nodding to him, Danny Boy quickly began working. "This will actually go faster. Not everything is hooked up. There was no point. The engine is shot, and this power cell is damaged. Should have it out in no time."

Carol cautiously looked around the room. Standing close to Justin. Gun drawn. She whispered to him, "I haven't even had time to recover from our first run in with an extra-terrestrial monster and we're stuck on a ship with another one. You aren't allowed to die, ok?"

"We're going to kill it, or get off this ship, or both. We brought it with us. These people are innocent, and we let it loose. I aim to destroy it," Justin said coldly.

Carol put her hand on his back affectionately. *A leader to the end,* she thought.

"I've got it," Danny Boy said quietly as he lifted the power cell out of the container it was housed in. "No problem. I'm getting pretty damn good at this."

Justin offered to take the power cell from the weakened Danny Boy. Instead, Danny shook his head and quietly mumbled, "I've got this. Just make sure no creepy crawly giant lizards crawl up my ass."

Nodding, Justin led the way, with Danny in the middle carrying the power cell and Carol bringing up the rear, sticking close to Danny. They headed to the cargo bay once again as the ship vibrated at the speed that Ramsey had it set to.

Justin unlocked the door and it slid open. Thankfully, the sliding doors on this particular freighter ship opened and closed with relative silence. Not so with the outer cargo bay hatch. All three of them walked in quietly as the door slid shut behind them. All the way down the hall, at the far end of the ship, a walking dead person roaming the operating systems room was about to make things significantly darker about the *Leo*.

Back up in the command center, Ramsey and Alex sat uncomfortably at their posts. Ramsey could cut the tension with a knife. Having had time to process what had happened to Sam, who was like a parent figure to her, Alex went from softly crying to herself to stone faced anger.

"Do you want to talk about…" Ramsey started.

"No. She's dead. Killed by that thing you brought on board with you. And now it's hiding like a coward. Probably going to try to pick us off one by one until we get the ship landed, then it'll escape," Alex spat the words at Ramsey angrily.

Contemplating his next words, Ramsey carefully said, "Hey, I can't express just how sorry I am for all of this. You're right, you know. We did bring this on board, and it is on us. But I know Justin, I know Carol. They're good people, and we all will do everything it takes to rid this ship of that creature and get us all to safety. You've got to believe me."

Hearing Ramsey take responsibility for the creature being on board softened her a bit. She sighed and looked over at him. He saw good in those eyes. Hardened by a hard life. And so incredibly beautiful.

Nodding, she said in a much calmer voice, as she quickly wiped bitter tears off of her lightly freckled cheeks. "Look, I'm not trying to come down hard on you. This crew is my family.

Much like your crew seems to be yours. So you get that, I am sure. Thank you for understanding."

"Oh Alex, seeing my own captain turned before my eyes into a monster, then later having to die to save us? That's one that'll stick with me till my dying day. Which, at the rate we're going, could be today," he replied back with a slight grin.

She shot a quick smirk back at him. "Well, I have no doubt, like I said earlier, that it's going to try to pick us off. The key word there is 'try.' Let's see what it thinks of this here Fusion Rifle jammed up its ass when I pull the trigger. It won't be thinking at all, because its brains will be splattered on the ceiling of this broken down old heap of a ship."

Ramsey's grin grew wider as he looked sideways at her. She returned the favor.

"Think the plan's going to work? Alex asked.

Nodding to himself, he said, "If there is a way, Justin's going to get it done. Meanwhile, I'm pushing this ship to its limits. I think we can all feel it vibrating and shimmying. That's probably not normal."

They both stared out into space. Nothing but stars and several planets in the far distance. Otherwise, total emptiness.

A psychic link seemed to have been made between the creature and the Sam corpse. It was faint but it was there. The black tar that flowed through the creature was the same that flowed now through Sam. It had been born from the stars. And now it gave back the gift of life to this unworthy being in the front end of level three.

Sam's corpse could now take certain commands from its creator on the most basic level. Obey. Do its bidding. Which is what it was doing now in the operating systems room. It sensed that it was to find a way to cut the main lights aboard the ship. Or as many as possible. To shroud themselves in darkness. All the better to attack. Hopefully one at a time.

It walked through the servers in the room. Black eyes staring out at the wiring, circuit boards and computing systems. Rows of various components were marked with makeshift labels. The ceiling was low and the heat in the room was making some of the black tar substance on Sam slowly liquify further and drop off to the floor. Its motor skills kept it walking, moving about the room. Almost instinctively, it found the correct circuit board. Marked above it were the words *Lighting Systems* scribbled onto a label. There were emergency lights on the ship that were not a part of this lighting board, but taking out the main lighting would be a major setback anyway for the livestock that it would soon be in control of. Or feasting on. Or both.

I need to get off this ship. Radar systems needed to stay active. Landing gear. Engine room. At least one of these beings to pilot it. However, their numbers needed to be greatly reduced. As well as the weapons they still possessed, destroyed. It could withstand them up to a point, but this husk of a once-living being would be obliterated. The creature had curled up into itself. Contracting until it fit tightly into a corner spot. Out of sight. In the darkness. Pulling the strings.

CHAPTER 19

LIGHTS OUT

Justin carried the power cell into the cargo bay along with Carol and Danny Boy. Once inside the large room, they inspected it. Primarily the open storage unit where the Marks had once been, which was now the entrance for wherever that alien had hidden itself.

They didn't make a sound as they walked forward towards the *Stormbringer*. Once inside, they could close the hatch and at least be a bit more protected. Once they got to the front of the hatch, Justin stopped and looked down at the locking mechanism connected to the front landing gear. He pointed to it so Danny Boy would look as well.

Danny looked at him as he said in barely a whisper, "We need to get that unlocked as soon as we know if the power cell liquid works in here."

Nodding back his response, Danny moved towards the outer hatch of the *Stormbringer* along with Justin and Carol. The ship creaked and they all jumped, looking in different directions. It must be the ship's acceleration. *Keep pushing it, Ramsey,* Justin thought.

The door slid open and Justin, Carol and Danny all peered into it. Not sure what to expect. Justin and Carol had guns drawn, standing on either side of Danny Boy, who was shaking from the strain of carrying the power cell. Normally, this wouldn't be too bad, but his body was wracked with pain, even if dulled by the pills.

"We've got to find a spot to set this down in the upright position here soon. My arms…" Danny said humbly.

They all stepped into the *Stormbringer*. Lights flickered on. It was a mess of blood and slime covering the walls and floor. Carol grimaced, revolted at the ghastly sight.

Justin tried to ignore it and Danny Boy exclaimed, in the same hushed voice, "Bloody hell."

"Bloody hell is right," Carol responded as the door slid shut behind them. "Before we do anything with the synth, let's find out a little bit more about our new enemy, shall we?"

She went over to the front of the hull, by the pilot's position. On the floor there was a compartment. She bent down, lifted it up and pulled out the Analyzation Cube. Setting it on the chair that Justin would normally sit in.

Before opening it, she looked at Danny Boy and spoke in a louder voice now that they were inside the enclosed hull.

"We need to find a spot for that. We're going to do a quick scan of this blood, then work on the synth, ok?"

Justin motioned for him to set it down in the back against the wall. On his way back, an already unstable Danny slipped on a bit of the bloody remains on the floor. He immediately started falling backwards. Justin instinctively reached out as he fell into his arms, almost sending Justin back towards the floor as well. Luckily, Justin was strong and able to hold his ground.

Jumping from the fright it had given her, Carol quickly went to check on Danny Boy. "Did you get lightheaded? What happened?" she asked, concerned, looking him over.

"I slipped on the bloody slime on the floor. Good thing this big brute was there to catch me." He shook his head, angry at himself at the catastrophe he had nearly caused.

This time, Danny was able to get the power cell to the back wall and prop it up. "We cannot, under any circumstances, let that thing fall. I'm going to hang onto it back here. Do your thing, Carol." He wiped his sweat covered brow.

Nodding, Carol opened the Analyzation Cube. It slid open with a hiss. She took a glass sliver housed inside the cube and bent down to the floor, scooping up some of the blood and clear sticky substance onto it.

Justin stood by as she entered the glass with the specimen on it into the Analyzation Cube and closed it. After a brief wait the cube spoke in a robotic non-human voice, "Compounds in sample are as follows: plasma, red blood cells, white blood cells, and platelets. Traces of unidentified compound located as well. No additional data."

"Human blood and whatever that thing is made of. The human blood must be Grant's," she said, glancing at Danny Boy sadly.

She opened the Analyzation Cube and took the sample out, discarding it, then looked towards the back where Danny Boy was propping up the power cell. Bright blue liquid filling most of the canister up. "Time to test it. The moment of truth, so to speak."

Danny reached into his pocket and produced a small tool with an odd shaped end that had several extended prongs on it. He held it up. "This is what will open the top lid. I got it out of the engine room. I can't stress enough how dangerous this is. Carol, do you have anything that's long and skinny that you can slide into the cannister if I just crack it slightly open?" Carol scanned the room, looking for something that might work. Then she spotted a food utensil and picked it up, holding it out to Danny. "Think this would be ok?"

He inspected it and nodded his head.

"Ok, Justin, can you get another piece of glass? I will carefully dip the utensil into the cannister, take it over and wipe it onto glass for the cube to analyze."

With the tool, Danny Boy began to disassemble the top lid. There were five bolts that needed to be removed, and they were tightened securely. Each one took time, but they did come loose. Finally, the fifth and final one was loosened and came out. Carol was holding the cannister upright through the process, careful not to shake it in any way.

Once all of the bolts were taken out, Danny put the tool away and popped the top lid. The bright liquid inside was steady, because Carol was holding it steady. Careful to not make any sudden movements. She let Danny Boy take over holding the cannister as he lifted the lid slightly.

She quickly headed up to the Analyzation Cube and wiped the substance off onto the glass Justin had procured and slid it into the opening, closing it once it was in place. "Here goes nothing," she said shakily.

They all looked to the floor in anticipation. Waiting for the results. After what felt like minutes, but in actuality was only a few seconds, the robotic voice spoke methodically, "Components in sample are as follows: Sillenopyrite, Bronvianite, Verorspar, Spring Blue Stepcophane."

Silence in the *Stormbringer*. Danny broke the silence. "Well? Come on! Do we have something here or back to square one?"

"Unhook the latch on the front of the ship. We have a way off of the *Leo*," Justin replied. Trying to contain his excitement at this bit of good news.

"You mean this stuff is that synth stuff that powers your ship? Really?" Danny replied, stunned at this development.

Carol was also trying to contain her excitement at this news and replied, "Those are the key ingredients of what we do in fact call synth. I guess in 100 years' time it was discovered either on our own moon or elsewhere in the galaxy and started being used in various ways. Not sure if we have the Scaagzil to thank for that or not. Regardless, if there isn't irreparable damage to the *Stormbringer* from what we went through out there, as well as that creature essentially being birthed in here from the looks of it, I think she'll fly, at least enough to get us off the *Leo*."

"Ramsey, come in," Justin said into the com system.

The com clicked on and Ramsey replied, "Give me some good news, sir."

Carol smiled at this, glancing over at Danny Boy, who was also relieved that something was currently going right after all of the death, deceit and general mayhem that had transpired since their fellow space travelers from another galaxy had come aboard.

"We have synth. Or at least a variant of it. Going to fill the tank up in the *Stormbringer*," Justin said evenly. He didn't want to get too excited just yet. Not without the ship properly powered up.

"Ok, ok good. So, if we continue as planned, we should be getting within an hour of the space port before the engine is done for on the *Leo*. But we should be long gone by then."

Justin came back in a hurried voice, "Hey Alex, that grenade you gave Ramsey. What was it called again? Wait, doesn't matter. Can it be set to detonate at a certain time?"

"Yes. I'm already seeing where you're going with this. I'm not a fan of destroying Sam's ship. Even with that thing onboard," Alex came back sternly.

"It's not Sam's ship anymore. Neither is it ours. It currently belongs to that creature. Otherwise, it could potentially just drift out here until some unsuspecting spacecraft stumbles across it," Justin responded firmly.

"Day just keeps getting better and better, doesn't it?" Alex shot back sarcastically.

"I'll keep you both posted on whether the synth is actually working once we pour it into our tank. We won't know for sure until we fire up the *Stormbringer*. Justin out."

And with that, Justin headed to the back and looked at Danny Boy and Carol. Time to pour their escape into the tank. They all nodded at each other.

In the server room, the Sam entity took hold of the circuit board that operated the lights throughout the ship and ripped it out of the motherboard. Immediately all lights onboard the *Leo* went out. Within seconds, small, dim red lights popped on throughout the ship. They only activated in emergencies such as this. However, seeing anything from a distance greater than a few feet in front of any individual onboard was nearly impossible.

Now, any forms of communication and transportation. Get rid of them.

The Sam corpse turned and walked down another row of hard drives and circuit boards until it found com systems. It ripped out the motherboard, sending sparks flying and more lights blinking in the server room. It then headed to the elevator control systems.

In the command center, Ramsey and Alex sat in near darkness trying to keep their cool. "Oh shit, oh shit, oh shit," Alex whispered to herself and Ramsey. Not trying to hide the terror she currently felt.

"Justin, come in! What's going on? Justin!" Ramsey yelled into the com. It was dead. No static, no crackling.

Both of them were armed and Ramsey had made sure the DPG was close by as he gave up on the com system. The *Leo* was continuing on its course at full speed, so creaks and shimmies continued reverberating through the ship's interior in the near darkness, making it sound utterly haunted.

Alex had gotten up from her seat and was standing by Ramsey, who was also out of his seat. Letting the ship pilot itself towards the space port.

"It got to the lights and com. I can't believe the radar is still operating," Ramsey said in a whisper, looking down at it.

"It wants us to find somewhere to land. Then it's going to try to do away with the rest of us," Alex exclaimed quietly.

Nodding, Ramsey replied, looking over at her coldly, "Agreed. And we aren't going to let that happen."

Justin, Carol and Danny Boy were still in the *Stormbringer*, attempting to pour out the synth into the tank when everything went to hell even further. While the lights remained on in the small escape pod, all other lights were cut. The dull, dim lights in the cargo bay kicked on, showing nothing more than black outlines on the sparse massive room.

As soon as the lights were cut, Carol tried contacting Ramsey and Alex as Justin was currently holding the cannister in the rear of the ship.

The com was dead. She put two and two together quickly and informed them, "Lights and com are down. It's gotta be that thing."

"Let's go. We don't have time. We don't know where it is right now, but we have to get this synth poured," Justin said urgently.

"Ramsey and Alex won't know if the ship works. And it might as well be a full day's walk back to the command center with no lights to speak of. Hell, at this point, I would assume it cut the elevator transportation. Emergency ladder only," Danny Boy said shakily, looking up at Justin.

Ignoring his grim assessment, which he guessed was probably accurate, Justin glanced at Carol, who was now by his side. "We got this, ok? We aren't going to give up. Can you help me pour the liquid?"

"Of course we're going to get through this." Carol mustered a warm smile for him as he tilted the container towards the synth tank in the rear of the ship behind a large panel that had been removed earlier.

The synth tank was a large tank made to securely store the volatile liquid. The problem was pouring it in without spilling a single drop, and the power cell housing was not designed to pour. It was designed to contain the liquid securely and safely.

"I can handle thirty-five pounds, but this is going to be awkward to say the least. Remember, both of you. Not a single drop. I will handle the majority of the weight of this thing. Carol and Danny, you stand on either side of me. Danny, you guide the power cell container so it stays in one place. Carol, you're going to ease some of the awkward weight off of it for me, ok? You just stand beside me, put your hands on my hands, and follow my lead as I pour the liquid into our tank."

Both nodded in reply as they got to work pouring. The liquid slowly trickled out into the opened synth tank of the *Stormbringer*. Then Justin tilted the cannister slightly more as the liquid was now rushing out into their own tank.

Sweat was rolling off Justin's brow and down his neck, but he tried to put the discomfort out of his mind. They were so close. As the cannister continued to drain, Justin continued to lift up more and more on it so the flow continued. Danny Boy steadied it and Carol's warm hands were on top of Justin's.

"Almost there," Carol said. Then a particularly fierce shudder through the *Leo* reverberated inside the *Stormbringer*.

Justin lost his grip on the power cell container as the nearly depleted liquid sloshed back down and around the bottom. Some of it kicked up, dangerously close to escaping the opened lid and falling to the ground. Danny, who had been in an awkward position kneeling on the ground, fell backwards and almost took the cannister along with him.

"Oh shit!" he yelled, once again falling backwards, although this time it was merely a minor misstep and he recovered quickly, carefully starting to guide the volatile liquid once again into the tank.

Justin and Carol kept a steady hold of the cannister. "Come on! Let's pour the rest in! We're so close!" Carol said with excitement and pure terror at just how dangerous this all was.

They poured the rest of the liquid into the tank and carefully set it back down, with Danny Boy immediately putting the top lid back on, sealing it up. Then, Justin put the cap back onto their own synth tank as Carol propped the back wall panel back into place. Once done they both slid down the interior wall of the *Stormbringer* to catch their breath, exhausted.

"Ok, so let's not do that again ever," Danny Boy said as he wiped his sweat covered face off from the immense tension-filled task that had just been completed. Then he added sarcastically, "We still have the lock on that front landing gear that needs unhooked. Oh, and a few extra passengers located about ten miles away."

"You always this sarcastic?" Carol shot at him.

"No, well, yes. Sometimes. I'm usually pretty even keel unless a huge alien lizard with horns is wanting to bite the brains out of the back of my skull. Yeah, then I get a bit snarky, I suppose."

Ignoring their banter, Justin stood up and headed towards to the front of the ship. "It's time to see if all this work is going to pay off. Come on baby, you've got one more mission we need you to accomplish," he said hopefully.

CHAPTER 20

NIGHT OF THE LIVING DEAD

Sam was dead, yet she walked the long hall of the *Leo*. On a mission. Possibly her final one. To add to her new master's numbers. The black goo that had taken over her lifeless corpse continued to twist her and contort her features. Doing this made the dead shell excrete blood through her mouth as well as other facial openings. She didn't need it anymore. All that was needed to exist was the black liquid that infected her like a virus.

She had arrived at the cargo bay as instructed and entered into the room as Justin, Danny Boy and Carol were busy in the back pouring the synth. It couldn't grasp what "good luck" was as three of her master's five prey were here, all located in one spot. It would continue to do its master's bidding until it was used up.

Meanwhile, deep inside the inner hull of the *Leo*, the seven-foot-tall parasite lay in wait. As powerful as it was, it needed to preserve itself. Great things lay in store for it. It just had to escape the confines of this vessel. It had crawled up to level two after contorting its body. Bones shifted and moved to adjust to the tight spaces it fit into. Along the way, it had seen several spots where it could easily pounce out and overtake one of the five remaining entities onboard. It slowly slithered up to level one, on the far side of the hallway from where the command center was located. There it waited, close to an air duct.

Danny Boy and Carol walked to the front of the ship and watched him as he clicked on the initial startup functions. More lights came on, including the outer lights in front, shining beams of light into the large empty cargo bay.

"Zark, you there?" he asked steadily.

"How may I be of service, Commander Justin Schwartz?"

Nodding in relief, he asked the *Stormbringer*'s A.I. system, "Zark, display ship diagnostics and synth levels."

On the screen in front of them, every aspect of the inner and outer hull damage was displayed. It was significant, but not enough to keep the ship grounded. Atmosphere could still be kept on board, even though the structural damage was extreme.

"Hey look, lucky us. We're at 13% hull integrity remaining. Up one percent for some reason," Carol said bemusedly.

"I'll take any percent increase we can get. 13% gets us somewhere hopefully safer than this ship," Justin replied confidently back to both her and Danny, who was looking over the schematics displayed on the screen.

"Synth level 50%. We're in business, gang," Justin said, pointing to the synth level readout.

Danny raised his eyebrows and replied, "Wow, with the other one we'd be at 100%!"

Putting his hands on the back of his head and stretching, Justin replied, "We would. But it's far too great a risk with that thing out there. We need to figure out how to get Ramsey and Alex back here and get going. That creature is certainly not going to let us just waltz right out of here. Danny, you're an engineer. What do you make of our damage?"

Carol put her hand on her sore neck and then her still bruised arm, noting the dull pain that it still caused and how it reminded her that not too long ago, she was stuck in a cave system deep inside a mountain trying to escape from a colossal monstrosity made of ice. And now here she was, squaring off against a chameleon-like monster in the tight confines of an old worn-out ship that had less tech than their 100-year-old ships back on Trilaxus.

Noticing Carol deep in thought, Justin stood beside her and put his arm around her. She leaned into him. "Why us?" she asked softly.

"The randomness of the universe, I guess. We're getting out of here. And we're going to kill this thing, and then we're going to find a planet that has a nice beach. We're going to stay up late and sleep in and not worry about a single thing. At least for a bit. That's my goal, along with keeping you alive."

"You know I love you, right?" she replied.

He kissed her on the head and glanced over at Danny Boy, who had read over all of the schematics on the ship. Turning to them, he nodded, saying, "I may not know this particular ship. But I'm fairly certain with the damage it's sustained, it's not gonna last long out there."

"Long enough to get us to that space port. Every passing minute is a minute closer," Carol exclaimed.

"And once we're off the *Leo*, we're gonna nuke it. That extra power cell is where I would like to leave it. It would inflict the most damage," Justin said coldly.

"Oh, that'll do more than just inflict damage. That would obliterate this ship. I wouldn't want this little *Stormbringer* escape pod anywhere near that explosion," Danny Boy muttered back.

"Time to get Ramsey and Alex down here," Justin said, lifting his Fusion Rifle.

"And time to release the lock on that front landing gear. I know how to do it, so yeah, that should be loads of fun." Danny looked out into the large empty cargo bay somewhat illuminated by the *Stormbringer's* landing lights. This, however, only lit up the immediate path straight ahead. There were far too many dark hiding spots in large, almost cavernous room.

Justin looked at Carol, sighed and cleared his throat, knowing how this discussion would go. He set the Fusion Rifle down and looked her in the eyes. "Carol, I want you to stay here. There's no reason for you to go along with me. You stay on the *Stormbringer* and back up Danny Boy."

"Absolutely not. There is no way I'm staying behind and letting risk your life. I let you go to put out the fire earlier against my better judgement. No!" Carol said angrily.

"Carol, listen to me. You need to survive. We all do. But it's an unnecessary risk. It's a long ladder climb up to level one. Your arm is hurting. I've seen how you've been favoring it. That creature had you by the throat. I don't want you to risk your life! I hate this. I hate the situation we're in. That we've put the *Leo's* crew in. But you have to be at the helm of the *Stormbringer* ready for us. Ready for when we all come back to take off. We only have one shot at this. I trust you, baby."

Justin stopped and stared at her, looked deep into her soft, sad eyes. She had been through so much, and now to separate again. With the creature loose. With all the death over the last week.

Tears began to drop from her eyes.

Justin put his hands on her waist and pulled her into him tightly. They kissed hard. Then she put her forehead against his and nodded briefly.

"Guys, we gotta make this happen," Danny Boy said quietly behind them, not wanting to break the moment.

Pulling away from her, Justin lifted the Fusion Rifle and said calmly, "Keep the *Stormbringer* warm for us. We're coming back soon."

"I love you," she said back as bitter tears continued falling. As he turned to walk out, she unsheathed her knife and belt, putting it in his hand. He was about to resist, but she backed away, shaking her head defiantly.

Justin and Danny Boy exited the *Stormbringer* together as the hatch slid shut behind them.

Up in the command center, Ramsey and Alex were deciding what to do.

"I think we should make a run for it. If the *Stormbringer* is back in business, we hop in and take off. The DPG could be set in the engine room for maximum damage. Set the timer and go," Ramsey said quietly.

Sighing, Alex replied only loud enough for him to hear, "I tend to go with that idea as well. But if the power cell doesn't jive with your tank, we are literally shit out of luck here. How much further to the space port?"

Ramsey glanced up at the screen. "Looks like a few hours. We're burning through fuel. Ship is continuing at max speed."

Outside through the viewscreen they passed a large gas giant planet. Green, orange and red swirls seemed to pulsate around it. In any other circumstance, it would have been a beautiful sight. But here, it made them feel even more alone in the deep vast emptiness of space.

"I know we have a bit more protection in this command center with the reenforced metal doors. What do you say we both get out of here? I have the *Leo's* course plotted towards the space port. Once it runs out of steam, then that's it. In the meantime, the synth will work, we plant the DPG, get out of here and kaboom, blow the ship and creature along with it into oblivion," Ramsey said with authority.

"Not that it will help us at all, but we have a hatch under the captain seat. Used for quick exits, but only on land. Worst case scenario, we wear space suits and bail through there. But I don't think it will come to that. Once we're out in space in our space suits, we're just as dead, only slower," Alex said grimly, looking over at Sam's seat and the thin circle underneath it virtually hidden from those not familiar with the ins and outs of the *Leo.*

"Let's not have to do that. Plan A for us, alright?" he replied back, eyeing the captain's seat as well, glad they weren't having to make that type of an exit.

Nodding, Alex slapped him on the back. "Let's do it."

They cautiously headed to the exit of the command center.

The door slid open to reveal darkness. Ramsey held the Electron Pistol out in front of him with the DPG strapped to his side. Alex was by his side with the Fusion Rifle pointed out. A small light on the gun stock illuminated their immediate surroundings as they began heading down the long hallway towards the emergency escape ladder leading down to the second and third levels at the far end. Dim red lights flashed around them, barely helping at all with the poor lighting situation.

The ship creaked and continued shimmying as it thundered through space on its way to the space port, growing closer and closer. Also nearing the *Leo* was the planet Thakitune, now visible on the viewscreen.

They walked past the bunks. Pitch black filled the rooms as they continued on slowly, trying to not make any sudden noises. Along with the creaking, there was a low growl. Deep inside the inner hull.

They both stopped. Alex glanced over to Ramsey. "What the hell was that?" she whispered.

Ramsey shook his head without uttering a word. Electron Pistol out in front of him, scanning the near darkness that surrounded them.

Inside the hull, it watched. Seeing a beam of light through the slots in the ventilation system. It was still a young creature, learning and not yet nearing its full potential. It instinctively knew that there would be stages of its evolution. Right now, it was small for what it was, but growing rapidly. It had limited telepathic abilities, but it was still vulnerable in its current state. It needed to be strategic in how it struck its potential victims. It continued to watch its prey move forward, inching closer to where it lay in wait.

The hatch had slid shut behind them. Danny walked over to the landing gear and nodded to Justin. It would take five to ten minutes to unlock it and set it aside, especially considering how dark it was underneath the escape pod the landing lights did little to illuminate. Justin cautiously walked the dark cargo bay. It was quiet. Only the sounds of the shuddering ship filled the air. The room smelled like blood, further reminding him of the horrors that had taken place in this room earlier. His feet stepped into the pools of blood, both from Grant as well as Sam.

Justin held the Fusion Rifle at his shoulder, ready to fire at anything that wasn't Ramsey or Alex. His eyes darted back and forth, his ears picking up every single creak on the hull. He made his way silently to the exit, with the stream of light from the *Stormbringer* lighting his way forward. The red glowing emergency lights were hardly noticeable as he continued walking.

The exit door slid open silently and he exited. Justin glanced back at the *Stormbringer*. Carol was standing by the front viewscreen watching him. He nodded at her as he exited the cargo bay into the long black hallway.

Justin took a breath, slung his Fusion Rifle over his shoulder then wiped off the beads of sweat that had formed on his nerve wracked brow. He glanced up into the darkness above him and began the long and dangerous climb up the ladder.

Inside the cargo bay the silence coupled with the shuddering of the *Leo* had Danny Boy continually glancing over his shoulder as he tried to work not just quietly but quickly. To make sure it would be disconnected properly, he needed to lift a particularly heavy bolt out of the large latch attached to the landing gear. He had it slid out most of the way and once again, a shudder rippled through the ship. The bolt was halfway out when it slipped and fell to the ground with a loud clang echoing through the cargo bay.

"Shit!" Danny Boy said louder than he wished he would have. He glanced up, thinking he heard something other than the stupid bolt. It sounded like heavy breathing.

The hatch to the *Stormbringer* slid open and Carol peeked her head out. "All good? What did I hear?" she said, as her eyes darted, scanning the seemingly empty cargo bay.

"Just my slippery fingers once again. Sorry Carol, I'm not normally like this. A probable concussion will do that to a person."

Carol breathed heavily and looked up towards the door where Justin had exited minutes ago. *I hate this. I hate it!* she thought to herself.

"Hey, I could use a hand here. I've almost got this thing unhitched." Danny Boy pointed at one more bolt that was still sticking to the hitch.

Carol looked back into the *Stormbringer*. Everything was ready to go. She was just waiting in there, nervous about Justin, about Ramsey. Everyone. "Sure." She nodded as she holstered her Electron Pistol at her side and walked out and joined him. The hatch to the small escape pod slid shut and she walked over to Danny, glancing around at their surroundings.

"Here, lift the anchor attached to the floor up a bit. I need to slide the bolt completely out of the anchor there." Danny Boy showed her the metal component latched into the landing gear that needed to be detached in order for it to leave the cargo bay at all.

Carol did as she was instructed and Danny was able to quickly slide the bolt out easily with her help, thus releasing the anchor. The *Stormbringer* was free of its constraints. Danny said quietly, "Thanks for the extra hand."

Carol was about the reply but was suddenly at a loss for words. Her eyes filled with terror. She tried to back up from her crouching position but fell backwards, her butt hitting the ground as she continued scooting back.

Directly behind Danny Boy, a newly reborn Sam stood. Blood oozing from her mouth, her tattered clothes covered in black tar. Hollowed out black eyes. In her hands she held a large wrench.

Once inside the cargo bay it had stood in the shadows, instinctively knowing darkness was its ally. It had ultimately decided that once the larger, more powerful looking human left, it was time to strike. It had slowly positioned itself behind the crouching man and raised the wrench in its hand. Then the woman saw it. It had to strike now.

Sam's corpse brought down the wrench onto Danny's bald head as hard as the black oozing slime wrapped around Sam's muscles could swing. It connected with a dull thud, immediately sending thick blood into the air as well as down Danny's surprised, horror filled face.

Carol was fumbling for her Electron Pistol, but the black tar inside Sam's body was faster. It leapt forward and swung the large, heavy wrench down onto Carol's still injured arm, making direct contact with the wound.

There was a second delay, as the pain was so intense that Carol almost fainted. Then then she let out a blood curdling scream as fresh blood began trickling out.

Through her pain, she was able to look up at the zombified Sam, standing over her, wrench raised above its lifeless head. It opened its mouth as more thick, dead blood oozed out onto the floor. A gurgled groan came out of its throat as it brought the wrench down onto Carol's upper thigh.

New pain shot through her body. Although the pain in her arm was so intense, this new blow paled in comparison. However, she was still near fainting, and she knew if she fainted, she was dead. *Fight through this agony, Carol!* she thought as she continued sliding backwards away from the dead Sam who followed her as she tried to make her way to the *Stormbringer's* hatch as well as reaching for her still holstered Electron Pistol.

She was able to pull the firearm out with her left hand and aimed it at Sam. The corpse of Sam was too quick for the injured Carol. She jumped out of the way of the laser fire that shot out of the electron pistol as the blast bounced off the back wall harmlessly. Carol then started firing randomly in the room, but Sam had vanished into the darkness.

Carol tried to sit up and fight through the pain in her right arm and left leg, these new wounds made the bruises on her throat seem minor. She could hear the Sam zombie groaning somewhere inside the cargo bay. She blasted again in its direction, not sure if she had made contact or not.

Looking over at Danny Boy, Carol momentarily forgot about her own injuries. Danny was certainly worse off than she was. The blow he had received had knocked him out, or worse, killed him. She couldn't be sure without checking his vital signs. But she could see that his skull was crushed in from the blow. Blood had sprayed out of the hole the wrench made on top of his head and was continuing to flow onto the floor. The sight was ghastly.

Feeling her stomach flip, Carol leaned over and vomited. Both from her own newly sustained injuries and the sight of Danny Boy, brains exposed from where she sat. After she wretched, she wiped her mouth off and began to stand up. "Danny," she tried to say weakly, seeing if he would respond.

In a gurgling grunt, Danny Boy moved his arms. He turned his head towards Carol. His eyes had filled with blood, yet he was still alive, barely. He began reaching for her as she stood by her own ship's hatch. Carol was about to attempt pulling him up and into the relative safety of the *Stormbringer's* interior, but a bloodied arm grabbed Danny Boy's leg and pulled him away into the darkness.

"Danny!" she screamed as she watched him being dragged away, his Fusion Rifle still slung over his blood covered shoulder. The Sam corpse looked up at her as it pulled Danny Boy away with way more strength than a normal person her size should have. Carol noticed that it almost looked like it had a slight smile on its black eyed, unblinking face.

The electron pistol didn't have a scope or light of any kind. She contemplated firing into the darkness, but was afraid of hitting Danny Boy. Although at this point, he was most certainly done for with the new head trauma he had sustained.

Keep it together, Carol, she thought to herself. "Danny!" she tried to yell again, but it came out in sobs.

In the darkness, Danny's life was quickly slipping away. Sam's corpse had pulled him out of the light of the *Stormbringer.* Away from the gun of the foolish woman she had injured. *You will be next,* it thought. It looked down at the blood covered head of what once was one of her dearest friends. Now however, it was meat, just as she was.

Sam opened her dead, already rotting mouth and bit down into Danny Boy's open wound on the top of his head, drawing fresh sprays of blood shooting into her mouth. But that wasn't the point. She had no hunger. The only desire it still possessed was to serve its master. And its master wanted more of what she had become.

Inside Sam's mouth, down her throat, inside her organs, the sticky, black substance came forward. Flowing from her mouth into the top of Danny's head. Immediately wrapping itself around his exposed brain matter. Making its way down his brain stem. Wrapping around his spinal cord. Sam's bite had instantaneously killed Danny Boy, who had already been nearing death from the immense loss of blood and major head trauma. His eyes had rolled up inside their sockets, now lifeless as fresh blood poured out of him open mouth.

The black goo acted quickly, wrapping itself around his bones, twisting through his organs. Sam was slumped over, waiting for her next instructions as well as a new creation to be reborn like herself.

She could sense her own creator ready to strike out at the other entities onboard. To conquer, kill and create new life. The Sam corpse's job wasn't complete. Not yet. But now she would have help. The woman with the gun was next. She was injured and vulnerable now. And the man that foolishly left her here. Sam's master would take care of him soon enough. If not, then the honor would fall on her if she was called to do so.

Danny Boy sat up. His eyes were still rolled back in his head. The whites of his eyes looking out lifelessly. Thin lines of black tar-like goo slid over his eyes until they were completely black, much like Sam's. The black goo, now controlling all of Danny's motor skills, moved his arms and legs as he stood to his feet. It twisted around his hands as they lifted the Fusion Rifle off of his shoulder and put the weapon in its hands as its eyes looked towards the *Stormbringer*.

CHAPTER 21

TROUBLE IN THE TUNNEL

As Justin continued his climb up the long ladder, unaware of the horrors currently unfolding inside the cargo bay he had just left, Ramsey and Alex were continuing their slow trek down the hall towards the emergency ladder. The thin light on Alex's Fusion Rifle lit the way forward.

As they passed air ducts, Alex whispered to Ramsey, "I feel like we're being watched."

"Tell me about it." His eyes darted back and forth. Then, trying to ease the tension a bit and calm both of their nerves, he added, "Still haven't told me your full name."

This made her grin and glance over at him. "You flirting with me?"

Raising his eyebrows, he whispered back, "You are a perceptive one, aren't you?"

Then they both fell into silence once again. Both aiming their respective weapons back and forth, continuing the journey down the long hallway.

They were three quarters of the way to their exit when it happened. The air vent directly in front of them burst out, smashing against the opposite side of the hallway that in the oppressive darkness more resembled a mining tunnel deep underground on a desolate planet.

The creature burst out of the open vent, ripping at the sides of the air duct it was escaping out of. Metal tore and crumbled as it was forced to make way for the large beast emerging. Its outer skin had morphed in the darkness of the inner hull and now the pale red glow of the emergency lights streaked across its entire body. It greeted the shocked Ramsey and Alex with fiery red eyes, a black line running through them. A feature that Ramsey recognized immediately from his time spent in deep in the cave of Mirnare in the Pivoron Mountains on planet TSR1, when he faced the mighty Hyzothan, the destroyer and one time conqueror of that world.

It had quickly crawled out of the inner hull where it had been stalking them and now it stood before them, mouth open, sharp teeth protruding and ready to attack. Alex and Ramsey, however, weren't waiting around to see what its next move would be.

Upon jumping out of its hiding spot, both Ramsey and Alex had their guns trained. Ramsey at its head and Alex at its chest. They immediately opened fire at point blank range, sending bright red streaks of laser fire through the hallway and smashing into the creature in front of them, sending it backwards away from them.

The laser blasts caught it by surprise, as it had hoped its mere presence would throw them off. Its large gaping mouth released incredibly high frequency shrill screams. It was as if several different tones emanated from the same being. So loud in fact, that it had an intensely negative effect on Ramsey and Alex.

They were unable to continue firing their guns and had to cover their ears due to the pain and pressure on their heads. The creature had stopped staggering backwards, but it was clearly injured due to the blasts it took at such a close range.

Sensing that it was vulnerable to the weapons, it continued to scream as a defensive measure, seeing that it had worked to stop the laser fire. It felt a wet substance on its chest. Black oozing tar-like blood was trickling out of the blasted areas of its injured torso. *Come to my assistance,* it spoke to the Sam zombie on level three.

Justin heard the smashing metal and laser and the shrill screaming sound, certainly not human. Ramsey and Alex were attempting to make their way down to the cargo bay and the creature had sprung on them. If he could get to level one fast enough, he could catch the creature off guard, hopefully as it was contending with their laser fire.

Nearly jumping from rung to rung up the ladder towards level one, he had passed level two now. He heard something down below him, something sounding like a gurgled yell or a loud distorted moan. Almost to the top. The creature on level one had started shrieking again, now beginning to affect his climb with how shrill it was.

There was something else, though. He felt the ladder he was on shimmy slightly. As if someone, or something else was climbing on it from down below. He looked into the darkness from where he had come and saw nothing. But he felt the ladder and heard moans. *Climb faster,* he thought as he continued upwards, sweat soaking his shirt. His hands were on fire from the climb and carrying around the power cells earlier. He was becoming desperate to reach level one, and started to have doubts he could make it.

On level one things weren't going well for Ramsey and Alex. They were unable to shoot due to the shrieking, and the creature itself was now strategically moving forward. Knowing now how to stop the laser fire.

"We can't get past that thing! It's figured out how to stop our laser fire!" Alex yelled to Ramsey.

"Back to the command center!" Ramsey shouted back at her.

They finally turned around, turning their backs to the creature and running as fast as they could towards the command center. The door slid open as they spilled in, landing on the floor. The creature was nearly to the command center as well when a new burst of laser fire erupted through the long tunnel they had attempted to traverse.

The blasts hit the creature squarely in the back. Justin had made it to level one, crawled out and after a brief pause to bring the Fusion Rifle up to his shoulder, aimed and fired. He wanted to make sure the blasts were controlled and hit the creature, not the opened command center door, for fear of hitting the vital components inside.

Four well placed Fusion Rifle blasts hit their target dead center on its back, knocking it forward off its large, clawed feet. Its tail was swishing in the air almost as if it were trying to figure out what had happened.

The creature was so stunned by this surprise attack from behind it had ceased shrieking, allowing Ramsey and Alex to climb to their feet. Both were still trying to get their bearings after the shrieking had disoriented them. In front of them lay the creature, black blood oozing and bubbling up from blasts on its back, dripping off onto the floor. It writhed around on the ground in pain with an open mouth and forked tongue slithering on the ground, its tail continuing to swipe back and forth.

Ramsey pointed at the sharp pointy end of the tail and yelled to Alex, "Another defensive mechanism. We have to stay away from that tail!"

Alex nodded in agreement, although she had only caught parts of what Ramsey had yelled. Her ears were pounding. She looked forward and saw only darkness and dim red lights down the long hall. However, approaching quickly was the shadowy outline of a person.

The creature sensed what was happening. It was being trapped on either side. It had been injured, but not mortally. It was immortal after all, it thought to itself. The human organism that had surprised it was nearly upon it. With a quick and deadly flick of its tail, it snapped out, connecting with Justin's side. Its tail wrapped around him faster than he or Ramsey and Alex had time to react. The tail lifted Justin in the air and smashed him sideways against the side wall beside one of the living quarters.

The pressure of its tail coupled with the sudden impact on the wall immediately knocked Justin out cold. He slumped over, dropping his Fusion Rifle to the ground. The creature stood to its feet and saw that Ramsey and Alex were about to open fire on it once again. It quickly pulled the unconscious Justin up in front of itself by its tail still wrapped tightly around him. Justin was now its protection against more gunfire knowing that it must keep the organism alive or its prey would shoot through it much like they did with the female earlier in the cargo bay where it had been birthed.

The creature made quick work of the Fusion Rifle Justin had dropped, once again stepping on it with all of its might, crushing it into pieces and swiping the parts with its large, clawed foot aside.

Ramsey and Alex held their ground, guns raised and both regaining a bit of their hearing. The creature was hissing now. Its serpent tongue flicking back and forth in its open mouth. Drool dripping from the long sharp and pointed teeth.

"What's it gonna do?" Alex asked shakily, not taking her eyes off the grotesque demonic beast in front of them. Its body was littered with black blood as well as the oddly morphing colors it was trying to use to mimic its surroundings.

Ramsey shook his head, but knew this was a defensive mechanism the creature was displaying. It could be hurt, and with it holding an unconscious Justin out in front of it, it was scared. And if that was the case, it could most certainly be killed.

It looked at Alex square in the eyes as she looked back at it, not breaking its gaze. "One way or another, we are going to kill you," she muttered. Then yelled, "You hear me, you ugly oversized lizard? And that's all you are!"

Sensing she was provoking it, the creature shrieked again, sending Ramsey and Alex cowering backwards away from it. It needed to get away from their guns, so it quickly turned and lunged into the nearest living quarters. Inside the room was a bunk and some personal belongings. It quicky scanned the room and saw the name "Samantha Howard" on the bunk head. The door had slid shut behind it. Seeing a mechanism on the wall beside the door, it pressed it, locking the door immediately.

It didn't have much time before the two with the guns would find a way inside. With Justin still unconscious and trapped in its tail, it started digging into the floor. Metal ripped away, peeling back and revealing piping and wiring underneath. Its arms flailed as fast as they could, ripping and tearing at the floor. Sparks flew and pipes burst open, sending steam out of them into the room.

There wasn't much flooring in between the levels, so breaking through to level two beneath it was relatively easy for such a powerful being. It ripped away more metal, revealing a room with tables and chairs. It kept tearing away at the metal until it was confident that its prey could be stuffed through. Once below, with a bit more time and safe hiding places, it would enjoy feasting on this large specimen's brains as well as changing it into another obedient follower, much like the woman that was on her way up to help it now.

The hole was big enough now and the room was littered with debris. With its tail still holding Justin, it shoved him through and dropped him to the floor beneath. Outside the room there was banging on the door. The creature slid through the new hole in the floor it had made and dropped down beside its latest soon-to-be victim. It glanced up at the hole it had just fell from. They weren't in the room yet. It had time to take this being and hide.

Outside the room, Ramsey and Alex were desperate to open the door leading into Sam's bunk. "It's locked! That thing, that alien animal beast can lock and unlock doors!" Alex screamed as she tugged on the handle to no avail.

Ramsey was trying to kick the door in, but that wasn't working either. "Time's running out. We have to blast this door in."

"Yep. I'm sick of this shit. Stand back." Alex raised her Fusion Rifle at the lock. Her ears still ringing from the shrieking.

"Oh, you're actually doing this?" Ramsey shouted back, surprised due to how close they were to the door itself.

"You got a better idea?" And then she pulled the trigger. The door exploded inward, smashing into most of Sam's personal belongings. The door was made of metal, so the shards of it embedded in the wall and her bed. Small fires had been lit on fabric and the entire room was covered in smoke.

Alex and Ramsey didn't bother with the small fires or the smoke, both stepping into the room and seeing that the creature had dug a hole in the flooring and escaped with Justin through it to level two.

"Where does that hole lead to, Alex?" Ramsey exclaimed, his ears also still ringing from the creature as well as the piercing blast of the laser against the meal door.

Looking through the hole in the floor, Alex shouted back, "That's the mess hall. There aren't many places to hide down there. We have to hurry!"

"I can't tell you just how much I don't want to jump through that hole. That's a drop and all I can make out from here are vague outlines of tables and chairs! We're going to have to land on a table to break the fall. That or take the long route down the ladder," Ramsey said as he looked down through the hole. Sparks igniting around it from the torn wiring and piping.

"Let's go, cowboy," Alex replied with a grin and jumped through the hole down to level two. She landed on top of a table, which crumpled around her from the fall. However, she was relatively uninjured and stood up, brushing herself off.

Ramsey was looking down at the incredible spectacle, shaking his head in disbelief. "You're nuts, lady. I mean, you are...nuts."

Alex quickly scanned the area to make sure there weren't any unexpected surprises in the small room, then looked up at Ramsey, who was peering down at her from above.

"Get your ass down here. Times a-wasting," she shouted up to him.

"Wonderful," Ramsey muttered to himself, then added, "First off, shine that light up here so I can see a bit better. I have that DPG strapped to me! So you're going to have to catch this. I'm not falling on no grenade!" He took the device that was strapped to his side and looked down at Alex.

"Here, catch!" He dropped the square shaped grenade that was housed in a secure enclosure. She caught it easily and slung it over her shoulder. Then, Ramsey positioned as best he could while watching the light source that Alex had provided and leapt down onto another flimsy table that crumped under his weight much more than the table Alex landed on.

The table had busted into pieces, with Ramsey laying on the floor in pain. "Ouch. That sucked."

"Get up, big boy. Time to hunt aliens."

"Ok, give me a second to get up. You weigh what? Maybe a little over 100 pounds? I'm pushing 200, so yeah, cut me some slack."

Alex reached down with her slim hand and held it out for him. Looking at it, he reached up, grabbed it and was hoisted up. Once up, he dusted himself off, glanced at Alex and said cynically, "Hunt aliens. Ok, let's do it."

He drew his electron pistol as Alex lifted her Fusion Rifle up to her shoulder, pointing the gun around the large room looking for signs of life, either from the creature or Justin.

More dim red lights glowed in the room. With the Fusion Rifle light on, it helped some. Much like all the other rooms and the long hallway, with the main lights out, it was incredibly difficult to see anything more than several feet in any direction.

The room was quiet. Sparks could be heard from above where the creature had ripped its escape route through the floor. Smoke had trickled down into the mess hall below, making it even more difficult to see anything other than glowing red outlines of what looked like more tables and chairs and other inanimate objects scattered throughout the room.

There was noise coming from outside of the room, in the hallway. They both trained their weapons towards the closed door leading out to the other areas on level two.

Looking over at Alex, Ramsey asked in a too-loud voice, "So what is on level two?"

"We're in the mess hall. Next door is the rec room, and finally at the far end are some restrooms. You know, for when you drink too much, just run down the hall for a piss," Alex replied, her voice equally too loud for their current predicament.

Ramsey nodded, his earing ringing then replied, "Looks like the room is empty. We've got to keep moving."

They both made their way to the door that slid open silently once they were in front of it. Alex and Ramsey both peered out, looking in either direction. They were near the front of the ship, to the right was the non-operational elevator and to the left was more dark and foreboding tunnel travel.

Alex led the way with her Fusion Rifle and its light with Ramsey slightly behind, continuing to glance back in case there was a sneak attack. They walked towards the rec room and Alex put her hand up, gesturing to stop. She pointed at the door and looked at Ramsey, who nodded back, understanding that this room was the next to be searched.

The door slid open and as they were walking in, Ramsey thought he saw the vague outline of a person down the long hallway. However, it was too dark to make out exactly what it might have been. He tried his best to hear any sounds from that area, but the ringing made it impossible to distinguish any sounds that were out of place.

Inside the rec room were couches and a viewscreen of some sort. That was all Ramsey could make out. They crept through the room, listening for anything out of the ordinary. Cold sweat had covered Ramsey's aching back and chest from the fall he took earlier. Alex was at his side, gun raised, the dim light scanning their immediate surroundings. This room in particular seemed far too quiet and unnerving due to the couches and chairs and overall number of places where unwelcome creatures could lie in wait, ready to strike.

Alex was about ready to motion to leave the room and continue heading down the hallway when she heard a slow, steady and quiet hiss in the far corner. She was about to shine her light in the direction of the noise when the sliding door leading into the rec room opened, making both her and Ramsey quickly turn to see what had caused it to open.

Red emergency lighting illuminated the outline of a woman standing in the open doorway. A garbled moan came from her throat as her dead black eyes focused in on her prey.

CHAPTER 22

EXIT PLAN

Carol trembled inside the *Stormbringer* as she peered out. It looked as if the dead being that used to be Sam was slumping out of the cargo bay. She saw the figure walk past the lights shining out from her ship. *Must be heading out to try to get Justin, Alex and Ramsey.*

"I've got to help them. But Danny Boy, and my arm!" she said out loud in frustration. Then she added, "Think, Carol, think!"

She had her Electron Pistol as her only defense. Otherwise, she had a fueled-up ship, but needed to open the hatch. On top of that, her crewmates weren't here, and she would die before leaving them stuck on this flying ship of horrors.

Whomever actually hit the button to open the cargo bay outer hatch would have precious few seconds to get from there to the *Stormbringer*, unless they had a space suit. The air would immediately be sucked out along with the poor soul stuck inside the cargo bay.

But that was later. Right now, Danny Boy was out there somewhere, severely injured or possibly dead. He had been dragged off by the Sam monstrosity earlier, leaving Carol to her imagination as to what happened out there in the darkness.

"Ok, if Sam was turned into, whatever she now is, it's safe to assume that's what she was doing to Danny Boy as well. That, or eating him." She shook her head, trying to get the awful image out of her mind.

"When she left the cargo bay, she wasn't carrying that Fusion Rifle. So, I'm guessing Danny Boy still has it. That's either a good thing or a very, very bad thing."

A figure walked out into the light shining outward from the *Stormbringer's* landing lights. She stood up straight, peering out, watching it move slowly. It was indeed Danny Boy. But she could already tell something was drastically different about him.

He lifted his blood drenched head with a hole on top from the wrench that Sam had brought down on it. She immediately saw round black eyes staring back at her. But that wasn't the only thing staring at her. His Fusion Rifle was aimed at the *Stormbringer's* viewscreen.

Instinctively she backed up, but held her gaze on the monster that had until very recently been Danny Boyd Asher. She drew her Electron Pistol, knowing she couldn't fire it inside the *Stormbringer*, but feeling at least a bit more protected with it in her grasp.

Danny opened his mouth as black slime spilled out along with his own blood. And then he opened fire on the *Stormbringer*. The laser blasts smashed into the front of the ship and erupted into flames. The small ship itself would easily have been able to withstand numerous blasts from a weapon this size, but the outer hull integrity was down to 13% and this would drop it further, resulting in its ultimate destruction if the thing outside shooting at it was left to continue firing.

Carol screamed at the blast hits that rocked the ship. Her arm throbbed with pain as she held the Electron Pistol in her right hand.

Zark, the ship's A.I., calmly stated, "Hull integrity at 10%."

"Nope, this isn't going to happen," Carol said firmly to herself, unlocking the hatch as the door slid open. Leaning out, she opened fire on what was left of the walking corpse now in front of her.

The first two green laser blasts from her electron pistol made contact, hitting Danny squarely in the chest and upper thigh. The blasts easily pushed through his body, exiting out through a new hole in his back. Red and black liquid flew out of both sides. His leg buckled at the intense blast as fresh blood gushed out onto the ground beneath him. Danny tried to gurgle a response, but all that came out was groans and grunts.

Her surprise attack on Danny Boy had indeed worked though. He had quit firing on the *Stormbringer* and was now focused on Carol herself, as that was his mission. To kill and change her into one of them.

It looked at the new wounds on its body as if they were minor distractions, then regained its composure, pointing the Fusion Rifle at Carol.

Carol had quickly realized the ship was of utmost importance. It couldn't take many more hits, and that was their ticket off the *Leo*. Furthermore, this new creation needed to be put down before her friends showed up. And her friends were going to show up. She had to believe that.

The Danny creature started to fire at her, but she was already on the run, drawing its attention away from the *Stormbringer*. While the cargo bay was relatively large and open, there were structural beams on the far side, which is where Carol headed. The blasts missed her and bounced off the outer hatch harmlessly.

Carol made it to the beams and propped herself up against it, out of range from the creature's laser fire. However, it was already walking towards her, still firing. It seemed that the creature was going on instinct alone and not nearly as cunning or agile as when Danny Boy was alive. It was walking in a straight line, firing.

Crouching down out of the line of sight of the blasts, Carol had a clear angle at the approaching entity. It was incredibly dark however, so getting a good lock on it was difficult. She assumed the same could be said for the Danny creature hunting her now. Neither could see the other well apart from the dim red lights in the room. Also helping Carol was that the light on the Fusion Rifle had not been activated. It didn't know how.

She glanced out to make sure she saw the location of the gunfire. Thus far she hadn't given up her current hiding spot but would once she started shooting back. Carol wanted to draw the creature closer to her for a more accurate hit with her much smaller firearm.

The creature must have figured out what her plan was, so it stopped firing. Smoke surrounded Carol from the Fusion Rifle's blasts against the outer hatch. The cargo bay fell uncomfortably silent. She noticed that whatever had become of Danny Boy was no longer walking towards her, but stationary. Probably waiting to see what she would do next.

It watched the foolish beings enter the dimly lit room. It was content to draw them closer to it as it hid silently in the shadows behind a piece of furniture. The creature was large, but not so large that it couldn't conceal itself. Its skin color had also adapted to this particular room, turning it into a dark red and black monster.

It would reveal itself soon, and when it did, it would eat this foolish entity's brain, just like it did the female back in the cargo bay. It reveled in other's pain and suffering. Even at this young an age, the creature felt the need to inflict the maximum amount of suffering on its soon-to-be victims.

With the wounds that had been inflicted on the creature from the weapons that the soft fleshed animals carried, it felt as though some of its strength had depleted. Carrying this bag of worthless flesh and using it as a shield with its tail had become strenuous, so it was time to rid it of its life. Then it would be reborn.

Alex had turned to see the silhouette of a person standing in the entrance of the rec room. She looked at Ramsey and motioned for him to keep his eyes peeled in the room for that creature and Justin. She would take care of whatever this was.

The human form walked forward as Alex's light from her Fusion Rifle hit it. There was Sam, standing silently in the darkness. Or what was left of Sam. A hollowed-out head with black sludge for a brain. It slowly made its way forward, towards Alex, who stood watching it with her mouth agape.

"It's Sam!" Alex exclaimed to Ramsey.

Glancing back to Alex and then to the entity walking towards them, Ramsey could also see that it was indeed Sam. What was left of her. He immediately trained his gun on her.

"That's not Sam, Alex. Whatever this creature is that we're hunting changed her. I've seen this thing before, back on TSR. Whatever this parasite is, changes its victims at will. Through scratches or bites or, in this case, whatever that black slime is that's covering her body," Ramsey said back coldly.

Alex's hands were wet with nervous sweat. Her best friend was walking towards them. The woman who had been like a mother to her for many years. Who had saved her from the street life eight years ago. That Alex had recently seen get the back of her head literally ripped out of her body. Here she was, continuing her approach.

"Shoot it, now! Or I will!" Ramsey shouted.

The Fusion Rifle was on Alex's shoulder, aimed at Sam's head. Alex shook her head. *I can't do this!* she thought to herself.

"Shoot it!" Ramsey yelled again.

The Sam corpse was nearly on them. Moaning and reaching towards them, it suddenly broke into a run right at Alex.

Alex pulled the trigger and a flash of searing red light erupted from the Fusion Rifle, connecting with the running Sam right in her throat. Red and black blood erupted from the gaping hole in the center of her neck as she fell forward in front of Alex's feet.

The Sam creature writhed on the floor and a pool of blood formed around it. Gurgled noises coming from its mouth and the hole in its throat. It slowly raised its head to look at Alex with blank, black eyes as torrents of black and red fluid continued to run from the hole in its throat.

It reached for Alex's leg. She looked down sorrowfully at it, then over to Ramsey. "Why her? It took her life then changed her into that!?! Oh Sam, I'm sorry!" she cried out.

Ramsey calmly yet firmly said, "Finish her."

She looked at him with new tears in her eyes as he nodded back at her. She looked down at the pathetic creation at her feet bleeding out, raised her Fusion Rifle at its head, and fired.

Sam's head exploded, sending the slimy black goo that had infested the cranial cavity flying in little sprays over the back wall. Whatever had controlled Sam released its grip on her internal organs and limbs and went limp. Slowly the remaining black tar substance began seeping out of the body in front of them.

They both started backing up when a hiss emanated from behind them. They quickly turned to see the huge creature that had started this terror onboard the *Leo* rising up from the darkness of a corner wall behind a large couch. The creature sensed the end was coming to one of its creations and was furious. It still had Justin wrapped in its long tail and, with some difficulty, was bringing him forward to place him in front of its body once again.

Ramsey and Alex, seeing their one second window of opportunity, didn't hesitate and opened fire on the beast, hitting it directly in its black blood covered chest. It was knocked back and started to scream in anger and pain. It hadn't noticed that Justin had come to already back when it was in the corner waiting.

As the creature had moved forward to reveal itself, Justin was able to unsheathe the knife attached to his hip that Carol had given him back in the *Stormbringer*. And now it was possibly the only thing between him and certain death. His Fusion Rifle was gone.

If Justin had been woozy from the injuries sustained at the hands of this monstrosity that had him wrapped up in its tail, the heavy gunfire certainly brought him back completely to rational thinking and the awareness of his current, grave situation.

The shrill screams of the beast beside him were almost too much for Justin to take. His head was right beside the ghastly beast as it screamed in rage and what Justin assumed was also pain. And then there was the smell. It smelled like blood and rotting, rancid meat. So strong in fact, that on top of the screaming, Justin was fighting back vomiting due to the intense smell. He had to keep his wits about him. He knew he had one chance to make this work before either the creature killed him, or he got hit in the crossfire.

With all the strength he could muster, he raised his right arm and, clenching the long, sharp knife, plunged it into the creature's throat, then, ripping the knife out, plunged it in again, and again.

The beast howled in pain and surprise. In its infancy, it hadn't yet fully grasped human ingenuity and resilience. Black blood sprayed out of the large slices in its neck. It couldn't continue carrying Justin by its tail and dropped him to the ground.

Justin hit the ground hard, but didn't release the knife. Instead, he took the opportunity to drive the knife into the creature's foot. Fresh blood pumped out of the wound as it continued howling in pain and anger.

Ignoring the intense ringing in her ears, Alex screamed obscenities at the creature as she continued firing her Fusion Rifle. "Die you murderous sonofabitch bastard piece of shit!" Laser blasts pierced the tough outer skin of the creature as it finally crashed to the ground.

As it hit the ground, the creature's tail lashed out, connecting with Alex, sending her flying backwards in the air and landing with a thud next to her dead, headless captain. Ramsey reached down and pulled her up quickly, but not before they both noticed the black substance wasn't lying dormant on the ground, but seemed to be moving towards Alex.

Justin stumbled to his feet and was backing away from the creature on the floor writhing in pain. He walked over to Ramsey and Alex, who were looking from the creature to the black tar. They all started backing away from it as it poured out of the stump where Sam's head used to be and moved in their direction.

"You have got to be kidding me," Ramsey said, astonished at yet another dramatic turn of events.

The black blood then trickled past them and made its way over to the creature and joined with the blood on its own body from the knife wounds and laser blasts inflicted on it. The flowing blood from the wounds slowed once the new substance connected with it. And slowly began oozing into the blast holes and knife wounds.

"It's regenerating itself. We can't kill it this way. We've got to run. Now!" Justin yelled.

The creature leapt up from the ground and roared as it charged towards Justin, Alex and Ramsey, who had turned to run towards the door. It slid open as they dove out. Alex, thinking quickly, turned and hit the lock button on the wall as the door slid shut a second before the creature made it to the exit, slamming its heavy body against the sealed door.

Justin shouted at Alex and Ramsey through the ringing in his ears. "It's going to tear through that door, and when it does it will literally stop at nothing to change us into one of those things! We have probably a minute. *Stormbringer*, now. Ramsey, when we get there, arm the DPG. This is it. Survive then escape. That's the plan."

They took off down the hallway in the darkness towards the ladder that would lead them to level three, the cargo bay, and ultimately, the *Stormbringer*.

Alex looked at Justin as they hurried through the near darkness. "Why the hell did it let you survive?" she asked loudly over her still ringing ears.

"Yeah, I thought you were a goner," Ramsey said, out of breath as they hurried along.

Justin glanced at them both with eyes filled with anger at this offspring, this distant relative of a creation they had destroyed so recently. "I think it was attempting to use me as a shield from the guns. When it had used me up as a shield I would have been changed, like Sam. But its plan didn't work. And I intend to make sure it doesn't get another chance with myself or anyone else. Like its big brother, it's quite arrogant. But it's just learned that it can take hits and regenerate. That's bad news for us. Come on, let's get down to the cargo bay."

They looked down the ladder into the darkness leading to level three. From where they had come from, the sounds of claws ripping apart steel and furious high-pitched shrieks could be heard echoing through the long hallway.

"Go," Justin said firmly to both Alex and Ramsey, motioning for them to start the descent down as he stared off in the direction the noises came from.

CHAPTER 23

CARGO BAY BATTLE

Carol continued to crouch down against the metal beam by the large cargo bay outer hatch. She was glad that this room had the added hull integrity of the Damaris metal. Otherwise, some of the blasts from Danny Boy would have undoubtedly made their way through the ship, and goodbye oxygen.

She had horrible images run through her head as she waited in the darkness. Images of Hyzothan, the monstrous parasite that had all but decimated the population of the world through the black hole. Its sickly red eyes with the black line through them. It's massive, curved horns that jutted out from the sides of its head and then pointed straight down. The stuff of pure nightmares. Which is what her and her shipmates had indeed all experienced.

If the creature onboard the *Leo* were left to survive, would their dreams be infected? Back on Thunder Stone Realm, they thought this was over. The beast was destroyed. The brilliant, mysterious glowing stone that it had possessed had been freed from its clutches. They had escaped, but it had cost them their captain and the captain of the Earth vessel, the *E.E.S Saros*.

But that felt as though it happened years ago. Now, here in this large tomb that glowed red, she cowered in fear. Literally shaking from the fright. But she and her crewmates wouldn't give up. They had gotten this far. Unfortunately at the cost of these innocent people. *We brought that thing onboard with us!* she thought to herself as she waited for the inevitability of a gun battle to the death.

She had to push the guilt out of her mind. That would come later, she told herself. Now, she needed to survive. To see Justin once more. To know that Ramsey would survive as well as the spunky Alex. *I will not die on this ship!* she thought as she gripped the electron pistol tightly in her sweat covered hands while trying to get the nightmarish images out of her head as well as the pain from her throbbing, injured arm.

She heard the footsteps again. It was on the move once more. It was moving closer and closer. She had to act even though she couldn't make out where the recently re-animated Danny Boy was. Her foot slipped slightly on the floor as she tried repositioning herself to run in case she missed.

The footsteps ceased. And then it opened fire once more with the Fusion Rifle. Red streams of fire shot through the air, smashing into the large pole Carol was crouching behind.

The blasts illuminated her target just for a second, which was enough time for her to get several shots of her own off.

The first shot connected with Danny's chest, sending him flying backwards to the ground, dropping his Fusion Rifle. This was Carol's opportunity to finish it off. She stood up and rushed over to where Danny Boy lay in a growing pool of black and red blood. But he was already getting to his feet and making his way to the gun.

Carol raised her Electron Pistol and pulled the trigger. The thin beam of green colored laser fire connected with the Danny corpse's stomach, shooting through and out the other side. Black slime poured out of the fresh wound. It gurgled and tried to yell at her, but all that came out of its mouth was more blood.

Then, to Carol's surprise, it changed course and immediately lunged at her instead of continuing its path to the Fusion Rifle, landing on top of her and knocking her back down to the ground. The Danny monster had a large laser blast in its chest and now stomach. The hole on top of its head continued trickling out blood onto his face and over his black soulless eyes. At this point, what used to be Danny Boy now barely resembled anything human.

Carol was struggling to gain the upper hand. Danny Boy's state was not helping. He seemed to Carol like his insides and whole exterior had turned to a soft gelatinous mass. Her fingers didn't just push back on its shoulders, they sank into his shoulders. Skin pushing inwards. She couldn't feel bones. Only squishy, thick cartilage.

The dead body that had been Danny Boy had finally pinned Carol down, so she wasn't able to lift her electron pistol up to fire at it. It stared at her with its dead eyes, then opened its mouth. Black oozing slime started to drip forward from its mouth. The substance was moving on its own. As if searching for another host body, hers. She needed to get away or she would become one of these poor unfortunate lost souls herself.

Her right arm that was pinned down dragged across the cold, hard metal floor. Scraping her wound. The pain was throbbing. *Don't pass out. Don't pass out. Keep fighting, Carol!* She struggled against the unsightly cadaver.

It made a garbled sound as the black tar seeped out of its mouth towards her own. At this point, she had closed her mouth tightly. *What happened to Sam and Danny Boy will not happen to me. I won't let it!* She continued her struggle with the undead being pinning her down. It moved closer to her, and she felt like she had only seconds left before whatever was seeping out of its mouth would land on her face.

Justin, Ramsey and Alex had made their way down to level three, opting to slide down the ladder quickly instead of a hasty time-consuming climb. Helping them to move as fast as possible was the sound of metal being ripped open and the howls of the creature about to escape the rec room. Luckily, the ladder ended close to the decontamination room, and then the cargo bay.

All three began to sprint for the closed door. Alex got there first as the door slid open. She glanced over to make sure Ramsey and Justin were at her side. She noticed that Justin was unarmed so she quickly pulled out her Electron Pistol and handed it to him. "You need this more than I do," she said coolly, lifting her own Fusion Rifle.

Justin didn't hesitate and grabbed the gun then ran forward past Alex and Ramsey to find Carol. The light from the *Stormbringer* continued to illuminate the vast space more than other areas of the ship, but it wasn't much help in the furthest corners of the large room.

"Carol!" Justin yelled as he ran towards the *Stormbringer*.

Before they could reach the small ship in the middle of the cargo bay, the weak, injured voice of Carol cried out, "Justin, I'm here, help!"

"There!" Alex shouted, pointing in the corner of the cargo bay. Two forms were struggling on the ground. She began to run forward and noticed more blood on the floor.

Alex, Justin and Ramsey arrived at the two struggling bodies on the floor. In the dim red glow, they all could make out Danny Boy, covered in both red and black blood. A black, oozing parasite hung from its mouth, trying to latch itself onto Carol's face. It looked up at Alex with dead, black eyes and a large mass of black slime hanging from its mouth.

The connection was made quicky and Alex screamed in both horror and anger at yet another close friend, a brother, who had been turned into a walking, infectious corpse by the creature laying waste to the *Leo*. The shock of seeing Danny in this grotesque, sad state gave Alex pause. But not Justin and Ramsey. Both had raised their guns. It sensed its end was near, so it spat the parasitic mass from its mouth onto Alex, the closest to it.

Justin and Ramsey froze for a brief second, looking at Alex and the mass of black goo that had landed on her chest and was already moving on her shirt. It was spreading itself. Looking to work its way inside of her. The slime slid up her shirt, making its way to her mouth.

The corpse of Danny Boy had been so distracted by the three new entities in the room that it took its black eyes off of the person in front of it. Enough time for Carol to break free of its grip. She raised her Electron Pistol to its forehead and pulled the trigger.

Danny Boy's head evaporated into a mist of red and black. The headless body went limp and began to fall onto Carol, but Justin caught it and flung it off of her as black slime gushed out onto the floor when it landed.

Alex and Ramsey were trying to pull her shirt off before the slime got to her face. She was able to pull the shirt off, revealing a dirty sports bra underneath, but no black slime.

Ramsey grabbed the shirt and threw it towards the headless Danny Boy, landing on his stomach. The thick black liquid was oozing out of the body and was heading towards the four survivors.

"We need to burn it! That might be the only way to stop that stuff," Justin shouted.

Carol ran towards the *Stormbringer* and went inside. Alex looked at Ramsey and Justin with an almost panicked expression on her face. Ramsey, however, put his hand on her arm and asked softly, "Hey, you ok, Alex?"

Somewhat taken aback by this kind gesture, she paused for a second, looking at him, then replied, "Yes. Thanks. That stuff was heading for my face. It gets inside you and takes over your motor skills."

They all looked up towards the *Stormbringer* as Carol came running back out. "Here," she said, handing Justin the empty power cell container. Justin took it and looked at it. It was empty. Almost empty. A few residual drops remained in the power cell, stuck to the sides.

Nodding at Carol, Justin laid the power cell on the ground and rolled it over to where the dead Danny Boy lay with the shirt on top of him. Sticky black slime coupled with human blood had already soaked through Alex's old shirt, leaking out onto the floor.

Once the power cell reached the body, it clinked to a stop by his side. Justin held out the Electron Pistol Alex had just given him and glanced at his crewmates. "Head to the ship, now," he said with authority.

Still holding onto Alex's arm instinctively, Ramsey pulled her to the *Stormbringer*. Carol, however, hesitated. Justin sensed her hesitation and glanced at her. "I'm right behind you." Then he winked at her. She reached out and gave his hand a small squeeze.

Then, nodding her response, she began running back to the ship. Ramsey and Alex were standing in the opened hatch, waiting. "We have to open the outer hatch and plant the DPG. We're not out of this yet," Ramsey said grimly.

Justin began backing up, holding the Electron Pistol out in front of him. Then when he felt he was far enough out of the blast area, fired the gun. The power cell exploded, incinerating the body that it had landed against. Igniting it into flames, including the black blood that had been trickling outward.

The initial blast knocked Justin onto his back on the floor. He started to get up, keeping his eyes on the burning flesh on the floor. Nothing moved.

He stood back up and headed to the *Stormbringer*. "Time to leave. Ramsey, we need to set that grenade's timer and then open the cargo bay. Alex, how many space suits are on this level?

"One spare. There had been four, but the other three are up on level one. Might as well be on another spacecraft," Alex said cynically as she shook her head.

"Here's the plan, everyone. I'm going to the decontamination room and will get into the space suit. Then I'll open the outer hatch from in here. If I make a sprint for the ship, I should be able to make it and get inside before too much oxygen escapes. You three will have to be strapped in. There'll be a mighty strong gust that will try to pull you out once I open the *Stormbringer's* hatch."

At once Carol began to protest. "Not again! Always you!"

"She's right. Justin, I've got this, ok?" Ramsey said. Then he added, "You barely made it out of that creature's grasp. You were literally unconscious not long ago. I've got the DPG, so I'll go and set it as soon as I get that space suit on."

Justin contemplated this and looked at Ramsey. "You're my responsibility. I don't want you to have to do this. But I know you can. You sure about this?"

Ramsey nodded quickly in reply and was about to head out when Alex leaned over to him, her mouth so close to his ear he could feel her warm breath as she whispered, "Last name is Tilly. Alex Tilly, ok hotshot? Hurry back."

He looked at her and raised his eyebrow, then smiled, nodded and ran out towards the cargo bay door exit to the level three hallway.

While Alex and Carol watched Ramsey head to the cargo bay exit door, inside the *Stormbringer*, on their radar system, three small red blinking dots were moving rapidly towards the *Leo*.

Ramsey hurried to the exit door and when he got there, it slid open, revealing, in all its furious glory, the beast. The black blood that had oozed out of the gun blasts had retracted back inside of it. Its full strength was nearly restored, and it was ready to strike.

It opened its enormous mouth and bellowed in anger at seeing one of its foes again, as well as seeing another one of its own creations burning to ashes in the corner of the room. Its fiery red eyes going from the burnt corpse of Danny Boy over to Ramsey. Thick saliva dripped from its hungry teeth, its tongue flicking inside the gaping mouth.

Ramsey's eyes widened. He heard Alex and Carol shout out to him. The creature grabbed him by his sides and lifted him in the air. Just as quickly, Justin, who was about to enter his ship, bounded out of the *Stormbringer*, grabbing Danny Boy's dropped Fusion Rifle off of the ground nearby and, running over towards the beast, opening fire with the Fusion Rifle aiming at its legs. The blasts ripped through its sticky tough chameleon-like skin, still showing red and black to blend in with its immediate surroundings.

Justin began focusing on one of its legs, continuing to fire. The beast shrieked and threw Ramsey at Justin, who landed on top of him, knocking both to the ground. Ramsey immediately slid back, trying to escape the creature's grasp. Justin, still on the ground, was firing once more at it.

The beast had stumbled back into the long hallway, unable to make progress forward with Justin, now back on his feet, Fusion Rifle in hand, continuing to fire on it. Back in the *Stormbringer*, Alex and Carol were shouting and beginning to run to their help.

Then, a huge shudder on the *Leo* knocked everyone except the creature down to the ground. Almost as if the ship was hit with a laser cannon blast from outside.

CHAPTER 24

SECOND WAVE ATTACK

Violent shockwaves rippled through the cargo bay, which made attacking Justin difficult for the creature. Ramsey had gotten to his feet and was behind Justin, yelling at him, "We've got to get to the *Stormbringer!* We're being attacked from outside. Probably Reaper reinforcements!"

Yelling over his shoulder, Justin said in reply, "Cargo bay is closed, and that creature is in our way! I think more of those Reapers were called in as reinforcements! We can't get off this ship with that outer hatch closed!"

Justin continued firing at the creature who was now backed into the hallway, but was able to avoid the blasts due to how shaky and off target the shots were. He continued pushing it back, hoping to drive it and himself out into the hallway, sealing it shut and opening the cargo bay. But now they had even more trouble to contend with.

"Give me the grenade, Ramsey!" Justin yelled urgently.

"Why? What are you going to do?" he yelled back.

"Just give it to me. That's an order!"

Ramsey unclipped the explosive device from his side and handed it to Justin.

Carol and Alex had run up and were close to Ramsey and saw Justin take possession of the DPG.

Carol yelled out, "No! Justin, what are you doing!?"

Justin looked back at her with a look of desperation across his face and yelled back, "Giving you all a fighting chance! Get to the *Stormbringer*, now. I love you, Carol!"

Before she had a chance to catch up to him, the cargo bay door slid shut behind Justin as she ran forward towards it. Locking it behind him. He reached over and hit the *Open Cargo Bay Hatch* button on the wall.

The creature ran forward at him, but Justin was faster. He raised the Fusion Rifle and hit it squarely in the face with a close-range laser blast. Black tar for blood splattered on the walls as it screamed in pain, knocking it backwards. He continued firing, pushing the creature further back into the hallway until it was past the decontamination room. He armed the small grenade by entering 927, then set it for sixty seconds. He quickly entered the room as the door slid shut behind him.

As quickly as he could, Justin ran to the lockers, opening each one until he found one with the space suit. He set his gun down then ripped the suit out of the locker and hastily started putting it on

In the cargo bay, the air was being sucked out. They had only a few precious seconds remaining before being sucked out into space. Ramsey grabbed Carol and dragged her screaming back into the *Stormbringer* with Alex already inside. The air pressure was being sucked out of the cargo bay, as was as the *Stormbringer*. As soon as they were inside, Ramsey hit the button on the side wall and watched their ship's hatch slide shut.

Once the hatch was closed the air was restored in the ship. Carol was pounding on the door. Furious at what was happening. Looking over at Alex, Ramsey said, "I've got to get us out of here. Help her."

Alex rushed to Carol's side as Ramsey took the pilot's seat. "Zark, everything ready to go?"

The cool, calming voice of the ship's A.I. responded, "Systems operational. Outer hull integrity compromised, 10% hull structure remaining. Rear landing gear damaged."

"Well, then let's not get hit," he muttered to himself as he lifted the damaged ship up off the ground and pulled back on the steering yoke and the *Stormbringer* slid with a low hum backwards and breached the exit of the *Leo* out into space.

The DPG went off right beside the creature. Sending pieces of it everywhere. The creature took nearly all of the brunt of the grenade when it exploded. It shrieked in pain as it dragged itself away, further into the darkness.

Back inside the decontamination room, Justin heard the explosion as he hastily finished putting the suit on and latching in the helmet. By his estimation they were close enough to the space port now that Ramsey, with some slick piloting, could get them to safety if they could avoid whatever was out there shooting at them. He grabbed the Fusion Rifle that he had swapped out his Electron Pistol for, slinging it over his shoulder, and ran out of the room, not sure what to expect from the damage done by the DPG. When the door slid open, the creature was gone. Only black blood and sickly entrails remained on the floor where it had received the brunt force of the DPG.

"It either completely exploded or it's gone to heal itself again, then hide. Good luck with that. I'm taking you down," Justin said to himself quietly as he made his way to the emergency stairway once again and began climbing up to level one as fast as his arms and legs could take him.

As quickly as he could, once the *Stormbringer* was outside the *Leo*, Ramsey circled the ship around to face whatever was firing at them. Two more Reaper ships were quickly approaching. They had been firing long range in the hopes of quickly taking down the *Leo*. Now they had another ship to contend with.

Alex looked at Carol, who was sobbing. "Look, I barely know you. But we are in survival mode here. We need your help! Please! Ramsey needs you. I have no clue how this thing operates!"

Carol attempted to compose herself, looking at Alex while wiping away tears. She headed to the front of the ship, sitting down next to Ramsey. "What are we up against?" she asked, trying to get herself focused.

"Two Reapers, bearing down on us. We can't take any hits, Carol, so hang on. Alex, strap in!" Ramsey yelled.

Quickly sitting down in an empty seat, she latched herself just in time, and Ramsey pushed up on the steering yoke, sending the *Stormbringer* rocketing straight up and out of the blast zone of the Reapers.

One Reaper ship ascended, chasing after them, while the other ship continued on its course to intercept the *Leo*. Laser fire erupted around the crew of the *Stormbringer* as Ramsey swerved the ship from left to right, avoiding the blasts from the Reaper in pursuit.

"Up there. I'm heading towards those several large meteors. Hopefully I can figure something out," Ramsey yelled at Carol and Alex, who were both clinging to their armrests as the ship careened back and forth.

Justin climbed up the stairs through the levels on his way to level one. This was even more difficult with a cumbersome space suit on, but he had no other options. He needed to get to the command center.

The bloodied creature had waited for Justin to leave level three. Then it slid back to where much of its black blood and entrails lay. *How can this be?* it thought. It was near death. It had to hide and recover. The organs and life blood of the creature slowly slid into its open wounds and began reconstructing themselves. This was good. However, the creature realized that it was mortal. It could die. It almost died at the hands of this worthless entity that still somehow continued to evade it and survive.

Once it had rebuilt itself, it retreated to the second level to further heal. The continual laser blasts and especially the explosion had brought it to the brink of its own demise, but it survived. It had made its way to the corpse of Sam, still laying in the rec room. It quickly picked up the headless corpse and began to eat it in large bites. Black tar poured out of the limbs it ripped off as it stuffed them into its mouth. This food was also revitalizing the creature significantly. It was once more learning. It could heal on its own slowly, but with meat such as this, the healing increased substantially. Then it heard something down the hallway. Not whatever was making the ship reverberate outside. *This must be that human!* it thought.

With new strength, it ran out of the room and saw him climbing at the end of the hallway. *I see you, and now you will die!* It thought as the silhouette of the human passed by, climbing up the ladder. It lunged forward, bounding towards the ladder with the black tar-like substance dripping from its mouth.

Justin passed by level two and was continuing heading up the ladder when the creature swiped out at him from the hallway of level two, narrowly missing his leg. The sight of the creature made Justin climb faster. He had to reach the command center on level one. It was a last-ditch chance of survival.

Ramsey continued zig zagging, avoiding the Reaper in pursuit. He had reached the meteors several clicks out from the *Leo* and rocketed for the largest one of the five that were floating in space.

"There. My scan shows that hole has an exit on the other side of this meteor. It's small, though." Carol pointed out of the viewscreen at a hole in the large meteor. Ramsey shot down and flew into the hole with the Reaper in pursuit. The hole was indeed small, and looked to be getting even narrower the further in it went.

"Not good, not good, not good!" Alex said louder and louder the narrower the tunnel got.

"Hang on!" Ramsey said as he pushed forward, rocketing the *Stormbringer* even faster through the tunnel.

Behind them, the Reapers opened fire. Laser blasts erupted around them as Ramsey pulled up on the yoke, seeing the tunnel take a sharp turn upward. A split second later and they would have smashed into the rocky surface of the meteor.

The Reaper wasn't as lucky. The ship pulled up as quickly as it could, but smashed into the side interior wall of the meteor and was obliterated into a ball of flames.

Ramsey flew out the other side of the meteor. The *Storm-bringer* had narrowly fit through the exit. "Woohoo!" Ramsey shouted to Carol and Alex. "You see that? That's right. You want to go toe to toe with me, you better pack your lunch, because you're gonna be here all day!"

"What in the bloody hell does that mean?" Alex replied back to him, laughing to herself.

Glancing over at her, Ramsey replied with a smirk, "Something I used to say to my opponents in the ring before a fight to psych them out."

"Did it work?" she replied back, curiously amused at this little phrase.

Ramsey tilted his head contemplating for a second before saying, "fifty-fifty."

Alex grinned and shook her head.

"Let's head back to the *Leo*. Maybe we can draw that other Reaper's attention away," Carol said restlessly.

"Carol, I think…" Ramsey started to say.

"Please, please. We need to try to help Justin."

Ramsey glanced at her, then to Alex. Alex shook her head sadly.

They rounded the meteor and saw the *Leo* in the distance. And the Reaper that had positioned itself below the ship, firing upwards. The bottom rear half of the *Leo* burst into flames as a large blast emanated from the hole the Reaper had just created. The ship slowly veered off course, with debris trailing from it into space.

Ramsey hung his head as Carol let out a gasp and a small scream. Quietly, Ramsey replied to what was unfolding in front of them. "We need to get to that space port. We got lucky. This ship is literally one minor misstep away from becoming space dust. Justin gave us the chance we needed. The *Leo* is done for. We certainly can't try to re-board. Look, the cargo bay has literally been vaporized. It's gone! My guess is that if Justin hasn't used it yet, he's going to destroy the rest of the ship with that DPG, along with the creature on board. That thing can absolutely not make its way onto any populated planet. Hell, it can't survive for any reason. You know as well as I do what it is and its origins."

"Not my Justin. Not him. All of this madness and now whatever that thing is that lives inside that black hole has killed the only man I have ever had feelings for and has killed all of Alex's crew." She shook her head in despair. Trying to come to grips with how things were unfolding.

Alex hung her head, not knowing how to respond.

They watched the *Leo*, the bottom of it engulfed in flames, drifting off, no longer on a plotted course. The Reaper, however, had spotted them and was turning to pursue.

"We need to go, now." Alex pointed at the Reaper ship turning to make off towards them.

Ramsey glanced at Carol, bitter tears streaming down her face. Without looking back at him, she nodded. Ramsey punched the accelerator on the *Stormbringer* and blasted upwards once again at full power.

The Reaper, as quick as it was, was no match for the engineering of a Trilaxian ship, even if it was a small escape pod. The *Stormbringer* pulled further and further away from it until it was out of sight.

"Those ships aren't normally used for long range space travel. It'll return to Darmus III and let them know the *Leo* was destroyed. They don't know this ship and have no way of tracking it at this point. Honestly, they will probably forget about it soon. They got their Marks and their weapons, then destroyed the ship that it was stolen from. A small, damaged escape ship like this probably means little to them. Let's just hope they don't want to further tie up any loose ends, I hate the Cambulons," Alex muttered.

"So, what's next? I need a bit of medical assistance for my arm," Carol grumbled, getting her emotions back under control.

"Space port. We make sure the coast is clear and there are no more Reapers there. Park the *Stormbringer* and get some much-needed help," Ramsey replied softly. Alex and Carol both nodded their agreement with the plan as Carol plotted a course for the space port under several hours away from their current location in space. The ship rocketed towards its next destination.

CHAPTER 25

SURVIVAL INSTINCTS

Justin made it to the command center. The door slid open as he rushed in, locking it behind him. "Ok, that buys me some time. If what Sam told Carol is accurate, this door should hold fast against that thing's claws," Justin mused quietly to himself.

He hurried over to the pilot's seat, awkwardly sitting down with his space suit on and looking over the ship's schematics. Warning lights were blinking all over the ship. Hull breaches in numerous spots from the creature on board burrowing through the hull, but that was minor compared to new damage from what most likely were Reapers attacking. Justin couldn't be sure.

"Ok, good news is that I don't see any more ships out there. Good job, Ramsey." He continued looking over the ship's layout grid, trying to figure it out. He knew the ship did not have an actual speaking A.I. system, which made it much more difficult to work through problems. Of which there were many.

Turning a knob near the bottom of the control panel, the screen zoomed in, and he was able to see the main structural damage on the underside of the *Leo*. It was significant. This ship was going down or would ultimately be lost in space.

The ship had run out of fuel from being continually pushed at maximum speed, and while it was relatively close to the space port, it wouldn't make it. Justin looked over the star map. "Come on, come on! Give me something!" he said tensely into his helmet, which he had contemplated removing, but thought it best to keep on with how things were continuing to go from bad to worse.

There it was, over to the left of the viewscreen. Thakitune. The planet that Willie had mentioned earlier. Significantly closer than the space port. Close enough, in fact, that if he could breach the planet's atmosphere, he might get lucky and survive the crash.

"First, let's take care of the oxygen on this ship, shall we? Make it a little bit harder for you to breathe," he muttered, thinking about the creature lurking on level two or possibly one by now.

The oxygen seemed to be stable even with the huge blast on the underside. Luckily the blast had missed the engine room and server room, but the cargo bay was gone. The door to the cargo bay had been closed, so currently, even with the ship in severely bad shape, oxygen levels remained breathable on all three levels, but the fire was spreading on level three, fueled by the oxygen.

It was only a matter of time until the fire hit the engine room, and once it got to the last remaining power cell, this ship would be obliterated. There was a *purge oxygen* switch for each level. Probably as a safety measure in case something drastic happened in the engine room to avoid a fire. Well, too late for that. *But that creature needs oxygen, and I need to get the fire extinguished,* Justin thought.

Justin hit the switch on all three levels. Even with his space suit on, he felt the air begin to rush out of the vents in the command center. The oxygen level readout on the screen in front of him began dropping on each floor of the *Leo.* Alarms began sounding through the ship.

Once that process had begun, Justin looked over the screen and quickly figured out how to plot a course. The controls on this ship were archaic and far less advanced than the Trilaxian ships. The good news for Justin, however, was the ease with which an old freighter such as the *Leo* could be piloted. Even when the ship was in duress.

Selecting the new destination as the planet Thakitune, the ship, which had run out of fuel, was still able to maneuver through space on its forward momentum. And now it glided forward on its new course towards Thakitune. Looking out of the viewscreen in front of him, the planet loomed large. Although it was a relatively small planet. No larger than an orbiting moon.

Justin quickly accessed the files on Thakitune. Green lettering appeared on the screen in front of him, stating the planet's surface was 25.5 million miles. It was primarily made of iron, magnesium, aluminum, calcium, and potassium. The surface consisted of dormant volcanoes, meteoric impacts, windstorms, and crustal movement causing quakes. Surprisingly, it had many small streams running through its tough outer crust, as well as several large bodies of water, though it was unclear if it was drinkable.

"Water!" Justin exclaimed, glad for this small bit of good fortune. Where there was water, there could potentially be some signs of life. Although the *Leo* wasn't able to pick that information up. The atmosphere consisted of low amounts of oxygen and nitrogen, as well as small amounts of other gases, including traces of argon and carbon dioxide. The readout claimed breathable air was minimal, however, one could potentially survive for a short period.

Justin stared at the screen. Breathable air. This planet had oxygen. Even at dangerously low amounts, the air could be breathed. And he had a space suit with air and possibly the two other suits that Sam and Alex had. If he could get those oxygen tanks as well… but that was a long shot, and he didn't intend to leave the command center unless he had to. He wondered if he could cycle the planet's air through the suit's oxygen tank and potentially make it last significantly longer. It would certainly be a way to survive a bit longer. If he even survived a crash landing. Or the creature didn't get to him first.

Next, he looked at the readout for temperatures on Thakitune. Daytime temperatures averaged 50 degrees Fahrenheit, but plummeted at night down to minus 60 degrees. "I can work with that, especially with a space suit," he said, studying the screen.

The alarms continued in the ship. Looking down, Justin saw that the oxygen levels were now at 20%. "Good. I hope you choke out there," Justin said coldly.

Outside of the *Leo*, in outer space, was the glorious sight of the ship expunging oxygen as well as fire being extracted and floating away. Both life giving and life taking elements glided silently into the icy cold vacuum of space.

The creature had finished off Sam's corpse as it continued healing. Bones and small bits of internal organs were all that remained of the once great but troubled captain of the *Leo*. The black tar that had controlled her body was now flowing once again through its master's own bloodstream. Instinctively, it knew as it grew larger and produced more of its black blood, it could easily make more of the beings like the two unfortunate souls it had murdered and transformed on this ship. Three, counting the man it had initially infected.

It needed a place to hide. Even if it would take years. Centuries, decades. It needed to wait. To learn. And then strike. It was too vulnerable right now. The weapons these animals used hurt it and could, after being subjected to their explosive devices and laser fire long enough, possibly kill it. In the short time it had lived, it had learned much. Learned what it was capable of in this current stage of its evolution. But it needed off this ship.

It sensed its breathing was becoming difficult. Which set the creature into a near panic. *I must find a breathable source or escape this vessel!* it thought to itself as it crawled up through the hole it had made earlier from level one to level two in the mess hall.

The ship continued gliding towards the planet Thakitune's atmosphere. The fire extinguished from the oxygen being sucked out into space, but the *Leo* remained in one piece, and its two inhabitants would soon meet gravity below. Justin noted that the planet was a sandy tan color, and already from space thin lines of blue could be spotted along with circles of larger blue water masses. This planet's nearest sun was 2.9 billion kilometers away. Luckily the star in this solar system was quite large and produced more sunlight and heat to the more distant planets in the HD-6549 quadrant.

"Come on…come on, get me to the atmosphere already!" Justin said to himself as he shook sweat from his brow inside the helmet. The air was nearly depleted off of the ship entirely. Smoke had seeped through ventilation and now covered much of levels two and three. *That thing must be here on level one now, trying to find breathable air.* Then he began hearing claws on the command center door, followed by shrieks of anger. The beast had indeed arrived at level one once again. But this time without the luxury of oxygen.

The creature was growing more and more desperate by the second, as breathing was nearly impossible. It smashed against the command center door, but the door would not budge. The ship was shaking more and more, and smoke was slowly wafting upwards to level three now. It wouldn't die this way, not now that its healing process was still working through its body. It frantically searched for a solution.

It was realizing that it was pointless to bang on the command center door. In its weakening state it was unable to claw through any metal, much less this far more durable compound that comprised this particular entrance. The creature bounded back down the long hallway, looking for something, anything to survive. Its long tail whipped back and forth with nervous energy. Its outer skin now took on a sickly grey tone, making it blend in with the smoke that had accumulated heavily throughout the ship.

At the very rear of the ship on the top level, it burst into the makeshift science lab which consisted of several small tables, and a significant number of bottles filled with liquids and other compounds. The room looked as though it was rarely used. Other supplies littered the messy area. Surgical instruments, several tools for machinery and first aid items.

One thing that did catch the creature's gleaming red eyes was a large silver tank in the far corner of the room that was attached to the ship itself. In black lettering on the outside of the tank, it read, *Water Filtration System*. The creature quickly looked over the sizable tank. It crouched down then leapt up, landing on the very top of the unit. It was sturdy and thick. Capable of handling the creature's weight.

It peered down at the large round hatch and quickly figured out this device could be turned and then simply lifted up. The creature's tongue slithered in its mouth. Sensing this could be the very thing that would shield it from the smoke and lack of air.

The round hatch opened up with a hiss. Inside was clear liquid. The creature's eyesight was quite good. Much better than the prey it had been stalking since its birth aboard the starship. Through its eyes the liquid shone as a gentle shade of blue. It plunged its head into the liquid to see what would happen, as this was something foreign to it up to this point.

The water filled its gaping tooth filled mouth and plunged down its throat. For a second, the feeling of drowning, another new sensation for it, filled its mind. But that soon passed. It realized it could breathe in this liquid. Thin slits had opened on the creature's thick neck as water pumped through them.

Thrilled with this new discovery and able to knowingly prolong its existence, it plunged the rest of the way into the cool liquid. It sensed that the ship it was traveling on was now doomed. However, this tank gave it newfound hope of survival. And its survival was the only thing that mattered. It must live. Its master inside the black hole had plans for it.

Its large claw hand reached out of the water, grabbing the round hatch, and brought it down on top of the tank.

Back in the command center, the readout for oxygen levels was now at 5%. It might as well have been 0%. Nothing could live onboard without assisted oxygen tanks like the one he was wearing. Justin hoped that one of his hurdles for survival was over. The death of the creature. He had been quite nervous when it was clawing and banging on the command center door, but the door had held fast.

"Thank you, Sam's dad. Whatever your name was. You just extended my life a little bit longer there," Justin mused to himself as he tried to control his breathing in the space suit.

Warning alarms continued to go off throughout the ship due to the loss of oxygen. However, Justin had noted that the fire was now under control. Better yet, it was nearly extinguished. That wouldn't make the ship flyable at this point, but it was at least not going to rupture the power cell that remained in the engine room.

The ship was ready to hit Thakitune's atmosphere. If it was a bumpy ride before, it was going to get a whole lot worse in a matter of minutes. *This is it. Time to see if I can crash land this thing.* As the ship hit the atmosphere, Justin centered his mind on Carol, hoping she was ok. Missing her dearly right now, but glad she wasn't next to him on this possible one-way ticket to instant destruction on the surface below.

"I hope you're not worrying about me, baby. You just need to survive," he said out loud in the lonely ship plummeting towards the light brown rocky planet now engulfing the viewscreen in front of him.

CHAPTER 26

THE SPACE PORT

The *Stormbringer* and her small crew continued on its trajectory towards the space port in the HD-6549 quadrant, which was now visible in the distance. The space port had a large circular center with plenty of windows around the top portion of it. It had four total ports that jutted out around the space station itself. A long and wide walkway connected to oval shaped docking bays where ships could land. Depending on the design of the ship, there were also ports on the sides of the oval docking bays that ships could connected with and then disembark from into the inner hull of the walkways leading into the main space port itself.

In extreme cases of ship duress there was one more docking station located near the bottom of the large orb shaped center. If the approaching ship had life threatening damage, it was granted access to the interior space port immediately, where a doctor was on hand, usually.

Alex had informed Ramsey and a quiet Carol that there would be a decontamination chamber and showers upon arrival. Also, this was considered a significantly smaller space port and that many of them in more populated regions of the galaxy could house up to twelve ships. This was an older one, and thus was showing significant signs of wear from being in outer space for many years. Its color was grey, but it had taken on more of a dirty grey from what they could all gather from inside the *Stormbringer*.

Staffing on this particular space port was minimal. They lived on the space station itself, which was the large center orb. Alex guessed that there would be a maximum of ten people and as little as four or five, possibly even less. Enough to take care of the lone, random spacecrafts that needed minor repairs until better, more well-equipped mechanics could arrive. Typically, there were small rooms for space travelers to bunk down for a night or two. Food was minimal and usually prepared by a short order cook that primarily took care of the onboard staff's meals.

All that mattered was that they could get off the *Stormbringer* and figure out their next move. Primarily, where were Ramsey and Carol going to go? Their home world was destroyed 100 years ago. Their acting captain, gone. Tough decisions were going to have to be made, but for now, a shower, food and a bed was what they all needed, even if they wouldn't admit it.

Ramsey had noted that all of the food rations were gone as his stomach rumbled. *Most likely eaten by the creature that was birthed inside this ship's hull,* he thought but refrained from saying out loud.

Most of the flight was met with silence from all three of them. Alex relived the past twenty-four hours while Ramsey and Carol quietly played back events from their abrupt wake-up in the hibernation tubes leading up to this point. So much loss. So much murder. So much evil, including the bloodshed smeared on the walls inside the small *Stormbringer*. Enough to last several lifetimes. Too much for any single person to ever have to endure.

"Space port docking procedures commencing," Zark said calmly to its crew.

"I can only see two of the docking bays. I assume the other two are on the opposite side?" Ramsey asked, glancing over at an exhausted Alex.

"Yep," she replied flatly.

"Zark, any other ships docked on the other side?" he asked.

"No ships detected on any of the four space port docking stations."

Carol, looking wearily at Alex, asked in as nice a voice as she could muster, "I'll be in need of some assistance with my arm."

Nodding in reply, Alex looked over at her and felt sorry. Even though she herself had lost so much in less than a day, her captain, her friends, the Marks and the *Leo*, she still felt terrible for what these people had also endured. Far more than she had.

"This is Space Port 771, HD-6549 quadrant. State your full name, cargo and reason for docking clearance," a cold voice patched through on the *Stormbringer's* com system.

Ramsey looked over at Alex and Carol. "Pleasant sounding fellow," he said sarcastically.

In the co-pilot's seat, Carol looked on as the space port loomed large on their screen. Behind it, distant planets she had never seen before, some with rings and some multi-colored. It made her think of the distant solar system where TSR1 was located.

"Space Port 771, please report back with requested information before docking procedures," the monotone voice said once more, agitated at the lack of a response from the approaching ship.

Ramsey sat upright in his seat, which made Alex smile. Clearing his throat and without thinking, Ramsey spoke in a clear voice, "This is Ramsey Connor of the Trilaxus spacecraft *Stormbringer* coming from quadrant 8478. Cargo is myself and two other passengers. One Alex Tilly and one Carol Blake. Requesting permission to dock for landing gear and outer hull repair and hopefully some food and bunks for the night." He paused, then added, "Or nights."

A long pause, then the voice on the other end spoke once more in the same monotone voice, but this time with a hint of curiosity, "We ran Trilaxus through our databank. That planet hasn't existed for 100 years. How can there be a ship still floating around out there that's 100 years old?"

"Long story. We can chat about it over drinks and food. So yeah, do we have permission to dock?" Ramsey came back, trying to hide his impatience.

"Ok, fine. Docking bay one. But don't expect us to have the right tools to fix up a 100-year-old obsolete spacecraft. From the looks of it in my seat, that thing's had it." The clicking sound of his com turning off echoed inside the *Stormbringer*.

"I'll show you obsolete," Ramsey muttered under his breath.

"I already have a mental image of whoever that voice belongs to. And I don't like him," Alex said coldly, staring ahead at the space port continuing to grow closer in their viewscreen.

Carol had been keeping quiet for most of the trip to the space port, due to the pain in her arm, the loss of Justin, and the enormity of everything that everyone around them had gone through. She finally added to the conversation, trying to keep her tone as upbeat as she could muster. "A warm bed and food. Never thought I would look this forward to the simple things. That and this arm. Wow, do I need a right proper doctor to help me out with it. I'm just glad we're here, all things considered."

Ramsey reached over and put his hand on her back, then gave it several gentle pats. He was at a loss for words for all of them. All the pain and loss. She looked over at him as he nodded at her, saying softly, "I can't tell you that it's going to be all right, Carol. That's not what you or any of us want to hear, I'm sure. But I can tell you that we're gonna push through regardless, ok?"

She nodded her agreement as Alex looked softly at him and his consoling words. She had known this man for a short period of time, but found him to be funny, soft hearted and quite attractive even in his haggard state.

The *Stormbringer*, piloted by Ramsey, glided into the first docking bay. Because of its damaged landing gear, the ship pulled up to the right side of the landing pad. Sure enough, there was a dirty white colored synthetic umbilical attachment waiting to connect with their hatch.

Ramsey slowed the ship to a stop as the arm on the space dock extended and the connection was made via a suction cup-like arm. A hissing sound was made outside the ship followed by the same man inside the space port once more giving orders.

With a sigh, the voice stated, "Ok, connection established. Oxygen levels stable in the umbilical arm. Once inside, proceed to decontamination chambers and follow instructions. Oh, one other thing. All weapons are to remain onboard your ship for the duration of your stay. There's a weapons scanner in each walkway into the space port, so don't even try it or you can turn right around and go back to wherever you came from. Welcome aboard Space Port 771." And with that welcome, the com clicked off once again, not waiting for a response.

"This should be a rip-roaring good time had by all. Come on, let's get off the *Stormbringer*. Not a fan of leaving the few weapons we still have onboard," Ramsey said, very irritated as he stood up and opened the hatch.

Alex nodded her agreement as her and Carol got up out of their seats and the three of them made their way through the extended space walkway on their way to the space port entry door. The walkway consisted of a thick, flexible white material that quite obviously was strong enough to connect to ships and withstand the emptiness of deep space although it looked as though it should have been replaced many years earlier.

They made their way through the tunnel, which indeed had weapons sensor detection lights on the side walls that remained green. Once they got to the entrance, the door slid open. Walking inside, they were met with darkness for a brief second before automatic lights kicked on. The door slid shut behind them as they walked forward towards the far wall that had a sign with instructions on it for gaining further entry.

"Welcome to Space Port 771 in the HD-6549 quadrant. Thank you for choosing us for your space travel needs. Please proceed forward for decontamination. If fresh clothes are needed, please see one of our friendly staff, and they will be happy to help you out in any way they can. Please note that all ship repairs, fueling, clothing, bedding, food, and drink supplies have pricing listed on forms one of our staff will supply if requested. Consider this before making any purchases."

"Blah, blah, blah," Alex said coldly at the smug sign in front of them.

"Come on, let's get this over with. I went through decontamination literally hours ago," Ramsey grumbled.

They moved to the next room and were surprised to see a choice between light green and white tee shirts and plain, grey pants that were offered at no cost. "Well, that's finally something pleasant, I suppose," Carol said bemusedly.

They each went into individual stalls for a quick decontamination spray. Once dressed, they made their way out of the large gray room and were met with a long flight of steps.

"No elevator?" Ramsey asked Alex, surprised.

"We're literally at the ass end of the solar system. Be glad this dump even exists. I can't wait to see our sleeping arrangements. That'll be rich," Alex said sarcastically as she stuffed her hands in her pockets on their way up the steps.

They made their way up the steps and through the door that slid open upon their arrival. At the end of the room was a man sitting behind a desk with several computer monitors in front of him. He looked up and motioned them forward.

The three of them walked towards the desk as the man eyed them up and down. "Wow, even with showers you three look like you've been through some hell," he said in a surprisingly pleasant voice. This was obviously not the individual they had spoken with briefly when they were arriving.

Ramsey responded quickly before Alex had a chance to say something that might get the man behind the desk to put his defenses up. "Thanks for the clothes. Our spacecraft is in serious need of repairs. Primarily the landing gear. The hull is a mess as well. On top of that, my friend here needs some medical assistance for her arm, and all three of us are hungry."

The man leaned back in his chair, looking them over while holding a small can that he spit some sort of greenish slime into that he was chewing on. "And my name is Ian Michaels. Just call me Ian. We can get you fed and housed for a bit. I've never seen a ship like that, and if I haven't, I can damn well guarantee our mechanic on duty hasn't either. However, we can get a specialist in. I know a guy. He's good. Can fix that thing up no problem. It'll cost ya, of course, but you'll be well on your way."

"Well, see, that's the problem," Alex said. "We don't have any Marks, currently. I mean, we did have some. A shit ton actually. But they were stolen. And then our freighter was taken over by an alien creature that killed half the crew. We managed to get off of it barely in one piece. And here we are. So, Marks and all that bullshit, we don't have. One night. Just give us a night to collect ourselves, get a little sleep and figure out our next plan. Because right now the only plan we got is us standing right here," Alex said forcefully but with enough pleading in her voice to make Ian take note.

Ian leaned back in his chair, spitting once again into his cup that was half filled with the green tobacco he was gnawing on. His long, greasy black hair pulled back in a ponytail and thin beard made his thin face seem much fuller. The man was skinny and even at an average height of 5 foot 8 inches, seemed much shorter due to his frail physique. He scratched his beard, then adjusted a dirty button-down white shirt several sizes too large that hung on his frame, looking up at Alex, contemplating how to respond.

"Look, it's just me and my brother Rex. He makes the food around here and could probably help you out with that injured arm of yours there," Ian said, pointing at Carol's badly injured arm.

"And then there's the resident hard ass, Judson, he's the mechanic. When I say we rarely get anyone out here, I do mean that. Most company we get is the supply drop offs every few months. There used to be more staff but out here, but there ain't nothing happening anymore. Used to be a trade route that ran through here that brought us more customers, but that route was changed up due to that damn dead star out there. Far enough from us, but close enough to chase away anyone with half a brain. So, we basically get the riff-raff of the solar system."

He paused, looking them over, then continued, "Anyway, look…if I let you guys crash here without paying, then the next broken-down ship will be requesting the same. I can get you a mechanic, shouldn't take too long, but we gotta get paid. Hey, here's an idea. You could ask the fellas that are here already. Made us park 'em in the main hub. They said they can pay immediately for repairs. Said they're gonna wait here until a small transport shuttle comes to pick one of 'em up. The other fella, nasty piece of work. He's staying behind to get his ship fixed. Jud's working on it now."

Alex was looking at Ramsey, who was looking at Carol. Connections were being made between them with this new bit of news. "Go on," Carol said in as calm a voice as she could muster.

Ian looked at them all, then after another spit into the can, set it down, stood up and hiked up his heavily worn brown cargo pants. "Ok guys, let me get you some grub. On the house. It ain't much, but it'll get your bellies filled up for now. We've been living off of it for years and we're still kicking."

Alex shot Ramsey a glance with eyebrows cocked. Ramsey grinned back slightly, then politely said, "That would be great. We really appreciate it. We just need to get our bearings and figure out the next move. We've been through a lot. But back to your other guests. When did they arrive?"

"Oh hell, less than a day ago. They seem to be in a hurry, and they aren't very talkative. Jud's working on their ship now. One slick looking little spacecraft if I must say so myself. Completely black. And supposedly really damn fast. Got their wing clipped. Claimed it was from a stray meteorite. Shouldn't take Judson too much longer to get it fixed. But we are expecting a shuttle here soon to pick the one fella up. I said that already, didn't I?" Ian said, grinning to himself.

Alex asked in as nonchalant a tone as she could muster, "So, where are your other guests now?"

Ramsey and Carol glanced at each other, both keeping poker faces, then looked at Ian for his response.

"Oh hell, I don't know. Probably in their bunks. Not much to do here, and they certainly don't want to make friends with us. Rex is the guy you talked with that cleared you for entry. He's not a friendly chap like I am. He tried lipping off to the one fella. Tall chap with the craziest haircut. They said they were from Darmus III, and that's all Rex got out of 'em. They can pay, and that's really all that matters to us."

Alex nodded. An icy stern look crossed her face as she glanced at Ramsey. He shot her a look as well. "Ok, just curious. We'll take you up on your food offer."

"Well good deal! I know Rex won't like my free food offer, but we're getting enough from the other fellas that we can help out a few folks in need. Which it seems like you are. Follow me."

Carol asked softly, "Do you think this brother of yours could meet us really quick? Maybe get me a few pain meds and a bandage for my arm?"

"Sure! Jud's working on those guys' ship. I said that already, didn't I? Rex is probably in the mess hall right now making us some grub. My brother, he likes to eat. You'll see," Ian said, chuckling to himself.

"Lead the way then. And thanks for your help." Ramsey masked his anger and tenseness at this new situation that was certainly going to play out soon.

Ian nodded and led them out of the sparse room with minimal decorations. Just a desk, computers, a water fountain, and some crooked wall hangings of purple haired women with bright green eyes and large ears, all in various stages of undress.

Ian noticed his guests scanning the pictures adorning the walls and commented proudly, "Them's Judson's pictures. He decorated this place to suit his own interests once the rest of our staff left and most of our customers quit flying through this quadrant. You just gotta love those Zequanonian women right!?"

"Sure. You just gotta love 'em, I suppose," Carol came back. Already not liking the crew of this all but abandoned old space port.

Once they exited the "greeting" station after their de-contamination and change of clothes, they were led by Ian through the main area of the station. Each landing pad and walkway was the same. A decontamination room, greeting station, then a large hollow open area inside the center, with connecting tunnels and stairs leading up to what appeared to be rooms and down to the enclosed interior docking bay.

Carol imagined that in its prime this place would have been hustling and bustling with space travelers from all over the galaxy arriving and departing. It was simply a place to relax a bit, eat, rest, get to know fellow travelers. Now however, it was desolate. Left to fall into near ruin. Dirty and rundown, with a musty smell. The viewscreens that encompassed the entire facility looked foggy from years of collected dust. She could only imagine what Rex and Judson would be like upon meeting them.

A long walkway led through the center of the circular main space port hub. Each walkway started at each docking bay leading to the large center where the bar and restaurant was located. Glass encompassed the tunnel, so people passing through could see the other tunnels all leading to the restau-rant. In its time this was a really novel design, Carol thought to herself as she gazed at the now outdated architecture.

All four of them made their way across towards the open-faced restaurant as Ramsey, Alex and Carol peered up and down, taking in the new sights as well as keeping their eyes peeled for several other recent guests.

The open-faced restaurant was more like a bar with several tables haphazardly set up around it. Each of the four walkways led to the large, round restaurant and bar. Low ceilings and dim lights encompassed the room. Many bottles of various alcoholic beverages adorned the back of the bar's wall. Roughly twenty barstools were placed around the long-curved bar top, although at one time, this could have fit many more stools for travel weary astronauts. Now however, the place was depressing and not appealing to any sort of drinker at all.

Once they got to the restaurant section of the space port, Ian led them to the bar. "Rex, meet our guests, Ramsey, Alex and Carol. You spoke with them earlier."

A burly man with messy hair and a mustache turned around on a stool from a computer readout behind the bar. His barstool came to a stop as he looked them over, stopping on Alex.

He ran his hands through his greasy hair as his eyes moved from Alex over to Carol and said in the same tone they were greeted with when they had approached the space port, "Your arm. Looks bad. I've got some meds and some gauze that'll help, I suppose. What the hell happened?"

Carol was slightly taken aback that he would start the conversation with her injured arm. She did appreciate the gesture, but certainly not the way his eyes fell over her body. "I would appreciate that, thank you."

Rex's eyes slowly fell from Carol's face and down the length of her body, making Carol immediately uncomfortable. *Don't let this clown intimidate you,* she thought to herself.

"I'll go let Judson know about their ship and see what he's able to do. He'll want to meet you three, I'm sure. What with the lack of guests and all. Good chance we'll have to send out a specialist regarding the ship you flew in on. I've never seen something that funky, and I've seen my fair share of funky out here," Ian said nonchalantly as he turned and shuffled towards the elevator.

"So, what's your story?" Rex said flatly as he peeled his eyes off of Carol and stood up. He proceeded to start scratching his large belly underneath a far-too-tight-for-his-physique grey shirt with what looked like a hole right in his left armpit. He sloppily poured himself a drink of something clear out of a short oval shaped bottle marked "Vinkenzza 110 proof."

He offered them glasses, which they all accepted as he poured shots out. Once poured, he reached behind the bar and handed Carol a bottle of unmarked pills. Taking them, she looked them over, noting the lack of any wording other than *Pain Meds* on the top of the cap.

"Trust me. They work. Grey market pain meds. Your arm will feel better. So will you. Only take one or you'll be knocked on your ass. Unless of course, that's what you're after," Rex said with a smirk then a wink. Through this all, Ramsey didn't break eye contact with Rex. He seemed to be relatively stupid, like his brother, but he could tell this man was already having some unpleasant thoughts about these two women standing in front of him that immediately made Ramsey uneasy, and angry.

Carol produced one pill from the bottle, popped it in her mouth and downed the shot of Vinkenzza, slamming the glass down on the table without flinching.

Raising his eyebrow at her, he looked at the rest of the new arrivals with renewed curiosity, focusing on Alex. His eyes walked their way up and down her slim, toned body. He grinned then shot her a wink. "So, good looking. Alex, right? You gonna tell me what…"

Stone faced and unmoving, she raised her index finger for silence, then picking up her shot glass, Alex also knocked it back, setting the glass down gently. Then in a calm, cool and entirely threatening tone asked him, "Where are your other guests?"

CHAPTER 27

WELCOME TO THAKITUNE

The creature stayed alert inside the large water filtration chamber in the rear of level one inside the makeshift science lab. Inside this large facility it breathed in the cool water easily. Doing this over a short period of time had healed it even further. It felt the holes riddling its body now begin to completely close shut. The black lifeblood that pumped through its two hearts was working as it should. Organs decimated from the DPG were rebuilding themselves. The left-over Sam corpse was good nourishment for it. That entity had attempted and failed at its task. Its last service to its master was becoming food.

This new discovery, breathing in water, was a welcome surprise to the creature as it continued to quicky evolve. It sensed a greater purpose for its birth. It welcomed that. Even if its goal on this vessel wasn't fully realized, it was confident that what was in its near future would more than make up for the worthless corpse's failures earlier. They were all expendable. It could make more, use them, then discard them, or better yet, use them as sustenance for itself.

It had nothing but contempt for these beings on this flying machine. They were less than. Weak. Easily disposable and even more easily manipulated to do its bidding. *I will rule an entire world,* it thought confidently as it floated in the water. It continued to wait. To hide itself. Until the next part of its journey was complete.

Justin did the best he could piloting the *Leo*. The ship had breached the atmosphere of Thakitune. Luckily, the fire was extinguished before entering this new planet's atmosphere, as new flames underneath the ship had started with the immense pressure and gravitational pull it was now experiencing.
The ship vibrated violently. Anything that wasn't locked down had fallen to the floor. Walls inside rooms were cracking. The server room was frying as numerous functions on the ship were rendered useless and inoperable. Meanwhile, the engine room was at a critical stage. The fuel had run out, but the power cell was shaking violently from the stress the rest of the *Leo* was taking on. The invisible guard on the inside of the cell was beginning to give way.

Justin tried in vain to steer the ship to a flat surface below to possibly soften the initial impact. Once the ship was through the atmosphere, the flames subsided a bit on the bottom half, but the *Leo* was picking up speed as it made its way to the planet's surface.

The ship began to point downwards, continuing to approach land. Justin remained strapped into his seat, peering out the viewscreen at the mass of tan, desolate rock fast heading his way. Water. He saw a small water basin below with a stream running off of it. The planet was riddled with these. The water, if he could land in it, would soften the blow somewhat. Justin frantically tried to plot a course for the water below. The lights on the monitors in front of him were blinking and cutting out, making this stressful task even more cumbersome, as time was running out.

Zooming in on the water mass below on the screen, he hit enter on the screen as it cut out again. However, the coordinates were logged and the ship, which still had the most basic of operating skills, was able to guide itself towards the looming body of water that was now less than one minute from impact.

He wasn't going to make the intended target. The ship was coming in too fast and would overshoot it. The system had done its best to steer itself towards the location Justin had selected, but it was now quite obvious it would hit solid rock.

Tightening his seat restraints, he braced for impact, looking over the gauges in front of him, most of which had turned dark and were no longer operable. The situation was grave. Thoughts of the power cell and the liquid similar to synth several decks below exploding. Incinerating him alive. Where had the creature retreated to? Had it figured out a way to stay alive? It certainly survived the DPG blast. And then Carol, where was she? Did the *Stormbringer* make it to the space port, or were they taken out by the Reapers? What would his commanding officer, Ben Newstead, have done?

He searched frantically over the control panel in front of him. The screens were now all dead. Many of the knobs and buttons were unmarked, or if they were, made no sense to him. He knew flight basics, but Ramsey and Carol were the real experts. On a bottom row of buttons was a red one that caught his eye marked *Cockpit Hatch.*

No time to think, press the button! Shaking his head, Justin reached down and pressed the button hard with his index finger. A hiss was heard throughout the command center below Sam's seat. He looked down and a circular hatch had unsealed around her seat.

"You've got to be kidding me! An exit inside the cockpit! Of course there would be some sort of easier way to get inside the command center from outside, instead of having to go all the way down to level three cargo bay to get out of here!" he yelled out loud. As fast as he could, he undid his seat constraints, stood up on unstable, shaky ground and ran to Sam's old captain's seat. He grabbed the chair, but was unsure how to dislodge it to open the hatch under her seat.

Looking up he saw land, closer and closer. He struggled with the seat. Shook it, pulled on it. Then, he turned it. The hiss grew louder. He turned the seat the entire way around until it was facing forward where it had started. The hissing stopped and a clearly defined seal had been completely broken around the perimeter of the seat in a perfect circle. Justin instinctively grabbed the seat and began lifting.

The seat and the circular flooring attached to its bottom lifted up, revealing a set of stairs leading down to the very bottom of the small command center's front end. On the underside of the opened hatch was a crank, obviously made to re-enter the ship from the outside. From the readouts on the side wall of the interior of the short tunnel leading down-ward were gauges and readouts that looked as though safety measures were taken into account in this design with regards to oxygen and depressurization. None of which mattered to Justin at this point.

Justin didn't hesitate. He slung his Fusion Rifle over his shoulder, climbed down the metal ladder attached to the side of the tunnel. The steps numbered ten and the tube he quickly climbed down through was no more than ten feet high. Once at the bottom, looking down, he saw another hand crank in the center of another circular hatch, exactly the same as the one attached to Sam's command center seat above.

Justin bent down, cranking the handle as fast as he could counterclockwise. It stuck at first but quicky moved in the intended direction smoothly. Several hard turns later, the hatch hissed open and dropped down on a hinge revealing open air and land seconds away. However, right now, the ship was passing over the large water mass. Justin didn't hesitate, dropping himself out of the hatch, plummeting towards the water below.

The ship's speed had made it essentially a missile, and the power cell in the engine room was the ignitor. Free falling at this rate of speed was suicidal, but the odds were slightly better than being on that ship. These thoughts went through Justin's mind as he fell the rest of the way to the water. He didn't know how deep it would be or how much impact these cumbersome space suits could withstand and cushion. He was about to find out in five seconds.

Back on the ship, at the end of level one, in the water filtration tank, the creature floated silently in the water. Its healing nearing completion, organs slithered back in place, black tar-like blood regenerated inside. It breathed in the water's oxygen. Waiting for its opportunity to escape. To live.

The last thing Justin saw before launching himself into the water below was the *Leo* smashing into a large boulder on the planet's surface slightly past the lake. A ball of intense fire erupted as the ship exploded. Sending debris up towards the sky and outwards. The power cell ruptured upon impact, thus making an already intense collision with the rocky surface significantly worse. Balls of fire shot in all directions and rained down from the sky. The rocks themselves around the crash site were burning.

Justin had plunged deep into the water. Mere seconds before he hit, he extended his feet towards the water, hoping to shoot into the water like a bullet. This is exactly what happened. Feet first, he sunk down, the water slowing his fall until he was over ten feet below the surface. However, he hadn't been knocked unconscious. He hadn't been killed. The suit had saved him.

He tilted his head upwards and saw a blanket of fire spread over the lake he was submerged in. Luckily, he had oxygen. What was on his back though would be it. He was sure the other suits and their oxygen tanks were incinerated by the massive explosion that had just taken place. Even more lucky for him was the Fusion Rifle that still clung to his shoulder. Chunks of the obliterated *Leo* splashed into the water. Justin, however, able to breathe, stayed submerged for a bit longer, waiting for the debris to stop raining down and the lake of fire to extinguish itself.

Deep in this lake, small beings swam. Small, white eel shaped aquatic life zigzagged away from the heat of the watery surface and zipped past Justin in the deep, blue water. He looked at them as they quickly vanished out of sight. *Life. There's life here,* he thought.

When the ship collided with the large boulder on the planet's surface there was a second, less than a second even, before everything ignited. The creature felt itself slide forward in the water tank it was submerged inside of. Crashing into the side interior wall. Then the power cell ruptured in the engine room, making everything go up in a ball of fire.

The water tank exploded, along with the rest of the ship. Fire engulfed everything, including the water the creature was housed in. On the back of the creature, large bat-like wings shot out of its back. Measuring seven feet each, nearly the size of the creature itself, the wings shot the creature upwards as it tried escaping the fire that surrounded it.

The parasite that had survived much aboard the *Leo* now shot out of the top of the explosion in a beautiful display of wings flapping, shrieking and ripples of fire cascading off of its entire body. Completely engulfed in flames. It continued its trajectory upwards, not knowing where to go, what to do. It flew as it was being burnt alive, away from the blast zone. Away from the water basin that could extinguish the flames charring its tough outer skin and boiling its internal organs as it launched upwards.

It flew through the air, like a shooting star breaching the atmosphere, until it fell from the sky. Out of sight of the crash. Behind a mountainous region on the planet Thakitune.

Justin swam up to the boiling hot water on the surface of the lake. His skin would be burnt if not for the space suit that had also saved his life from the plummet out of the *Leo*. Even through the water running off of his helmet, he could see the huge flames off the shore. A cloud of black smoke had funneled up into the atmosphere as fire continued burning the already charring remains of the ship.

Starting to swim in the heavy space suit was a frustrating and cumbersome ordeal, but he slowly made his way to shore after what seemed like an eternity of paddling through the liquid. Once on shore, his gloved hands sank into the sandy beach of this strange new world he now inhabited. Currently with no single way of escape.

Justin stood up and surveyed the area. The sky was a haze of sand-colored clouds, much like the surface, as well as grey smoke in the immediate area from the massive explosion.

His eyes fell onto the demolished *Leo*. The fire was still raging and burning whatever was left of the hull. Once it was finally extinguished there would only be the charred metal skeleton of what once flew through the galaxy. Memories of a father and his daughter on numerous adventures. Lost to time. By the beast they had unwittingly brought onboard. Justin hung his head in shame at the destruction this species wrought wherever it went.

Justin turned his helmet sideways and released it, realizing he was breathing heavily inside the suit and using far too much oxygen. He had to check the air quality as well as conserve what he had in the tank. He breathed in the air. It hit his lungs and felt good. But he could tell almost immediately the air here was much thinner. *I'll try to filter the air here through my tank later.*

His mind went to the creature on the ship. Those eyes, the same as Hyzothan on Thunder Stone Realm. It had hitched a ride when they went through the wormhole, traversing through the dead star. It was a race of creatures, born from a black substance floating inside that black hole. How many more were there in the known universe?

He contemplated these things as he dropped to the sand beneath him. Exhausted. His mind drifted from the creature, much like the one that James Korvell had destroyed on TSR1, surely burnt until it was ash, to warm thoughts of Carol. She had survived the Reaper attack. She was alive. He knew it. He sighed as he watched the smoldering remains of the *Leo* in the distance.

CHAPTER 28

UNPLEASANT REUNION

Rex stared at his guests, not knowing how to respond. Seemingly not allowed to respond. Very quickly his fake type-A personality was crumbling in real time. The look on the black man's face was grim. Same with the blond lady with the gnarly looking injury. But it was the thin woman with the flowing red hair. The one that looked like she was going to jump across the bar, grab the knife used to cut slices of rotting fruit for drinks, and stab him in his throat. That was the one he was most intimidated by.

"Um, why do you need that information?" Rex said in a shaky and already unsure voice. He had immediately lost the upper hand with this group of three space travelers. His brother had left. It was him and these three.

Rex handed Carol some gauze from the first aid kit under the bar, then tried changing the subject and stuttered out, "S-so, um, here, this should help that arm as well. So, sleeping accommodations are located one level up. Repair work is below. You said your ship needs some work? And food, we've got food here. What do you like? I can fry you up some…"

"You can shut the fuck up is what you can do. After you tell us where Willie Petros and his pilot are. That's what you can do. Now," Alex said grimly, with unblinking eyes and a stone face.

Rex shifted his eyes back and forth from Alex to Carol then to Ramsey. Ramsey, seeing he was looking for help, added, "I'd do what she says there, partner. We've all had better days, and yours is likely to get worse here in about five seconds."

Rex had a sawed-off Thermal Blaster behind the bar. While he continued to shift his eyes back and forth, now between Ramsey and Alex, his right hand shakily grasped the stock of the thick, dull gray colored weapon. He pulled it slowly towards his large gut, hidden behind the dirty bar top.

He tried to stall for time and build up his nerve. "Look guys, I know I could have maybe been friendlier on the com on your way in. But not many travelers stop by here anymore. And if they do, they're running from something, so you just can't be too sure who might pilot their way through our doors. We're just trying to survive here, ok?"

Carol had finished wrapping her bruised arm and was watching him from a slightly different vantage point. She noticed something her companions did not. A glimpse of the grey weapon sliding out from the shelf below the bar top.

Opening her eyes wide at the sight of the firearm, she started to back up and yelled, "Ramsey, Alex, look out!"

Drawing the weapon to his upper chest, Rex pumped the Thermal Blaster back and aimed it at Alex. "Now! No one moves, you hear me!?"

Carol had flinched and backed away from the bar. Ramsey had both hands raised as a defensive reflex, but didn't break eye contact with the very nervous and most likely trigger-happy Rex. Alex, however, hadn't moved an inch. Holding her icy glare.

"Ok, look, the two that have holed up in this space port. They stole from my friend here," Ramsey stated, shifting his eyes over to Alex.

"Yeah, well that has zilch to do with myself, my brother and old Judson down below. My advice is you turn around, hop back in that broke down heap you landed in, and fly outta here. We don't want trouble and you three, especially you. Trouble," he said, regaining some confidence as he looked at Alex.

Carol tried to defuse the escalating situation and moved slightly forward. Immediately Rex's Thermal Blaster trained onto her. "Not another move, sweet cheeks," he said in an edgy tone. Sweat now forming on his greasy brow.

"Look…Rex. Our freighter was lost. Her Marks were stolen. Her crew killed, one of which was by the man that's currently somewhere here on this space port. We have had one hell of a last twenty-four hours. Actually, scratch that, last week. I'm apologizing for Alex here. We mean no harm. We just want a little help. Ok?" Carol said in as kind a voice as she could conjure in front of this clearly repulsive pervert.

"She's telling the truth," Alex added. Still in an icy tone.

Rex's gun immediately went back to being trained on her. "Get that gun out of my face," she spat, then glanced at Carol and shot her a quick grin.

"I'll point this here gun anywhere I…"

In one swift move, Alex lunged forward, grabbing the barrel of the Thermal Blaster and yanking back, pulling the gun out of a stunned Rex's hands. She quickly flipped the gun in the air, grabbed the stock and aimed it at Rex's head with her finger on the trigger.

Taken aback by what was happening, Rex decided to lunge forward. A foolish choice. Ramsey the professional boxer delivered a devastating right-hand blow to the side of his face, sending him backwards, crashing into the bottles on the shelf behind him and knocking him out. An unconscious Rex dropped to the ground, hitting it with a thud.

"'Get that gun out of my face.' That line sounds familiar," Carol said with a grin, glancing at Alex and sighing.

"Pretty badass sounding, so I stole it," Alex replied without taking her eyes off of the unconscious Rex.

"What's going on here?" a voice from behind them said in a deep, bellowing voice.

Alex whipped around with the Thermal Blaster pointing at whatever was behind them. Ramsey and Carol both spun around as well to be greeted by Ian and a large, tan skinned muscular gentleman with a greying beard and grey hair combed back over his head. He looked to be roughly in his mid 50's, but from his physical appearance, this man took quite good care of himself. Wearing a skintight cut off shirt monogrammed with what appeared to be a ferocious wolf-like animal baring its teeth, the words *Animal Instinct* blazing above the creature.

In his hands were two pistols. Boxy looking, long barrels, black in color. "I asked a question. Why is Rex on the floor and why in the hell are you holding his gun?"

"You must be Judson," Ramsey said in as calm a voice as he could muster, considering the escalation of this entire visit to Space Port 771, another in the long list of bad situations they found themselves in since waking up in their hibernation tubes onboard the *Cauldwell*.

Ian cautiously moved forward. "I just want to check my brother out, ok? I knew I shouldn't have left you two pretty little ladies alone with him. He has a soft spot for the cuties," he said, trying to calm things down. It didn't work.

"Why don't you come over here and call me a *pretty little lady* again, slim," Alex yelled back at him defensively, continuing to hold the Thermal Blaster, aiming it at both Judson and Ian.

"Ian, will you kindly shut the hell up?" Judson said, calmly glancing over at him.

Ramsey quickly made a mental note: Judson was the smart one of this bunch. It was time for him to try defusing this standoff, "Look Mr. Jud, we'll give back this gun here. Ok?

We don't want any trouble. Alex here, she's been through a lot. We all have. We're sorry if we came across the wrong way, but Rex here was being a bit disrespectful and at this point, we simply aren't really wanting to deal with disrespect. At all."

He paused, waiting to see what would happen next. Ramsey's hands were still partially raised. He glanced at Carol, who was standing close by, also raising her hands slightly up.

"That Vinkenzza drink you stock at this fine establishment is pretty tasty. Mind if I have another one?" Carol asked calmly. Almost pleasantly.

Silence fell over the bar area. Rex was starting to come to. Propping himself up on his elbow and shaking his head at the blow he took at close range, full force from an ex-boxer in peak physical fitness.

"Well shit! We have a fellow Vinkenzza fan here, let's get you another one, then!" Judson said as he lowered his dual pistols and walked forward to the bar, all but ignoring the Thermal Blaster Alex still held out.

Ramsey shot Alex a confused look. Carol slowly lowered her hands, also stunned that her defusing the situation seemed to be working. She walked forward towards the bar where Jud stood as he poured himself a drink into a dusty shot glass.

"Ian, go help numb nuts up, will ya?" Judson said, pointing over to Rex, who was now in a sitting position and rubbing his jaw.

Ramsey also had lowered his hands and put his right hand on the barrel of the Thermal Blaster Alex had raised. He pushed it down then looked at her and quietly said in a composed tone, "Let's see this play out. This guy seems ok. Might actually save some lives going this route, ok?"

Alex stared at him for a few seconds, and out of the corner of her eye she saw Ian go behind the bar and help his ego busted brother Rex back to his feet. Alex finally nodded back and quickly put the Blaster on the bar top close to Judson. Before she could change her mind.

"Well, all right then. That's more like it. We run a business, and you three are our customers. We obviously got off on the wrong foot. Once again, compliments to this piece of work here," he said sarcastically as he rubbed his well-kept greying beard while glancing over at Rex, who hung his head in shame.

"I was just asking them where they was from and what their busi…" Rex started to justify himself.

As with Alex, Judson cut him off mid-sentence, shifting his gaze to him and coldly stating, "Rex, I know how you are. We all do. And in the, what, maybe two minutes you interacted with our guests here, you probably undressed both of these here ladies in that thick, brain-cell-deprived head of yours. So, I'm sure they were both uncomfortable from the get-go. That probably pissed off their male friend, Mr. Punchy here, so you had to play big ol' alpha male with my Thermal Blaster. Yeah, *my* gun. Not yours. Hell, you barely know which end to point. Kinda like your pecker. So, yeah. Kindly shut the fuck up, ok?"

With that, Alex took a seat at the bar beside Judson and slid the glass she had downed earlier over to him. "Hit me with another one, too. Put it on my tab, alright?" she said in a much calmer tone than mere minutes before.

Ian led Rex from out behind the bar, and as they walked over to a nearby table for Rex to take a seat and collect himself from the punch to the face and the verbal thrashing he had just received, he said in an almost overwhelmed voice, "I gave blondie pain meds and some gauze for that messed up arm of hers!"

"Name is Carol. Carol Blake. I happen to have blonde hair. But that's not my name. Ok?"

Stuttering, Rex replied, "Um, yes, Carol. Um, Carol Blake."

The three of them proceeded to sit down at the bar as Judson made his way behind the bar and poured them all a double shot of Vinkenzza. He raised his glass and said, almost jovially, "Cheers to new acquaintances. May we not have to do that whole cowboy bullshit again."

"Here, here," Ramsey said as he knocked his shot back and grimaced, with the rest following suit.

"A few more of those and you three will think this place is a bar on Vella Capella beach," Jud said, snickering.

They all nodded and were thankful that more level heads had taken over here on Space Port 771.

There was a pause in the conversation that Alex broke. "So, Judson. Look, I do agree, things got off sour. But here's the deal. There's a guy here, Willie Petros. He was a pilot on my ship. We had just made a weapons run. Dropped them off on Darmus III. We got paid. In the meantime, we pick up these two and um…" She stopped and glanced over at Carol.

Carol gave her a small smile as if to say, *It's all right, keep going.*

She nodded slightly and continued, "And another crew member. That ship out there was what they flew in on, called the *Stormbringer*. Anyway. They, um, they had just come out of the black hole in quadrant HD-8478."

Ian looked up and exclaimed, "Wait, what? Did you just say they went through that black hole that's been out there since, well, since forever, so it would seem?"

"Twice," Ramsey chimed in, then added, "and on the way back through, we picked up some sort of parasite on our ship that was living, if you can call it that, inside the black hole. Stuck to our hull. Traveled back with us. I'm not even getting into what we dealt with on the other side of that black hole. Needless to say, the creature that emerged from the black mass that clung to our ship, well, we fairly recently had to contend with its big brother on another planet, but this one took out the rest of the crew of the *Leo*. That's Alex's freighter ship. Guess I cut you off there, Alex."

"It's ok. We all have lots to tell, I suppose," Alex responded as the events played back in her mind as she fidgeted with her glass. Judson poured her another shot of the clear 110 proof liquor that tasted like liquid lava.

Then, Ian added to the discussion, speaking gravely, "You know about that there black hole and what's inside of it? Them things? There's stories about 'em. That whatever it is that lives in that big ol' dead star, well, it's been around since before time or some such shit. Before anything really. Pieces of it escape from time to time and burrow down on planets. Create chaos. Planets end up being burnt to ashes so the stories go. One of the reasons space travelers go out of their way to avoid being in any remote proximity to it. Supposedly whatever's inside that black hole looks for ways out. Them's the stories Momma and Pops used to tell us as kids, remember Rex?"

He looked over at Rex, who was still hanging his head in shame. However, he nodded back in agreement with his brother.

Alex was watching Ian and Rex skeptically, but they both seemed rather sincere with the tale. Then Alex continued, "So Willie killed my crewmate, Grant. Stole our Marks and tried to shoot us down. This was all before this creature was hatched. I know it all sounds crazy because, well, it is. Willie escaped through our air lock in the cargo bay. I was able to clip their wing with one of the *Leo's* onboard weapons, and the sneaky bastards that they are, came here for repairs. Or extraction, or both." Alex stopped to catch her breath as she was spilling it all out for Judson, but also as a way for herself to come to terms with all that had happened over the last twenty-four hours. She sipped the current glass of booze instead of shooting. She needed to keep her wits about her. Willie was somewhere onboard, and she hoped this new back and forth with these guys would lead to the information she needed.

Judson, Ian and Rex were silent, waiting for more of their tale to unfold.

"So you guys are the crew of the ship that this Willie fella got all those Marks from, huh? How can we be sure this isn't just some bullshit story and you three are out to steal this Willie fella's Marks? You are right, he is indeed here. When we asked him what happened to that slick little ship of theirs, he mumbled something about space debris," Judson said as he continued processing this information.

"Bring him in here, see how he reacts. Regardless of if you believe us or not, we intend to stop that murderous thief before he leaves. You're fixing up the ship he came in on?" Alex responded quickly.

"Oh, not just that. They've got a transport shuttle on its way here to pick him and those Marks up. The other fella will leave on his own ship," Judson answered quietly.

"So, the question is, where are they?" Alex said back as the room got once again very quiet.

"Well, hello there Alex. We meet again, so it seems," Willie said, walking towards the bar with a tall man with long straight black hair and a scar running across his face. Both were carrying small Cambulonian Close Defense Phaser Pistols.

CHAPTER 29

STAND OFF

Justin had figured out that cycling the thin air of the planet Thakitune through his own oxygen tank on the back of his space suit worked well. He wasn't sure how long this would work, but this, coupled with regular intervals of removing his helmet and breathing the thin air resolved the oxygen issue for now.

He was thirsty and hungry. "Time to sample the water. What have I got to lose?" he said to himself as he cupped his hand in the clear liquid from which he had recently plummeted. He raised it to his mouth, hesitating for a few seconds, then took the liquid into his mouth and swallowed the cool water.

It tasted like cool, clean water. "Ok, another positive I suppose." He lowered his head to the edge of water basin and drank in his fill. Leaning up, he wiped off the water dripping from his mouth and scanned the area again.

Time to go look through the smoldering remains of the *Leo*. He walked towards the wreckage, still burning. There was nothing left. The power cell that had ignited added to the destruction, incinerating literally every part of the ship.

Justin couldn't get too close to the remains, but even from the distance he was at, the heat was intense. What about the creature? Had it survived? "There's no way. If James Korvell crashing into one of these things worked back on TSR, then the *Leo's* explosion surely was the end of this much smaller one," he said to himself, hoping it to be true.

Black smoke continued to waft up to the light tan clouds above. Scanning the terrain, he saw nothing but rocks, dirt and sand and, in the far distance, craters. He wondered how the water existed here, but different worlds in different solar systems functioned differently. *How do I get off this rock?* was the main question that plagued his mind.

Back on Space Port 771, Willie and an unnamed individual walked towards the open bar area in the center of the space port. The man walking beside Willie was wearing odd attire that consisted entirely of the color black. Tight, black pants, large black boots, a tight black shirt and a black pilot's jacket adorned his body. His nose was very pointy, and his eyes were spread far apart. Which were typical physical traits of a Cambulon.

Behind the bar, Judson looked ahead at the new arrivals entering the bar. His hands were immediately at his sides where both firearms were holstered. The Thermal Blaster was still on the bar top, close to Alex, where she had set it earlier.

Willie and the silent man both stopped when they reached the table where Rex had sat down, nursing his injured face and ego along with his brother Ian. Both of which had turned to see them enter. They were unarmed but saw quickly that their new customers had indeed found a way to get weapons through the detectors in the interior docking bay where the Reaper ship was parked below.

Willie saw the shocked looks on Ian and Rex's faces as he stopped beside them. "What, never seen a Cambulonian Close Defense Phaser Pistol? Ingenious little things. They're actually modified Emulow handguns. Virtually undetectable when passed through archaic detectors like this trash heap of a space port has. The Cambulonian government thanks the crew of the *Leo* for helping supply more of these wonderful little creations to their soldiers." He smirked at them.

Alex stared at him. Eyes filled with rage. He had the upper hand. And she let this happen! She glanced at the Thermal Blaster still sitting on the bar. She could grab it. She knew she could.

"Uh, uh, uh," Willie said smugly, shaking his head at her and raising his pistol directly at her head.

"I didn't like you two fellas the moment you walked in here. Had a bad feeling your story was bogus. That wing you claim got clipped by a stray meteor looked like a laser blast from another ship. But Marks are Marks, I thought. I fix your ship, my doofus cousins and I get paid, and you go on your merry way," Judson said in an unruffled tone, hands still near his two side arms.

Ramsey and Carol stood their ground. Unarmed. Ramsey calculated that if Willie or this other guy started shooting the place up, he would have precious few seconds to tackle one of them. But then what? Hope that Alex grabbed that Thermal Blaster and get a shot off? Carol was in no shape for some sort of crazy shootout, but he knew she would do all she could, regardless of the arm.

Willie cocked his head to one side as if deep in thought then answered Judson in an almost lighthearted tone. "Well, see, that's the problem. Which had a solution, until these three showed up. So now we have to step up the timeline, unfortunately."

The Cambulonian pilot who was standing within three feet of Rex and Ian's table immediately turned the Phaser Pistol on Rex, aiming it squarely at his head, and pulled the trigger. A thin green stream of electricity shot out of the barrel, connecting with Rex's right ear. The results were devastating, as the stream of green death immediately fried his brain on its way out through the other side of his head through the left ear. Blood and a thin line of smoke exited his head, and he slumped over, smashing his face, expression frozen in a stunned look against the table, dead before it hit.

Less than a second after firing the first shot, a second shot was fired, this one hitting Ian in his slightly opened mouth as he was about to protest what was occurring. Once again, the green shot of electricity pierced through his mouth and exited the back of his head as a stream of steaming hot blood shot out from the entry and exit wound. Ian had tilted back in his chair at the surprise shot and had fallen over backwards at the sudden and lethal impact to his head.

Willie, meanwhile, kept his Phaser Pistol trained on Judson, with an eye on Alex, hungry to end her soon. The Cambulonian pilot had executed both men in the timespan of two seconds. He was quite obviously an expert shot, trained by the Cambulonian military for just this type of cold-blooded murder. Hence, the initial reason for the crew of the *Leo* to supply the guerilla rebels of that world with their own weapons to fight back. This however, was the outcome. More weapons in the hands of the oppressive fascist government.

Ramsey glanced at Alex with a *don't do anything stupid* look on his face. She didn't move. Remaining stone faced and unflinching at what had just happened. The Thermal Blaster still within reach, yet far enough away that it would be her death sentence if she attempted to retrieve it.

Carol gasped at the ferocious and sudden execution of the two brothers, putting her hands to her mouth at the horror that was now unfolding in this run-down dump of a bar in an even worse run-down dump of a space port. Regardless of her feelings for the two men, it was cold-blooded senseless murder.

Judson kept his wits about him. They would surely have killed him already if they didn't have need of his services. He was fixing their ship. Now, obviously, for free. That was why he was still breathing. After that Reaper ship was repaired, which would be soon, he was a dead man walking. This was the plan all along.

Like Alex, Jud didn't move a muscle. They had one shot at this. If they messed up, they were all dead. He needed to stall them, or these three new arrivals would be killed next.

Alex beat Judson to the punch of breaking the silence, speaking in a calm and still quite threatening tone. "So that's how it is? No honor, just cowardly execution-style murder? That checks out perfectly. You were always a cowardly little swamp rat. You know, I can always tell someone's character by their eyes. And you Willie, you've always been a little shifty eyed sonofabitch. Right from the get-go. What Sam saw in you I'll never know. I didn't trust you from day one. And you knew it." She paused. Waiting for the response. Buying time.

The Cambulon was unblinking, Phaser Pistol aimed directly at her. His icy stare would normally be intimidating. But Alex was tough and had been through a lot. She was unphased. The question was, what about the mysterious tough-guy Judson who had two guns at his side?

"I'm starting to like you and your bunch," Judson said with a grin, impressed at this firecracker of a lady.

Sighing, Willie said evenly, "Ok, so I suppose your little rant, something you excel at, ranting, helped me choose in which order you all will die. Not you, Jud. You're gonna fix our ship. I can guaran-damn-tee that. No, Alex, what I'm going to do is shoot this one here first."

He pointed his Phaser Pistol at Ramsey. "Yeah, you, hot shot. Then this one here gets it." Pointing at Carol, who was standing upright as defiantly as she could.

"Then you last." He said slowly as his eyes shot daggers into her.

"Was it worth it, Willie? All of this for those Marks?" Alex said defiantly.

Willie glared at her and replied with a smirk, "Oh, not just the Marks, which I will be getting half of, but also an extra twenty-five percent on the back end once I succeed, as well as full immunity with the Cambulons moving forward. Let's just consider them my muscle now. Lovely deal, if you ask me."

Alex fell silent but didn't break her gaze at the traitor amongst them.

Ramsey yelled out, "Well then, best get on with it, you coward! Both of you. Pathetic cowards! Unless of course, you want to throw down with me there, tough guy."

He stared at the Cambulonian pilot. Wearing black, head to toe. With this long black hair and large biceps. This man was quite obviously strong. But Ramsey knew he could take him.

"Toss the Thermal Blaster over here. And your sidearms. Yeah, I know you're packing," Willie said arrogantly as his gaze fell to Judson.

Judson piped up from behind the bar. "Why don't you come over here and get 'em?"

Willie walked over to Carol and put the electron pistol to her temple. "I said, toss them over here. Now, I won't ask again."

Carol was shaking. She had kept a cool, calm demeaner through this, but time was running out for them. She knew it. She glanced over at Willie, who had a sneer on his cold face.

Ramsey had attempted to rush to her aid, but the Cambulonian pilot moved forward, stretching out his arm with the Electron Pistol at the ready. "Go ahead, do it," the man said in a garbled, low, bass-heavy voice that was almost undecipherable.

Ramsey stopped where he was and glanced over at Alex and Judson. Judson had pulled both pistols out of their holsters and raised them into the air, non-threatening.

A voice from somewhere on the space port came through on the PA system in a soft woman's tone. "Ship arriving off port side towards docking bay four. Requesting landing clearance."

There was a split-second pause at what the voice said from everyone as it sunk in. This was the Cambulonian Transport Shuttle arriving. Surely with, at the very least, one or two more Cambulon fighters.

The unnamed pilot with Willie took his eyes off of Ramsey for a second, glancing up at the PA system. And then Ramsey struck.

With a lightning-fast blow, like the one inflicted on the recently deceased Rex, Ramsey's right hand, now a tight fist, delivered a stunning punch to the pilot. Connecting with and smashing his nose. A sickly orange blood erupted from the man's smashed nose, spilling down over his long chin and running down onto his black shirt.

As this was happening, Carol moved her left foot out behind a now distracted Willie and, with her left arm, elbowed him in the stomach, which caused him to lose his balance, with the blow knocking the wind out of him while he tripped backwards over her foot at the same time.

Alex reached across the bar and grabbed the Thermal Blaster at the same time Judson had taken both of his pistols into shooting positions. One in each hand. The Cambulonian pilot had now regained some composure as Ramsey came in with a hard right-hand blow to his stomach, followed by a hook to his jaw. He went down to the ground, but not before starting to fire his Phaser Pistol. Green bolts of lightning erupted from it as he fired in any direction he was able to on his way to the ground.

Jud didn't hesitate, pulling both triggers on his own pistol. Simple, but effective bursts of red fire erupted from both barrels, slamming into the falling long haired man's chest as orange blood exploded outwards and through. Four shots were fired, all four connected. Two in the chest, one in the throat, and one landing on his forehead.

The man was dead as he hit the hard floor of the bar, blood pouring out from the large holes Jud's gun had produced as well as Ramsey's hard punch to the nose.

Carol had jumped back, away from a stunned and furious Willie's grasp. Ramsey was too far, with no weapon. Alex was in Jud's line of fire, but with her own weapon she lunged over at Willie, Thermal Blaster in hand.

Willie was quicker though, already on his feet, and seeing he had lost control of the standoff, he turned and ran, his own Phaser Pistol still in his hand. He bolted out of the bar area, looking forward as he held the pistol in his left hand, firing it behind him as he ran. Hoping to get lucky.

Alex was in pursuit behind him, dodging the random green streaks of electricity zinging past her as he ran down the open corridor. Ramsey had taken pursuit as well after the fleeing Willie. However, one of the green bolts from Willie's gun that narrowly missed Alex grazed the side of Ramsey's neck, instantly burning the skin.

Ramsey shrieked in pain and surprise at the searing hot electricity that burned onto the side of his neck, grabbing ahold of the fresh wound and dropping to the floor in pain.

Judson had run from behind the bar towards Ramsey, and was joined by Carol, who had grabbed the dead pilot's Phaser Pistol on her way. When she saw Ramsey yell out in pain and drop to the floor, she shouted out at him, "Ramsey, no!"

"This is Cambulonian Transport Shuttle 557, request docking authorization. Do you copy, Space Port 771? Picking up passenger and light cargo. We'll be out of here in less than an hour. Reply."

Carol and Judson ran up to the badly injured Ramsey and knelt down to look over his wound. "This here is one lucky sonofabitch. A fraction more to the right and that shot would have killed him instantly. But we also have this transport ship to contend with," Judson said.

Ramsey was still coherent as Carol gently rolled him over and he looked at her. "Did Alex get him?" he asked quietly. His eyes told her that he was in a state of shock from the intense pain.

"Lay still. I'm going to get you help. Alex will take care of him. You're gonna be ok," Carol replied in a hopeful voice as Ramsey laid his head back down onto the floor, squinting in pain. A large patch of flesh was smoldering on his neck from the nearly fatal shot from Willie's gun.

Judson had glanced up to see Alex pursuing Willie out of sight down the hallway. "Willie's going to make a run for that Reaper ship in the interior docking bay. It's locked up tight, and they didn't take anything off of the ship, so those Marks are still onboard."

"Space Port 771, do you…" the agitated Transport Shuttle pilot started to say.

Quickly, Judson pulled out a small rectangular communicator from his pocket. It was gray and had a view screen as well as what looked like a built-in microphone under the screen. Pressing a little red button on the side, the screen lit up and there was the ship, heading towards the space port, viewable from an exterior camera system that was clearly past its prime. The image was filled with static and fuzz.

"This is Judson Brooks. Chief Engineer of Space Port 771. Permission granted. Please proceed to docking bay two. Extending arm now. Please await further instructions once you've powered your ship down. Judson out." From the small communicator, Judson was able to access the space port's external docking ports. He pressed docking port two and hit enter.

Jud looked gravely at Carol. "You stay with him. I think you saw the med kit behind the bar? That's where that gauze ol' Rex gave you came from. There'll be some anti-burn meds in there. I need to take care of these guys coming in. If they think anything is amiss, they'll send for more back-up and we're all dead. I'll stall for time."

Jud got up, holstered both of his sidearms and started towards the Welcome Center. He had a plan for handling the new arrivals.

Looking down at Ramsey, she calmly said, "I'm going to go get some things from the bar. Welcome to the burn victim club. Now party of two."

Ramsey tried to grin at this, but was only able to mutter, "Alex. Is she ok?"

CHAPTER 30

FINAL WORDS

Willie had darted down a long flight of stairs. He cursed this old dump. *No elevators!* he thought as he bounded downwards towards the Reaper. He could gain access to the ship. He remembered there was a spare co-pilot suit inside, as were the Marks. His own space suit was back in their rooms on the top level.

He had a good head start from the pursuing Alex down the spiraling stairway that wrapped around the outer hull of the space port. This was one of the very smallest spaceports in the solar system, so navigating through it was relatively easy, even though this one lacked the most basic of amenities, like an elevator or even clean living quarters.

Typically, there were several space ports in each solar system with substantial life that had space travel capabilities. This being on the outer rim of the HD-6549 quadrant nearest to the desolate planet Thakitune as well as the dreaded black hole further out at the edge of this solar system, it was rarely used by anyone anymore.

Carrying his Close Defense Phaser Pistol, Willie bounded down the steps. He had left the Electron Pistol aboard the Reaper ship as he'd been instructed by that bozo Rex upon landing. He hadn't needed it with the newer and much more advanced Close Defense Phaser Pistols. Undetectable on this old space port.

Willie made it to the bottom of the stairs. All that was left was a short hallway where the weapons detector was located. The interior docking bay decontamination room was off to the right side of the hallway instead of straight ahead like they were in the four outer docking bays. He hated having to even go through that stupid, useless formality, but at the time they had wanted to keep a low profile. Follow the rules. He hated following the rules. With the Marks in his possession, there were no more rules, for a while at least. Until the next long con. There was always another one on Willie's horizon. He had gotten good at it, even with this current setback.

He made his way to the door as it slid open upon his arrival in front of it. He quickly ran into the interior docking bay. This area was quite large and, unlike the rest of Space Port 771, was quite clean and tidy. There was certainly enough room to park a larger ship than this small Reaper fighter. The ship was parked in the middle of the room with a ceiling seventy feet high and 20,000 square feet inside. The area made the Reaper ship look relatively small in comparison.

Judson had gotten started on the clipped wing. The damage wasn't significant, and the ship would fly, especially with the minor repairs already underway. They would have to do. Willie needed a quick exit off the space port. He had heard the transport shuttle requesting clearance to land over the port's com system, but they might as well be on another planet. There would be no way to get to them with Alex in pursuit and Jud armed with two pistols. Good chance that Carol lady or the black fella got the pilot's Phaser Pistol. He was outnumbered and outgunned, with time working against him.

If he could make it into the Reaper ship and access the communications inside, he could warn the Cambulonian Transport Shuttle about the four individuals onboard that had murdered one of their pilots and were out to get the Marks. He knew his life was meaningless to a race like the Cambulons, but the Marks and the dead pilot, that would get their attention quick.

He ran through the brightly lit room filled with fluorescent lights adorning the ceiling towards the ship. He wasn't sure how close Alex was behind him in pursuit. *Get inside the ship, then I'm safe!* He thought to himself, continuing to run.

The Reaper ship Willie had used as his escape sat inside the space port in Judson's repair bay. The Cambulon government had larger and more deadly fighter ships but none as fast and agile. These were what made up the core fleet on their home world. Cheap and quick to build while not being all that comfortable inside, they were certainly deadly with the right person at the helm which included Willie.

Willie ran up the five steps that Judson had extended when they had connected to the hatch, which was locked. The Marks were inside, and he hadn't trusted the three dirty grease monkeys living on this old space port. "Shit! What's the code for this damn hatch? 520…I need one more number!" He shouted as his mind went blank looking at the keypad in front of him.

He pressed 5201. A small red light flashed above the keypad, signifying he had entered an incorrect code. 5202, the red light blinked again. 5203, once more, the red light blinked. "Come on, come on, damnit!" Willie shouted frantically as he glanced back, waiting for Alex to run into the room, then wiped cold sweat from his brow.

His hand was now wet with sweat as he continued working his way through the possible entry codes. 5204, red light. 5205, red light. 5206, red light. 5207, red light. 5208, red light. He held his breath, "It's got to be 5209!" he said excitedly as he entered the numbers, waiting to hear the hatch unlock and slide open. The red light blinked.

"No! It has to be that! Wait a minute." He glanced back again. No Alex. He punched in 5200. A green light blinked as the hatch unlocked and slid backwards against the outer hull. He had gained access to escape. He started to climb into the Reaper and shouted back, "Good riddance, you lousy bitch!"

A thunderous shot rang through the room as the explosion from the Thermal Blaster connected with Willie's lower back, ripping through him and spraying blood all over the interior of the small two-seat cockpit of the Reaper.

Willie froze in place, realizing what had happened. He looked down at the hole in his stomach, then up to see crimson bits of himself splattered inside the ship. Splashed on the stolen Marks stacked directly behind the pilot's seats.

He tried to lift up the Phaser Pistol at his side, but his motor skills were abandoning his body quickly. He could hear footsteps approaching behind him. Not running. Walking. Stalking. And then he fell backwards off of the steps, landing on the cold hard floor and scattering some of Judson's tools he had set aside for the repairs.

He lay still. Alive but feeling a puddle of warm blood soaking through his shirt and expanding outward onto the floor. He tried to raise his Phaser Pistol in the air, but his arm fought him. A shadow loomed over him now. Alex stood silently, looking down at the mortally wounded Willie. She had the Thermal Blaster at the ready.

Coughing up blood, Willie tried his best to speak in a garbled dying voice. "You can still do the right thing here, all you need to do is…"

Alex didn't hesitate, aiming the gun and pulling the trigger. Willie ceased to have a head. "I had a feeling this day would come shortly after I met you, and here it is. Wish I could say I feel some relief. But it won't bring back my crew, you dirty murdering thieving bastard," she said calmly. She had been out of breath from the chase, but had time to gain her composure as she waited for Willie to unlock the ship, watching him frantically enter numbers. Ensuring she would gain access to the Marks as well as the ship itself.

She walked up to the Reaper and peered in, looking at the remains of Willie splattered throughout. And then there were the Marks, as well as the space suit from the *Leo* Willie had been wearing upon his theft and escape. She stepped back out of the ship and looked at the keypad. It read, 5200. She hit lock and the outer hatch slid shut.

She left in a hurry, grabbing Willie's bloody Phaser Pistol on the way out and avoiding the violent bloody carnage spread out across the floor where Willie lay dead. She made her way back up the long stairwell. "Time to help that Judson fella intercept the new guests," she said quietly to herself as she continued her climb.

CHAPTER 31

DECISION TIME AT SPACE PORT 771

The Cambulonian Transport Shuttle glided into docking bay two. Three Cambulon soldiers were aboard. One female and two males. All had similar features. Pale, yet muscular skin, long straight black hair, pointy noses, eyes wide apart and chins and dressed head to toe in black. Signifying they were military.

The transport ship was significantly smaller than the *Leo*, but they were essentially used for the same purpose. To haul things. In this case, one man and his stolen loot back to their home world. The ship was slightly narrow and long. With two large round engines on either side. Two large exhausts jutted out the rear of the ship. Because of its smaller size, any transporting of goods was loaded and unloaded on the large side entrance.

Because this was a transport ship, it didn't offer much in the way of protection other than a strong outer hull and two blasters on the front of the ship under the cockpit area, which itself had a large, thin rectangular viewscreen. As with every Cambulonian ship, the colors were the same. Either dark green or black. This particular transport shuttle was black.

The lead pilot on this ship noticed the small *Storm-bringer* connected to the side of docking bay one. "What's the odd-looking wreck?" she said mockingly at the heavily damaged Trilaxian escape pod.

"Whatever it is, it's not going anywhere soon. But it does mean there will be some more visitors. Hopefully we don't even have to see them. That fool Willie should be ready and waiting. If this goes as planned, we just open the hatch, he hops in and we leave," the co-pilot responded in a deep voice.

The ship came to rest on top of docking bay two. Once it landed, the platform lowered until the ship was inside the round platform. Above, a panel slid shut, covering the top of the platform as a way to re-establish oxygen to the arm and docking bay area for safe passage into the space port.

On the com system, Judson cleared his throat and spoke. "Welcome to Space Port 771, this is Judson Brooks. Before entering our space port, you will need…"

"We only have one getting off of our ship to oversee the rest of our Reaper's repairs. We're here to pick up a passenger and his cargo. Let's make this quick. I don't want to be here. None of us do." The female Cambulonian pilot tilted her head a bit, waiting for a response.

"We have a problem with your vessel here. I need to have you all come aboard and check it out. Won't even make you go through our decontamination process," Judson said calmly.

Groaning loudly, the female pilot responded in an increasingly agitated tone, "You can't fix a clipped wing? What kind of outfit is this? Fine. But I don't want to be here more than an hour. Do you understand?"

Judson grinned to himself then said in a still, even and calm voice, "I totally understand. In and out in under an hour. If you would be so kind as to leave all weapons onboard, thanks in advance."

The Cambulon crew grinned at each other, placing their undetectable Close Defense Phaser Pistols inside their black jackets that all had concealed holsters on the inner pockets.

As the Cambulons exited the ship and made their way towards the decontamination room and Welcome Center, Alex had made her way up to Carol and Ramsey.

Carol had given Ramsey something for the pain and had put a large bandage with salve from the first aid kit behind the bar on the fresh wound. Alex ran over to see how they were holding up.

Putting her free hand on her side from all of the running, she looked down at Ramsey. "What happened?" she asked, concerned.

Carol looked up at her, then down to her feet, noticing the blood on Alex's boots. "Get him?" she asked, raising her eyebrows.

Alex nodded in reply while continuing to stare at Ramsey. She set her Thermal Blaster down as she knelt beside the resting Ramsey, looking over the bandage.

"When Willie took off, he was firing the Phaser Pistol randomly in all directions. This lucky fellow here got grazed on the neck by a stray blast," Carol told her as she herself looked over at her handiwork on his neck.

Ramsey opened his eyes slightly, looking up at Alex kneeling over him. He mumbled, "Well hello there, good looking. You got him, right?"

Smiling warmly at the injured Ramsey, she steadily replied back, "Oh, I got him. He's down in the interior docking bay by the Reaper on the floor. Well, most of him is."

Ramsey opened his eyes a bit more as he studied her tired face, then a smile crossed his. He put his hand on hers and weakly said, "Good job. I knew you would be taking care of business."

Alex felt her face turn flush from his warm hand on hers. She gently squeezed it, then stood up along with Carol.

"Jud. What happened to him? I've got the Marks and a Reaper ship that's flyable from what I was able to assess. Not 100%, but she'll fly," Alex said coolly.

"I think he went to intercept the transport shuttle over in docking bay two that showed up with some more of those wonderfully pleasant Cambulons," Carol responded bitterly.

Alex's face turned determined. "We're close, you guys. I know it's been a hell of a rough go for all of us. But we are getting off this space port and we're going to do it on that transport shuttle. Carol, stay with Ramsey. I'm going to finish this."

She took the bloody Phaser Pistol and handed it to Ramsey, saying, "Here you go, tough guy. Compliments of one headless Willie. I'll tell you all about it later."

He took the weapon in his hand, looked up at her and said woozily, "You come back, ok? I need to buy you dinner at the fine dining establishment over there behind us."

"It's a date," she shot back, walking away, hurrying towards the Welcome Center docking bay two with Rex's hand cannon, the devastatingly powerful Thermal Blaster. She wished she had the Discharge Fusion Rifle or the low frequency Electron Pistol that sat in the *Stormbringer*, but time was of the essence. This would have to do. And she was confident it would do just fine against their latest, and hopefully last, batch of Cambulons.

Looking down at Ramsey, Carol put her hand on his chest. "You're going to be ok, there. The pills are kicking in, and probably mixed with those Vinkenzza shots, you're going to feel a bit woozy."

"Carol, go help Alex. I'm gonna be ok. Her and that Jud character need you," Ramsey muttered quietly.

Nodding, Carol got up from kneeling down by Ramsey and, holding the dead Cambulonian pilot's Phaser Pistol, ran out to meet up with Alex.

The three Cambulonian pilots made their way past the security check with their weapons going undetected, then on to decontamination and finally onward towards the Welcome

Center where Judson sat at the desk previously occupied by Ian.

Judson watched them with a keen eye as they made their way forward, knowing full well all three of them were armed with their own Phaser Pistols. He gently rubbed his slightly greying short beard, then lowered his hands to his own pistols on either side of his belt.

They approached the Welcome Center desk. "What's the issue? What could possibly be important enough that you required all three of us to exit the transport shuttle and subject ourselves to this dump?" the leader of the three spat out. She was tall and rather attractive for a Cambulonian woman.

"Yes, I was the only one that was supposed to stay behind with the pilot currently on your space port to make sure our work on the damaged Reaper was adequate. Which, judging by the appearance of this room, will be sorely lacking," the third Cambulon said. This one was shorter than the rest, but stocky. All three wore expressions of anger for having to deboard and set foot on Space Port 771.

Judson stared at them coolly. Not wanting to play his hand yet. He knew once they found out their fellow pilot and Willie were dead and the Marks were in jeopardy of being reclaimed by Alex, they wouldn't hesitate to execute every one of the survivors here. *Come on Alex, where are you?* he thought as his hands gripped the pistols under the desk.

Carol had caught up with Alex before they arrived at Welcome Center Two. "What are you doing here, Carol?" a surprised Alex asked.

"I can help you more than I can help Ramsey. He's fine. We need to secure this space port if we want to get out of here alive, so I'm with you," Carol came back assuredly.

Nodding her approval and smiling back at Carol, she looked ahead at the door leading into Welcome Center Two. "Here we go," Alex said confidently, and headed towards the door.

On his computer screen, he saw the women approach and nodded to himself. "Well, you see. Here's the thing, that ship of yours that I started working on. You said it got clipped by a stray meteor. One, you pilots are better than a misstep like that and two, I know a laser blast when I see one. I know all about you Cambulons. You might think I'm some backwards mechanic working a dead-end job on a dead-end space port. But I know a heist when I see one. The other fella that came here with your pilot, shifty eyed bastard. He was keen to keep that Reaper ship locked up tight. Even though I need to get inside to complete some minor repairs."

The looks on the Cambulonian crew's faces shifted from disdain to cunning quickly. Judson could sense his time was running out before he would be executed.

The lead pilot, the one in charge, spoke in a deep and intimidating voice, glaring at Judson. "You seem to know a lot about us. Or think you do. We've suppressed the rebels on our world. And we've done it well. You see, Mr…what was your name? Doesn't matter. We will do what we want, take what we want, and you will not do a thing about it. Because you are indeed a backwards mechanic working on a backwards…"

Alex and Carol burst into the room, Alex with her Thermal Blaster raised and Carol with both hands on the Phaser Pistol. Neither said anything. Judson got up out of his seat holding his two pistols.

"You would be wise to hand over those Phaser Pistols you've got stashed in your jackets," Judson said calmly, staring directly at the female pilot.

Fury had crossed her face. The co-pilot and short stocky soldier waited to see what their captain would do next. She spoke quietly to Carol, "Where did you get that Phaser Pistol?"

"From the dead pasty-faced guy inside this space port that's dressed quite similar to you three," Carol retorted calmly.

The female slowly raised her hand to her jacket towards the Phaser Pistol not so hidden inside.

"I would think hard about your next move there, lady," Alex said grimly.

The Cambulonian woman was now staring daggers into Alex, who had the Thermal Blaster at shoulder level with her finger on the trigger.

She pulled her own Phaser Pistol out from her jacket, holding it up slightly above her head, which prompted the other two Cambulons to do the same. Then she hissed at Carol, Alex and Judson, "You don't know what you've done. Our government, my commanding officer, Tenebris will personally see to it that each of you is disposed of. Slowly. Not quick like with these Phaser Pistols. Oh, you'll suffer. We won't stand for this, and we won't be taken alive!"

"Yeah, that's kind of what I figured," Alex said.

At that, the three Cambulons tried in vain to lower their Phaser Pistols from their surrendered positions to get a clean shot of Judson, Carol, and Alex. But they all three had guns trained on them already, with fingers on triggers.

The Cambulons weren't able to get a single shot in. All three dropped to the floor dead from the multiple blasts. Judson took out the co-pilot with both of his pistols, covering his chest with blast holes. Carol had one well-placed shot to the co-pilot's forehead. Alex hit the pilot square in the chest, sending her flying backwards and hitting the wall of the relatively small room. The female pilot dropped to the ground as if sitting on the floor, and her Phaser Pistol slid out of reach.

A light haze of smoke had filled the room from the gunfire. Judson came around the desk to inspect the carnage as Carol kept her Phaser Pistol drawn, aiming at the mortally wounded Cambulonian woman bleeding out on the floor.

Alex had walked over the where the woman lay. A pool of dark orange blood flowing from the large hole in her chest. Her blood had sprayed against the wall where she was propped up in a sitting position.

"Choice was yours. You made your decision, I'm glad you did actually. Less hassle for us now," Alex said grimly down at the woman as blood trickled out of her mouth.

"My government will come looking for us. Mark my words, you will pay for this," the nameless Cambulon muttered as her life was fast slipping away.

"Maybe. But not today." Alex turned around, leaving the bloodied Welcome Room of Space Port 771 with Carol and Judson.

CHAPTER 32

NEW MISSION

When Ramsey saw the three of them heading towards him, he sat up, grimacing at the pain of the fairly severe burn on his neck from the stray Phaser Pistol blast.

Carol bent down to check on him. "How are you holding up?"

"Oh, I'll be fine. How's your arm?" Ramsey replied, looking at the gauze wrapped around Carol's right upper arm.

"I feel as though I've had this injury for over a year. It's been what? A week maybe? It'll be fine. Just like your neck."

Ramsey looked over at Alex and Judson, who were now standing over him. "You get them?"

"Oh, we got 'em, all right," Jud came back.

"I figured when I heard the shooting start and end just as quickly that you three made short work of them," Ramsey said, grimacing as he tried to think of something other than the fried flesh on his neck.

Alex nodded at him as she clung to the Thermal Blaster, then looked over at Judson and with a slight grin asked him, "So, I very much like this here gun. I'd be happy to buy it off of you. I've come into a large sum of Marks quite recently."

Grinning back at her, Judson retorted, "It's yours. Belonged to Rex, but he never used it. Won't do him any good anymore. Poor fella."

"Look, I have to say, you seem like a pretty good guy. I am truly sorry for all of this insane bullshit that we've put you though, and I am sorry about Rex and Ian," Alex said remorsefully, and she looked down towards the floor when she gave thought to the sheer magnitude of what they had been through.

Judson thought on it for a bit, then said in his deep grizzled voice, "Things happen. Some are out of our control. Such is life. I'm glad to be alive. I don't know you three all that much, but you do seem to be some of the good ones, as I like to call 'em."

Ramsey stood up and looked at everyone. "Now what? I mean, what's the plan?" he said as he held the bandage on his neck.

"I have the Marks in the Reaper ship. But the *Leo* is gone. My crew is gone. Literally my whole life was on that ship. My past before it means nothing," Alex said sadly as she looked from Ramsey to Carol and Judson.

Judson chimed in next. "My cousins are gone. Dumbasses that they were, they were still my cousins. All I had. I've spent the better part of my adult years aboard this heap fixing up ships. Getting drunk, rinse repeat. I can guaran-damn-tee that the dead gravel-voiced lady in the other room was telling the truth about their government. The Cambulons aren't ones to be messed with. And we just did a lot of messing. When they don't check in, and I mean Willie and that other fella over there as well as the three orange bleeders in the Welcome Center, they'll send reinforcements here. Lots of 'em."

Carol nodded in agreement and added, "I can't imagine what each of you has had to deal with. We've lost so much. With my crew, Ben and now…" She paused, then continued, "Justin. But we can't stay here. Ramsey is right. We need a game plan."

"Way I see it, we have three ships. One needs just a bit more repairs, one is good to go and the one you three flew in on, well…that's gonna need some significant repairs. Something we don't have the time for. Follow me, down to my office." Judson headed over towards the stairs before adding, "Ramsey, you good to walk downstairs? I have to show you all something."

Ramsey nodded, as did Carol and Alex. They all followed Judson as he led them down the stairs that Alex had recently traversed. Once they were at ground level, they headed into the large interior docking bay. There, in front of the Reaper, lay a headless Willie.

"Wow, not much left," Ramsey replied as he walked beside Alex.

Alex glanced over at him and muttered, "Trust me, he had it coming. That was for Grant."

"Here's my office. Come on in." Judson led them into a small office in the corner of the room past the Reaper ship against the back wall.

The room was simple and basic, but clean and tidy, unlike a lot of the rest of Space Port 771. Judson noticed them looking around the room. "This is my space. The whole lower level, actually. And I keep it nice and clean. Rex and Ian let everything else go to hell up top when the rest of the staff slowly trickled off. I can't keep the place clean all by myself, but this here is my area," he said proudly.

He sat down at his small desk. A computer screen was mounted to it as well as a keyboard and several other toggles and switches.

"I can run most of this space port from right here. In fact, I would have probably been the one to clear you all upon arrival, but I was busy working on that ship out there. Anyway, I did monitor your correspondence with Rex. I've screened all travelers myself, regardless of what Rex and Ian did. Which was precious little. So, upon playing back the recording of your transmission requesting landing access, you mentioned you had come from quadrant HD-8478. That's black hole territory. No one goes out there, and if they do, they don't live to tell about it."

Ramsey looked at him gravely. "Oh we have stories to tell, trust me on that one."

"That I am sure of. But I tracked your route. From near that black hole to here. Just looking for any abnormalities, due to where you said you're coming from. Anyway, only planet close by from this here space port to that quadrant is Thakitune. Well, on a whim, I did a quick scan of that planet. This image was taken three hours ago." He pointed at the screen.

The screen displayed a frozen image of the planet Thakitune. A tiny portion of it seemed to have a dark grey cloud over the area. Jud zoomed in on the cloud as it got larger and larger as well as more pixelated.

"Sorry about the quality, we aren't up to date on our computing systems here, haven't been for some time. Otherwise, I would be able to get a much clearer image," Jud said, not really looking for a reply back from anyone.

Ramsey, Carol, and Alex stared at the screen as Judson continued zooming in closer and closer. Then he stopped and pointed. "That's a smoke cloud, which itself is odd for this particular planet. There, I know it's just a black blob on this screen, but I know for a fact, that planet is uninhabited. I mean, there is water, but life there is limited to small Polixio Eels in some of the water masses and a few other tiny aquatic species. The evolution on Thakitune is quite slow, or nearly non-existent, due to its proximity from this solar system's sun."

Carol's eyes widened. She shot Ramsey a look. Even in his heavily sedated state, the astonishment was visible on his face.

Judson continued, "Anyway, that little black dot, that's something burning, an explosion. What happened to the ship you came from?"

Ignoring his question for the time being, Carol exclaimed, "Justin. He must have crash landed the *Leo* on Thakitune!"

"Wait, slow down there, Carol," Ramsey said. "What if the ship crashed with him in it, and he had no control over the situation? The ship was going up in flames the last time we saw it. And let's not forget about the creature that was hunting us down and quite literally turning us into diseased walking corpses. It could very well still be alive on that planet. These creatures, they're nearly impossible to kill. James knew that, and look what happened to him back on Thunder Stone. 'Kamikaze,' that was the word James used. What if that's what Justin did? Have you considered that?" Ramsey hoped to dissuade her from what she was thinking and planning in her head.

"Maybe. Maybe that did happen. Maybe Justin did crash the ship and maybe the creature survived. Maybe it didn't. All I know is that he might still be alive. Our captain, Ramsey. We owe it to him to at least look! And if he is alive, he can't survive long there with no food and that one oxygen tank." She paused, with tears beginning to well up in her eyes. She was desperate.

"I'll ask again: what happened to your ship that would cause it to have crashed on Thakitune?" Judson asked calmly but firmly.

Alex looked over at him. She liked this guy. She could tell the guy was no nonsense and liked knowing what was up in any situation he was a part of. She responded to his question, "The *Leo* is my ship, and after a few more of those Reaper bastards showed up to finish the job that the dead bloke upstairs failed to do, we abandoned ship. Minus Justin Schwartz. Commander of that little silver orb we flew in on. He stayed behind to save the rest of us from the creature that hitched a ride through the black hole. Or something like that. I don't know. It's all a blur right now. But I'd bet all the Marks in that Reaper ship over there that the smoke cloud and black dot is in fact, the *Leo*."

Carol continued to stare at the frozen image on the screen in front of her. The pixelated dark grey smoke and the black dot under it. "That's the *Leo*, and Justin is alive. I know he is," Carol said matter-of-factly, without looking up.

Silence fell over the small office. Then Ramsey shook his head and crossed his arms sighing heavily. He could tell by the look in her eyes no amount of arguing and reasoning would work. She had made up her mind, and what if she was right? What if Justin had survived and needed their help? Time was, once again, not on their side. He finally looked over at her and said calmly, "Ok Carol, what do you have in mind?"

Carol glanced around the room while trying to hide the new wave of emotions she was dealing with. Looking at Judson, she pointed out into the interior landing bay. "How long until that Reaper ship is operational?"

Glancing out at the Reaper, then back to Carol, he shrugged and replied, "I could have it patched up and flight ready in a few hours. Which is about how long we have until the Cambulons figure out something is amiss here when no one checks in with them back home. I'm sure there are radars on both of their ships, so they'll be tracked, and then another round of reinforcements will be sent in. This time to certainly destroy the space port and hunt down those Marks."

Chiming in, Alex added, "I know the Cambulons all too well, and what Jud says is correct. The clock officially started ticking when that transport shuttle was granted docking access. Hell, there's a good chance their higher ups have been trying to reach them, and they'll be met with silence. Carol, I know what you're thinking, but I'm going to let you spell it out."

Carol looked over to Ramsey, Judson, then Alex, and nodded. "Here's the plan, Jud: finish repairing the Reaper ship and make sure the tracker is disconnected or figure out a way I can go undetected by any other Cambulon vessels, same with that transport shuttle up there. Alex, there're space suits inside the Reaper ship?"

Alex nodded and added, "Two of them. A Cambulonian pilot's suit and Willie's. The suits must be worn inside those ships. No cabin pressure. Cost cutting by the Cambulons for their numerous rather expendable pilots."

Ignoring Alex's jab at the Cambulons that she had come to loathe, Carol responded with urgency in her voice, "Ok, got it. When the Reaper ship is fixed up, I take it to Thakitune and look over the wreckage and, more importantly, get Justin. He's there. I know it."

She glanced over to the other three in the office to gauge how they would receive the plan. When no one objected, she nodded, then continued, "Alex, you and Ramsey get some supplies here, if that's ok with Jud, and pack it on that Cambulonian Transport Shuttle."

Jud nodded his acceptance at the request when Carol looked at him.

"So, I take off to get Justin, you two head to Geshan T-32. That's where you were originally heading, right Alex?" Carol asked, quickly glancing over at her.

"Yep, in the HD-6549 quadrant."

Carol continued, "I recall you said the indigenous people there don't take kindly to strangers. Well, they're going to have to get to know us and make up their minds later. But we need someplace to head to, and that sounds like the best option, especially if they were expecting you already."

Alex nodded and put her hands on her hips, thinking, then added, "They know me. Not as good as they knew my captain, but we're going to explain the situation. We'll make them understand."

"So, let me get this straight: you want to take that fighter ship out to an uninhabited planet in the hopes of finding Justin. And we load the shuttle up in bay two and take off towards Geshan T-32 with Marks in tow, disconnecting the trackers and I assume keeping off the coms, hoping no Cambulons follow either of us or pick up any transmissions. What about this here Space Port 771?" Ramsey asked, exhausted, looking at Judson.

Judson thought through his answer, then responded with a sigh, "Well, I've been wanting a career change, and you three fell into my lap. I'm not quite ready to die like my cousins up there, and this space port is done for. It'll officially be a target for more Cambulons. I say we pack up, like Carol is suggesting, and nuke Space Port 771 from orbit."

Everyone looked at Jud, who shrugged and added, "Hey, I'm a damn good mechanic. I'll find work somewhere better than this dump I've wanted off of for years now. Until then, I say we team up for a bit. All in favor?"

Carol replied first, "Yes."

Alex was next, "I'm in."

Ramsey contemplated a bit more, then followed, "Justin would do the same for any one of us. It's risky and I've laid out my concerns. Having said that, let's do it."

Judson nodded in agreement. "We have a lot of work to do in a very short period of time. Before we get to it, Ramsey, Carol, how do both of you feel about using that little ship of yours to create a fireworks show for us on our departure? I'm assuming it can't be fixed, at least not in time, and a well-placed shot on our way out of here will cause a chain reaction. I've got plenty of fuel stored here for passing ships."

"We're going to do what needs to be done to survive. I'm sure Justin would agree." Ramsey looked over at Carol, who smiled and nodded.

Jud looked at everyone once more, took a deep breath and said, "Ok then, let's get to it, times a' wastin."

CHAPTER 33

NEW CREW

They got to work. Each one chipping in. Carol's arm hurt, Ramsey's neck burn throbbed, Alex was exhausted, and Judson, while hard at work on the Reaper, was contemplating this completely strange turn of events this last day had brought him. The loss of his cousins and soon the loss of his home. Or what had been his home for a great number of years. Jud had always believed in fate.

And this was a turning point in his life. He knew it. He knew that these three much younger space travelers needed him. It felt good to be needed again. He had also noticed the looks that Alex and Ramsey gave each other, which made him chuckle to himself. *Those two will undoubtedly be sleeping in the same bed once we're out of the shit,* he thought.

Jud got to work on the Reaper ship. Much of the damage to the wing was cosmetic, but it did need some parts that he was able to supply from his warehouse of spare parts he had collected over the years. The main goal was to get the ship flying in a straight line, and fast.

While Jud worked fast on the Reaper in the interior landing bay, Ramsey, Alex and Carol loaded up the supplies needed on the transport shuttle. They were all impressed with the build of the medium sized ship. It certainly wasn't the size of the much larger *Leo*, or the *Cauldwell* for that matter, but it was in tip top shape. It had heavy artillery on the front sides, as well as a loading area. Nothing more, nothing less. It was a typical ship an authoritarian government such as the Cambulons could offer its well-trained, highly disciplined, and quite expendable soldiers and pilots. A fact they all were aware of and accepted.

"Man, even something as simple as a transport shuttle is made to look like a dangerous fighting vessel. I'm digging the look of it, and looking even more forward to flying this thing," Ramsey said coolly as he ran his hand along the side of the ship before entering through the side hatch which featured the Cambulon motto, *Unity Through Power*, written in their native dialect.

His neck pain was subsiding somewhat due to the medication and salve that Carol had applied. It would certainly heal up well, but a scar was inevitable, and should have been treated by a doctor at a legitimate hospital. But that was a luxury they hadn't had since leaving their home world several years ago aboard the *Cauldwell*.

Carol's re-injured arm was once again feeling better also. "No more bruises to this arm. I don't think I can take it," she had commented to Ramsey when he had asked her in passing how she was doing.

Alex was quick to scan the transport shuttle for the tracking system and, once found, she had quickly blocked all tracking from any and all Cambulonian vessels. All of which were located on the system's databanks.

Commander Kar from Cambulon had several times connected with the com system, requesting updates. Each time he was met with silence and each time he grew more impatient, until his most recent transmission. "I'm not sure with whom I'm speaking, but I assume it isn't one of our soldiers. I see that recently you've blocked all tracking of the shuttle number 557. So, if you're hearing this, rest assured, we're coming, and there will be no mercy."

"Go for it," Alex replied back flatly.

Carol walked into the shuttle to see Alex looking over the weapons system and layout of the shuttle. She was trying to learn the ins and outs to better equip herself to help out once they were airborne as quickly as she could.

"I gathered a few things from the *Stormbringer* while you and Alex brought up the Marks from the Reaper ship and loaded them in the back. Not much over there, but I wanted something to remember it by." She set a few tools and the Analyzation Cube down on an open space near the front of the cockpit. Ramsey glanced over and smiled.

The transport shuttle had two pilots' seats up front with a large assortment of navigational and flight tools in front of each station, as well as two piloting yokes. Any firing of the two blasters on the front of the ship was done by either the pilot or co-pilot. Behind the front two stations was a middle seat. This could either be the captain's seat, with several functions on the armrests, or just a spare seat used for a third crew member, much like the three Cambulons that had arrived in it earlier.

Back slightly from the middle seat, against the inner hull on either side of the ship, were two more stations. Primarily used for extended crew helping with navigation or watching over the cargo. Be it transported items or prisoners. There was also a small washroom and captains' quarters as well in the far back of the ship.

The ship had a complex engine system that used similar methods of fuel to the *Leo*. One power cell sent the required power to a large, fuel powered engine. Carol wondered if any ships in the galaxy had figured out how to power their ships with magnetic propulsion and synth liquid combined. It may have been 100 years ago, but she felt that the technology used to power Trilaxus vessels was far superior to what now appeared to be quite archaic technology. Almost as if space travel had regressed in that time span.

"So does this thing have onboard A.I. that can be interacted with?" Carol asked Alex as she continued scanning over the interior of the vessel.

"557, do you copy?" Alex asked without glancing up from the station she was at.

A flat, robot voice replied, "557 copies. Please state your request."

Alex looked over at Carol. "Yep, it does."

"Before we all leave, I have an idea. I'll be right back. Ramsey, I'll need your help," Carol said as she made her way to the exit hatch on the side of the ship.

Alex yelled back, "Time's ticking you guys! Make it quick!"

Outside of the transport shuttle, Carol walked quickly towards the *Stormbringer*. "Ramsey, I have an idea. How difficult would it be to take out the A.I. of the *Stormbringer* and integrate it into our new ride? We need to name that thing, by the way."

Ramsey looked over at her with an almost surprised look on his face. "You want to hook up Mr. Zark into that thing's computer banks?"

"Yes. Ramsey, there is a wealth of information on our ship's interface. It's lost once we take off. This is quite possibly our only link to our heritage. To the build structure of the magnetic propulsion systems that might not be used anymore. This information might be some of the last ties to our home word!" Carol said, pleading her case.

"I've got to hand it to you Carol. If there's one thing I've learned about you since waking up in the hibernation tubes back on the *Cauldwell*, it's that you are quite the resilient lady. That's a great idea. Let's do it," Ramsey said, smiling at her.

She returned his smile. Glad he was onboard even if time was running out for them to leave the space port before more Cambulonian ships arrived and, more importantly, time was running out for Justin. *He's alive!* she kept repeating to herself silently.

Ramsey and Carol had made it through the hall and were heading over to landing port one where the *Stormbringer* rested. Still mounted to the side of the arm extension. They quickly made their way in through the umbilical cord then into their old ship. The lights clicked on when they entered.

Walking directly to the ship's computer banks, Ramsey opened the panel located on the inside rear of the ship close to the magnetic propulsion unit. "Zark, power down completely and await reboot of system," Ramsey stated to the ship's A.I.

The cool, calm voice of Zark came through the *Stormbringer*: "Powering down all functions now."

A small green light on a large drive turned red. Ramsey looked over at Carol, "Here goes nothing," he said as he detached the ship's A.I. drive from the rest of the databank. It was roughly the size of a brick, and easy to carry.

On their way out, Carol turned to the ship, put her hand on the ships outer hull and with reverence said softly, "Thank you for getting us this far." Then, they walked out of the quiet, lifeless, bloodied and beat-up *Stormbringer* and made their way back to Transport Shuttle 557.

Jud was working as quickly as he could on the Reaper. Alex had joined him and was helping him out while Ramsey and Carol began the installation of the *Stormbringer's* interface into the transport shuttle.

"Hand me that wrench there, Alex," Jud requested.

She handed him the wrench as she continued a small welding process on a piece of metal that had been pulled back by a blast she herself had inflicted on the ship earlier. "I'm literally repairing damage I caused. Crazy times," she said with a grin.

"What was that?" Jud replied, looking down from the ladder he was on, hearing her mumble to herself.

She glanced up at him and replied, "Oh, it's just…I was the one that shot this ship all to hell, and here I am. Fixing it."

Jud returned her smile. "Hey, I know we don't have much time to chit chat, but what's the story on your own ship and its crew? Other than what I've already been told. I had to handle that headless fella down there earlier. That was…unpleasant. So, I'm all ears if you want to share. If not, no biggie."

Alex silently nodded and the grin left her face. She began telling Jud the sad tale that began with the Cambulonian weapons purchase, to their new arrivals onboard the *Leo* to fighting for their lives, battling a nearly unstoppable alien presence that ended with the loss of her entire crew and spacecraft.

As Jud continued making final repairs on the Reaper ship, he looked over at her as she made her way up the side of the ship with the welder tool and said, "What happened to you all is tragic. But I've gotta believe everything happens for a reason. Those two in there, they need you. And quite honestly, you need them. At least that's how I see it. Good people are hard to come by. Trust me on that one. Them two you came here with, they're the good ones."

Her thoughts went to Ramsey. So awkward in the beginning. Her catching him making eyes towards her. The small bits of flirting. And Carol, strong and determined even through everything that had happened. She hadn't lost hope. "You're right, Mr. Judson. They are good people." She went silent and continued to work on the ship.

An alarm rang through the space port. Judson looked up towards the speaker in his interior docking bay, then quickly over at Alex. "We're out of time. I set an alarm to trip at any spacecraft within thirty minutes of our location that's heading towards us. It's them."

Alex responded urgently, "Do you think this Reaper ship here is flyable?"

"It's going to have to be. At least until we're all somewhere safe and not being hunted. Carol's gotta go now. So do we." Jud climbed down from the ladder and headed to the com system.

"Carol, come in. You and Ramsey heard the alarm. It's time to go. We need to be out of here as soon as possible. Head on down and I'll go over the minor repairs made."

Carol and Ramsey were finishing up the install of the *Stormbringer's* A.I. drive into the transport shuttle with relative ease. They would create a more permanent spot for it later once they were safe and clear of any Cambulonian pursuers. But for now, it was quick and dirty.

They both heard Jud's message and looked at each other. Less than thirty minutes. It was time to get Justin. Carol tried to keep a cool and calm demeanor, but she was overtired and anxious to get to Thakitune, a ninety-minute trip in the Reaper at nearly maximum power the whole way.

"On my way," Carol replied from the transport shuttle.

"Carol, you sure about this? I mean, he could be alive. I'm just scared for you. With everything we've been through. We lost Ben on TSR1, and I don't want to lose you and Justin. You promise me you make your way to Geshan in the, what was it? HD-6549 quadrant, I think?" Ramsey asked soberly.

She hugged him tightly. Not caring about her injured arm. "I'm getting Justin and we're going to find you. Ok? Count on it."

Ramsey nodded, noticing that he himself was getting emotional. Wiping his eyes, he quickly looked back down at the A.I. drive they had plugged in and were attempting to boot up when Jud's voice came over the com.

Carol left the transport shuttle without looking back. A new, even more determined look crossed her face. She was going to get her man. The commander of the *Stormbringer* was alive and waiting on Thakitune, and she was going to find him.

She made it down to the interior docking bay where Alex and Judson waited. Running over, Alex handed her the suit that Willie had stolen from the *Leo*. "Here. This will fit you better than the Cambulonian pilots. That one will be for Justin. Remember, you have to wear the suits and helmets in that ship. I put some water and some food from the bar in there for you and Justin. You might need it."

"Alex, I…" Carol started, not knowing what to say.

"You're a good person, Carol. Now you go find him, ok? We're going to be fine." She grinned as she glanced over at Judson, who was grabbing a few more tools and throwing them into a container to take with them.

Carol nodded back to her, taking the space suit and putting it on. Before she put the helmet on, she looked at Alex and grinned. "Hey, I'm putting you in charge of renaming our new ship. 'Transport Shuttle 557' doesn't work."

Alex returned the smile, nodded, and then headed up towards landing bay two where Ramsey awaited.

Jud walked over to her and put his hand on her shoulder. "We've gone over the ship's diagnostics with you already. Just remember, complete radio silence, ok? They may not be able to track us, but until we're safe and out of this quadrant, absolutely no communications. They'll be scouring this area of space and most likely the surrounding quadrants. It's not just about the Marks. They now have dead soldiers, so I am assuming revenge is high priority for them. Understood?"

Jud waited for a nod of agreement before he continued, "Ok, otherwise, you know what to expect when piloting this crazy little thing. With the quick and dirty repairs I made, it'll fly, and I think you're ready. Good luck, Carol. Till we meet again."

He held out his hand. She took it in hers, smiled and nodded at him and said warmly, "Look out for each other, ok?"

Judson nodded and watched her head over to the Reaper and put her helmet on as she climbed into the cockpit and closed the hatch behind her. Once he knew she was ready, he took one last look at what had essentially been his home for most of his adult life, turned and walked out the sliding door, heading up to his new crew.

CHAPTER 34

A NEW ADVENTURE AWAITS

Fifteen minutes until the Cambulonian reinforcements arrived at Space Port 771. They had said their goodbyes and it was time for the next leg of their journey. Ramsey and Alex were seated in the pilot and copilot stations on the transport shuttle. Judson had taken a seat over to the side closer to the engine bay in case they ran into any unexpected trouble early on. The Marks had been secured in the rear of cargo bay, and all systems were functioning optimally.

Carol sat in the Reaper ship's pilot seat. Beside her was the Cambulonian pilot's suit and helmet. Soon to be Justin

Schwartz's. Judson had gone over with her briefly the ship's primary functions. Enough to get an already well-trained space pilot up to speed on the technology found on such a ship.

This ship, like the others ever since James Korvell's small ship, the *Rescue 1* back on Thunder Stone Realm, had felt archaic compared to the way more advanced tech of Trilaxian ships. She hoped she could someday implement some of these advances into spacecraft in this current time.

With the flip of a knob, the engine on the Reaper ship roared to life. The hatch had been opened when Judson was safely out of the docking bay on his way up to the transport shuttle.

Pulling slightly back on the yoke that was quite small and agile, likely made for sharp maneuvers in space battle, the ship raised up off of the platform and hovered, waiting to be taken out into space as Carol did last minute flight checks to ensure a safe exit.

Ramsey had quickly tested out their own A.I. drive and whether it could be assimilated into the transport shuttle's own system. Luckily, there were no issues and they synched up perfectly, adding extensive knowledge of Trilaxian spacecrafts as well as a databank filled with valuable information on their trip through the black hole and the world of Thunder Stone Realm.

"Zark, pilot Ramsey Conner here. Do you copy?"

The soft voice of the *Stormbringer's* A.I. responded back, "Hello, Ramsey Conner. How may I be of assistance?"

Ramsey grinned and looked over at Alex. "Thank you, Carol, for that one. Just good to hear your voice, Mr. Zark."

"We've got to work on that 'Zark' name. It's ridiculous, even if it's from some movie. Alex shot back.

Ramsey acted shocked at the comment. "Oh, someday, somehow, you're going to watch *Trooper Command*. And when Zark shows his ugly face in the movie, you'll laugh and then call it a genius move naming our ships A.I. after him."

"If you could fully grasp just how much of a long shot me doing that actually is," Alex said back to him with a bit of lighthearted sarcasm.

Ignoring her taunts, a grinning Ramsey took the ship upwards, off of the landing bay it had rested on.

Jud piped up, "Hey guys, I've got multiple ships approaching our location. Tracking is disabled, but if we don't get out of here soon, they'll be able to see us out of the viewscreens on their ships. As it stands now, they might be able to pick up vapor trails off of our exhausts, so yeah, time to go."

Alex looked down and, sure enough, multiple unidentified spacecraft were approaching on their monitors. She counted eight in total. If they were spotted, they would be destroyed.

"As soon as Carol is clear of the space port, we nuke it and plot our course for the HD-6549 quadrant. Destination, Geshan T-32, ok?" Ramsey said tensely.

No sooner had the rhetorical question escaped Ramsey's lips than Carol's jet-black Reaper ship emerged from the bottom interior docking bay.

Carol brought the Reaper ship upwards until it was parallel with the transport shuttle. She looked over and saw all three of them at the front viewscreen looking out at her.

"I sent over the coordinates for Geshan T-32 to Carol," Jud said as he peered out at her.

"You get Justin, and you get back to us, ok?" Ramsey said, looking out at her Reaper ship, trying to hide his deep concern for her solo voyage.

"Good luck out there," Alex whispered to herself, with genuine care in her voice.

Inside the Reaper ship, Carol looked from the Cambulonian transport shuttle over to the *Stormbringer*. Taking one last look at the ship that had saved their lives numerous times, a deep feeling of sorrow and thankfulness welling in her chest.

And with that, Carol pushed forward sharply on the yoke. The thrusters kicked in and the ship blasted forwards, out into space on a course for Thakitune.

"Time to go. Let's check out the firepower on this here ugly brute," Jud said, leaning forward in his seat, awaiting the destruction of Space Port 771.

Ramsey nodded at him as he backed the ship up and Alex hit the blaster buttons in front of her.

Green streams of laser fire shot out in front of them, connecting with the *Stormbringer*. The ship exploded, causing a ripple effect down the arm of the space port it was still connected to, leading into the main hub. The entire space port burst outward in an enormous ball of fire and smoke. In the span of five seconds, it was all over with. The transport shuttle had moved back out of the blast radius as the three inside looked on at the massive destruction their ship had caused.

"And that's that. Let's get out of here. The Cambulonian fleet heading our way will have seen that for sure," Jud said with remorse in his voice. He knew this chapter of his life had just closed permanently. His future was now intertwined with these space travelers who had also lost their homes and their families.

Ramsey and Alex nodded solemnly as the ship turned away from the remnants of Space Port 771. Smoldering debris floated in space aimlessly as smaller explosions still erupted around the area where the port had once existed.

As the transport shuttle shot forward, away from the oncoming Cambulonian ships and in the opposite direction of Carol's Reaper as it traveled towards Thakitune, Ramsey and Alex looked on. Both knowing their lives were forever altered. Not knowing what lay ahead for them. Silently, similar thoughts went through their minds. *I'm glad he's with me. I'm glad she's with me.*

Breaking the silence, Jud piped up from the back, "Hey, I was thinking about transport shuttle names. We can't call this ship that. Zark is weird enough for the ship's A.I., but does anyone have a suggestion for this thing?"

Alex chimed in immediately, "Glad you asked. Carol put me in charge of the rename."

"What?" Ramsey said, half laughing and looking over at her.

She laughed and replied teasingly, "Hey, Jud's right. Zark's a weird name. I told you that before. No weird names for this thing."

Judson scratched his scruffy greying beard and tilted his head, contemplating for a second, then said, "Well, got any ideas? What I lack in creativity I make up for with mechanical knowhow and well, being able to kick some ass now and again."

Both Alex and Ramsey laughed at this. The guy had a sense of humor for as grizzled as he looked and acted.

"I would like to call this ship *Storm II*."

Ramsey glanced over at Alex with a sly grin. "Now that I like. Jud, what do you think?"

"Works for me," came the reply from the back.

"*Storm II* it is," Ramsey said boldly. Alex smiled at her station sensing that Ramsey was looking at her and felt her face flush. He then shifted his gaze to the viewscreen and the stars in space.

"Oh, I almost forgot to mention, once we get to Geshan I should note that, well…they don't speak our language. This ship has a universal language translator, but that's mainly for communicating with other ships in space. Once we get to Geshan, let me do the talking. I speak their language fluently, alright?" Alex said as she looked over at the universal translator knob on the right-hand side of her station.

Both Ramsey and Judson nodded in response. Thus far, they were working quite well as a team.

✦

On Cambulon III, Commander Kar had sent eight ships to intercept Space Port 771 and get to the bottom of the complete lack of communication from any of his pilots. "Commander, this is Captain Tenebris reporting in. We've arrived at the location of Space Port 771."

"And?" Commander Kar responded hastily.

"It's gone, sir. Only thing left here is space debris. Whoever did this had help. We can't pick up anything on our radars, but there were two small traces of vapor trails heading in opposite directions from this location. We can't track them with how faint they are, but we can tell they took off from this space port."

Commander Kar calmly sat down in his seat in a large barren office. The Cambulonian flag hung on the wall behind him, the top half black, the bottom half dark green. In the middle was their planet. "Unity Through Power" was written below in the Cambulonian language.

After thinking a bit, he responded to his best captain, Tenebris of the ninth squadron, "I am sure our pilots were killed. And I'm also sure the Marks that belonged to us were taken. We are going to find them. Is that clear?"

Captain Tenebris, in his deep and thick voice, answered, "Yes, sir. And one other thing. The vapor clouds, we're fairly certain they originated from the transport shuttle and one of our Reaper ships. The one that was docked here, undoubtedly."

There was a long pause before Commander Kar spoke again. "Begin your sweep of the quadrant. Any planets remotely inhabitable where these thieving, soon to be executed cowards might flee to, search them. Understood?"

"Yes, sir. Tenebris out."

Commander Kar contemplated this information alone in his office, silently. There was a glass of a clear liquid on his desk in front of him. Looking at it, he picked it up and threw it as hard as he could against the wall in front of him. The glass shattered as liquid splashed against the wall.

Justin continued searching for anything he could use out of the smoldering wreckage that continued kicking up large plumes of smoke into the desolate sky. Even the Damaris metal in the cargo bay appeared to be on fire. Recycling the air through his oxygen tank worked well enough, but he could tell that after prolonged use, he was finding himself taking deeper breaths and running out of breath quicker.

This was not sustainable in the long run. Especially with no food, unless he could figure a way to catch some of the small sea creatures he had seen upon his initial plunge into the water mass close to the wreckage of the *Leo*. He still had the knife Carol had given him back on the *Leo*, but little good that would do trying to catch eels deep in this lake. Still, he was glad he still had the knife.

Eventually it would get cold here. Too cold for humans to survive for any extended period of time. Luckily, Justin had the warmth of the burning remains of the *Leo* to keep him warm through the night as darkness had descended on this planet so far away from the star it orbited. Stars shone in the night sky, partially masked from the dark cloud that continued to waft upwards to the heavens. No other planets could be seen from this lonely vantage point.

He lay beside a large stone near the burning rubble, hoping for sleep to come quickly. The sheer enormity of what had happened to the crew of the *Cauldwell* and then the *Leo* was difficult to fully comprehend. His exhausted body lay still, but his mind remained active. He tried to push thoughts of Carol out of his mind for now. *Where was she? Did she survive the Reaper attack?* Now it was about survival, his own survival. Another foreign world with limited to no resources. No one else to rely on. *Just a few dreamless hours of sleep. That's all I ask for right now,* he thought to himself as darkness washed over him.

CHAPTER 35

THE BEGINNING OF THE END

Justin was not alone. Something wanted him. Something hidden on this desolate planet wanted to be found. He felt its presence. An object. A presence he hadn't felt since…

He was standing on a tall sand dune, overlooking a cavernous region of the planet Thakitune. No gloomy tan thin clouds to be found above. Stars twinkled in the clear night sky with glowing planets now visible behind them. He could breathe normally, and he no longer wore a space suit. He scanned the terrain he found himself in. This wasn't close to the wreckage of the *Leo*. No smoke filled the sky. To his eyes, it looked as though there was a hole inside the base of the furthest crater. It was a great distance from where he stood, but unmistakable. It wasn't just the hole in the side of a large rock wall inside the crater that had his attention. It was a dim, glowing light emanating from it. A light he hadn't seen since…

He continued to study the hole in the side of the cliff. He was drawn to it. Needed to get to it. But there was another presence. He felt something watching him. However, for as far as his eyes could see, there seemed to be no life. Except something glowing deep inside that rock wall.

"It belongs to me. Do you understand?" the presence spoke in a slow soft whisper, sounding as if the voice was inside Justin's head.

Looking around, he still saw nothing. Then his eyes raised once more to the heavens. An immense object floated in the night sky, high above him. It was nearly featureless due to its height in the sky as well as it being pitch black nighttime. Justin squinted up, trying to get a better look. It looked as though the being had large wings, not like a bird, but a sea creature. Possibly fins? They slowly moved up and down, keeping the entity afloat. It had what Justin assumed was a long tail connected to a thick, flat body with a truncated, slightly oval head-like appendage above the wings. The being looked to be over two kilometers in length, but it was hard to tell for sure from Justin's vantage point. Justin also felt an intense heat radiating down onto him.

Small glowing lights emanated from its body, illuminating it enough for Justin to see what appeared to be a slick, wet black substance covering it.

It spoke again. "You…I sensed you and the travelers you were with. I've waited patiently for eons, and then you arrived. One of my offspring was released and traveled with you, through the black hole I will soon be free of. I've waited for another to find the other stone. To take possession of it. And then I will call them home to me with the stones. And my healing will finally be complete."

"What…are…you?" Justin spoke out loud, but it continued to sound more like just a thought in his mind. As if they were communicating telepathically.

"I am the eternal hunter, once nearly destroyed but now confined inside the very thing that nearly took my life countless ages ago. To complete my transformation, I will at long last take possession of both stones. You and your kind killed my child in your flying machine of destruction. Murdered it on the mountain! Even though my offspring failed in its task of bringing the stone to me, I know its location, and now I know the location of the second stone. They want to be found, to be reunited with me, only me! They are connected to me. They are a part of me, and I them! Much like my offspring. I sense my children and through them, my precious stones," the floating entity gently whispered.

Dread had fallen over Justin. He felt cold sweat on his forehead. The thing inside the black hole had indeed sent something out with them. Something that had crashed with him on this cold, nearly lifeless planet. *But it was dead, right?* he thought to himself as he felt himself getting hotter from the heat source of this alien being hovering over him.

"Why are you telling me these things?" Justin shouted up at the heavenly being.

"You killed my child and attempted to kill another newly born creation of mine. You will be tormented, knowing what is to come of all living things under my rule. I will murder everything, and their blood will fall on you and those you traveled with. Including the man you left stranded on my dead child's world."

It's vain, proud, and arrogant. Just like its offspring back on Thunder Stone Realm. That pride was Hyzothan's downfall, Justin thought.

"Ben! What about Ben Newstead!?" Justin shouted at the being. But nothing had come out of his open mouth.

It responded coldly, ignoring Justin, "You need not concern yourself with anything but me. You burn my children, but I live and there will be no mercy."

Shaking his head in despair, feeling the entities telepathic grasp growing stronger, Justin shouted, "What are you?"

"I am a conqueror of all life. I have always been, and I will forever live. Long after all life in the universe ceases to exist, I will continue. Always. When I reclaim what is mine and complete my healing, I will take my rightful place in the stars. Every living thing in the solar systems and the galaxies they inhabit will bow down and worship me. I will repopulate the universe in my image, with my children!" it hissed boastfully as the embryotic lights that littered its huge body lit up with excitement.

Justin thought of the small lights Ramsey had spoken of on the entity inside the black hole. This was that very being. The frightening reality of this nightmarish vision was coming full circle to Justin now. *But why didn't Hyzothan taken the stone to this being inside the black hole? Unless it was unwittingly protecting the stone until the second could be found. That, or the greedy evil monster that it was, had hoarded the powerful stone all for itself. Then, we defeated Hyzothan. Now the stones are…where?* Justin thought to himself as he gazed up at the floating being above him. Lording over him, throwing intense heat rays onto him.

"I am the mighty Zîā, and I am coming for both of my precious life restoring stones. And worlds shall burn. You shall burn!" it said, as it instantly shot straight up into the black night sky out of Justin's vision. The being's violent departure upwards sent a cascade of heat waves down towards Justin.

How can such a small stone like the one on Thunder Stone Realm give power to such a huge being? This thing dwarfs Hyzothan! Justin began to wonder before the heat blast hit him.

Screaming in agony, Justin erupted into flames that immediately burned the flesh from his muscles. Intense flames engulfed him. He felt his insides exploding in fire. His brain melting inside his skull. He collapsed onto the rocky, dirty, sand covered ground, nothing but a pile of sizzling, charred bones that continued to burn until ashes flew away in the breeze of the desolate planet.

Justin opened his eyes and abruptly sat up, covered in cold sweat. Quickly scanning the area, he realized he was alone. It looked to be dawn on Thakitune. He was groggy, but immediately felt rested, even with the terror-filled dream, or vision he had just been a part of. And he was hungry. *When was the last time I ate?* he thought to himself, continuing to scan his surroundings as he picked up the Fusion Rifle at his side.

The intense fire that had burned through the rubble of the *Leo* was now nearly out but still sending a thick cloud of smoke into the atmosphere. Even the Damaris metal that lined the cargo bay had begun to melt under the intense heat emanating from the rest of the ship. The sky above him was as clear as it would be on a planet this distant from the star in this solar system. The cloud cover was minimal, but what clouds there were consisted of thin tan-colored lines in the sky. Above them, distant stars were visible from Justin's vantage point.

"Ok Justin, think. There's small aquatic life in this water, water that luckily is drinkable. Gotta re-circulate my oxygen as well." He nodded his approval. He walked over to the shore, took off a glove from his space suit and scooped up water into his hand, drinking the cool liquid down. After taking in his fill, he stood up and once more scanned the terrain.

The dream was so real! He replayed the entity's monologue to him about what lay ahead. He thought of the evil being that had infested the *Leo* that they unwittingly brought along on the trip back through the black hole. It was only an infant and had nearly wiped them out. And it came from something much, much larger. As did Hyzothan on Thunder Stone Realm. A being he had just witnessed in all of its horrifying, monsterous glory. Something that called itself Zîā. *It named itself,* Justin thought, shuddering.

He began walking around the base of the water mass, making his way to a higher point to better look out over the surrounding area. That might possibly jog his memory as to his location in the dream he'd had. And the hole in the side of the face of a large boulder. *It was a boulder, right?* He continued to walk several kilometers and saw a larger hill.

He made his way up a steep incline with the Fusion Rifle in hand, the wreckage of the *Leo* still visible in the distance. As he climbed, his mind drifted to Ben, alive if he was to take the dream literally. *That thing hinted that Ben was alive?!?* Justin wondered. Was it true? Or was this a lie? Possibly a taunt from what appeared to be an evil set about to destroy all known life.

Justin spoke to himself on the climb, "And he mentioned two stones. That *something* pulled us into that black hole for a reason. It wanted us to go back through so it could send a part of itself along with us. The creature that I hoped was incinerated and turned to ashes somewhere here, It could still be alive, or part of it at least."

He pondered these dreadful thoughts as he reached the top of the large hill and looked across the sandy barren valley. He hoped something on this desolate landscape would click with him. So far, it was smatterings of water masses with lots of rocks, dirt, and sand. And very thin air. He put his helmet back on, needing better air quality after the climb.

Speaking to himself again after sucking in the fresher air, he said quietly, "I'm here for a reason. The stone. What if that thing is here for a reason as well, unbeknownst to it currently? If it still lives, of course. But nothing could survive that crash."

The dream, while quite vivid, still had foggy parts to it that he struggled to either remember or comprehend. "That hole with the glowing light on the cliffside. Surely that's not the location of another…"

He heard something in the distance. *What was that rumbling and where did it come from?* Justin thought as he looked up, scanning the sky. It sounded like an engine.

Carol approached Thakitune. She had successfully navigated the Reaper ship away from the space debris of Space Port 771, kept radio silence and avoided any detection to her knowledge. She breached the planet's atmosphere close to the wreckage visible on her monitor.

She had gotten good at piloting the Reaper ship since leaving the space dock. Pushing down on the small yoke in front of her, the ship began its descent onto the planet's surface, near the wreckage of the *Leo*. Dust kicked up as the ship circled the area close to the ground.

Carol scanned the area for life signs at the crash site. Nothing. She glanced over at the Cambulonian pilot's suit and helmet. She could imagine him sitting here, beside her, leaving this bleak planet on the edge of the solar system behind, leaving the nightmare that had been their reality since awakening inside their hibernation tubes aboard the *Cauldwell*. She clicked on the com on her space suit, sighed and spoke, "Justin. Do you copy?" She waited for a response. She was met with dead crackling air through the com system in her helmet.

After a long pause, a distorted and cracking voice filled her helmet through the internal speaker: "Carol, is that you?"

While Carol maneuvered her ship to prepare for landing on a safe, flat area close to the wreckage several miles away, on the very bottom of a nearby water basin, the remains of the creature that had brought about the destruction of the *Leo* and much of its crew lay dormant. Its charred remains resting silently after plummeting from the sky, fully engulfed in flames. Small eel-like beings, white in color, with their tiny organs shining through their thin, nearly clear bodies zigzagged around the carcass, investigating the new, unmoving life form.

Three of the tiny life forms were bold enough to nip at its body in the hopes of a new food source. Through the crusted over, charred outer skin, thin lines of a black, sticky tar-like substance latched onto the eels, pulling them all together tightly. They were trapped, stuck against the pulsating tar. The tar wrapped around the squirming eels. Ingesting them. Assimilating them. The three tiny aquatic creatures became part of the small amount of unburnt and freed black tar. The gooey substance lay still once more, waiting for more life to ingest, regardless of how small.

The adventure across time and space continues…

ABOUT THE AUTHOR

Eugene Weaver was born on August 8, 1974 in Millersburg, Ohio. He and his wife Joani have been married for 20 years and have two boys. They currently live in North Canton, Ohio.

Eugene has been an avid lover of movies, music, and the arts nearly all his life. At 12 years old, he wrote his first novel, Pivoron Mountain in longhand cursive. With the persuasion of his boys, he has decided after 36 years to take another trip to that magical world he created in the basement of his childhood home where all he had was his imagination, a pencil and some paper. The basement has been replaced with a home of his own and the pencil and paper are now his laptop. His first novel, *Thunder Stone Realm*, was published in 2023. Survivors of the Realm is book two in a three-book series.